The Accordionist's Son

Bernardo Atxaga

The Accordionist's Son

TRANSLATED
FROM THE SPANISH
BY

Margaret Jull Costa

Harvill *Secker*

LONDON

Published by Harvill Secker 2007

2 4 6 8 10 9 7 5 3 1

First published in Basque with the title *Soinujolearen semea* in 2003
First published in Spanish as *El hijo del acordeonista* (translated by Asun Garikano
and Bernardo Atxaga) in 2004 by Alfaguara, Madrid

First published in Great Britain in 2007 by
HARVILL SECKER
Random House
20 Vauxhall Bridge Road
London SW1V 2SA

www.rbooks.co.uk

Addresses for companies within The Random House Group Limited can be found at:
www.randomhouse.co.uk/offices.htm

The Random House Group Limited Reg. No. 954009
A CIP catalogue record for this book is available from the British Library

ISBN 9781843432807

The publication of this work has been made possible through a subsidy received from the Directorate
General for Books, Archives and Libraries of the Spanish Ministry of Culture.

The Random House Group Limited makes every effort to ensure that the papers used
in its books are made from trees that have been legally sourced from well-managed and
credibly certified forests. Our paper procurement policy can be found at:
www.randomhouse.co.uk/paper.htm

Typeset in Perpetua by Palimpsest Book Production Limited,
Grangemouth, Stirlingshire

Printed and bound in Great Britain by
Clays Ltd, St Ives plc

Quotation from *Steppenwolf* by Hermann Hesse, translated by Basil Creighton.
Revised translation © Holt, Rinehart and Winston Inc, 1963

The Death and Life of Words

This is how they die,
the old words:
like snowflakes which,
after hesitating in the air,
fall to the ground
without so much as a sigh.
Or should I say: without a word.

Where are they now
the one hundred ways of saying butterfly?
On the Biarritz coast
Nabokov collected one:
miresicoletea.
Look, it lies under the sand,
like a splinter of shell.

And the lips that moved
and said precisely that –
miresicoletea –
the lips of those children
who were the parents
of our parents,
those lips now sleep.

You say: One rainy day
when I was walking
along a road in Greece,
I noticed that the guides to a temple
were wearing yellow raincoats

with a big Mickey Mouse on them.
The old gods also sleep.

New words, you say,
are made of such commonplace materials.
And you mention plastic, polyurethane,
synthetic rubber, and declare
that soon they'll all end up
in the rubbish bin.
You seem a little sad.

But look at the children
shouting and playing
by the front door,
listen carefully to what they're saying:
The horse rode off to Garatare.
What's Garatare, I ask them.
It's a new word, they say.

You see, words don't always emerge
out of remote industrial estates;
they're not necessarily the products
of advertising agencies.
Sometimes they are born out of laughter
and float like dandelion clocks in the air.
Look how they rise into the sky,
look how it's snowing up there.

Contents
(the piece of string)

The beginning

It was the first day of term at school in Obaba. The new teacher was walking from desk to desk holding the register in her hand. 'And what's your name?' she asked when she came to me. 'José,' I replied, 'but everyone calls me Joseba.' 'Very good.' The teacher then addressed the boy sharing my desk, the last member of the class left to ask: 'And what's your name?' The boy replied, imitating my way of speaking: 'I'm David, but everyone calls me the accordionist's son.' Our classmates, boys and girls of eight or nine, greeted his answer with giggles. 'So your father's an accordionist?' David nodded. 'I love music,' said the teacher. 'One day, we must ask your father to visit the school and give us a little concert.' She seemed very pleased, as if she'd just received a piece of wonderful news. 'David can play the accordion too. He's an artist,' I said. The teacher looked amazed: 'Really?' David elbowed me in the ribs. 'It's true,' I said. 'In fact, he's got his accordion over there by the door. After school, he usually goes and rehearses with his father.' I had difficulty finishing my sentence because David was trying to cover my mouth with his hand. 'Oh, but it would be lovely to hear some music!' exclaimed the teacher. 'Why don't you play us something? I'd really like that.'

As if her request filled him with sorrow, David slouched reluctantly over to the door to fetch his accordion. Meanwhile, the teacher had placed a chair on the main table in the classroom. 'You'd be better up here, where everyone can see you,' she said. Moments later, David was, indeed, up there, sitting on the chair and holding the accordion ready to start playing. Everyone began to clap. 'What are you going to play for us?' asked the teacher. '"Padam Padam",' I called out, anticipating David's reply. It was the song my friend knew best, the one he'd practised most often because it was a compulsory piece that all accordionists had to play in the local competitions. David couldn't help but smile. He enjoyed being the school champion, especially in front of all the girls. 'Attention, everyone,' said the teacher, like a master of ceremonies. 'We're going to end our first class with a little music. I'd just like to say that you seem very nice, hard-working children. I'm sure we're going to get on well and that you're going to learn a lot.' She gestured to David, and the notes of the song – 'Padam Padam' – filled the classroom. Beside the black-board, the leaf on the calendar showed that it was September 1957.

Forty-two years later, in September 1999, David was dead, and I was standing by his grave along with his wife, Mary Ann, in the cemetery belonging to Stoneham Ranch, in Three Rivers, California. Opposite us, a man was busy carving the epitaph that was to appear on the grave-stone in three different languages, English, Basque and Spanish: 'He was never closer to paradise than when he lived on this ranch.' It was the beginning of the funeral oration that David himself had written before he died and which, in its entirety, read:

'He was never closer to paradise than when he lived on this ranch, so much so that he found it difficult to believe that life could possibly be any better in heaven. It was hard for him to leave his wife, Mary Ann, and his two daughters, Liz and Sara, but, when he left, he had just the tiny necessary sliver of hope to ask God to take him up into heaven and place him alongside his Uncle Juan and his mother Carmen, and alongside the friends he once had in Obaba.'

'Do you need any help?' Mary Ann asked the man carving the grave-stone, shifting into English from the Spanish we normally spoke together. The man made a gesture with his hand and asked her to wait. 'Hold on,' he said.

There were two other graves in the cemetery. In the first lay David's uncle – Juan Imaz. Obaba 1916–Stoneham Ranch 1992. 'I could have done with two lives, but I only had one'; in the second, the first owner of the ranch – Henry Johnson, 1890–1965. Then, in one corner, there were three more tiny graves, like toy graves. They belonged, as David had explained to me on one of our walks, to Tommy, Jimmy and Ronnie, his daughter's three hamsters.

'It was David's idea,' explained Mary Ann. 'He told the girls that

2

their pets would sleep sweetly beneath the soft earth, and they accepted this gladly and felt greatly consoled. However, shortly after that, the juicer broke, and Liz, who must have been six at the time, insisted on burying that too. Then it was the turn of a plastic duck that got burned when it fell on the barbecue. Later, it was a music box that had stopped working. It took us a while to realise that the girls, especially the little one, Sara, were breaking their toys on purpose. That was when David invented the business about words. I'm not sure if he talked to you about that or not.' 'I don't think he did,' I said. 'Well, they started to bury words.' 'Which words do you mean?' 'Your words, words from your language. Did he really not tell you?' I assured her again that he hadn't. 'I thought you talked about everything on those walks of yours,' smiled Mary Ann. 'We talked about things that happened in our youth,' I said. 'As well as about the two of you and your idyll in San Francisco.'

I'd been at Stoneham for nearly a month, and my conversations with David would have filled many tapes. Except that there were no record-ings. There were no documents. There were only traces, the words that my memory had managed to retain.

Mary Ann looked down towards the banks of the Kaweah, the river that flows through the ranch, where, in a field of green grass, five or six horses grazed among granite rocks. 'It's true about our idyll in San Francisco,' she said. 'We met while we were both on holiday there.' She was wearing a denim shirt and a straw hat to protect her from the sun. She was still a young woman. 'I know how you met,' I said. 'You showed me the photos.' 'Oh yes, of course, I forgot.' She wasn't looking at me. She was looking at the river, at the horses.

He was never closer to paradise than when he lived on this ranch. The man carving the stone came over to us carrying the piece of paper on which we'd written the epitaph in three languages. 'It's a strange language this,' he said, pointing to the lines in Basque, 'but kind of beautiful too.' He pointed at one of the words; he didn't like it, he wanted to know if there was another better word that could replace it. 'You mean *rantxo?*' The man put his finger to his ear. 'Yeah, it doesn't sound good,' he said. I looked at Mary Ann. 'If you can think of a better one, go ahead. David wouldn't have minded.' I racked my brain. 'I don't know, perhaps . . .' and I wrote *abeletxe* on the piece of paper, a word which the dictionaries translate as 'fold or shelter for cattle, separate from the farmhouse'. The man muttered something I couldn't understand. 'He thinks it's too long,' Mary Ann explained. 'He says it's got two more letters than *rantxo* and that there's barely enough room on the gravestone as it is.' 'I'd leave it as it is,' I said. '*Rantxo*, it is then,' said Mary Ann. The man shrugged and returned to his work.

The path that connected the stables and the houses that made up the ranch passed by the cemetery too. First came the houses of the Mexican ranch-hands, then the house that had belonged to Juan, David's uncle, and where I was staying; and finally, higher up, on the top of a small hill, the house where my friend had lived with Mary Ann for fifteen years; the house where Liz and Sara had been born.

Mary Ann left the cemetery and went out on to the path. 'It's supper time, and I don't want to leave Rosario on her own,' she said. 'It takes more than one person to get the girls to turn off the TV and sit down at table.' Rosario, along with her husband, Efraín, the ranch foreman, was the person Mary Ann depended on for nearly everything. 'You can stay here a while, if you like,' she said when she saw I was about to follow her. 'Why don't you dig up one of those words? They're behind the hamsters' graves, in matchboxes.' 'I don't know if I ought to,' I murmured doubtfully. 'As I said before, David never spoke to me about them.' 'He was probably afraid of looking ridiculous,' she said, 'but there was no reason to. He invented the game so that Liz and Sara would learn something of your language.' 'In that case, then, I will. Although I still feel like a bit of an intruder.' 'I wouldn't worry. He used to say you were the only friend he had left on the other side of the world.' 'We were like brothers,' I said. 'He didn't deserve to die at fifty,' she said. 'It was a dirty trick.' 'Yes, a very dirty trick indeed.' The man carving the gravestone looked up. 'Are you leaving?' he asked. 'No, not yet,' I replied and went back into the cemetery.

I found the first box of matches behind Ronnie's grave. It was in a pretty bad state, but the tiny roll of paper it contained was perfectly preserved. I read the word David had written on it in black ink: *mitxirrika*. It was the word used in Obaba to mean 'butterfly'. I opened another box. The roll of paper contained a whole sentence: *Elurra mara-mara ari du*. It was what people in Obaba said when it was snowing softly.

Liz and Sara had finished supper, and Mary Ann and I were sitting outside on the porch. The view was really beautiful: the houses of Three Rivers nestled beneath enormous trees, for the road to Sequoia National Park ran parallel to the river. On the flatter ground, I could see vineyard upon vineyard, lemon grove upon lemon grove. The sun was gradually setting, lingering on the hills surrounding Lake Kaweah.

I could see it with pristine clarity, just as you can when the wind blows the atmosphere clean and everything seems newly minted. Except that there was no wind, and my perceptions had nothing to do with reality. It was all because of David and my memories, because I was thinking about him, about my friend. David would never see this view again: the hills, the fields, the houses. Nor would the songs of the birds around the ranch reach his ears. His hands would never again feel the warmth of the wooden boards on the porch after a day of sun. For a moment, I imagined myself in his place, as if I were the one who had died, and I felt the awfulness of that loss even more keenly. I couldn't have been more affected if a great crack had suddenly opened up in the earth, swallowing fields and houses and threatening the ranch itself. I understood then, only in a different sense, what is meant by the words: 'Life is the greatest thing there is, whoever loses life loses everything.'

We heard a whistle. One of the Mexican ranch-hands – wearing a cowboy hat – was trying to move the horses away from the river bank. Immediately afterwards, however, everything fell silent again. The birds stopped singing. Below, cars with their headlights on were driving along the road to Sequoia National Park, filling the landscape with bright red splodges and lines. The day was drawing to a close, and the valley was at peace. My friend David was now sleeping for ever. Accompanying him in that sleep were Juan, his uncle, and Henry Johnson, the ranch's first owner.

5

Mary Ann lit a cigarette. 'Mom, don't smoke!' shouted Liz, leaning out of the window. 'It's one of my last ones. Don't worry, I'll keep my promise,' replied Mary Ann. 'What's the word for "butterfly" in Basque?' I asked the girl. From inside the house came the voice of Sara, her younger sister: '*Mitxirrika*.' Liz shouted: 'Hush up, silly!' Mary Ann sighed. 'Her father's death has affected her a lot. Sara's coping better. She hasn't really grasped yet what his death means.' There was the sound of neighing and another whistle from the Mexican ranch-hand in the cowboy hat.

Mary Ann stubbed out her cigarette and started rummaging around in the drawer of a small table on the porch. 'Did he ever show you this?' she asked. She was holding an A4-size book of about 200 beautifully bound pages. 'It's the edition the friends of the Three Rivers Book Club were preparing,' she said, a half-smile on her lips. 'It had a print-run of three. One for Liz and Sara, one for the library in Obaba, and a third copy for the friends of the club who helped publish it.' I couldn't suppress a look of surprise. I didn't know anything about this either. Mary Ann leafed through the pages. 'David used to say jokingly that three copies were three too many, and that he felt a complete fraud. He said he should have followed Virgil's example and asked his friends to burn the original.'

The book had a dark blue cover. The title was in gold. At the top was his name, David Imaz – using only his mother's maiden name – and, in the middle, the title in Basque: *Soinujolearen semea* – *The Accordionist's Son*. The spine was made of black cloth and there was no lettering on it at all.

Mary Ann pointed at the title. 'Needless to say the gold lettering wasn't his idea. When he saw it for the first time, he clutched his head and again quoted Virgil and said what a fraud he felt.' 'I don't know what to say. I'm really surprised,' I said, examining the book. 'I asked him several times to show it to you,' she explained. 'After all, you were his friend from Obaba, the person who would present the copy to the library in the village where he was born. He kept promising he would, but only later, when you were getting on the plane to go home. He didn't want you to feel obliged to offer an opinion.' Mary Ann paused before continuing. 'And maybe that's why he wrote it in a language I can't understand. So as not to put me in an awkward position either.' The half-smile returned to her lips, but this time it was sadder. I got to my feet and paced up and down the porch. I found it hard to remain seated, hard to know what to say. 'I'll take the copy to the library in Obaba,' I said at last. 'But first, I'll read it and write you a letter giving my impressions.'

There were now three ranch-hands rounding up the horses by the river bank. They seemed to be in a good mood. They were laughing loudly and pretending to fight, swatting each other with their hats. Inside the house, someone turned on the TV.

'He'd been toying with the idea of writing a book for ages,' said Mary Ann. 'Probably ever since he arrived in America, because I remember him mentioning it to me in San Francisco, the first time we went out together. But he didn't do anything about it until the day we went to see the carvings made by the Basque shepherds in Humboldt County. You know about those carvings, don't you? They're figures and inscriptions carved with knives on tree trunks.' I did know about them. I'd seen a programme on the *amerikanoak*, the Basques in America, on Basque TV. 'At first,' she went on, 'David was really happy, and all he talked about was what those inscriptions meant, about the need every human being has to leave his or her mark, to say "I was here". Suddenly, though, he changed his mind. He'd just spotted something on one of the trees which he found really disturbing. There were two figures. He told me they were two boxers and that one of them was a Basque and that he hated him. I can't remember his name right now.' Mary Ann closed her eyes and searched her memory. 'Wait a moment,' she said, standing up. 'I've been sorting through his things and I think I know now where I can find the photo we took of that tree. I'll be right back.'

It was getting dark, but there was still some light in the sky and a few clouds lit by the sun, small, round, pink clouds, like the little cotton wool balls you might use to plug your ears. Below the ranch, the trees and the granite rocks blurred into one, as if their shadows were all made of the same material, shadows that filled the river bank, where

7

there were now no more horses or ranch-hands wearing cowboy hats. The loudest sound was the voice of a TV presenter describing a terrible fire near Stockton.

Mary Ann turned on the porch light and handed me a photograph of a tree trunk. It showed two figures with their fists raised as if squaring up to fight. The drawing was fairly crude, and time had so distorted the lines that they could have been two bears, but next to the figure, the shepherd had carved their names, along with the date of the fight and the city where it took place: 'Paulino Uzcudun–Max Baer. 4–VII–1931. Reno'.

'I'm not surprised David was upset,' I said. 'Paulino Uzcudun always sided with the Spanish fascists. He was one of those people who claimed that the Basques themselves had been responsible for destroying Guernica.' Mary Ann watched me in silence. Then she told me what she remembered: 'When we came back from Humboldt County, David showed me an old photo in which his father appeared along with that same boxer and with some other people. He said it had been taken on the day the sportsground in Obaba was formally opened. "Who are these people?" I asked him. "Some of them were murderers," he said. I was surprised because that was the first time he'd ever spoken about anything like that. "And who were the others? Thieves?" I said, half joking. "Probably," he said. The next day, when I came back from school, I found him in the study, setting out on his desk the files he'd brought with him to America. "I've decided to make my own carving," he said, by which he meant this book.'

The porch light glinted on the gold letters of the cover. I opened the book and started leafing through it. It was in very small print, and almost every inch of the page was used. 'What year was that? I mean the trip you made to see the carvings and when he started to write.' 'I was pregnant with Liz, so that's about fifteen years ago.' 'Did he take long to finish it?' 'I'm not sure,' said Mary Ann. She smiled again, as if amused by her own reply. 'The only time I helped him with it was when I translated the story you heard the other day.'

The story you heard the other day. Mary Ann meant 'Obaba's First

American', a story she'd translated into English for publication in the anthology *Writers from Tulare County*. There had been a reading of it at the ranch, in David's presence, only two weeks before. Now he was no longer there. Nor would he ever be there again. Or anywhere. Not on the porch, not in the library, not in his study, sitting at the white computer Mary Ann had given him and which he had been using only hours before he was taken to hospital. That was the nature of death, that was the way death behaved. No sweet talk and no niceties. It simply arrived at a house and bawled: 'That's it, it's over!', then set off to another house.

'Now that I think of it, I did translate a couple more things for him,' said Mary Ann. 'I helped him translate two stories he wrote about friends in Obaba. One of them was called "Teresa", and the other . . .' Mary Ann couldn't remember the title of the second story, only that it was someone's first name. 'Lubis?' She shook her head. 'Martín?' Another shake of the head. 'Adrián?' 'Yes, that's right, Adrián.' 'Adrián was part of our group,' I explained. 'We were friends for nearly fifteen years, from primary school through university.' Mary Ann sighed: 'A colleague of mine at college wanted to publish them in a magazine in Visalia. There was even talk of sending them to a publisher's in San Francisco, but David got cold feet. He couldn't bear the thought of them appearing for the first time in English. It felt to him like a betrayal of the old language.'

The old language. For the first time since my arrival in Stoneham, I heard a note of bitterness in Mary Ann's voice. She spoke perfect Spanish, with the Mexican accent of the ranch-hands. I could imagine how she must have said to David on more than one occasion: 'If you can't write in English, why don't you try writing in Spanish? After all, Spanish is one of your languages. And it would be easier for me to help you then.' David would have pretended to agree, but then postponed the decision again and again. To the point, perhaps, of causing irritation.

Rosario appeared on the porch. 'I'm off now. Efraín can't even make himself a sandwich, and if I don't make him one, he'll go without any supper at all.' 'Of course, Rosario. Joseba and I have talked longer than we thought,' replied Mary Ann, getting up from her chair. I stood up too, and we both said goodbye to Rosario. 'I'll present the book to the library in Obaba,' I said afterwards. Mary Ann nodded: 'At least someone there will be able to read it.' 'In the old language,' I said. She smiled at the irony in my words, and I set off down the hill towards Juan's house. I was leaving America the next day and had to pack my bags.

Mary Ann returned to the subject of 'the old language' the following morning, while we were waiting at the airport in Visalia. 'You must have thought me really rude yesterday, the typical minority-hating reactionary. But don't get me wrong. When David and Juan used to talk to each other, they always spoke in Basque, and I found it a real pleasure, like listening to music.' My flight was being called, and there was no time for any long disquisitions. 'Perhaps you were right yesterday,' I said. 'Given that David had no intention of returning to his native land, it would probably have done him good to write in another language.' But Mary Ann ignored my comment. 'Yes, I really loved to hear them talking,' she said again. 'I remember once, when I'd just arrived at Stoneham, I said to David how strange that music sounded to me, all those k's and r's. Had I never realised, he said, that both he and Juan were, in fact, crickets, two crickets lost in America, and that the sound I heard was of them rubbing their wings together. "Yes, as soon as we're left alone, we start rubbing our wings together," he said. That was his humour.'

I had my own memories. The 'old language' had been a major topic of discussion between me and David. There were references to it in many of the letters we'd exchanged since he left for America: Would Schuchardt's prediction come true? Would our language disappear? Were we, he and I and our fellow countrymen and women, the equivalent of the last Mohican? 'Writing in Spanish or English would have been very hard for David,' I said. 'There are so few Basque speakers, fewer than a million. And every time even one of us abandons the language, it feels as if we were contributing to its extinction. In your case it's different. There are millions of you. You'd never hear a speaker of English or

Spanish saying: "The words that were in my parents' mouths are strange to me".' Mary Ann shrugged. 'Well, there's nothing to be done about it now,' she said. 'But I would like to have read his book.' Then she added: 'There can't be many American wives who've had to say: "The words that were in my husband's mouth are strange to me".' 'Well put, Mary Ann,' I said. 'Well complained, you mean.' And her American accent seemed suddenly much stronger.

They started calling for the passengers to board; there was no time to continue our conversation. Mary Ann gave me a goodbye kiss on the cheek. 'I'll write to you as soon as I've read the book,' I promised. 'Thanks for being here with us,' she said. 'It's been pretty tough,' I said, 'but I've learned a lot. David was a man of real integrity.' We embraced again and I joined the queue to board the plane.

The pink clouds I'd seen the previous evening in Stoneham were still there. From the plane window they seemed flatter, like flying saucers in a blue sky. I took David's book out of my hand luggage. First came the dedications: two pages for Liz and Sara, five for his Uncle Juan, five or so more for Lubis, the friend of his childhood and youth, two for his mother . . . and then the body of the story, which he described as a 'memorial'. I put the book away again. I would read it on the flight from Los Angeles to London, in that ethereal region ploughed by great planes and in which there is nothing, not even clouds.

A week later, I wrote to Mary Ann to tell her that David's book was now in the library in Obaba. I told her, too, that I'd made a photocopy for my personal use, because the events described were familiar to me and because I appeared in some of them as a protagonist. 'I hope you don't mind me increasing the print-run to four.' The book was important to me. I wanted to keep it near me.

I then explained my interpretation of David's behaviour. As I understood it, he'd had other reasons for writing his memoirs in the Basque language, apart, that is, from the reason I'd given her at Visalia airport – his desire to defend a minority language. David had preferred not to mix up his first life with his second, American life; and since she'd been

11

the person mainly responsible for that feeling he'd had at Stoneham of never having been closer to paradise, he hadn't wanted to implicate her in matters that had nothing to do with her. Lastly, out of the possible alternatives – Virgil wanting to burn his original script – he'd chosen the more human one: giving in to the impulse to publish his writings, but in a language that would prove hermetic to the majority, but not to the people of Obaba, or to his daughters, if the latter fulfilled his wishes and decided to increase their vocabulary and go beyond *mitxirrika* and the other words buried in the cemetery at Stoneham.

'He felt that the book would mean very different things to the people of Obaba and to your daughters,' I argued. 'The former had the right to know what was being said about them, whereas in the case of Liz and Sara, the book might help them to know themselves better, because it's about their progenitor, a certain David who would inevitably continue living through them and influencing – at least to some extent – their sense of humour, their tastes and their decisions.'

At the end of the letter, I copied out the words David had used as a coda to his book: 'I've thought about my daughters as I wrote each and every one of these pages, and from that "presence" I've drawn the courage I needed to finish the book. That, I feel, is only logical. One mustn't forget that even Benjamin Franklin, hardly the most devoted of fathers, included in his list of valid reasons for writing an autobiography the need to leave a record of the circumstances of his life "for his posterity".'

Mary Ann answered with a card sent from the post office in Three Rivers. She thanked me for the letter and for having made David's wishes reality. She also asked me a question. She wanted to know what I thought of the book. 'Very interesting, very dense,' I wrote back. She sent me a second postcard: 'I see. So events and facts have all been crammed in, like anchovies in a glass jar.' The description was fairly accurate. David was trying to tell everything, leaving no gaps; but some facts, which I knew first-hand and which seemed to me important, weren't given the necessary emphasis.

*   *   *

Some weeks later, shortly before the twentieth century came to an end, I wrote to Mary Ann setting out the project that had first begun to take shape in my mind on my return from the United States: I wanted to write a book based on what David had written, to rewrite and expand his memoir. Not like someone pulling down a house and building a new one in its place, but in the spirit of someone finding a tree, on which some long-vanished shepherd had left a carving, and deciding to redraw the lines so as to bring out and enhance the drawing and the figures. 'If I do it like that,' I explained to Mary Ann, 'time will so blur the difference between the old incisions and the new that eventually there'll only be a single inscription on the bark, a book whose main message will be: "Two friends, two brothers were here".' Would she give me her blessing? I proposed starting as soon as possible.

As always, Mary Ann replied by return of post. She said she was thrilled by the news, and told me that she was sending me a batch of papers and photographs that might be of use to me. She also said that she was acting purely out of self-interest, 'because if you write the book and it's later translated into a language I can understand, it won't be too difficult for me to identify the parts that correspond to the life David led before we met in San Francisco. Your corrections and additions may leave almost no scar at all and be invisible to a stranger, but I shared more than fifteen years of my life with him, and I'll be able to tell the two styles apart.' In a postscript, Mary Ann suggested a new title, *My Brother's Book*, and reminded me not to forget about Liz and Sara, 'because, as you yourself said a few months back, they might one day be readers of the book, and I wouldn't want it to cause them any unnecessary suffering'.

I wrote to Stoneham reassuring her about her daughters. Like David, I would think about them on each and every one of the pages, and they would be a 'presence' for me too. I wanted my book to help them to live and feel more at ease in the world. Naturally, not all my desires were so noble. I, too, was motivated by self-interest. Rejecting the other option, that of becoming a mere editor of David's work, meant that I didn't have to relinquish the chance to make my own mark. 'There will be people who won't understand what I'm doing and who'll accuse me of tearing the bark off the tree, of stealing David's drawing,' I explained to Mary Ann. 'They'll say I'm burned out as a writer, incapable of writing a book of my own, and that this is why I'm having to resort to rewriting someone else's work; and yet the truth is quite different. The truth is that, as time passes and events become more remote, the protagonists begin to resemble each other; the figures grow hazy. That's what is happening, I think, with David and with me. And also, although in a different way, with our friends from Obaba. Any lines I add to David's drawing must be true to the original.'

Three years have passed since that letter, and the book now exists. It still has the title it started out with and not the one suggested by Mary Ann. However, as regards everything else, her wishes and mine have been respected: there's nothing in it that could hurt Liz and Sara, nor has anything been omitted of what happened in Obaba in our time and in our parents' time. The book contains the words left by the accordionist's son as well as my own.

Names

LIZ, SARA

Liz, the older of our daughters, was two and a half and Sara, the youngest, was only one. Liz was with me at home; Sara was in hospital in Visalia with Mary Ann. Sara had been there for about twenty-four hours, inhaling salbutamol and, intermittently, connected up to an oxygen tube. The mucus blocking her bronchial tubes was preventing her from breathing, and her little seventeen- or eighteen-pound body just didn't have the strength to get rid of it. Her cough was truly terrible to hear.

As on other afternoons, I suggested to Liz that we go for a walk. I did so, moreover, with a certain enthusiasm, pretending a good humour I didn't at all feel. I assumed she hadn't noticed the ruckus at home on the previous night, with Rosario weeping and screaming – 'Oh, dear God, the child's suffocating!' – and that she knew nothing about what was going on. 'How's Liz? Is she missing us?' Mary Ann asked when she phoned from the hospital. I told her 'No', she was perfectly calm and had eaten well.

Liz isn't particularly interested in looking at sweeping landscapes. She prefers studying the ground to contemplating the mountains or the valley. She crouches down again and again and scrutinises whatever pebbles, twigs or other insignificant objects happen to be near her feet, cigarette ends included. If, during these observations, an ant or some other insect appears, so much the better. She greets this novelty with joyful laughter.

We walked along at our usual slow pace, stopping every few yards. It took us half an hour to reach the swing near the river. Then, when she got bored with playing there, we went over to the paddock where the new-born foals are kept, and after that, to the garden where the stone gnome 'lives', beside Rosario and Efraín's house. This is another of Liz's habits: she goes over to the gnome, talks to him for a few minutes, kisses him and comes back. 'How's your friend?' I asked her. 'Fine,' she said. 'And what did he say to you?' 'He said Sara will get better very soon.'

I was so touched. Both because of the unexpectedness of the reply and because her words – the words of a little girl of two and a half – seemed to me to have a beauty I'd never known before. 'Of course she will, she'll be back home in no time,' I whispered in her ear, holding her in my arms. Through my mind passed a multitude of thoughts, as if I had many souls, each with its own voice, or a single soul endowed with many tongues, and I couldn't rest easy until I'd made myself a promise: she and Sara would receive from me something more than the ranch and its sixty or seventy riding-horses. I would take up my pen again and try to finish the 'memorial' I'd been thinking about writing ever since my arrival in the United States.

JUAN

In the last few months of his life, the deterioration in Uncle Juan's state of health was so marked that Liz and Sara were always saying: 'What's wrong with him? He's stopped telling us stories.' One day, Mary Ann told them the truth. His heart was very weak, and any effort, however slight, wore him out. 'It's best to leave him alone,' she told them. 'So I don't want you playing at his house any more.' Liz and Sara took this advice very seriously indeed. They would do as their mother asked. 'I knew Juan was ill. Nakika told me,' explained Liz. 'She said "ay-ay-ay Juan doesn't play golf any more ay-ay-ay that's a bad sign. And he doesn't go out to see how the horses are running ay-ay-ay".' Nakika was the name of her favourite doll.

She was right. Juan had given up his two favourite occupations months before, when he was still in good health. First, golf and then horses. More than that, unusually for him, he began hanging around our house. He was, to all appearances, the same as ever: a man concerned about current affairs, about politics and the economy; an attentive conversationalist with his own ideas. But he tired very easily, and after a while would sit down in front of the television or phone for Efraín to come and fetch him in the Land-rover.

In June, his condition worsened. He came to the house one afternoon, asked Mary Ann for a coffee and sat down on the porch to watch the horses – 'I used to know all their names' – or to look out over the valley. His remarks began to sound, to use Efraín's word, *bizarros* – bizarre. He said for example: 'I bet those men riding along the river are Indians. They probably want me to offer them a cup of coffee. Coffee makes them crazy.' His voice grew gradually weaker until it became – as Mary Ann put it – as flimsy as cigarette paper. Towards the end of June, a few days before he died, he asked me to play something on my accordion. 'There's a tune I want to hear,' he said. 'Which one?' I asked. 'The one you played the other day, the one about *café*.' At first, I didn't know what he meant. I hadn't played the accordion for years. 'I don't know which one you mean, Uncle,' I said. He took a deep breath and started singing: '*Yo te daré, te daré, niña hermosa, te daré una cosa, una cosa que yo sólo sé: ¡café!*' – 'I will give thee, I will give thee, lovely girl, I will give thee something, something only I can give thee – coffee!'

Finally, I remembered: I'd played that song shortly after my arrival at Stoneham Ranch, the day of Efraín and Rosario's wedding. After the meal, Juan had told us about his encounter with Indians in the Nevada desert, and how frightened he'd been when he realised that a large group of them were following him. 'The worst part was when it got dark and I began to see shadows creeping around the encampment. My horse got real jumpy, and so did I. In fact, I took the safety catch off my rifle. But the redskins weren't interested in attacking me, they just wanted some coffee. They whooped with joy when I picked up the pot and started making some.' He had followed this story with that song – *yo te daré . . .* – which Juan had sung in a strong voice, very different from his voice during those last few days. I fetched my accordion and did my best to repeat my performance at Efraín and Rosario's wedding. He seemed really pleased.

On the day before he died, he was sitting quietly on the porch, not wanting to eat or drink anything. 'Do you want me to get my accordion?' I asked. He shrugged. He didn't feel like listening to music. He was staring off into the distance, past the vineyards and the lemon groves to the hills surrounding Lake Kaweah, behind which the sun had just disappeared.

'So stupid!' he said suddenly. It sounded more like a sigh. 'Mary Ann, have you ever heard of the Spanish civil war?' he asked. I felt sad for him. Mary Ann's father had fought in the International Brigade, and we'd often discussed the war. 'Uncle, why don't you tell us about the colts you were looking at this morning,' I suggested. 'Efraín told me you'd been to visit them.' He took no notice of my remark. 'When the fascists entered Obaba, a lot of young men fled into the hills to see if they could join the Basque army,' he said. His voice was stronger now. 'But I stayed on in the village because the party asked me to, and that's how I came to see that dreadful scene. A captain arrived, Degrela he was called, and he started haranguing us from outside the town hall, in the same place where, only hours before, he'd ordered seven men to be shot, amongst them, my friend Humberto, a good man who'd never done anyone any harm. Anyway, this captain said he needed young men who were prepared to give their lives for religion and for Spain. "I need your red blood," he said. "I cannot promise you life, but I can promise you glory." And they all went crazy, pushing and shoving to be the first to reach the table and sign up. It was as if they had only one desire in the world – to die for the Spanish fascists.'

He stopped speaking, as if he'd stumbled upon an obstacle his voice couldn't overcome. Then he went on, gesturing with his hand: 'One of those young men from Obaba was excitedly urging me to go with them. "I can't," I said. "I'm lame. I can't go to the front on crutches." Because I happened to be using crutches at the time. According to a certificate I had in my pocket, which was completely false, but which bore the signature of a real doctor, I had a very serious cartilage injury. That's how I got out of it. All the others marched off to the front, I've no

18

idea how many, perhaps a hundred. Before the year was out, half of them were dead and buried.'

Efraín came to fetch him in his Land-rover. 'The girls are fast asleep,' Efraín said when he came into the house. So Liz and Sara would be spending the night at his house, in Rosario's care. 'How are you, boss? Feeling better?' he asked Juan. 'There are a lot of innocents in the world,' Juan said. Efraín thought he was referring to a prisoner in Texas, whose picture we kept seeing on TV because he was about to be put to death in the gas chamber. 'And a lot of guilty people too, boss,' he replied, helping him to his feet.

'He's going to die soon, isn't he?' I said to Mary Ann when we went to bed. She nodded. 'Yes, I think so, but I wouldn't want today's conversation to be our last one.' I agreed. His story about the young men who'd marched off to war as if to a fiesta – that dark 'carving', that sinister inscription – wasn't like Juan. He'd always been such a cheerful man.

The following day, 24 June, as if we were under the protection of some kindly genie or even of God himself, our wish was granted. Just hours before he died, Juan felt much better. As soon as we saw him, we knew he was in a good mood. He called for champagne. 'Great! Why not?' said Mary Ann with exaggerated enthusiasm. 'What are we celebrating?' 'You Americans forget all the important dates,' he said. 'In case you don't know, today is San Juan. My saint's day! A very special day in the Basque Country!' 'It's true, I'd forgotten as well,' I said, 'I must be getting too American.' 'Congratulations, Juan!' cried Mary Ann. Afterwards, while the champagne was chilling, we sat on the porch and amused ourselves watching the Mexicans who were, at that moment, training the horses. In the paddocks on the other side of the river, there were ten men, all wearing cowboy hats, and each carrying a rope. The horses were trotting round and round.

'How many have we got right now?' asked Juan, indicating the horses. 'Counting the colts, exactly fifty-four,' I said. 'Excellent,' said Juan. 'That was my idea when I came to America. To have horses, not sheep like the other Basques. Wandering around the mountains with two

19

thousand sheep to look after is no life at all! Breeding handsome horses and selling them off for ten thousand dollars a head is a much better bet!' We got the bottle of champagne out of the icebox and poured three glasses. I looked across at the valley: the vineyards were in darkness; the sky was rose-pink; the sun had just slipped behind the hills.

'What was the name of that Hollywood actress who used to have a house on Lake Tahoe?' asked Juan, after taking a sip. 'A fantastic-looking woman. A real sex-symbol.' We knew who he meant, but just then Efraín arrived in search of some pyjamas for Liz and Sara, and he was the one who provided the answer to the question: 'How can you have forgotten? It was Raquel Welch!' Juan hesitated for a moment. 'I mean the actress that Sansón, that rather crude shepherd, was so keen on.' 'Yes, Raquel Welch,' repeated Efraín. Juan nodded, laughing. That was the woman!

He started telling the story: Sansón had arrived in the United States straight from a village in the Basque Country and got a job helping a man who owned some sheep and who was called Guernica, because that was where he came from in Vizcaya. Shortly after he arrived, the two of them were herding their sheep near the shores of Lake Tahoe when they saw something strange. A riderless horse came galloping wildly towards them. Sansón managed to stop it, and they both waited for its owner to appear. The person who appeared was Raquel Welch. She was the owner of the horse. She was walking along, alone, wearing only a black bikini. 'The smallest bikini in the whole United States,' according to Guernica. Sansón was transfixed, like a statue. 'Paralysed,' to use Guernica's word.

Juan burst out laughing, as he always did when he reached this part of the story. Then, imitating Guernica's Vizcayan way of speaking, he continued. 'Sansón still hadn't moved, so I went over to the actress and the only thing I could think of to say was: "He's epileptic, very epileptic." "Oh, dear," she said and stroked his cheek, the way grown-ups do with children, as if to say "Aren't you sweet," and then rode off on her horse. I grabbed Sansón's arm and said: "Come on, we've got to go after the sheep." He looked at me like an idiot and said: "Sheep? What sheep?

20

Weren't we herding pigs."' Juan collapsed in laughter. 'Honestly, how could anyone confuse pigs with sheep!'

We poured ourselves some more champagne and stayed out on the porch for another half an hour.

'Do you remember that time we were travelling in Spain and we came across a ruined castle?' Mary Ann said to me the following morning over breakfast. I said I wasn't sure that I did. 'It was a really isolated place,' she went on, 'really desolate. The stones looked so terribly heavy. Suddenly, a stork arrived and started strutting around on one of the towers. All it took was that tiny movement to bring all the stones to life again.' 'What made you remember that?' 'It's exactly what happened yesterday with Juan. The joy he felt in retelling the Raquel Welch story transformed him. He seemed so full of life.' 'What you're saying is that it was his last story.' She nodded.

Mary Ann would make an excellent sibyl. Her elegiac words were spoken at exactly the right moment. We were still having breakfast when Efraín arrived and started shouting to us from the porch: 'Come quickly! All the lights are on at the boss's house, but there's no answer!' We went down to Juan's house with little hope of finding him alive.

During the funeral, I told the story of the stork and the ruined castle, and talked about Juan's life: 'he was so full of energy and hope that he deserved to have a second, even longer life'. Then I picked up my accordion and, in his memory, played the hymn to San Juan.

MARY ANN

I

A soft rain was falling on San Francisco. A young woman who looked either Swedish or Icelandic was standing on the corner of the street holding a camera. The camera was a Polaroid; the district, Haight-

21

Ashbury; the cross-streets, Ashbury and Frederick; the young woman, Mary Ann.

When I walked past her, she held out her camera to me. '*Puede usted, por favor, hacernos una fotografía?*' – 'Would you mind taking a photograph of us, please?' – she said in very correct Spanish, but with a strong American accent. I rejected the idea that she was a citizen of Sweden or Iceland. 'How did you know I spoke Spanish?' I asked. 'I'm a very observant tourist,' she replied with a smile. Her hair was blond, as were her eyebrows and eyelashes; her eyes were an intense blue, the eyes not so much of an Icelander or a Swede, but of an inhabitant of North Cape.

She went and stood next to a woman who couldn't have been more than forty or forty-five, but who looked terribly thin and drawn. I framed them both in the viewfinder. When they linked arms, the two women formed a kind of emblem. They were joy and sadness intertwined.

Mary Ann was rubbing the woman's back as if trying to warm her. She was wearing a transparent raincoat. Underneath, she had on a denim skirt that came just above her knees and a white, embroidered blouse that matched her white ankle boots.

'Are you Argentinian?' she asked when I'd taken the photograph. 'No,' I said, 'I'm Basque.' She needed a few seconds to connect that word with something. 'Shepherds!' she said, with the look of someone who has just guessed the winning number. 'Yes, I keep my sheep over there in that park,' I said, pointing towards Buena Vista. 'You can come and see them, if you like.' I issued this invitation in a jokey, nonchalant tone, as if it were a matter of complete indifference to me, but I felt very nervous. I could hear inside me the 'wise voice' which is, according to Virgil, the voice that speaks of presentiments. 'Stick with this woman,' the voice said.

'Why not?' said Mary Ann. 'We could do with a photo of us with some sheep, couldn't we, Helen? Besides, we look pretty awful in the photo our shepherd here has taken of us.' She again rubbed her friend's back. I had the feeling that the sole purpose of all her dynamism was to instil her friend with some energy. 'What do you think, Helen?' she

22

asked again. 'If that's what you'd like, Mary Ann,' answered the woman. It was the first time I'd heard her name. *Mary Ann*. I thought it was really pretty. 'Although, personally, I'd rather go to a café in Castro,' said Helen. 'I have certain needs that would be hard to meet in an American park.' Mary Ann agreed, and so did I.

We introduced ourselves as we walked down the hill. They told me they were both teachers in a college in New Hampshire. Helen taught Latin American literature, and Mary Ann taught literary translation. They were only in San Francisco for a few days. 'And to be perfectly honest, we're very annoyed with the horrible weather we've been having,' added Mary Ann, moving closer to me and taking shelter under my umbrella. The rain didn't stop. 'Don't worry. The weather's going to improve tomorrow,' I said. 'Are you sure?' 'We Basque shepherds are never wrong about such things.' 'But how do you know? By studying the direction of the wind?' 'Studying the direction of the wind helps, but the most important thing is to listen to the weather reports on the radio and to study the meteorological maps on TV.' She laughed. Her raincoat smelled new.

'You're both teachers and both from New Hampshire, but you're cheerful and she's the exact opposite,' I said to Mary Ann while Helen went off to the bathroom. Mary Ann looked very serious. 'Her father's gravely ill. That's why we're in San Francisco.' I was filled with apprehension. I was getting ahead of myself in my desire to establish some complicity between us, and my remark had been a clumsy mistake. If I didn't put it right, as soon as she'd finished her coffee, she'd leave, a disappointed woman, and without giving me her phone number or her address. In order to remedy my mistake – people who consider themselves to be sensitive souls always turn to 'deep' topics of conversation when they want to create a good impression – I started talking about death.

I can't repeat what I told her. I can't remember what I said. I doubt that the moment even reached my memory. The only thing I know for sure is that I was afraid we might lose the incipient affinity that had sprung up between us as we stood on the corner of Ashbury and

Frederick, and so, during all the time we were together, I watched every change in her North Cape eyes, trying to capture each tiny movement. My uncertainty lasted until I mentioned Dylan Thomas' famous poem – 'Do not go gentle into that good night' – or, rather, until I gave a rather inept recital of the first few lines. I noticed a change then in the North Cape area. 'Helen's father might like to hear that,' she said. 'We could perhaps buy the book,' I said. 'Dylan Thomas seems to be better known here than he is in Europe.' I was seeking her approbation. 'We'll see what Helen thinks, but I reckon it's a good idea,' she said. Harmony between us was restored.

'What do you think?' Mary Ann asked when Helen returned. 'My father might take notice of what the poem says,' she said. 'After all, like Dylan Thomas, he was born in Wales, and the Welsh tend to be very patriotic. What they won't do is follow their daughter's advice.' She ended this sentence with a sigh. Then she explained that her father's main problem was a lack of will. He wasn't fighting the illness. He had lost the will to live.

Helen spent most of her time at the hospital, and so Mary Ann and I would meet up at about nine o'clock at the hotel in Lombard Avenue where she was staying. Over breakfast, we'd consult the guidebook and set off, usually on foot, along that day's chosen route.

The agreement between us was a tacit one. I didn't really know why she agreed to go out with me, but I imagined that the prospect of trailing around a strange city on her own must have seemed rather unappealing and that she appreciated having someone to talk to. On one of our first days out, we were drinking hot chocolate on the terrace of the Ghirardelli when the waiter suddenly addressed us as if we were a married couple. 'I think your wife would rather be inside.' And Mary Ann laughed gaily, and that made me hope that there were other, deeper reasons behind our expeditions. We usually went our separate ways at about seven in the evening: she set off to meet Helen, and I grabbed something to eat in Chinatown or in the Marina itself, then walked back to my hotel to rest.

The hotel Uncle Juan had chosen for me enjoyed a very privileged position. The windows of my room looked out over the bay, and to one side I could see the lights of Alcatraz Island and to the other the lights of the Golden Gate Bridge. While I watched them – the lights on Alcatraz were fainter – I would go over the events of the day in my mind, analysing every detail, pondering every word, wondering ceaselessly about the feelings of this woman whom I'd met on the corner of Ashbury and Frederick. I did something else too, something that has been parodied and mocked a thousand times: I took a sheet of the hotel's headed notepaper and wrote her name on it. Sometimes I would write the whole thing: Mary Ann Linder, sometimes simply Mary Ann. I also tried, without success, to write a poem. The only vaguely acceptable part of my various attempts at poetry was my way of describing her eyes and lips: North Cape Eyes, Thule Lips. However, I wasn't sure about that second image, because I associated the word 'Thule' with the colour blue, rather than with red, which is the colour that has been used to describe lips in nearly every poem ever written anywhere in the world.

We walked from one end of the city to the other, and I took lots of photographs of her. At first – 'I'm your official photographer' – these were snapshots in which she appeared outside such places as the City Lights Bookshop or Mission Dolores, while others were more personal, unposed close-ups – 'Sorry, I'm a member of the paparazzi and I have to earn my living somehow.' One afternoon, sitting outside a café – the weather had improved since the second day – the camera fell off the table. 'We'd better check it's not broken,' Mary Ann said, picking it up and training the lens on me. 'It sounds all right,' she added, when the photo emerged from the camera. We waited while the photograph developed. 'Hey, I think the fall improved it! You look great.' She was right. It was a really good picture of me. 'I'll do a deal with you,' I said. 'I'll give you this photo of me in exchange for one of you.' There was a lot of cheerful coming and going between Thule and North Cape. 'I don't need it,' she said, opening the bag she usually carried and taking out an envelope full of photographs. I appeared in many of them. 'Sorry,

25

I'm a member of the paparazzi as well, and I, too, have to earn my living,' she said. Then she added, laughing: 'Besides, I've got plenty of photographs, thank you, so, no deal.' 'That's not fair,' I said. 'I don't hang on to yours. I hand them over straight away.' There was more coming and going between Thule and North Cape, this time of a mocking nature. 'We all have our own way of doing things,' she said. 'You give me no choice, then,' I said. 'I have no alternative but to become both paparazzo and thief.' 'That won't be possible,' she replied. 'From now on the camera never leaves my bag.' 'What do I have to do to get a picture of you, then?' 'You have to earn some Brownie points,' she said.

I began to be conscious of time passing. After my first year at the ranch, Juan had thought it a good idea for me to take a holiday and go to San Francisco, but he wanted me back in Three Rivers for the so-called Community Recognition celebrations. He wanted to introduce me to local society and for me to make friends with people in the village, many of whom were craftsmen and artists. That way, he said, I would stop wasting all my free time playing poker with the Mexican ranch-hands. This meant I could be away for a maximum of ten days. And of those ten days, six had already passed. The time was fast approaching for me to go back to the ranch, to Stoneham. It was the same for Mary Ann: her college classes in New Hampshire awaited her. Over 3000 miles separated the two places.

'It's always a bad sign when we start thinking in numbers,' Joseba had said to me once, apropos a poem he was writing. 'When we're about to lose something good or something we really love, we start to count: only another so many days, we say. And the same thing happens when we're in a situation we don't like: we start to calculate how many days until the end. In either case, thinking in numbers is never good.'

In the spring of 1983, when, after my sixth day on holiday, I went back to my hotel, numbers started going round and round in my head more furiously than ever. It was true that I only had another four days' holiday left; it was true that New Hampshire was over 3000 miles from Stoneham. On the other hand, I was on the verge of embarking on the third serious relationship of my life, and if the previous two were anything

26

to go by – neither had been particularly satisfactory – my chances of success were very low, about twenty per cent, more or less. They might be even less if I took into account one particularly negative factor: we came from such very different places, miles apart from each other, she from Hot Springs, Arkansas and I from Obaba, in the Basque Country. This reminded me forcibly of the brutal maxim that appears at the beginning of one of Cesare Pavese's novels: 'Take both wife and horse from a local source.' What's more, as I'd guessed on our first meeting, she belonged to a family that had emigrated from Sweden to Canada, and from Canada to the United States; her real surname – 'which a pragmatic grandfather decided to shorten' – was Lindegren. These thoughts and calculations mingled with what my eyes could see: the darkness of the water in the bay and the faint lights from Alcatraz.

I moved away from the window and turned on the TV. I wanted to distract myself, to concentrate on something else and stop thinking. I knew myself well, and was all too aware of what happened to me in such circumstances: something would start going round and round in my head and insist on showing me the same situations and the same faces over and over, as if it were a *tiovivo*, what Liz and Sara call a carousel.

On the TV screen appeared the figure of a man walking along the deserted shore of a river. He started to sing: 'Mary, queen of Arkansas . . .' The landscape shown on the screen, the tune and the words of the song all oozed melancholy. I recalled what a fellow student at the School of Economics in Bilbao used to say: 'It's terrible, every time I fall in love, I turn up in a song in the Top Ten.' I decided that I should simply resign myself to the absurd nature of the situation.

I turned off the TV and lay on my bed in the dark, waiting for sleep to come. The wheel in my head kept spinning; it was no longer talking about numbers now, but about names: Teresa, Virginia, Mary Ann. To put it in the words of a Top Ten song, these were the names of the women 'whose lives had once crossed mine'. The first of them soon disappeared, and only Virginia – *the queen of Obaba* – and Mary Ann – *the queen of Arkansas* – continued turning. Both of them were physically strong and had very clear, open faces. The difference was that Virginia's hair and eyes were dark, and Mary Ann's were light. I fell asleep still worrying away at this comparison.

On the seventh day of my holiday, Mary Ann asked me to go with her to the hospital to pick up Helen, so that we could all go out to supper together. 'She's feeling really sad, and it would do her good to talk to you. You know how to cheer people up. Better than I do.' This was the first compliment I'd received from her since our meeting in Haight-Ashbury, and from that moment on, I did nothing but ponder the best way of carrying out the task I'd been charged with. But nothing occurred to me, or, rather, I could only think of 'deep' subjects, in particular death – the least suitable topic given the circumstances. Cheering Helen up suddenly seemed very difficult indeed.

We walked from the hospital to an Italian restaurant in Mission District. As soon as we went in, we heard music, a tarantella. A man in a red waistcoat was sitting in one corner, playing the accordion. The wheel that had been turning inside my head – like a kaleidoscope, you might say, although without the bright colours – changed at once. All the arguments, ideas and quotes I'd been juggling with as a way of cheering Helen up vanished. 'My father was an accordionist,' I said. We were sitting a short distance from the man playing the tarantella. 'How neat!' exclaimed Helen. 'Well, not really,' I said. 'We never got on very well.'

I continued talking about my father. 'When I was a child, I used to make lists,' I said. I regretted having said this before I'd even finished the sentence: there, in an Italian restaurant in Mission District, to the sound of a tarantella, this confession seemed out of place. However – like spilled water and a thrown stone – a word once spoken is difficult to take back. Mary Ann and Helen were looking at me intently, waiting for me to go on.

'My mother called them my lists of favourites,' I said, unable to stop now. 'I used to list the names of the people I loved: first, the person I loved most, then the person I loved a lot, but slightly less than the first

28

person, and so on. Well, my father soon disappeared from the list entirely.' Mary Ann looked at Helen: 'You see, I told you, he's a perfectly normal guy.' She stressed the word 'perfectly'. Helen smiled.

Having dipped a toe – or perhaps, if I wanted to make a rather bad joke, put my foot – in the subject of lists, I made another confession: I was going to write a book about the life I'd led in the land of my birth before coming to America. I said this because it was true, and because I wanted to impress Mary Ann. It was time to start accumulating the Brownie points I needed to obtain her photograph, her attention and her love. Someone like her was bound to warm to the idea of me writing a book.

Mary Ann turned to Helen. 'I don't trust this man. I don't know if he's telling the truth. Does he look like a writer to you?' I added quickly: 'I didn't say I was a writer. Like I said, I'm the manager on my uncle's ranch . . .' I stopped talking. There was another thought in my head. 'But I *am* an accordionist, like my father.'

As a Caribbean song in the Top Ten used to say: 'I found another way to impress her.' 'Is that true?' asked Mary Ann, opening her North Cape eyes very wide. 'Now you're contradicting yourself, Mary Ann,' said Helen. 'If you don't trust him, why ask?' She seemed in a brighter mood than when we'd picked her up at the hospital.

Mary Ann had stood up. 'If you want to take it back, you've still got time,' she said. She went over to the man in the red waistcoat. 'You shouldn't doubt me,' I retorted. Before I knew it, I was sitting on Luigi's stool – he told me his name when he shook my hand – with the accordion, an old but lovingly cared-for Guerrini, on my knees. 'I know this instrument well. I had one almost the same,' I told Luigi, after trying it out. I mentally reviewed the tunes I used to play at dances in Obaba and finally opted for 'Padam Padam'.

As soon as I'd finished playing, Mary Ann and Helen burst into applause, as did the people sitting at the other tables, and Luigi again warmly shook my hand. Nevertheless, I felt bad. I was furious with myself for having broken the promise I'd made at Stoneham that I would never again play the accordion, especially not 'Padam Padam'. Suddenly,

I was no longer in that Italian restaurant, in San Francisco, in the United States. I was back in Obaba with my friend Lubis.

Mary Ann noticed my change of mood. 'Come on, you didn't play *that* badly,' she joked. 'I should have chosen another song,' I said. 'Why?' she asked. The waiter came with our order, and I took advantage of the interruption to consider my response. Now was not the time to tell Lubis' story. I didn't want to return to the past and say: 'A friend of mine, now dead, really liked that song.' 'Why was it a bad choice?' Mary Ann asked again. 'It'll all be in the book,' I said, managing to sound light-hearted.

I turned to Helen. 'Your father must be very happy,' I said. 'Here you are, having come all the way to San Francisco to be with him. The years have passed, but he still has your love. How many other people could say as much? Five per cent? Ten maybe?' Mary Ann was listening to me, holding her glass level with her nose.

'I wish that were true, but I'm not sure,' said Helen. She wiped her lips with her napkin. 'When I was a child, my father and I were very close. I remember once going to the station with my mother to meet him off the train, but when we arrived, he wasn't there. We'd got the times wrong and arrived late. The platforms were all empty, not a soul on them, and the sight of those deserted platforms so alarmed me I thought I'd never see him again. Then, suddenly, there he was, calling to me. I ran to him and hugged him as hard as I could. It was a wonderful moment. One of the most wonderful moments of my life.' Helen paused. Luigi was playing an accordionist's classic: 'Barcarola'. 'Then we grew apart,' Helen went on. 'We always grow apart from the people we love. I don't know why, but that's what happens. It's one of the lessons life teaches us.' I said nothing; there was no point arguing with her.

For the rest of the meal, we talked only of banalities. About their classes at college, about the workings of a ranch devoted to breeding riding-horses.

Our hotels were in the same part of town, and so we decided to share a cab back. 'I'll sit in the front,' said Helen, getting in beside the driver.

'You two have to make plans for tomorrow.' Mary Ann and I got in the back. 'Lombard 1080,' said Helen. The taxi drove off quite fast. I wanted to say something, to talk about those plans, but I didn't know how to start. 'How many days' vacation have you got left?' asked Mary Ann, as we drove along. Her head was full of numbers too. 'I leave the day after tomorrow,' I said. 'Me too. Helen's staying on for longer, but I have to get back to my classes.' We drove into Lombard Avenue. Their hotel was at the far end.

'What do you think? Shall we do something tomorrow?' I asked. The vacation was coming to a close, and decisions were becoming difficult to make. It was no longer enough to say: 'We're tourists, let's discover San Francisco together.' Now we were going back to ordinary, everyday life. 'No, I don't think I'd better. I have to buy some souvenirs,' she said. Her mind was already in New Hampshire. One of those presents would probably be for her boyfriend.

Those Top Ten songs are right: when the woman you've fallen in love with turns you down, your heart breaks in two. 'Well, if you change your mind, call me at the hotel and we can have supper together,' I said. I was surprised that I was capable of coming out with those words. I felt as if something – a bone, a splinter – had got stuck in my throat.

The cab had stopped, and Helen was paying the driver. Mary Ann and I got out. 'Anyway,' I said, 'if you fancy having supper somewhere, call me. Or if you feel like going for a walk beforehand.' She was avoiding looking me in the eye. 'Don't Basque shepherds buy souvenirs?' she asked. 'No, never!' I exclaimed. 'We've worked hard to gain our reputation as solitary souls. We wander inhospitable mountains and arid deserts with only our faithful dogs for company.' 'Campuses can be inhospitable places too,' she said, rummaging around in her bag. 'Just in case we don't see each other again, this belongs to you,' she added, handing me the envelope full of photographs. 'Oh, so you're not a real paparazzo,' I said. I wanted to ask her if she was going to give me a photograph of herself, but she'd already turned to speak to Helen and I didn't dare. Our good-byes – in line with those Top Ten songs – were very sad.

*   *   *

31

The telephone in my hotel room rang for the first time at five o'clock in the afternoon. 'How's the vacation going?' I heard a voice say. It took me a moment to recognise the voice. It was Juan, phoning me from the ranch. 'Really well,' I said. I knew that I'd been away from Stoneham for nine days, not nine years, but I found it hard to believe. It was as if the numbers had escaped their usual framework, their normal dimension. 'And how are things with you there?' I asked. Juan answered with one of his favourite phrases: 'We're all fine and the horses are even better.' 'I'm glad to hear it.' 'Do you know why I'm calling?' he said, with a change of tone. He didn't like long phone conversations. 'To remind me that the vacation is over and that the account books await,' I said. 'You obviously don't think much of your Uncle Juan. I asked you to come back promptly so that you could go to the Community Recognition party. Who knows, you might meet a nice girl and get married.' He was in a good mood.

He started talking about a friend of his, Guernica. 'You know the one I mean. The shepherd who used to work with Sansón, the one who met Raquel Welch. You remember the story, don't you?' 'You told it to me on Christmas Day, Uncle.' 'Well, I suddenly remembered this morning that he's opened a restaurant in San Francisco. Over the bridge, in Sausalito. Go and have supper there and give him my best regards.' 'I'll see what I can do. But what's the restaurant called?' 'Guess.' 'Guernica?' 'Well done!' 'If I do go, I'll tell him you said "Hi".' 'Great. Drive safely.' And he hung up.

It was raining, just as it had been when I met Mary Ann for the first time. I imagined her wearing her transparent raincoat, looking for souvenirs in shops on Hayes or in Union Square, scouring the shop-windows, her thoughts fixed on her boyfriend in New Hampshire. Would one of those baggy shirts she'd seen in Castro suit him? Would he like the latest recording by the San Francisco Symphony Orchestra?

According to the alarm clock in my hotel room it was five fourteen. I lit a cigarette and sat down opposite the big window. If Mary Ann didn't ring in an hour, or possibly before that, if she didn't ring by six, then she never would.

The boats crossing the bay left very straight wakes behind them, white lines on the grey surface. An image passed through my mind, leaving an even fainter wake than the boats in the bay: I saw myself walking through a city, turning a corner and bumping into Steve McQueen and Ali MacGraw, who were strolling along, hand in hand, oblivious to the fine rain falling. I saw Joseba, who turned to watch them move off and said: 'I wish I was as happy as them.' I could, I believed, even remember the raincoat Ali MacGraw was wearing. It wasn't transparent like Mary Ann's, but white, or, rather, cream.

I called reception to ask them to reserve me a table at the restaurant Juan had recommended. I spelled the name of the restaurant according to the old spelling – G–u–e–r–n–i–c–a – but warned them that it might be spelled another way, without the 'u' and with a 'k'. 'For how many people?' the receptionist asked me. He seemed very professional. 'For two.' 'At what time?' 'At eight o'clock.' 'I'll call you back to confirm the reservation.' The receptionist put down the phone.

Another memory surfaced in my mind. A man who was almost too big for his seat in the train compartment once said to me: 'Do you know why I'm so fat? It's all because one day, I invited a girl out to lunch and she stood me up. I was so upset I ordered two entrées, two main courses and two desserts, just as if she were there. And that's where my race towards twenty-three stone began.' 'So love's made you fat.' 'Exactly.' The memory sank in my memory like a coin in water.

The telephone rang again. Mary Ann's voice came clear as clear down the phone line: 'How are you Basque shepherds doing over there? I hope you've brought your sheep in out of the rain?' Far off, on the other side of the bay, a ferry was chugging along beneath an almost black sky. 'It takes more than a bit of rain to frighten Basque shepherds,' I said. 'Our sheep are grazing tranquilly in the parks of San Francisco.'

The people walking along beside the bay started to run. It was suddenly raining really hard. 'If the Basque shepherds of today were as wise as those of yesteryear, they would have guessed that a storm was approaching. There's thunder around and the wind's blowing hard,' said Mary Ann. I imagined her lying on her bed in her room, barefoot. 'How

33

was your day?' I asked. 'Oh, I've known better. I discovered that Basque shepherds make rather good company.' 'I'll tell my friends in Nevada and in Idaho. They'll be pleased to hear that.'

The ferry was speeding across the bay now. 'How would you like to have supper in Sausalito?' 'I'd love to.' 'I have my car here in the hotel car park, or else we could get a taxi.' 'I've never been in the car of a Basque shepherd. I'd like to see what it's like.' 'And I've never done any simultaneous translation,' I said, 'but I'm going to have a go. The fact that you would prefer to go in my car means that you're prepared to move on to the plane of everyday life. From now on, we'll no longer be tourists.' 'That strikes me as a very bold interpretation, a very large interpretative leap.' And she burst out laughing. 'What time shall we meet?' I asked. 'I need thirty-seven minutes to get ready.' This, according to the alarm clock, was the number of minutes until six o'clock. 'Fine. At six outside your hotel, then.' 'Have you got an umbrella?' I didn't. 'In that case, I'll borrow one from Helen. She's going to spend the night at the hospital.' On the other side of the window, the lights of Alcatraz were beginning to come on. 'So her father isn't getting any better.' 'No, on the contrary.' 'The restaurant we're going to is called Guernica,' I said. I didn't want to talk about sad things. 'Now where have I heard that name before?' she said. I liked her sense of humour more and more.

The ferry disappeared behind one of the sandbanks in the bay. The streets and walkways were deserted. The telephone rang a third time. 'Your reservation is confirmed, sir. Restaurante Guernica. Sausalito. At eight o'clock,' said the receptionist. 'Old spelling, I presume.' 'Indeed, sir. As in the painting by Picasso.' He was a real professional.

II

I have before me the photograph Mary Ann and I had taken in Sausalito, the first photo of us as a couple. I'm dressed fairly formally, in a white polo shirt and the dark suit I used to put on when I went to Three Rivers and Visalia on business. I'm looking at the camera rather inexpressively, although I have my hands in my pockets and give the impression of being relaxed and happy. Mary Ann is wearing a tight-fitting, pale blue dress, a linen jacket and white heels. She has her arms folded and is leaning against me. Our heads are very close.

The table they'd reserved for us at the restaurant was next to the window, and we could see the boats crossing the bay, and, beyond that, reaching up to the sky, the pearly lights of the city. I wasn't interested in the view, though; all I wanted was to look at her, frankly and directly. I delighted in – a slightly old-fashioned phrase, I know, but I can think of no other – the kind of details, which, in the photo, are imperceptible: her blue eyes – North Cape – her earrings – two simple pearls – her lips. Especially her lips, because she was wearing blue lipstick, just as I'd described them when I'd sketched out that poem and written 'Thule lips'. 'We college professors are more imaginative than people think,' she said when I mentioned her lipstick. The coincidence between the imagined and the real seemed to me a good omen. 'Those blue lips will give me a kiss,' I said to myself. 'This very night,' I added.

The meal passed quietly. We had crossed a line, and we both felt that our time, which had been on the point of stopping, had once more been set in motion. Nevertheless, I was incapable of holding on to my good humour. I would have liked to tell Mary Ann, right there, in Restaurante Guernica, about the incident of the shepherd who'd been left speechless by his encounter with Raquel Welch, but I couldn't find the right moment. We'd spoken, in the narrow streets of Sausalito, of Helen's father's worsening condition. – 'They've told her to prepare for the worst.' – and I found it difficult, yet again, to avoid 'deep' topics of conversation. Mary Ann felt the same. In the end, when those same topics got mixed up with the name of the restaurant, our conversation turned to the Spanish civil war. 'We have a *Guernica* at home,' she said, pointing to the reproduction of the Picasso painting on the wall. 'My father carved it out of wood. Now he's just a retired doctor who won't leave Arkansas, not even to visit the college where his daughter works, but when he was twenty-five, he set off for Spain with the International Brigade.'

I was afraid she might ask about my father, about his role in that same civil war, and so I tried to change the subject. 'A friend of mine in Obaba used to work in wood too,' I said. 'Now he's in charge of his father's sawmill, and I think he's given it up. But he was a real artist. He made some really beautiful carvings.' 'Not like my father,' said Mary Ann, laughing. 'He made the copy of the painting during the Second World War because he was bored with being stuck in barracks.' There was no avoiding the subject. From the Second World War, we passed to the First – 'Have you read Robert Graves' memoirs? He says it was the cruellest war in all history' – later to the Vietnam War and back again to the Spanish civil war. Fortunately, she didn't ask me any direct questions, and so I didn't have to tell her that my father had been on the side of the fascists.

We ordered dessert. Mary Ann asked me then for the exact meaning of the word *gudari*, which I'd used during our conversation. I explained that it had come into popular use during the civil war and added a few philological details. 'So it means Basque soldier.' 'Leonard Cohen wrote a poem in their honour,' I said. 'He was shown a photograph of fascists shooting several *gudaris*, and that's where he got the idea for the poem.' Mary Ann was surprised. 'I didn't know that,' she said. 'If you like, I'll send it to you. I've got it in one of my files at Stoneham.' 'Yes, I'd like to read it.'

The wearisomely solemn tone that had so far dogged our evening finally dissolved. We abandoned the subject of war and spoke about the possibility of writing to each other. 'Are you serious when you say you'd like to get a letter from me?' I asked. 'Yes.' Her eyes – North Cape – held my gaze. 'You must give me your address then.' 'And you must give me yours.' 'We'd better do it before dessert arrives.' I could see the waiter hovering near a display cabinet. He'd just taken from it a raspberry tart and a chocolate one.

I had cards which gave all my personal details and my title as Manager of Stoneham Ranch, but these seemed inappropriate and so I started feeling in my jacket pockets for a piece of paper. 'Write on this,' said Mary Ann, folding up a publicity postcard for the restaurant and tearing it in two. It didn't tear evenly down the fold, and the result was two pieces of paper of unequal size. She gave me the larger one. 'If we ever arrange to meet again,' she said, 'we must each bring our half of the postcard and that way we'll be sure we really are us. If they fit together, I mean.' She seemed very pleased. 'Is it going to be that long before we see each other again?' I said. 'Won't we recognise each other by sight?' 'Yes, but the postcard option is safer.' She was writing the address, her head bent. Her hair was North Cape too. Very smooth and blond.

'Pardon me,' said the waiter, who was waiting until we'd finished writing. 'Raspberry tart?' he asked with a smile. I indicated that it was for Mary Ann. 'And chocolate tart for you, sir,' he said, putting the plate down on the table. I asked if he was Basque. Not just because of where we were, but also because of his appearance and his accent. 'People often ask me that,' he said, 'but I'm Greek.' Then he informed me that the owner was Basque, but that he was away at the moment. He'd gone off to the family cottage to see how the grass and the flowers were doing in his home country. He made the trip every spring. Mary Ann took a raspberry from her tart and put it in her mouth. 'I've got nothing against grass and flowers,' she said, looking at us, 'but I prefer fruit, especially raspberries.'

We paid the bill, and the waiter asked if we'd like to try a Greek liqueur. Picking up on Mary Ann's comment, he wanted to know how we liked that 'fruit' from his own country of Greece. 'Very strong and very good,' I said, after taking a sip. The waiter refilled my glass and left us alone. 'Do you want to smoke?' asked Mary Ann, and we both lit a cigarette. Outside, it had grown dark. Not far off, the lights on the bridge lit up the foaming crests of the waves. There were red lanterns on the boats in the bay.

Mary Ann took short puffs on her cigarette. She seemed slightly uneasy. And I felt the same. Time was passing. According to the clock in the restaurant – a large wall clock, doubtless brought from the Basque Country – it was eleven twenty. The swinging of its pendulum seemed almost violent, more powerful and more baleful than the delicate flow of sand, say, or water. The moment when we would have to part was getting closer and closer.

On the wall of the restaurant was a calendar bearing the image of the tree of Guernica. The message I read into that mitigated the message from the clock: the seconds and minutes would pass, the hours would pass, that day would end, but other days would come, April and May, June and July, summer and autumn would come. There was time. All I needed was a thread, a way of staying in touch with her. It was over 3000 miles from the college in New Hampshire to the ranch at Stoneham, but letters travelled by air, at top speed.

Mary Ann stubbed out her cigarette. There was a very faint smudge of blue on the end. 'And what about you? Don't you feel the need to go and see how the grass and flowers are doing in your country?' She clasped her hands together and held them beneath her chin, although without leaning on them. She had a strong neck. Strong shoulders too. One hundred years ago, I thought, the Lindegrens would have been peasants.

I didn't respond directly to her question. I lit another cigarette and started talking about people who leave their native land. I said that emigrants always take with them a childish idea – 'The people here are bad, where I'm going the people will be honest; here I just about scratch a living, there I'll live high on the hog' – and out of this fantasy emerges a first idea of paradise. Later, after many years, when they had grown somewhat disillusioned with the new country and conscious of the difficulties of starting anew, there was a contrary movement, just like the pendulum of that clock, and then it was the home country that began to take on the qualities of paradise.

I'd finished my cigarette. 'Now I want to ask you a question, Mary Ann,' I said. 'Why am I talking about this?' She raised her finger like a student in a class. 'Because you don't want to tell me the truth? Could that be it?' 'No, I don't think so. I think I've just lost the thread. I'm probably drunk. This Greek liqueur is pretty strong stuff.' 'I feel kinda woozy too,' she said, laughing. She hadn't been bored by my discourse on the 'two paradises'. After all, she was finding it equally hard to tackle the real subject that had brought us to that restaurant in Sausalito. It was easy to talk about emigration, much less easy to ask a concrete question before she returned to New Hampshire and I to Stoneham.

The weight of all these unasked questions made the journey back to the hotel difficult. We could see before us the lights of the city which, at that hour of the night, seemed sad in the rain and transformed the inside of the car into a good place for conversation, a place where we could say something about our feelings, except that neither of us had the courage to take the first step.

We reached the other side of the bay and started across the park. Lombard Avenue ended there; we were nearly at her hotel. 'Let's see what kind of music our accordionist listens to in his car,' said Mary, with a slightly embarrassed laugh.

The cassette was one I'd chosen a few hours before in the hotel car park. It was an old Ben Webster recording. The man in the music shop in Visalia had recommended it to me, saying: 'So you can dream about your girl.' Every track was a gem, and whenever I listened to it, I regretted not having known about records like that when I lived in Obaba and played dance music like 'Casatschok'.

The hands on the car clock kept moving. And the tape kept turning in the cassette player too. The first song finished as we drove into Lombard Avenue. 'That's a lovely song,' she said. 'What's it called?' It was 'The Touch of Your Lips'. 'It's a love-song,' I said, incapable of pronouncing those five words: 'the touch of your lips.'

I parked the car about twenty yards from the entrance to her hotel. There was little traffic, only a few taxis driving through the puddles. It started to rain harder, and the tapping of the raindrops merged with the music. I turned off the engine and put the parking lights on.

The next track was gently rhythmic. It aided conversation. 'You still haven't answered the question I asked you in the restaurant. What are your plans?' asked Mary Ann. 'Are you going to stay in America?' She was sitting slightly turned towards me. Her linen jacket lay folded on her lap, and her hands rested on top. 'Are you really interested?' 'If I wasn't really interested, I wouldn't have asked the same question twice.' I felt like smoking another cigarette, but decided not to move. The pack was next to the gear stick, about four inches from her knees. 'I feel good here. Stoneham Ranch is a nice place. Three Rivers and Visalia are nice too, well, the whole region is.' It was the truth, although not the whole truth. But I couldn't say to her: 'The situation in my own country was so bad that I couldn't go on living there.' It wasn't the right moment.

'Is your mother still alive?' Mary Ann asked. 'No, she died about three years before I came to America.' I forgot my decision not to light another cigarette, and reached over for the pack. 'How do you lower this window,' she asked, having accepted and lit the cigarette I offered her. 'If we don't open it a crack, the car will fill up with smoke.' 'Allow me.' As I wound down the window, my arm inadvertently touched her stomach, only very lightly, but enough to feel its softness.

'I thought of your mother because of what you told Helen and me in the Italian restaurant,' she said, by way of apology, as if afraid I might have found her question painful. 'Do you remember? Just before we forced you to play the accordion, you were talking about your father. You mentioned the lists you used to make of the names of the people you loved, and how badly you and he got on. I don't know, sometimes we move simply to get away from our family.'

The hands on the car clock were still turning, as was the tape in the cassette player. It was half past midnight, very late for her. She had an early flight. Yet she didn't appear to be in a hurry. 'Although, that's a silly idea really,' she said. 'There's never only one reason. It's just that, probably because of Helen's situation, we've often mentioned our parents in the last few days. Anyway, that's why I asked the question.' She returned to her former posture, sitting slightly askew. From time to time, she held her cigarette to the crack in the window and flicked off the ash. 'You're right, there's always more than one reason,' I said. 'That's why I want to write a book, to have a chance to think about those reasons.'

A patrol car sped past, lights flashing. It was a strange thought, but there I was in America, in San Francisco, in the company of a woman with blue lips. Mary Ann. Mary Ann Linder, from Hot Springs, Arkansas. From the Lindegren family, originally from Sweden. A woman to whom, paradoxically, I felt very close. I thought: 'The half of the restaurant postcard she has in her bag fits the half I have in my jacket pocket.' I mustn't forget that; I must cling on to that symbol.

'The trouble is I can't seem to find a way of starting to write,' I said. 'As you said in the Italian restaurant, it's probably because I'm not a real writer . . .' I broke off and took her hand. She had held it out to me in protest at my words. 'I'm sure that's what it is,' I went on. 'But isolation has a lot to do with it too. I have no friends at Stoneham. I can talk to my Uncle Juan about a lot of things, but not about the book. And to be honest, who would be interested in anything I might write? A good friend of mine, Joseba, writes books and has lots of readers, but that's certainly not the case with me.' I finished my sentence; Mary Ann's hand was still clasped in mine. 'I could be your first reader,' she said.

Side one of the tape had finished, and all we could hear was the sound of the rain on the windscreen and the roof of the car. Mary Ann threw the stub of her cigarette out of the window. She took my hand in hers.

'I've had the best time these last few days,' she said. 'So have I, but what will happen after tonight?' I asked. She turned in her seat so that her head rested on my shoulder, her knees touching the door. 'I can't make any decision right now,' she replied. Her voice was barely louder than the rain, and I could only just hear what she said. She squeezed my hand. 'If I'm not mistaken, I have no option but to accumulate more Brownie points,' I said. Her head was still resting on my shoulder, and her knees, pressed against the door, looked now like two small peaks. West Cape? East Cape? No, they were smooth and white, not like rocky, rugged capes. She didn't answer. She remained silent, as if asleep. I couldn't hear her thoughts.

It was ten minutes to one. She sat up in her seat. I freed my hand from hers and opened the car door. 'Do you know how my parents met?' she said, shaking her head, as if waking up. 'It was during the war in Spain. When he went off with the International Brigade, my mother was asked to be his sponsor and they started writing to each other. My father says it took only seven letters to win her heart.' She sat looking out at the rain. Her pearl earrings glinted in the lights of Lombard Avenue. 'I think I must be a bit nervous. I'm talking nonsense,' she said. She didn't know how to say goodbye.

Then I spoke the most practical and sensible sentence of the evening: 'You and I have fallen in love, haven't we?' I struggled to keep my voice neutral. 'Maybe,' she said. 'And as usually happens in these cases,' I went on, 'there are complications, especially on the New Hampshire side. But if we keep on collecting those Brownie points, the problems might resolve themselves.' 'So what are you going to do?' she asked. 'The same as your father. I'm going to write you long, long letters,' I replied in a less serious tone. 'Not bad,' she said.

We stood underneath the canopy at the hotel entrance. I closed the umbrella and handed it to her. 'And what do I have to do to get Brownie points?' she asked me. I was about to give in and confess to her that she was for me the 'golden bough' of the poem and that she didn't need to do anything. But I said nothing. 'I'd like to send you my translations,' she went on, 'but that would probably be too much work for you.' 'Not at all,' I said. 'But send me a photograph or two as well. We've taken so many in the last few days, but the only one of us I'm carrying back with me to Stoneham is the photo of us today in Sausalito.' 'It's a deal,' she said, going over to the reception desk. The receptionist gave her the key to her room and a message. She read it quickly and sighed. 'Helen will be flying back with me tomorrow. Her father didn't make it.' 'Give her my condolences.' We kissed, and I went out into the street.

On the drive back to Three Rivers, I didn't stop thinking about Mary Ann for an instant. I remembered how she'd called me a 'Basque shepherd' and how that small joke had filled the first few hours we spent together. And how later, almost like a game, we'd taken photographs of each other while we visited all the tourist spots in the city. When the trees on the hill at Stoneham and the granite rocks of the Kaweah river came into view again, there was only one thought in my mind: what I would write about in my first letter.

LUBIS AND OTHER FRIENDS

In Obaba there was a man who earned his living selling fire insurance. I saw him for the first time one summer's day when I was playing with my friends at the Hotel Alaska; he was in a room full of empty chairs, busy preparing for a talk he was about to give. He would have been in his seventies then. He was wearing a black suit and a white shirt.

Out of his leather briefcase he took some papers and a cord which was about three feet long. Threaded on to this cord, rather like a rosary, were various small objects, amongst them a series of figures – made out of cardboard, plastic, wood, and iron – in the form of butterflies. We all thought it strange.

'Why do you need that piece of string?' asked Teresa. She and her brother Martín had been born in the hotel. They were at home, on their home territory. 'It isn't a piece of string, it's a piece of cord. Didn't they teach you the difference at school?' The man spoke slowly, as if he were tired. His eyes were a very pale blue. They seemed weary too.

'String or cord, what I want to know is what's it for?' replied Teresa. She must have been about eleven or twelve at the time. She was an extraordinarily inquisitive child, the one who always asked most questions at school. 'Come over here,' said the man, pointing to the first row of chairs, and we all sat down in front of him: Teresa, Martín, Lubis, Joseba and me. The only one missing was Adrián, a schoolfriend who was in hospital in Barcelona at the time because of a spinal malformation, the name of which – scoliosis – we regularly bandied about.

The man picked up the cord by one end and held it up. 'What do you think this is?' he said, pointing to one of the 'beads'. 'A piece of coal,' said Lubis, slightly embarrassed at having to answer such an obvious question. He was older than us, and after school he looked after the horses kept by my Uncle Juan, 'the American', in Iruain, the house

43

where my uncle was born. 'Correct,' said the man. 'And this? What would you say this was?' 'Another piece of coal, of course! It's certainly not a butterfly!' retorted Martín. 'Well, you're wrong. It's a charred splinter of wood.' Martín grabbed the cord from the man and started examining it. 'It's makes a very ugly necklace!' he said, pulling a face. Teresa, his sister, got angry and yelled at him: 'Why call it a necklace when you know it isn't? Why do you always say such stupid things?' She was very quick-tempered.

'Let me explain,' said the man, taking back the cord. 'What you have here is a tool for remembering things.' 'A tool? What, like a hammer?' Martín looked at Joseba and me, seeking our support. 'The guy's mad.' The man continued, unruffled: 'In a while, I'll be speaking to an audience, and my fingers will touch this bit of coal. Then I'll think: coal is good, as good as the fire that's born from it. It's useful for cooking and for heating a house. If this sort of fire hadn't existed, the world wouldn't have been able to progress. I'll think about that and I'll tell my listeners. Then . . .' 'A coal fire can also burn your bum,' Martín broke in again. 'That's what happened to our teacher last winter. She sat down on the stove and burned her bum.' 'That's not true, Martín! That isn't what happened at all!' cried Joseba. He was a very diligent pupil and adored his teacher.

The man ignored Martín's comment and went on with his explanation: 'After the piece of coal, my fingers will touch this blackened splinter, and I'll remember how bad fire can be. In fact, this piece of wood came from a house that burned down a few years ago. The owners were reduced to poverty and forced to emigrate. And do you know why?' 'Why?' asked Lubis, his eyes wide. 'Because they didn't have decent insurance cover, that's why.' The man smiled wanly. Regardless of the expression on his face, what always shone through was weariness.

On the next section of the cord were two coins, one large and one small. 'Do you need a lot of money to buy an insurance policy?' I asked. 'Very good, young man. You've understood perfectly,' he said. 'And what about the butterflies? Why do you think they're here?' He held the cord

44

up in front of my eyes. 'To represent the different kinds of policies?' I ventured. Amongst his papers I could see a few advertising flyers with butterflies on them. 'Very good indeed,' the man said, putting his hand on my head. His eyes filled with tears, as if he were moved by my answer. Martín sneered: 'Own up, David, you were just guessing, weren't you?' I didn't have time to answer him back. The doors opened and the people who had come to hear the talk started taking their seats. The insurance salesman stood up. Clasped behind his back, his hands concealed the cord, his memory tool.

We stood at the door, waiting for the talk to begin. The room soon filled up. 'Fire is a good and necessary thing, ladies and gentlemen,' the salesman began. 'Without fire, the world would not exist . . .'

Later that afternoon, I had a surprise. I was playing with my friends on the hotel mirador when the fire insurance salesman called me over. He was heading in the direction of the hotel car park, where a taxi was waiting for him. 'Keep the cord,' he said, holding it out to me. 'It might come in handy one day.' 'Thank you very much,' I said. I felt uncertain, not daring to take the present. 'That was my final talk. I won't be needing it any more,' he explained. 'Why?' 'I forget things, and even with the cord I get muddled,' he said. I waited for a moment; it seemed to me that he wanted to go on. 'Do you know how old I am? Seventy-four.' I wanted to say something, but could think of nothing. The taxi-driver came towards us. 'Where am I taking you?' he asked, helping the salesman into the car. 'Home,' the man said.

The taxi drove off down the narrow road that led to the centre of Obaba. I didn't know what to think. I sensed with my child's logic that the insurance salesman had chosen to single me out for that honour, but I was troubled by the sadness with which he'd spoken – 'I won't be needing it any more' – and by the fact that I'd been selected to be the heir to that memory tool.

'He was right to give it to you,' Lubis said to me on the way to Iruain. That summer he was teaching me to ride. 'What would *I* want it for? To remind me when to feed the horses or groom them? With you, though, who knows . . . you might well get a job in an insurance company one day and then it would be really useful.' I laughed. Lubis' way of thinking always amused me.

I could declare now, in that emphatic way in which people sometimes write: 'From that day on, I kept the cord with me. It was the first thing I put in my suitcase when I decided to go and live in America.' But, as is always the way – for events never quite live up to ideas or secret promises – the truth was more prosaic. I put the cord away in the drawer of my bedside table, and there it stayed for years. Then I took it from my parents' house to the house in Iruain, to show it to some friends of Lubis', and I never thought about it again until I was living in America and had started writing my book and decided to apply that method of remembering: I would go from subject to subject just as the fingers of the insurance salesman had gone from the piece of coal to the charred wood or the butterflies. 'Keep the cord. It might come in handy one day,' the man had told me. His prophecy would come true.

Internal dedication

Who would have thought it, Mary Ann, that our story would one day be the germ of my book, and that what the ancient poets wrote would once again prove to be true: 'Without a city, no province; without a founding father, no law; without a muse, no song'? Who would have thought that from the distance of Stoneham Ranch I would one day remember my first home, Obaba, and the friends I left behind there, especially Lubis, and that thanks to that distance, I would succeed in crossing a far greater and more dreadful gulf, the gulf separating life and death?

A piece of coal

My first homeland, the land of my childhood and my youth, was a place called Obaba. On the few occasions when I left it for any length of time, like the summer my parents sent me to a school in Biarritz, or the following winter, when I travelled with them to Madrid, I felt no happier than those victims of the Roman *relegatio*, banished temporarily to the Black Sea, and not a night went by without my wondering when I would be able to return.

I remember that around the same time, or perhaps a little later, when I was thirteen, they employed a psychologist at the De La Salle school I attended, and I was sent to his office by the prefect of studies not because I was a lazy or difficult student, but because of my lack of interest in making friends with my classmates, because of my misanthropy, to use the prefect's word, which was new to me. After interviewing me for forty minutes, the psychologist attributed my lack of sociability to my deep attachment to the rural world, and noted in his report that the old values were all mixed up in my head with modern ones.

The terminology may have been new to my parents, but not the problem. They knew about it and were concerned. 'You've been on a farm again, haven't you, David? I just don't understand it,' my father said a few weeks after the psychologist's report, when he saw me come in with bits of straw stuck to my clothes. Then he said what he always said, his favourite refrain: 'You're not a child any more, but you still don't know which world you belong to.'

He meant that I came from a good family. And it was true. As well as being a professional accordionist, my father was a man with political responsibilities, who had influence both in Obaba and in the rest of the province. My mother, for her part, ran a sewing school that occupied a large room in the house where we lived, Villa Lecuona. However, when I was thirteen or fourteen, I was indifferent to the benefits of social position, and whenever my father trotted out his usual reproach, I told him so. He would get angry then and threaten me with confinement to the house or with boarding school, until, that is, my mother intervened and brought the discussion to a close: 'Leave him alone, Ángel. Remember what my brother says. You can take a horse to water, but twenty men can't make it drink.'

My parents tried to get 'the horse' to drink and continued sending me to the provincial capital – which had and has a lovely name: San Sebastián – to study at the De La Salle school, even though the journey there and back took me more than two hours, and even though there were other schools nearer to home that I could have gone to. They also invited over Martín and Teresa, from the Hotel Alaska, or Adrián, the son of the owner of the local sawmill. However, although I didn't entirely refuse to drink that water, and although I did go out with these friends from the same social class as myself, I still preferred, as the psychologist had noted, that other world, the rural world. I knew nothing about pasturing; I didn't know how to prepare a bottle of milk for a calf or how to help a mare give birth to a foal, but I felt a nostalgia for those simple tasks, as if once, in a former life, I'd been one of those 'happy peasants' praised by Virgil.

The lists I drew up of the people I loved most – my lists of favourites – were proof of the same thing. In the list I copied down in my diary at the age of fourteen, first place was occupied by my friend Lubis, who, by then, was already in charge of Juan's horses. In second place came his brother, José Francisco, or Pancho, who worked at the sawmill and whose sole task was to take lunch to the woodcutters felling trees in the wood. And Lubis and Pancho were followed on the list by a woodcutter, a boy who measured 6' 2" and weighed 220 pounds and was known to everyone as Ubanbe, because he'd been born in a house of that name. My list of favourites, then, was headed by three country boys. My other friends – Martín, Teresa, Adrián, Joseba – came after.

*   *   *

49

In the magazine for the Basque shepherds of North America, I read an article once, signed by a priest, in which he stated that the enormous change the world had undergone was not a gradual one, and that rural villages like Obaba had changed less in the twenty centuries from the birth of Jesus to the coming of television than in the ensuing thirty years; and this, he wrote, was the reason why he, in his childhood, had played the same games as those depicted on the frescos in Pompeii.

This seems to me no exaggeration. In 1960, and even in 1970, the country people of Obaba had an ancient air about them that made them appear to belong, in the strictest sense, to another country. They fulfilled L.P. Hartley's definition: 'The past is a foreign country: they do things differently there.' Examples of this were Lubis, Pancho, Ubanbe and many others in Obaba. They would look at the sacks full of various kinds of apple and be able to distinguish each sort: 'This one's *espuru*', 'this one's *domentxa*', 'this one's *gezeta*.' They looked at the butterflies fluttering about and said unhesitatingly: 'That one's *mitxirrika*', 'that one's *txoleta*', 'and that one over there's *inguma*.' These names were meaningless to people like my schoolmates and, to some extent, myself, who, although they still lived in Obaba, had assimilated 'modern values'.

But it wasn't just what they said, their ancient lexicon; it was also what they didn't say. Many words in frequent use now never left their lips. They simply didn't know them. When I go to Visalia to buy something at the mall or at the music shop, I notice that verbs like 'depress' or adjectives like 'obsessive', 'paranoid' or 'neurotic' are on everyone's lips, and are unavoidable in any conversation, whether personal or not. Well, I never heard them on the lips of Lubis, Pancho or Ubanbe. They would sum the situation up in two simple sentences: 'I'm happy' or 'I'm not happy'. They never went further than that, they never went on to expound on their innermost feelings. They were from another country; they were ancient, from an age before the proliferation of personal diaries. Even though I inclined the other way – since I started attending the De La Salle school, I'd been writing a diary entitled 'The days pass' – I nevertheless admired their reserve.

One day – it was summer and intensely hot – the two brothers who

50

headed my list of favourites, Lubis and Pancho, asked me to go up into the hills with them because they wanted to show me something. I went and, after walking for nearly an hour, we came to a rocky outcrop. 'Are you going to climb up there?' I asked Pancho. He liked heights. I'd often seen him scramble up a tree. 'Don't look up, David. Look down,' said Lubis. He was speaking slowly, seriously, like a grown-up. In Obaba, it was said that, after the death of his father, he'd taken on the responsibility of looking after his brother and his mother, which is why he was as he was – older than his years.

Pancho lay down on his back on the ground and started wriggling feet-first into a hole in the rock. A moment later, only his head was visible. He had a very broad face, all out of proportion, in which his eyes were like two small slits and his mouth and jaw were far too big. 'Now you see me, David,' he cried, 'now you don't!' And he disappeared into the rock.

'Do the same as Pancho,' Lubis said, 'I'll help you.' 'Do you think I'll fit?' I asked. 'The hole is bigger than it looks. Wait, I'll go first.' He did as Pancho had done, and stood inside the rock, looking up at me. 'It's a cave, and it's really, really cool inside,' he explained, laughing. He didn't look like Pancho. He had a neat head, and in his face only his eyes were out of proportion with his nose – which was small – and his mouth – equally small – for his eyes were very large and tranquil. If they'd been blue, like Mary Ann's, and not brown, they would have dominated his whole face.

I slipped inside the cave too. It was blissfully cool, and I could hear what sounded like a fountain bubbling. About thirty or so feet above the ground, the roof formed a vault with a natural 'lantern' that let in the light and created a soothing half-darkness. I saw then that next to one of the walls there was, indeed, a fountain, whose waters flowed into a deep pool – *putzua*, in Lubis' language – which covered Pancho up to his neck.

Lubis got undressed and joined his brother. Infected by their high spirits – the echo in the cave gave back no gloomy responses – I, too, got undressed and slipped into the pool. 'Watch this, David,' Lubis said.

51

He struck the water with the flat of his hand. In the light coming in through the 'lantern', the drops of water glittered as if they were made of glass. 'Fantastic!' I exclaimed.

I felt closer than ever to the two brothers. I said to myself that, in future, I would seek out their company alone, rather than waste time with Martín and the other boys and girls from my own social group. What's more, I didn't want to go back to the De La Salle school, and when summer was over, I would help Lubis look after Uncle Juan's horses or else get a job at the sawmill so as to be with Pancho, Ubanbe and the others who earned their living felling trees in the wood.

I knew, however, that these plans were completely unrealistic. Once October came, I would have to set off to the De La Salle school again, by bicycle, by train, on foot; along with Martín, Adrián and Joseba, and with all the other boys studying in San Sebastián. Worse, my father had announced that, after school, I would have to attend accordion classes, and on Saturdays and Sundays – the only days when I could get together with my country friends – I would have to play with him at the dances held in the Hotel Alaska. I was only fourteen; I was not the master of my own life. I felt like crying. I slapped the water hard with my hand. The shimmering drops splashed the walls of the cave.

When, in 1964, aged fifteen, I drew up my next list of favourites, Lubis, Pancho and Ubanbe retained the top three places. At the time, though, there was something that worried me: I wasn't sure if they accepted me. Lubis was working for Uncle Juan, and his brother Pancho, along with Ubanbe and the other woodcutters, took advantage of every spare moment to go and see his horses – such magnificent creatures had never been seen in Obaba – and so their friendliness might simply be due to my status, as if they'd said to themselves: 'He's the owner's nephew. We'll have to put up with him.' It seemed to me, though, that they really did like me for myself, and that they behaved quite differently with Adrián, despite his being the son of the sawmill owner, but I couldn't be sure. Then Palm Sunday arrived, and my doubts were dispelled.

The feast day commemorating Jesus' entry into Jerusalem was celebrated in Obaba on the last Sunday in Lent. Since we had no palm leaves proper, most people went to the church bearing branches of flowering laurel, which the priest blessed during the *missa solemnis* and which we then took home to protect us from storms and other dangers. It was a very beautiful ceremony. People wore their best clothes; the priest put on a red chasuble; the choir and the organ filled the brightly lit church with songs.

In the face of such solemnity, the young country boys from Obaba amused themselves by giving the ceremony quite a different and distinctly un-Christian tone. First, they would compete to see who had the biggest laurel branch with the most flowers; then, once mass was over, this competition degenerated into fighting, and about ten to fifteen boys would battle it out, wielding the laurel branches as if they were spears or swords.

This fight usually took place about a hundred yards from the church, in some discreet place. That year, however, in 1964, they were too impatient and started fighting in the church porch as soon as they came out of mass. I looked at Ubanbe. He was carrying a laurel branch that measured at least fifteen feet, at the same time keeping an eye on one of his fellow sawmill workers, nicknamed Opin. Opin's laurel branch wasn't as long as Ubanbe's, but it was much stouter. Moreover, he had whittled away the end of the branch to make it thinner and easier to grasp.

The opponents formed two lines: on one side stood those from the Iruain district or thereabouts – amongst them Ubanbe and Pancho – and on the other, with Opin at their head, those who lived in the houses near the church. The people who had just come out of church and were standing in the porch, looked at them, not quite sure what was going on. 'Why the funny face, Opin? Are you afraid?' said Ubanbe challengingly. Some girls – for, as well as being strong, Ubanbe was also very good-looking – burst out laughing. 'I'm not afraid of loudmouths!' cried Opin, scything through the air with his laurel branch and thus signalling the start of the battle.

The floor of the porch was soon covered in leaves and flowers, and the sickly sweet scent of laurel filled the air. The blows that were dealt and which had, at first, seemed quite gentle, started to sound harder, because the branches were gradually becoming stripped of leaves and they were hitting wood on wood. We all fell silent; no one wanted to miss a moment. You could hear the breathing of the boys engaged in the fighting.

Opin dealt a rather low blow and injured Ubanbe's hand. 'You did that on purpose!' Ubanbe roared, dropping his laurel branch and shaking his fist at Opin. 'Sorry,' said Opin, opening his arms wide in a gesture of contrition. Ubanbe withdrew to a corner, clutching his injured hand under one armpit. Then he suddenly turned to me and said: 'David! You're from Iruain! Take my place!'

Iruain was nearly two miles from the centre of Obaba, and both my mother and my Uncle Juan had been born there, in the house that bore the same name as the district. Uncle Juan maintained a close relationship with both district and house, thanks to the horses he kept there, tended by Lubis, and to his yearly summer visits. But it wasn't my district or my house: I belonged to Villa Lecuona. And yet Ubanbe wanted me to take his place. I felt proud, like one of the chosen ones.

I hesitated for a moment. The municipal council usually presided over the Palm Sunday ceremony, and I was afraid that my father, one of the councillors, might be hanging around somewhere. He'd be furious if he saw me there fighting in the church porch. Normally, he wouldn't allow me to play any kind of sport. As he said over and over: 'Accordionists have to take good care of themselves, because just one clumsy move could put an end to their career.' And he was perfectly capable of bawling me out in front of everyone.

Lubis came over to us. 'Don't hassle David,' he said to Ubanbe, 'he's not a rough peasant like us.' The word he used for 'rough' was '*salastrajo*', a term that doesn't even appear in dictionaries which make a point of collecting the words people used to use in the past. 'What do you reckon?' Ubanbe asked the girl next to me. It was Teresa, Martín's sister, from the Hotel Alaska.

At the time, Teresa was in the habit of sending me little scraps of pastel-coloured paper containing deliberately enigmatic messages: 'What were you reading yesterday, sitting on the stone bench in the hotel garden?' 'What do girls like me think about when they're alone in their room?' When Ubanbe and his friends talked about her, they used to say that she was *pantasi aundiko neska*, 'a very imaginative girl'. And they were right. She revealed this even in the clothes she wore. That day, she was wearing a white trouser suit, a rare sight in the Obaba of 1964. And unlike everyone else, she was carrying a yellow palm adorned with a red ribbon.

'Go on, David,' Teresa said, holding up the palm. 'If you win, I'll give you this trophy.' I bowed to her – Lubis and Ubanbe laughed – and took Ubanbe's place on the side of Iruain.

Opin struck my laurel branch so hard that I could barely keep a hold on it. Although I was taller than him, my muscles weren't as strong as his or Ubanbe's: I didn't load wood on to trucks in the forest, I didn't chop down trees with an axe. Five or six blows were enough for my wrist to begin to hurt and for me to start to get worried. I could imagine the telling-off my father would give me: 'How could you be so stupid? How are you going to play now with a sprained wrist?' Fortunately, I didn't have to suffer the humiliation of laying down my laurel branch. The fight ended before I had time to surrender. I noticed suddenly that Opin was standing very still, head bowed, his eyes fixed on the leaves and flowers scattered about the floor.

Don Hipólito, Obaba's parish priest, was watching us from the stairs leading down from the church's main door. 'What have you done with the laurel branches I blessed during mass?' He didn't speak very loudly, but we could all hear him. Don Hipólito was an important figure in Obaba, with as much power as my father or any other politician. 'I want to see you all in church this afternoon. And make sure that everyone who took part in this outrage is there.' His words rang out clearly in the porch. We were all quiet, and even Ubanbe seemed contrite. 'You should send them all back into church now without any lunch,' said one of the people present. 'No, they're too young to be fasting,' retorted Don Hipólito. He was a prudent man, who disliked excesses.

*   *   *

55

'Pray to God to forgive you,' said Don Hipólito that afternoon, before leaving us alone in the church. There were about fifteen of us boys, all kneeling before the altar. St John and St Paul, each perched on his own glittering column, gazed down on us tenderly from the retable. As did the Virgin from her glass display case. In the centre of the altar, on the altar stone, lay a small laurel branch covered in white flowers. It wasn't a particularly oppressive atmosphere and, after a while, my fellow delinquents started making jokes. The slightest thing made them laugh.

'I've prayed enough,' said Ubanbe after a quarter of an hour, and sat back on the pew. It wasn't long before the others followed suit. 'Tell me the truth, David,' he said, putting his arm around my shoulder. 'If the priest hadn't turned up, how much longer would you have lasted with that laurel branch?' 'Not very long,' I admitted. 'I'm not surprised. Opin isn't exactly an easy opponent. When he can't get you any other way, he goes for the low blow.' He showed us his swollen hand. 'The only "low" thing here is Lubis,' joked Opin. Despite having taken no part in the porch battle, Lubis had chosen to accompany his brother Pancho to the church. He looked at Opin with his large, tranquil eyes, but said nothing.

A low blow. The fight between Cassius Clay and Sonny Liston had just taken place in Madison Square Garden in New York, and the excitement provoked by that distant event was still much in evidence. As some San Francisco freak might have put it: 'they were all still high on it', especially the country boys. Along with their more ancient words, Ubanbe and Opin now used other words learned while watching the fight on TV: low blow, clinch, left hook, right, Cassius Clay, Sonny Liston.

'Cassius Clay! That's all I ever hear, Carmen!' Don Hipólito had said to my mother at a choir rehearsal a few days before the fight. 'Who is this man? The new Messiah?' Luckily, the priest didn't walk into the church at six o'clock on that Palm Sunday evening, and was thus saved the distasteful sight of Ubanbe – Cassius Clay – and Opin – Sonny Liston – pretending to box right there, in front of the altar. Some of those doing their 'penance' in church hadn't seen the fight on television and wanted to know the details.

The largest window in the church, whitish in colour, was growing dark. The flame of the candle burning on the altar seemed to have gained in strength. 'Do you fancy having a go on this, David?' asked Lubis. He was standing underneath the pulpit steps, next to the harmonium.

Ubanbe said, as loudly as if he were in some remote place in the country or in the middle of a wood: 'What are you talking about, Lubis? How can you expect him to play a piece of junk like that? He's got enough to do with the accordion!' The conversation about boxing had excited him and he was in provocative mood. 'I'll have you know that I play a piece of old junk like this in the school chapel. I know it well,' I retorted.

There was a song, 'Angelitos negros' – 'Little black angels' – that had been made popular throughout Spain by a Cuban singer called Antonio Machín. It seemed rather appropriate for a church. I sat down at the harmonium and began to play.

Then the unexpected happened. Silence fell, a profound silence through which the melody of 'Angelitos negros' flowed easily. I looked up: Don Hipólito was staring at me. He was standing right in front of me, arms folded. Ubanbe, Pancho, Opin and the others had returned to their pew. Kneeling down, leaning forward, they all appeared to be praying devoutly.

I stopped playing and stood up. 'No, David, don't get up. That's a really lovely tune,' Don Hipólito said kindly. He was a musician too. He'd studied at the Jesuit university in Comillas. I obeyed and continued playing. 'Your mother mentioned that you could play, but I had no idea how well,' he said when I'd finished. 'Why don't you come to Sunday morning mass? You could play that tune during communion.'

He was a tall man with curly, white hair. He turned to the choirstalls. 'How are you on the organ?' 'Hopeless,' I said. He shrugged. 'Well, you can't play it now anyway, it's broken. After a hundred years too.' 'I should think it had a right to break after working for as long as that,' remarked Ubanbe. He'd left the others kneeling in the pew and come over to join us. The priest patted his cheek, as if he were a child. 'We'll get it mended when we've collected enough money. Then I'll teach David to play. He could become a good organist. Anyway, what do you say, David?' he said, turning to me. 'Will you come and play the harmonium in church?' I told him I would.

II

I've mentioned the cave with the hidden pool inside, and what happened on Palm Sunday at the church in Obaba, but the reality was that I had very few opportunities to spend time with my country friends. Encouraged by the advice of the school psychologist, my parents insisted on finding me other friends: on one day they'd despatch me to the sawmill to teach Adrián how to ride a bike: 'We have to help those in need'; on another, they'd send me to a meeting of young accordionists, or to the private French classes that Geneviève, Martín and Teresa's mother, had organised at the hotel. However, I still did my best to spend more time with Lubis, Pancho or Ubanbe.

When my fifth-year exams were approaching, I went to my mother and asked her permission to go and study at the house in Iruain. 'I can concentrate better over there. The only things to distract me are the horses, and I don't imagine *they'll* bother me much.' She peered at me over the top of her glasses. 'And where will you eat?' She was sitting by one of the windows in the sewing workshop, and on her lap was a bridal dress decorated with embroidery. 'I'll talk to Adela,' I said. Adela was the wife of the shepherd who lived in the same hamlet as Lubis, Pancho and Ubanbe. She cooked for Uncle Juan when he came over from America. 'Can I?' I asked again. My mother wasn't sure. 'I'm going to have to spend hours studying Physics. It's been really hard this year,' I said.

The word 'study' was sacred to my mother. She attributed her success as a dressmaker to the fact that she had a diploma, and on one wall in the workshop she had hung a small poster bearing a maxim aimed at the apprentice dressmakers: 'Knowledge is no burden.' She was also flattered by my desire to spend time in the house where she was born. She gave her consent.

At first, I spent only the occasional afternoon there, then whole days, and later still, when Uncle Juan arrived at the end of June, I would stay for three or four days at a time. And these visits didn't end when the exams were over. Throughout the summer, I travelled the road to Iruain again and again.

Ángel – I prefer to call him by his name rather than 'father' – got angry with me: 'There you are off to the farm again. And your accordion left on a chair, gathering dust.' He called Iruain a farm even though there were only horses there. My mother wouldn't budge: 'You know my views on the matter, Ángel. Music is all very well, but it's not the most important thing in the world. You've seen what good marks he got this year. And the other day, I phoned Monsieur Nestor and he told me that he's making real progress.' Monsieur Nestor was the man in charge of the French classes being held at the hotel. That was the one condition my mother had imposed on me: whether I was at Villa Lecuona or in Iruain, I mustn't miss his classes.

Ángel fell silent. He was free to devote his time to music or to politics, but he had no hand in my education. If, for some reason, she needed to speak to someone, my mother would go to the church to ask Don Hipólito's advice, or she would phone Uncle Juan in California. Or rather, while she occasionally spoke to Don Hipólito, she always talked to her brother. They were very fond of each other, fonder than brothers and sisters usually are. Ángel would joke about this sometimes: 'The only reason you get on so well is because he lives in California and you, Carmen, live here. It's easy enough to get on with someone when they're 6000 miles away.' My mother would deny this categorically: 'He was nine and I was seven when we lost our parents and were left all alone in an isolated place like Iruain. Ever since then we've been inseparable.'

An isolated place like Iruain. It was a small, green, bucolic valley, which seemed custom-made to welcome Virgil's 'happy peasants'. To get there, you had to take the road from Obaba to San Sebastián and then, after about a mile, turn left down a road which didn't even appear on maps of the region. Then, immediately after a wood of chestnut trees, the little settlement would appear, a line of farmhouses built along either side of a stream and surrounded by meadows and maize fields. The house belonging to my mother and to Uncle Juan was the last in the row. After crossing a bridge, the road came to an end at their door. Beyond, the landscape reverted to hills and woods – of beech trees this time, not chestnuts.

Whenever I got on my bike and cycled over to that house, I felt as if I were crossing a frontier and entering a territory in which the past still reigned. This wasn't just because of the friends who lived there – Lubis, Pancho, Ubanbe – it applied to everyone. There was something ancient about them all. They would sit in Adela's kitchen – she was the shepherd's wife who cooked for me – and tell stories about wolves; in the first house, a mill known as Beko Errota, they still used to grind maize; many of the people who came to see Uncle Juan's horses knew no other language than Basque, and if they found me there rather than Lubis, as they were expecting, they would point to one eye in order to explain the reason for their visit: '*Ver caballo, ver caballo*' – 'See horse, see horse.' They imagined, given my appearance, that I was from somewhere else, from the city.

During the whole of that summer I lived in a dream, similar in every respect to the dreams which, according to Virgil, enter our mind through 'the ivory gate' and keep us from seeing the truth. Because around that time – 1963, 1964 – the truth was that those ancient people living in Iruain were already losing their memory. The names they gave to different sorts of apples – *espuru*, *gezeta*, *domentxa* – or to butterflies – *inguma*, *txoleta*, *mitxirrika* – were fast disappearing: they fell like snowflakes and melted when they touched the new ground of the present. And if it wasn't nouns, it was the various meanings of words they were forgetting, the different nuances acquired over centuries. And in some cases, it wasn't just words or meanings, it was the language itself that was being erased.

I behaved like someone who doesn't want to wake up. I could hear the noise of the new world very close, in the construction of a sports-ground just opposite my house, in the clatter of cranes and trucks, but I didn't consider the ultimate meaning of all that activity. Had it burst in on my dream, that image of the cranes and the wheels of the trucks crushing words as if they were snowflakes and plunging them into the mud, I would have been forced to see how unequal the battle was, how little hope there was for the world of those 'happy peasants'. But that image, which should have woken me, never arrived, and I remained inside the dream, as if I were in the delicious cave Lubis and Pancho had shown me.

My affection for their world continued to grow. I grabbed every chance I could to help Lubis out or to go to the restaurant in the square that provided a meeting place for Ubanbe, Opin, Pancho and most of the other woodcutters from the sawmill. And on Sundays, when I played the harmonium in church and the girls got up to take communion, I only had eyes for the country girls, despite their old-fashioned clothes and hairstyles. I felt drawn to them, much more than I did to the girls in my French class. Teresa, Susana, Victoria – the daughters of the best families in Obaba, and favoured both by my parents and by the school psychologist – were never more to me than classmates.

Teresa soon noticed this 'excessive' fondness and, in particular, my predilection for country girls. Her messages written on pastel-coloured bits of paper became more frequent: 'I'll be waiting for you at the door of the church', 'I'll be wearing a miniskirt to communion', 'I'll look at you when I walk past the harmonium'. She suspected that behind my attitude lay some 'specific love'; she thought I was in love with one of those girls. She was wrong though. There was no Selene, no one had as yet hypnotised me. The reason behind my dream, my hypnotic state, was the delicious cave that concealed a pool; it was the ancient world – the homeland of Lubis, Pancho and Ubanbe.

Teresa sent me a longer note: 'You're always in Iruain, David. You only stay in the hotel for as long as Monsieur Nestor's class lasts. Adrián and Martín say you'll have to go to the psychologist again, that you haven't yet got over your misanthropy. You may not realise it, but you're treating your friends very badly.'

She wanted me to wake up. As did the school psychologist, as did my parents. And in the end, I did wake up; I emerged from my dream; I settled into my proper time. I wasn't driven into doing so by the noise of the cranes and the trucks going back and forth on the sportsground, nor by the songs I played on the accordion, nor by the entirely new sound of television sets, which were beginning to be heard everywhere, but by other voices that had their origin in our parents' war.

Liz, Sara: I didn't know anything about that war, the Spanish civil war. I lived near Guernica – a plane would cover the distance between there and Obaba in ten minutes – and in 1964, the year of the Clay–Liston fight, it was only twenty-five years – 'Twenty-five years of Peace' according to the propaganda – since the end of the conflict. More than that, it was a war in which many people in Obaba itself had taken up arms. But I knew nothing about it. If someone had said to me then that Nazi Dorniers and Heinkels had killed hundreds of women and children in Guernica, I would have been astonished.

One day in July, in that 'year of peace', 1964, I went with Martín – the fourth friend on my list of favourites and Teresa's brother – to visit the sawmill-owner's son, Adrián, who had just come back from hospital in Barcelona after an operation on his spine to try to correct his scoliosis. It just so happened that a film about the Second World War was being shown on TV. We were watching it when the manager of the sawmill, the father of our friend Joseba, came into the room. 'I don't know how they can show films like that,' he said. Martín looked at him boldly and said: 'Well, I like them.' 'Even though the Nazis always lose,' retorted Adrián, just to needle him. The three of us laughed. Joseba's father suddenly started shouting: 'That's enough! War is no laughing matter. If you'd lived through the war here, you wouldn't think it was so funny.' And with that he stormed out of the room.

Shortly afterwards, three of our fellow French students from Monsieur Nestor's class turned up – Joseba and two girls, Susana and Victoria;

they, like Martín and me, had come to visit Adrián. 'I can't bear these films. I hate wars,' said Victoria as soon as she sat down on the sofa. Adrián smiled mischievously: 'Victoria doesn't like the Germans losing either. Although, of course, in her case, that's perfectly understandable.' Victoria was the daughter of a German engineer employed by a factory in Obaba. 'Well, I think the same. And I'm not German,' said Susana. She was the daughter of the doctor in Obaba, a very quiet girl. She was also very pretty, and a big hit with the boys at the dances held in the Hotel Alaska. 'I know why you say that, Susanita,' Martín said. 'Because your father lost the war. If he'd won, you might quite like wars.' He was trying to imitate Adrián's playful tone, but he lacked his light touch. 'My name isn't Susanita, it's Susana,' she said, getting up from the sofa. 'And I'll say it again: I hate war. In this village alone, nine innocent people were shot.' Martín winked at Adrián: 'You can tell what kind of family she comes from, eh?' 'And you can tell that you're your father's son,' said Joseba, joining in the argument. He stood up and so did Victoria. 'Me? And why is that, may I ask? Tell me, please, José,' Martín paused. 'Forgive me for not calling you Joseba, but just as Susanita is another name for Susana, Joseba . . .' 'And what do people call your father?' Joseba said, interrupting him. 'Why don't you tell me?' said Martín, standing up. I knew that his father was known as Berlino, because he'd made a trip to Berlin in his youth and come back telling everyone how marvellous it was there. But also because it rhymed with his real name, Marcelino. However, Joseba was clearly referring to something else.

Adrián turned off the television. 'Since it's impossible to watch the film in peace, let's have a look at the latest football news,' he said out loud, picking up a sports newspaper. 'Barcelona's going to beat Juventus 3-0, that's for sure.' No one took any notice. 'Shall we go out on to the balcony and smoke a cigarette?' Joseba said to the two girls, and all three of them left the room. I went after them. I'd been shocked by what Susana had said about people being shot in Obaba. It was the first time I'd heard anything about this.

From the balcony we could see the piles of planks and the warehouses belonging to the sawmill, as well as a large part of the village and the surrounding hills. On the side of one of those hills there was a white mark: the Hotel Alaska. 'I can't believe how crude Martín can be sometimes,' said Joseba. 'How did Geneviève manage to have a son like that?' Geneviève, the mother of Martín and Teresa, was much admired in the village because of her French origins and, above all, because she had Russian ancestry. 'I'm not going to the hotel any more,' said Susana. 'I don't see why the French classes have to be held there anyway. Just because it suits Geneviève?' She was still angry. 'They could be held here at the sawmill,' suggested Joseba. 'Especially now that Adrián is convalescing. I could mention it to our teacher, if you like.' 'That would be great,' said Susana. 'And if Geneviève doesn't agree, we'll just form another group.'

They fell silent, feeling somewhat placated. I said to Susana: 'Why did you get so angry with Martín?' She looked at me, as if wondering what I was doing out there on the balcony. 'My father suffered a lot in the war. His only brother was killed by the Nazis during the bombing of Guernica. He was a doctor too.' She paused before going on: 'But I suppose it's not really Martín's fault. We all know what his father was.' I glanced over at the hill and the hotel. 'It's Teresa I feel sorry for,' said Victoria shyly. If someone had asked her at that moment if she was German, she would probably have denied it. 'I'll talk to Teresa,' Joseba promised. 'She doesn't get on with her brother either.'

It was windy, and the alder trees growing along the banks of the river were swaying gently. *We all know what his father was*. But I didn't. I had to find out.

III

The message coming from Lubis, Pancho, Ubanbe and the other 'happy peasants' came through only faintly, drowned out by the daily hustle and bustle; but the message coming from our parents' war came through loud and clear from the moment I learned that people had been shot in Obaba. I would say it was like a dog barking, were that not offensive to Susana and to the messenger who arrived soon afterwards: my Uncle Juan.

It was the third week in July, and barely ten days had passed since that conversation at the sawmill. I went to my French class at the hotel as usual – the idea of forming another group had come to nothing – and then back to Iruain. When I reached the house, I heard noises upstairs, as if Juan were moving some furniture. This struck me as odd, because it was happening in the room I was using, not in his. He slept in the room next to the kitchen.

'What are you up to, Uncle? Shifting furniture?' I asked when I joined him. The wardrobe had been moved. After a moment's hesitation, he said: 'I do it every summer. I always like to have a look at the old hiding-place, just to see how it's doing.' The word he used for 'hiding-place' was *gordeleku*.

There was an opening in the floor, and he had leaned the missing section of flooring against the wall. 'What do you think this is, David?' 'A secret room, I suppose,' I said. He nodded. 'It was built more than a hundred years ago, apparently, at the time of the third Carlist war.' I was all eyes. 'You see this trapdoor?' Juan pointed to the section of flooring by the wall. 'You just have to close it behind you in order to vanish from the world.'

He turned on a torch and shone it into the hole. 'Look inside. It's about time you started finding out about these things.' I saw some steps. Down below, there was a piece of cloth, or something that looked like cloth. 'What's that down there?' I asked. 'Can't you see? It's a hat,' said Juan. 'Get it for me, will you, you're more agile than I am.' I placed my foot on the first step and started to climb down.

The hiding-place was very narrow. If I leaned to one side, I immediately touched the wall with my shoulder. 'It's like a tomb!' I said. Juan laughed, 'Well, if you're not careful, I'll leave you in there.' 'How could they get out if the wardrobe was on top of the trapdoor?' 'They couldn't, unless they had good friends outside,' he replied. 'And what if those friends let them down?' Juan gave a sardonic laugh: 'They'd be stuck down there for ever!'

65

It was a grey felt hat, made by J.B. Hotson, as I could see from the lining. A small label indicated the seller: *Darryl Barrett Store. Winnipeg. Canada*. These names shocked me. Iruain belonged to Lubis, Pancho, Ubanbe and the other farmworkers, woodcutters and shepherds; it was the space in which the old ways of saying butterfly or apple – *mitxirrika* or *domentxa* – still floated. But Hotson? Winnipeg?

Juan was looking out of the window. 'How old did you say you were, David?' he asked. 'Fifteen,' I said. 'When I was fifteen, I was working a full day on horseback taking food and equipment to the woodcutters. And your mother, who wasn't even fourteen, used to spend every evening sewing until midnight. She'd go to school, then run home and start sewing. That's what life was like when we were orphaned.' He picked up the hat and brushed off the dust. 'I'm not Obaba's first American,' he said. 'The first was the owner of this hat. We called him Don Pedro. He had a terrible time during the war, because there were people out to kill him. But I hid him in here, and they couldn't find him.'

In his hands, the hat became a familiar, friendly object. He span it round, turned the brim up and then down, squeezed it and then released it. I thought that he probably wore a hat like that on his ranch in California. 'My sister tells me that you spend a lot of time at the Hotel Alaska. Why is that, David? If you don't mind my asking, of course.'

I remembered what I'd heard Susana say on the balcony of Adrián's house, and sensed that I should be on my guard. 'It was Geneviève's idea to have the French classes there, and that's why I go,' I said. 'And you play the accordion when there's a dance there too, don't you?' 'Yes, my father likes me to go with him.' I was speaking carefully, aware that there was clearly something my uncle wanted to tell me. 'And how about Old Red-eyes? How do you get on with him?'

Teresa and Martín's father had an eye disorder, a chronic form of conjunctivitis which meant that his eyes were always red. The first time I saw his eyes when I was a child – which wasn't easy: he concealed them behind glasses with dark-green lenses – I went home and found my mother cleaning a fish in the kitchen sink. 'It's got the same eyes as Martín and Teresa's father,' I said. She put one finger to her lips: 'Sh! David. Don't say that.'

'I mean Berlino,' my uncle explained. 'Do you talk much to him?' 'No, never.' It was true. If I needed anything during the dances or the French classes, I would go to Geneviève. 'He disgusts me,' I said, remembering his red eyes. 'He does me too,' he said, going over to the hole in the floor. He crouched down slightly and dropped the hat inside. Then he put the trapdoor back in place. 'Shall we move the wardrobe as well?' I asked. 'No, it's fine in that corner. If you ever need to hide, it'll be easier for you to get in.' My mother used to say that every now and then Juan would grow sullen. And that's how he looked just then, frowning and tight-lipped.

Outside the house, against the front wall, was a stone bench, and we sat down there. It was a particularly lovely, sunny day, and the laughter and bustle of Adela's three children added to that pleasant feeling, as if those childish sounds were part of the landscape, the voice of the earth and the grass.

By the picket fence surrounding the paddock where the horses were grazing, the children were playing, bringing pebbles from the stream and arranging them around the stakes. 'Sometimes I find it hard to enjoy this place,' said my uncle, watching the children. 'I keep remembering the war. They were really bad times.' He turned to me: 'What about Ángel? Hasn't he told you anything about it?' 'No,' I said, 'we only talk about the accordion. That's our one topic of conversation.' My uncle started telling me about the war in general, rather as Joseba's father had spoken about it. He said that wars were a real disaster, especially civil wars, that people killed each other, out of greed and in order to steal.

Lubis appeared, walking along the road, and went over to the horses. As soon as Adela's three children saw him, they raced after him. 'Lubis is doing a fine job. I'm really pleased with him,' said my uncle, raising his arm to wave to my friend. 'They're very elegant, aren't they?' he said, meaning the horses.

There were five horses, and all five were trotting towards the fence to meet Lubis. Two were white, another two were chestnut, and the fifth was black. My uncle asked if I'd ever learned how to ride, and I was ashamed to have to tell him that I'd tried it when I was at school in Obaba, with Lubis in fact, but that Ángel considered it an inappropriate activity for an accordionist. 'So I had to give it up, which was a pity.' 'And why don't you tell Lubis that you'd like to try again?' 'Aren't I too big? I weigh more than fourteen stone.' 'Well, I don't exactly see you as a jockey,' said my uncle, laughing. 'You have some very funny ideas about horses. They can carry people much heavier than you. The American in the hiding-place was a huge man, and he rode to the French frontier on horseback.'

We were returning to the same subject. 'Who was after him? Berlino?' I asked. My uncle got up from the stone bench. 'You've seen the hotel, haven't you?' he said, pointing to the building on the hillside. 'It's pretty, of course. It was a sort of folly, really. Anyway, it belonged to the American, to Don Pedro. He found a silver mine in Alaska and made a fortune. Then he came home and built that hotel. It was his until Berlino and the military took it away from him. He's a thief, that Berlino, a criminal.'

He walked over to where the horses were, and I followed him. When we reached the bridge, he stopped and whispered in my ear, as if afraid that Lubis or Adela's sons might be watching us. 'And isn't what they're doing now tantamount to robbery? I mean, how much is that new sportsground going to cost? I'd like to know how much he's pocketing.' 'Are you sure?' I asked, slightly frightened. He was talking about Berlino, but Berlino and Ángel were inseparable. Besides, as a local councillor, Ángel was involved in all the public works carried out in the village. 'Of course I'm sure!' cried my uncle, not bothering to whisper any more. 'There was no call for tenders for that work. It was awarded to one company directly. How do they get away with it? It's just jobs for the boys, for fellow fascists. Things like that don't happen in California.' Suddenly, as if he were in a hurry, he strode on ahead of me, shouting. He was calling each horse by its name: 'Blaky! Faraón! Zizpa! Ava! Mizpa!' His favourite was Faraón, the largest of the white

68

horses. The horse put his head over the fence, and my uncle gave him a sugar lump.

'Why don't you teach David to ride?' my uncle asked Lubis. Before Lubis could reply, Adela's oldest son, Sebastián, yelled: 'Let me teach him!' He had very curly hair and my mother always used to talk very tenderly to him because he reminded her of 'a Murillo angel'. However, at only ten years old, he already swore like a trooper, stole cigarettes and had a sassy remark for anyone who stood in his way. He was nothing like the meek child who went to Villa Lecuona with the cheeses and eggs my mother used to buy from him. 'I don't believe you can ride!' jeered my uncle. 'Better than you can, old man!' replied Sebastián. – '*Ik baino obeto, aguria!*' – Lubis flinched. It was disrespectful of the boy to speak like that. The term *aguria*, meaning 'old man', was highly pejorative. But my uncle wasn't bothered. 'I can imagine you astride a sheep,' he said, winking at us, 'but not a horse.' Sebastián hurled one of his store of expletives at him. Then he leapt over the fence and on to Faraón's back. 'Stay!' Uncle Juan told the horse.

All the boy's efforts were in vain. Faraón wouldn't move a step. Sebastián's younger brothers, the twins, burst out laughing. 'He got you there, Sebastián!' said one of them. 'Yes, he got you there!' echoed his brother. Lubis sternly asked the boy to dismount: 'What are you playing at? Are we supposed to just stand around while you act the fool? Come here at once!' Sebastián hurried back to our side and said to my uncle defiantly: 'I'll make you a bet whenever you like. But no tricks, eh?' The twins again roared with laughter.

'Do you think your parents would let you ride, David?' Lubis asked. His uncle answered him: 'Do you mean because of the accordion? Don't worry about that. My sister says David prefers books anyway. And quite right too. Playing the accordion is all very well, but reading books is more profitable.' 'I'd love to learn,' I said. 'I really envy you when I see you ride.' The five horses were watching us, waiting for more sugar lumps. 'We could start right now if you like,' Lubis said. He looked at my uncle. 'Are you going for a ride?' My uncle said he wasn't. 'Then I'll take Faraón. He needs some exercise.' He climbed nimbly on to the horse, like a real jockey. 'Wait here a moment, David. I'm going to get a saddle from the pavilion.'

The 'pavilion' was their name for the wooden stables Uncle Juan had had built, 'like in America'. It was set a little back from the house, and, seen from outside, it resembled a small church. Inside, it was very functional: three stalls on one side and another three on the other, with a wide corridor down the middle.

'David should learn on Ava,' said my uncle. 'Good idea,' said Lubis. 'She's nice and quiet.' 'And what about me, Juan? Aren't you going to let me ride too?' Sebastián stood looking at my uncle, his chin lifted. 'Do what you like, as long you leave me in peace.' 'I'll take Zizpa, then.' Unlike Ava, Zizpa was very highly-strung, with a tendency to shy. 'Aren't you going to let us ride as well?' asked one of the twins. 'No!' cried my uncle. 'Then give us a sweet for our mother!' said the other twin. Adela was calling them from the door of her house. 'Here you are then! For your mother!' said my uncle scornfully, giving each of them a sugar lump, and the two boys raced off.

My uncle grabbed my arm. He was serious again. 'Just one thing, David. Don't tell anyone about the hiding-place, no one.' I gave him my word. 'Although I'm sure there won't be any more wars,' I added foolishly. He smiled: 'Do you imagine that war is something you know about beforehand? Do you think that, in 1936, we were all hanging out of our windows waiting for the first shot to be fired?'

IV

My mother, Carmen, used to say: 'I think we have another pair of eyes alongside those we have in our head, a set of nocturnal eyes that mostly show us only troubling images. That's why the night frightens me, because I can't bear what my Second Eyes see.' Perhaps I've inherited her character, because the same thing happens to me, and has done ever since the day my uncle first showed me the hiding-place and talked to me about the civil war. I suddenly began to be afraid of the night, because my Second Eyes would show me a dark place that prevented me from sleeping: a filthy cave full of shadows, utterly unlike the delicious place Lubis and Pancho had shown me. Obaba's first American was there, as were the nine executed men of whom Susana had spoken; and there, finally, was Teresa and Martín's father – Berlino – and my own father – Ángel. In my imagination, the former were crying and the latter were laughing.

In the discussions that Juan and I used to have during my first years at Stoneham, I even reproached him for the abrupt, unceremonious way in which he'd woken me from my sleep. The story he told me that day – I would say – led me to suspect Ángel of having been involved during the war in persecutions and executions, something for which no adolescent is prepared, however cool his relationship with his father might be. But when I think about it now, I believe he was right: if I hadn't had those suspicions about Ángel, I would never have struggled. If I hadn't struggled, I would never have become strong. If I hadn't become strong, I would never have been able to move on.

One day, we were sitting on the porch at Stoneham, and Mary Ann said to my uncle: 'Sure, David had to grow up, but the bad news could have waited, couldn't it? He would have been far better equipped to receive that news at twenty than at fifteen.' 'Does fifteen seem young to you? I was eight when I started working.' Mary Ann replied: 'My point is that you weren't concerned about whether he was old enough or not. You had political motives for talking to him like that. You were proselytising so that David wouldn't go over to the other side.' And my uncle: 'I do hold certain views, but I've never been that political. Besides, what else could I do? Leave the boy in the hands of Berlino, Ángel, and the other fascists?' *The boy.* Juan used those words without thinking. For me, though, it was the best possible proof that when, on that day, he acted as a messenger for what happened during the war, he was also thinking like a father.

Throughout that summer, there were many days of suffocating heat, and Lubis and I became fond of going riding in the hills around Iruain, where we could enjoy the cool of the wood. At first, when I could barely stay in the saddle, we chose the lower paths, which were broad and fairly straight, then, as I grew more confident, we tried the more difficult tracks. After a week or so, Lubis said to me: 'Right, today we'll go to the highest point in the woods.' And so we did, abandoning the paths, and riding up into the woods. We moved, from then onwards, with complete freedom, discovering previously unknown places.

We would saddle up Faraón and Ava and set off in the morning and sometimes – much to our pleasure – find ourselves in the wood with Ubanbe, Pancho or even Opin, who were felling trees for the sawmill. It wasn't long before we were arranging to get together with them each morning at around eleven, when they stopped to rest and have lunch beside a spring known as Mandaska. When we arrived, Sebastián would usually be there too, because he was in charge of bringing the men fresh bread and putting the cider to cool.

We removed the cider bottle from the spring, shared out the bread, cheese and sausage, and started eating: Lubis, Ubanbe, Opin and I ate slowly, taking our time; Pancho and Sebastián ate as quickly as they could, because they could hear the birds singing and found it hard to stay put. As soon as they'd finished, they would hide amongst the ferns, looking up, examining every branch of the beech trees, and often – Pancho was particularly skilled at this – would return holding several nests. If I close my eyes, I can see them still: the goldfinch's nest made of moss; the long-tailed tit's perfect oval of a nest; the magpie's, large and coarsely made. Some days, we drank too much cider, Sebastián as well, and the stupidest things would make us roar with laughter.

'I'm surprised at you, David,' Lubis said to me after one of these outings, when we were unsaddling the horses in Iruain. 'You seem really happy in our company. I would never have thought it.' 'Why, Lubis?' 'Oh, I don't know. Your friends spend their time going to the cinema and swimming in the Kramer pool. Not a bad life. I wouldn't mind it myself.' Kramer was the name of the German company run by Victoria's father. 'I prefer the cave that you and Pancho showed me the other day. Bathing in that was better than any swimming pool,' I said. Then he gave me a piece of bad news: 'You won't be able to bathe there any more.' 'Why, what happened?' 'The water doesn't reach the cave any more. Didn't you know? They diverted the spring because the village is expanding so much it needs more water.' I felt as sad as if I'd been told of the death of a living being.

Utter calm reigned in the stables. Ava was eating grass from the manger; Mizpa was brushing away flies with her tail. There was the odd murmur, the sound of breathing, but no other noise broke the silence. 'Forgive me if I'm being indiscreet,' said Lubis with a slight smile, 'but are you in hiding?'

I misunderstood the meaning of his question. I thought he'd read my thoughts, not the thoughts that were passing through my mind at that precise moment, or those that came to me during daylight hours and when I was with him, but those that had assailed me almost every night since Juan had shown me the hiding-place; as if my suspicions regarding my father were now written on my forehead, like a tattoo. 'You're right,' I said. 'I come here so that I don't have to be at Villa Lecuona.'

Lubis' eyes, normally so tranquil, looked suddenly uneasy. They scrutinised first the stalls and then the ground, as if searching for something. 'Sorry, David. I was just joking. I thought it was because of that girl who's after you, because of Teresa, because she's always sending you letters and dropping hints.' He didn't know where to put himself; my confession had embarrassed him. 'Anyway, it's true,' I said. 'I'm not quite sure how I feel about my father at the moment, and I'd rather not see him.'

The truth was much harsher than that, because my suspicions gave new meaning to each and every one of Ángel's gestures. He was no longer my father, Obaba's accordionist, but the close friend of Berlino, a fascist and possibly a murderer. I found it unbearable to have to sit opposite him in the kitchen at Villa Lecuona. But I said nothing of this to Lubis. It was clear that he didn't want to hear another word about it.

I knew that he disliked confidences, not only because he'd been brought up in the country and belonged to a place and a class where

73

things were done differently, more discreetly, but also because of his own character. Even so, his reaction seemed extreme. 'Do you have a problem with Ángel?' I said. 'No, why should I?' he replied, calmer now. I wondered if perhaps he knew something; if he, like Susana or my uncle, was awake, alert, and already informed about Ángel and Berlino. He didn't give me the chance to ask. He'd gone over to the other side of the stable and was giving Faraón some feed. Our conversation had ended.

During the summer, our rides and our meetings at the Mandaska fountain became more and more necessary to me. In the end, I decided to stay in Iruain, rather than have to keep coming and going between there and Villa Lecuona. In order to do this, I resorted to a lie. I told my mother that there was a short story competition commemorating 'twenty-five years of peace in Spain' and that I was thinking of entering. 'But I need to be alone,' I said. 'And what about your French classes? Are you going to abandon them too?' I nodded determinedly.

If Monsieur Nestor had given the classes somewhere else, at the sawmill, for example, as Susana and Joseba wanted, and not at the Hotel Alaska, I wouldn't have minded. I now saw the hotel as home to Berlino, 'Old Red-eyes', the largest of the shadows in the cave that haunted me at night. 'I don't need the classes. My French is fine. I'd prefer to spend the time writing.' My mother frowned. She didn't like my plan. 'I won't go to Urtza either,' I said. Urtza, a pool in the river beyond the sawmill, was our favourite place to bathe. I said this so that she would believe that I really did want to write, and was prepared to give up our main source of fun in the summer in Obaba. 'Do what you like,' she said, but she continued to look concerned.

The following Sunday, Don Hipólito came to meet me as I was going into the church, and immediately, almost without bothering to say hello, began talking to me about confession, as if it were something he'd been wanting to talk about for a long time. He said that there was nothing more beneficial and healthy, which was why Jesus Christ had instituted it as a sacrament. He warned me, too, that I must be careful not to let the demons living inside me multiply into legions, 'as happened to that

74

poor man from Tiberias'. 'If you have a problem, tell me about it. It will do you good,' he said.

We were in the sacristy; he was putting on his vestments for mass, and I was sitting on a bench. When I didn't reply, he went on: 'Young people should have friends their own age. It's not good to live apart.' 'Has my mother been talking to you?' I asked. They usually met at choir rehearsals and were good friends. 'Yes,' he said, 'Carmen *is* worried about you. Why don't you want to go swimming at Urtza or at the Kramer pool? Your mother says that, last year, she couldn't get you out of the water, and that swimming's your favourite sport.' 'I'd rather spend this summer writing,' I said. 'But your friends will be going swimming, and you'll have to rest sometimes. Remember, even Our Lord rested on the seventh day.' 'I won't be alone in Iruain,' I said. Don Hipólito had put on a white chasuble and was preparing the chalice he would carry to the altar. 'Oh, I don't doubt that Lubis is a fine companion,' he said, then added: 'So you consider your soul to be in a healthy state, do you? You feel no need to confess?' 'No, Don Hipólito,' I replied, 'I don't.' He took up the chalice and went over to the altar.

It was a lost opportunity. If, that day, I'd told Don Hipólito the truth – 'I've heard about some really terrible things that happened during the war, and an awful doubt keeps gnawing away at me: I wonder each night if perhaps I'm the son of a murderer' – if I'd confessed this to him, my mind might have found a way of healing itself. Don Hipólito – a Jesuit – was a practical, prudent man and would have immediately found some argument capable of reassuring a boy of fifteen – 'During the war there were 10,000 men like your father, and 10,000 more who were far worse.' Had that happened, the doubt would not have stayed lodged inside me, attached to me like a foreign body.

Far from acting sensibly, I kept all these things to myself and sought refuge in Iruain. I found it easier to forget there. I could always find something there to occupy me: mucking out the stables, going to the woods with Lubis, fishing for trout with Pancho or visiting Adela's house with Lubis, Pancho and Ubanbe. And when night came and there was an increased risk that I would start seeing the world through my Second

Eyes, I would go to bed and read until two or three in the morning, keeping my eyes trained on the words, the lines, the chapters, the books, until I fell asleep.

Books. One of these, which I found in my uncle's room, became indispensable to me. It was by a poet called Lizardi and was entitled *Biotz-begietan – In the Heart and in the Eyes*. It seems incredible now, sitting here in Stoneham Ranch, where I can see the bookshelves crammed with Liz and Sara's hundreds of children's books, but it's true: that summer of 1964, at the age of fifteen, was the first time I'd seen my mother tongue in print.

I found *Biotz-begietan* a difficult book to read, and had to decipher the words – words, as I say, written in my mother tongue! – as patiently and stubbornly as if they'd been written by an Ovid or a Martial, like someone rubbing away with water and vinegar at the face of some long-buried coin. The very difficulty of reading Lizardi, however, had the virtue of making me forget about everything else. The sinister shadows, 'the demons that could become legions', disappeared from my head and left me alone.

One morning, I was reading the book in the kitchen at Iruain when my uncle came in, accompanied by the doctor, Susana's father. He used to visit Juan now and then to check his blood pressure, or so my uncle said, but also in order to chat or go off on trips together for the day. He was a laconic fellow in his sixties, who always wore plaid jackets and dark ties. His name was Don Manuel, but the country people called him *mediku iharra*, 'the thin doctor'.

He glanced at the book I was reading, and as he walked past me on his way to my uncle's bedroom, he clapped his hands together several times. At first, I didn't understand the gesture. I only realised what it meant when he closed the bedroom door and left me alone. Don Manuel had been silently applauding me.

That same night, my uncle came up to my room and told me that he'd just got back from Biarritz. He was holding a hardback book. 'I've brought you this. It will come in handy if you want to learn to read in our language.' On the cover it said: *Dictionnaire Basque–Français. Pierre Lhande S.J.* 'A Basque-Spanish dictionary would be more useful, of course, but, as you know, the military who are in charge in Spain won't allow it,' he said. I thanked him and said that it didn't really make much difference, since my French was pretty good. 'But be careful, don't go around telling everyone you're reading Lizardi. People have been reported for less than that.' 'I'll bear it in mind. And if there are any problems, I'll just climb into the hiding-place with the book and a torch, and problem solved.' 'Don't joke about it.' My uncle wagged his finger at me. I had better keep alert.

V

I was looking out of the stable window when I saw Ángel's grey Mercedes emerging out of the forest of chestnut trees and driving down into the valley. It passed by the mill and by Ubanbe's house. 'You know, David,' my uncle said, coming over to me. 'That car used to belong to our friend with the red eyes.' 'Which car, Juan?' asked Lubis. He was on the other side of the stable, tending to a cut on Zizpa's leg. 'My uncle says that my father's Mercedes used to belong to Berlino,' I explained. 'Oh, I see,' said Lubis, glancing out of the window for a moment. 'And before it passed into Berlino's hands, it belonged to the current owner of the hotel,' added my uncle.

The car was moving fast, churning up the dust on the road, past Lubis and Pancho's house and past Adela's house. In another hundred yards, it would be at the door of Iruain. 'I seem to be having difficulty understanding you today, Juan. Do you mean Berlino isn't the owner of the hotel?' asked Lubis. He was still crouching down, rubbing some antiseptic cream into the mare's injured leg. 'The real owner lives in Madrid, a certain Colonel Degrela. That's what Berlino and company call him.' Lubis concentrated harder on the task in hand. He didn't seem to be in a mood to talk. My uncle said to me: 'He's angry with me because I let Sebastián ride the horse.' Lubis shook his head vehemently:

'I'm angry because you let that boy go off on his own with her. And this is the result. He took Zizpa along all the most dangerous paths. We're lucky she didn't break a leg.' 'Who's Colonel Degrela?' I asked my uncle. 'Hasn't he ever visited your house?' 'Not that I know of.' 'He was in charge of the troops that entered Obaba. Berlino became his right-hand man, or should I say his wrong-hand man.' My uncle laughed at his own joke, and stood looking at me, as if daring me to ask another question.

The car was almost too big for the bridge over the stream, but Ángel didn't even slow down. 'I don't know the man with your father,' said my uncle. 'It's Monsieur Nestor, my French teacher.' I was slightly unnerved by this visit and pronounced my teacher's name in a some-what ironic tone. 'He's a very decent, very cultivated man,' I added quickly, to avoid any misunderstanding. My uncle went over to the stable door: 'Let's go out to greet them; these gentlemen are far too elegant to be met in a stable.' 'Wouldn't you like to meet Monsieur Nestor?' I asked Lubis. He replied with an abruptness unusual in him: 'Another time perhaps.' I thought again about what had happened a few days earlier. There was something going on between Lubis and Ángel. That's why he didn't want to see him.

Ángel was wearing a dark suit that looked completely out of place in Iruain, and my uncle again remarked on his elegance. 'Because I'm wearing this suit, you mean?' my father said. 'This is my work uniform I'll have you know.' Then he introduced his companion. 'And this gentleman is Monsieur Nestor.' 'I'm not elegant either. I'm merely poor,' said Monsieur Nestor, taking a step towards my uncle and holding out his hand. He pronounced his r's like a Frenchman. 'Poor and elegant? How is that possible?' asked my uncle as they shook hands. Monsieur Nestor raised one finger theatrically, as he did in class: 'As Petronius so rightly said, elegance is the last hope of the poor. If I dressed in accordance with my bank account, no one would employ me.' He was a bulky man, with fair, curly hair. He was 'in uniform' too, wearing what he always wore: a cream-coloured suit, white shirt, dark red silk tie and white shoes to match his shirt.

'So you're still alive, then!' Ángel said, as if he'd just noticed me. He was smiling, but, as my mother sometimes said, only in order to keep himself from yelling. 'How long are you going to be staying here? Until Christmas?' 'I'm not sure,' I said. I felt inhibited with my uncle and Monsieur Nestor there as witnesses to our conversation. 'Lately, everyone seems to be asking after you,' he went on. 'Your mother asks. Martín asks. And that's why I've brought your teacher today. Because he's been asking after you too. It's true, isn't it, Monsieur Nestor?'

My uncle pushed open the door of the house. 'Leave your son alone, and tell us how the work's going on with the new houses and the sports-ground,' he said to Ángel. 'How much money have you made?' Ángel smiled: 'As I've told you many times before, we're not all like you. We work for the good of the village, we're not interested in business.' There was no apparent hostility between them. Addressing Monsieur Nestor, my uncle asked: 'Won't you join us?' My teacher declined. He preferred to stay outside. 'But you'll have a drink, won't you?' 'Yes, a beer. But in a glass, please, I don't want to drink from the bottle like a barbarian.'

'What do you think would be the most effective way of wiping that dreadful name "Monsieur Nestor" from the face of the earth?' said my teacher, once we were alone, sitting down on the stone bench. He asked the question in French, just as if we were in class, and the word he used for 'dreadful' was *épouvantable*. 'Although, the fault, I realise, is entirely mine,' he went on. 'The first day I arrived at the hotel, Teresa and Geneviève came out to meet me and said: "Monsieur Nestor?" And all I could think of to say was "Yes", instead of telling them: "No, please, just plain Nestor will do." And now, as you see, I'm stuck with it. Even the waiters in the restaurant in the square call me "Monsieur Nestor". Worse, they pronounce "Monsieur" *mosie*, *Mosie Nestor*. Things really can't go on like this.' I laughed, but he was, in a way, being serious. 'Why don't you like it?' 'For the simple reason that it's a name better suited to a hamster.' He took a white handkerchief from his pocket and wiped the sweat from his brow.

Ángel came out of the house carrying a bottle of beer. 'Oh, the glass!' he cried and went back inside again. 'As I've told your father,' explained

Monsieur Nestor, 'one shouldn't drink beer the way people in Obaba do, straight from the bottle. That way you just swallow all the gas.' He was speaking in Spanish now, using expressions like 'beber a gollete', literally 'to drink from the neck of the bottle', which I'd never heard. 'Your bottle and your glass, Monsieur Nestor,' said Ángel, when he returned. 'What has this son of mine got to say for himself? Why doesn't he fulfil his obligations?' he asked, without even deigning to look at me. 'He says he's very happy living here,' Monsieur Nestor replied, inventing an answer. 'Yes, like all idlers. Well, I don't like idlers,' said Ángel, turning his back on us and going into the house again.

'We don't call you Monsieur Nestor,' I told my teacher. 'Teresa does, but the others don't. We call you *Redin*.' He frowned, then his face lit up. '*Redin*? You mean, like Reading, the town in England? But I can't think why.' 'Don't you remember? In one of our first classes, you were comparing French and English pronunciation. You said that English was much harder and told us what had happened to you the first time you were in England. How you kept saying *Redin*, and no one knew what you meant. And then at last someone understood, and said: "Oh, you mean Reading!" Anyway, that's where your nickname comes from. Pretty silly, as you can see.' 'But better than Monsieur Nestor, much better!' he said and drank the rest of his beer.

He sat looking at the landscape. 'What a lovely place! It makes one feel like lying down on the grass,' he said. He produced from his pocket a pack of cigarettes – Virginia tobacco, unfiltered. 'Sometimes, you know, I fancy becoming an animal. Right now, for example. Look, how happy those horses seem to be!' He lit his cigarette in one smooth movement. His index and middle fingers were stained yellow with nicotine.

The three mares, Blaky, Ava and Mizpa, were standing together on one side of the paddock, while Faraón was grazing in the middle. In a few days' time, when Zizpa was better, that state of equilibrium would once more be undermined. Zizpa was showing signs of wanting to replace Faraón as leader.

I felt sorry for Monsieur Nestor. It was said that, years before, when he was still a Jesuit priest, his 'excessive intelligence' had caused him to go mad, and he'd got it into his head to go to the station at San Sebastián and catch the first train he saw. His students at the Hotel Alaska knew the story, and most thought that he'd hung up his cassock precisely because he'd gone crazy. When Adrián and Martín wanted to make fun of him, they used to call him '*Trenes*' – 'Trains'.

'I must be a terrible teacher,' said Monsieur Nestor, or as he would prefer, Redin. 'Susana was the first to stop coming to the class. Then it was your turn. And Adrián, who's still convalescing, doesn't come much either. It's disastrous.' His cream-coloured suit was distinctly worn, as was his shirt, the cuffs of which looked to me as if they'd been darned. He was not exaggerating when he spoke of poverty. Losing the class at the Hotel Alaska really could prove disastrous for him.

'It's not because of you,' I said. 'Susana stopped going because of Martín – they don't get on, you see. She and Joseba considered starting another group.' 'That's not a bad idea. Another class would certainly suit me. I need to buy some new spectacles. They're incredibly expensive here. They're much cheaper in England.' He paused, as if making calculations. Then he asked: 'And why don't *you* come any more?' I repeated my lie: 'I'm trying to concentrate. I want to write.'

'In order to write one needs money,' he said, still looking at Faraón. 'Remember Hemingway. I've often read that he was so poor when he lived in Paris that he used to go pigeon-hunting in the park so as to have something to eat. Bah!' Redin made a gesture indicating that the story should be treated with scepticism. '*Légendes!*' he exclaimed. Or perhaps he said it in English, given that he kept moving between languages. 'Are you sure?' I asked. 'Absolutely. As I've often told you, I came to know him rather well.'

There was disagreement amongst those of us who attended his classes. Some considered Redin's stories about his friendship with Hemingway to be pure fantasy. Unsurprisingly, Martín and Adrián were among them, but so was Joseba. Joseba said that they might have met a few times, perhaps during the fiestas in Pamplona, and that this would doubtless have made a great impression on Redin, because Hemingway was very popular in Spain. I had my doubts too. 'Hemingway at the bull-running,' was the caption of a photo that appeared every summer in the newspapers. It was hard to imagine such a famous man going around with Redin.

'How could a man with dollars in his pocket be poor!' cried Redin, getting up from the stone bench and speaking as if he were arguing with someone. 'When he first started coming to Spain, twenty people could eat for one dollar! Twenty people!' He pointed to Ángel's Mercedes before concluding: 'It's the same with you. You're lucky enough to be rich. You *could* become a writer.'

Ángel and Juan came out of the house, still arguing. Ángel said to Redin. 'We're going to erect a new monument in the square to commemorate those who died in the war, and we want to unveil it at the same time as the sportsground. But Juan here thinks it's a bad idea.' My uncle winked at me. He was less excitable than Ángel. 'It's a waste of money. Who needs monuments? You'd be better off building a playground.' 'A playground!' cried Ángel, as if he'd been expecting such a comment. 'That's exactly what we're going to build. In fact, we're building one right now!' 'And where are you going to put it? I haven't seen it.' 'Where? Inside the sportsground, near the river, opposite Urtza!' 'That's fine, Ángel, but a monument is a waste of money,' repeated my uncle. He looked at Redin: 'What do you think, sir? Are you for or against?'

Redin gazed off into the distance, towards the woods. He disliked arguing, even in jest. 'When it comes to monuments, I'm very Roman. I like them,' he said at last. 'You see?' said Ángel to Uncle Juan. 'He's in favour too. 'Yes, in favour of the Romans,' added Redin, but he said this in a whisper that only I could hear.

Ángel took the accordion out of the boot of the car. 'It's time you did something, don't you think? You haven't practised for weeks,' he said. My uncle winked at me again: 'Oh, great, now we'll all be dancing in Iruain!' Ángel left the accordion case by the door. 'The only reason *you* would dance is if they paid you,' he told my uncle. I said angrily: 'Can't you talk about anything else? You're boring us all to death.' He took no notice. 'A dog will dance for a bone, and anything else he's thrown,' said Redin suddenly. Ángel applauded, laughing: 'Very good!' My uncle laughed too, and started walking towards the stables. 'I'm going to see how that horse is. Adela's son is too confident for his own good and took her into some really risky places. She could easily have broken a leg. Would you like to see her?' Ángel declined the invitation. 'I have to drive Monsieur Nestor back.' He got into the car. Redin did the same. 'Your son's been learning to ride,' said my uncle, 'and he's doing really well.' 'Well, I'm glad he's learning something,' muttered Ángel, starting the engine. He turned to me: 'You can stay here until the fiestas start. After that, you're coming back home.'

From the passenger window, Redin beckoned me over. 'I almost forgot,' he said, 'Teresa would like to come and see you, if you don't mind, that is.' 'No, that's fine,' I said, without thinking. It had never occurred to me that Teresa would need to ask my permission before visiting me.

They left as they had come, churning up the dust along the road. I went back to the stable to join my uncle and Lubis.

Teresa arrived alone, walking calmly along, and remained seated on the stone bench while Lubis and I finished whitewashing the walls of the kitchen in my uncle's house. Then, when we came out, she handed us each a bunch of wild flowers. 'What does a girl have to do to be admitted to the team of builders?' she asked. Lubis burst out laughing: 'I've never seen a girl whitewashing walls. Besides, you're much too refined. Just look at the pretty dress you're wearing today.' Lubis had cheered up again. The cut on Zizpa's leg was healing. Teresa kissed him on the cheek: 'Thank you for saying that I'm refined.' Lubis laughed again: 'From now on, I'm going to go around covered in whitewash stains all the time. I might get more kisses that way.' Teresa was wearing a yellow dress and jacket, and had a white bag over her shoulder.

'How is everyone?' I asked. 'Who's "everyone", David?' 'Who do you think, Teresa? Our friends. Have you all been swimming at Urtza?' She looked at me for a moment. She was wearing make-up, and the dark eye-liner emphasised her greenish-yellow eyes, the colour of olive oil.

'A lot of people have been at Urtza. In my opinion all the *inessential* people have been there, but the one *essential* person has not. I'm referring, of course, to you.' Lubis shifted on the bench. It shocked him that a girl should speak so frankly. It shocked me too.

'I wasn't going to come,' said Teresa, in a different tone of voice. 'Girls aren't supposed to go chasing after boys, but what's a girl to do when the boy takes no notice.' This time Lubis made as if to leave. I grabbed his arm and forced him to sit down again. Teresa gave us a mocking look. 'You see? David's embarrassed to be left alone with me.' 'That's not true,' I protested. She was making me nervous; she kept staring at me.

Teresa got up. 'Anyway, the visit is over. The truth is I came to give you a letter.' She took the letter out of her bag and handed it to me. Then she walked away, taking short, rapid steps, as if she were in a hurry.

We watched her move off along the river bank. She crouched down now and then, apparently to pick flowers. 'She's brave. Like her brother Martín, only in a different way. I like her,' said Lubis. As if she'd heard him, Teresa turned and waved to us. 'I don't mean that I don't like Martín,' explained Lubis, 'but Teresa has more class. Martín is like his father, and she's like her mother.' We remained sitting on the bench. A quarter of an hour later, Teresa's outfit was just a small yellow stain against the woods.

Teresa's letter — I quote from memory because I haven't been able to find it amongst my papers here at Stoneham — began with a poem from the anthology we used in our French classes: *Est-ce que les oiseaux se cachent pour mourir?*, 'Do birds hide when they die?' Then, in a similar tone to the poem, she said how sorry she was that I no longer went to the hotel, but remained 'determined to live the life of a peasant', with no consideration for 'our dear Monsieur Nestor'. 'I don't know if you realise,' she said more or less, 'but you're leaving our teacher at the mercy of people like my brother Martín, who's going around saying that it's impossible to learn anything from Monsieur Nestor because he

84

keeps shifting in and out of English and French and doesn't even realise he's doing so. And do you know why he's invented this calumny? Because he's found someone to replace him. As you can imagine, the person in question is an *explosive* young woman of twenty-five.'

The letter ended as it had begun, on a sad note, and at the end, she mentioned the fact that had probably provoked her into writing in the first place: 'I've just realised: you've stopped coming to the French classes and so has Susana. I had no idea you were so in tune.'

There was no basis for her suspicion. If I was 'in tune' with anyone, it was with one of the country girls who went to mass. Her name was Virginia, and she was the same age as Lubis, two or three years older than me. She would take communion at the altar-rail and return to her seat via the aisle where I was playing the harmonium. When she passed me, she would turn her head slightly and look at me. Every Sunday, without fail. After the third or fourth time, I began to respond: I would look at her too or play some variation on the harmonium, which would, of course, be noticed in the church, but that was all there was to it. Teresa's suspicions were, as Lubis would have said, *pantasi utsa*, pure fantasy.

VI

On 15 September, six men went up the church tower to ring the big bell and announce the start of the Obaba fiesta. The bell rang for half an hour and then, when the six men left it to swing freely, it rang less loudly and less regularly. A little later, when it was ringing only in fits and starts, someone sent three rockets up into the air. That was the signal for the festivities to begin.

My uncle hated the big bell, or, rather, not so much the bell itself, as the dogs, who would start barking and howling. He said they gave him a headache and that he was afraid of all those hysterical dogs; one year, some dogs had got into the paddock at Iruain and bitten one of the mares. Deep down, though, the problem lay in himself, in his heart and in his eyes. *Biotz-begietan*. He disliked fiestas, no, more than that, he loathed them. He only stayed in the village until 16 September for my mother's sake, because the family meal held on that day at Villa Lecuona was important to her. However, by then, he was usually all packed up for the flight home As soon as the meal was over, my mother would take the Mercedes and drive him to San Sebastián airport. Twenty-four hours later he was back in California. And in 1964, things unfolded as they normally did.

After the fiesta and Juan's departure, everything seemed sadder. It felt as if the water in the stream at Iruain flowed only reluctantly, as if Lubis were depressed, as if the horses didn't neigh as much, as if the birds had hidden away somewhere – *pour mourir* perhaps.

I took up walking. Leaving the houses behind me, I would walk to the point where the Iruain stream met the Obaba river and there, in the nearby woods, I'd collect the first glossy chestnuts of the year. I would walk as far as Urtza and sit down on the small pebbly beach.

Without the lively bustle of the hot summer days, Urtza seemed to me a doubly silent, doubly solitary place, as though the voices and hubbub of the people who'd enjoyed themselves there during July and August had left a void, a kind of hollow in the water. Sometimes, 'perhaps stirred into life by the god Pan', the alders on the banks would begin to move and whisper, and I'd feel on my skin the first cold wind of the year. Then I'd walk back to my parents' house – Ángel wouldn't let me stay at Iruain – to ponder my immediate future. I had no choice. I'd have to go to school every day, by bike, by train, on foot, with Adrián, Martín, Teresa, Joseba, Susana, Victoria and the whole Obaba group. And at night, home again, on foot, by train, by bike, this time alone, because I came back later than the others, after the last class of the day at the accordion academy.

As the date for the start of school approached, my Second Eyes, as if emboldened by Uncle Juan's departure, no longer waited for the dark of night to show me the filthy cave and its shadows, these appeared now at any time of the day; there was Martín and Teresa's father, Berlino

– Old Red-eyes – as frightening as ever; there was the 'American', who had sought refuge in the hiding-place in Iruain; and the men shot by firing squad of whom Susana had spoken. And there was one last shadow, that of Ángel, my father. There were moments when what my First Eyes saw blended with what my Second Eyes saw, and the darkness of the waters of Urtza mingled then with the events of the civil war, and the whispering of the alder leaves with my suspicions about Ángel.

The day before my return to school, I went to the house in Iruain and suggested to Lubis that we visit the spring at Mandaska to see Ubanbe and our other friends, who would be where they always were, felling trees in the woods. Lubis agreed, and we set off along the path we'd taken on other days, with him mounted on Mizpa and me on Ava. However, it turned out not to have been a good idea. At Mandaska, they were all drunk, Ubanbe, Opin, Pancho and even Sebastián.

'The fiesta's over, but it seems no one's bothered to tell these idiots here,' said Lubis, without getting off his horse. Ubanbe started yelling: 'We've been hunting, Lubis! Look at what your brother's caught!' He was wearing a white shirt, unbuttoned, with a large wine stain down the front.

Pancho came towards us. He was holding a little field mouse by the tail. 'Give it to me,' Lubis said. 'Oh no you don't!' cried Opin, coming between the two brothers. He was holding a long-handled axe and waving it around in the air. The gleaming blade came very close to Lubis' head. 'Put it down on that trunk, Pancho, and watch me cut off its head,' said Opin. He was the drunkest of all and seemed incapable of taking a step without staggering. 'Give it to me,' Lubis said again, ignoring Opin's axe. 'Lubis wants the mouse so that he can set it free,' said Sebastián. 'He likes animals. Besides, you know what category *he* is – *flyweight*.' This incomprehensible remark was greeted by the others with loud guffaws. 'No, let *me* have it. I'm going to see if it can swim,' said Ubanbe, snatching the mouse from Pancho. There was a barely perceptible squeak: a tiny red thread in the forest air. 'What's up with you, eh? Be quiet!' exclaimed Ubanbe, shaking the mouse. He strode over to the spring. The little creature squeaked again.

Lubis tugged on Mizpa's reins in order to turn and ride back. Before setting off, he looked at his brother. 'You haven't been home for three days. Your mother's very angry.' Pancho replied furiously: 'What do I care what the old cow thinks!' With his massive jaw, he looked quite frightening. 'We'll talk again when you're sober,' said Lubis, loosening his horse's reins.

Ubanbe yelled: 'Grab him! Grab him!' Then he started cursing: 'How could you have let him get away, Opin? You're getting slow, you are, you're useless!' Sebastián came running after us. 'Lubis! Don't tell Adela you've seen me here.' Without turning round, Lubis said: 'Come and ask me if you can ride Zizpa and see what answer you get! I forgave you for that cut she got on her leg, but I won't forgive you for what happened today!'

Even when he was angry, Lubis still spoke in the same measured way. He merely said the words slightly more loudly. 'You're annoyed because I called you a "flyweight", but I didn't mean it,' said Sebastián, almost in tears now. He seemed to be feeling much worse than he had a few moments before, as if under the renewed effects of the alcohol in his veins. He was pale and his hair was all dishevelled. 'Get up here with me, and we'll go home. That'll be best for everyone.' Sebastián tried to get on the horse, but had to turn his back on us in order to vomit copiously.

We rode home in silence. When we reached the valley, Lubis took Sebastián to Adela's house, and I went to Iruain. I took up the Lizardi book and tried to concentrate on reading.

I was still reading when I heard the sound of a car engine. I thought it would be Ángel, angry with me for having gone to Iruain without his permission. However, when I went over to the window, I saw two cars, not just the Mercedes. The other car was a maroon Peugeot, which I recognised at once. It always occupied the same parking place at the Hotel Alaska. It belonged to Berlino. The two cars stopped outside the house.

Ángel burst into the kitchen. 'What *are* you thinking of? Come outside this minute!' he said. 'Come and meet Colonel Degrela! Now!' I stayed where I was at the table. I didn't understand why he was so upset. I didn't know who he was talking about. Or, rather, I couldn't remember who this Colonel Degrela was, although I'd heard his name before. 'Move!' shouted Ángel.

I went outside. Standing with their backs to the house, Berlino and another older man were gazing out at the valley. Ángel made the introductions: 'This is my son, Colonel. He comes to this peaceful little place to practise playing the accordion.' He was making an effort to speak very good Spanish, but couldn't disguise the accent of a man born and bred in Obaba, and he lapsed inadvertently into alliteration.

I reckoned the colonel must have been about sixty. He was thin and bony and immaculately dressed, all in grey, with a silk shirt and tie. His spectacle frames were a pinkish colour. Although his short hair gave him a rather military air, he looked more like an aristocrat. 'How are you?' he said gravely. We shook hands. His grip was firm but brief.

A woman of about thirty-five got out of the Peugeot. She was wearing a pair of tight, dark red trousers and a jacket in the same colour over a beige polo neck. She had a round, pretty face. She made an even odder impression on me than the colonel.

'Where are the horses?' she asked, without even bothering to say hello, and making clear the real reason for their visit to Iruain. 'They'll be in the field at the back,' said Ángel. 'No, they're not,' I said, 'they're in the stables.' Colonel Degrela turned to me: 'Be so kind as to bring them out, will you? My daughter would be thrilled. She prefers horses to people.' The mere transcription of his words might suggest that there was in them a hint of affability, some suggestion of sympathy for his companions. This was not the case. He spoke in a soft, clipped voice. Despite this, both Ángel and Berlino laughed. 'Pilar, go and see the horses,' the colonel said. 'I'd like a quiet chat with these gentlemen here.' He wasn't looking at his daughter, but at the countryside. 'Go with her, will you?' he said to me, then went into the house with Ángel and Berlino.

We walked over to the stables. Lubis was standing in the doorway, looking worried. 'This is the man in charge of the horses. He's more qualified to show them to you than I am,' I said to the woman. Lubis stood in front of me and said: '*Bakarrik utzi bear al nauzu oilo loka onekin?*' – 'Are you leaving me alone with this old broiler?' He was feeling annoyed. 'I can't stop,' I said. I wanted to go back to the house to keep an eye on Ángel and on the other two men. 'What did your friend say?' the woman asked me. 'I was talking about chickens,' answered Lubis. 'We'll go and see them later. Now show me the horses,' said the woman.

I went into the house through the back door and straight to my uncle's room. There was a small window there that gave on to the kitchen; it had a revolving shelf, like the kind that used to be built into convent walls to receive foundling children, and I sat down there, intending to hear every word.

The three men were talking quite normally. They were discussing the various public works projects being carried out in Obaba. Colonel Degrela said how important it was that the new houses and the sports-ground should be completed at the same time, and both Berlino and Ángel agreed. 'The new houses are coming along well, although work on the sportsground is running slightly late,' explained Ángel. 'But don't worry, it'll all be ready within a year, if not before.'

Colonel Degrela said something I didn't quite catch. 'Yes, of course,' said Berlino, 'and the monument as well. And you're absolutely right. The current memorial plaque is in a dreadful state. Some of the names of the fallen are almost illegible, the names of my two brothers, for example. The colonel's quite right, Ángel. We should have taken more care of it.' 'We mustn't be found wanting in such matters,' said the colonel. 'And we won't,' promised Ángel. 'It's all decided. Down to the last detail. The monument will be in black marble with gold lettering. And it'll be unveiled at the same time as the other projects.' Berlino's voice sounded cheerier now. 'How about getting Paulino Uzcudun for the inauguration?' Paulino Uzcudun was a famous boxer who had been born near Obaba. He'd fought with the likes of Primo Carnera, Max

Baer and Joe Louis. 'An excellent idea, Marcelino!' declared Colonel Degrela authoritatively.

I stopped listening. I began to wonder what I was doing there, glued to the window, crouched there like a thief. Why didn't I just go into the kitchen and say to them: 'What are you doing sitting in this kitchen? What right have you to be here, Berlino, you who sully the very floor you walk on, you who one day, doubtless accompanied by Ángel, came to this house looking for the real owner of the hotel? By the way, the hat you didn't manage to take from him is still here . . .'

The thoughts coming into my head were making me dizzy, and I had to go and sit down on the edge of the bed. The cave I could see with my Second Eyes was coming into view again and there was a new shadow in it now, possibly the main shadow: that soldier called Degrela. Ángel and Berlino were merely his servants.

I heard a door slam in the kitchen. 'Papa, I want to buy that horse! He's wonderful. I've never seen a horse like him!' said Colonel Degrela's daughter. 'Don't worry, Señorita! If you like him, you shall have him,' said Berlino. 'We'll sort it out,' added Ángel. 'And he has such a lovely name! Faraón!' exclaimed the woman. 'We have no choice, gentlemen! When my daughter gets an idea in her head, there's no shifting it. We'll have to go and see this horse,' said Colonel Degrela. I don't know if I actually heard him sigh or if I imagined it. 'Pilar, give us five minutes. We've got just one last thing to discuss.' 'He's a really fine horse,' insisted the woman. I heard Ángel's voice again: 'Don't worry, we'll sort it out. I'm sure the owner will make us a special price.'

I couldn't believe it. I found Ángel's behaviour completely unacceptable. How dare he promise someone a horse that wasn't his! What right had he to speak on behalf of Uncle Juan! I left the bedroom and ran to the stables.

Lubis was sitting on a saddle on the ground. 'Do you know what that woman wants to do? She wants to take Faraón!' Yes, I said, I'd heard them talking. 'More than that, she wants to take him with her right now. I've warned her, though, that no horse leaves here without Juan's permission.' 'I don't know, Lubis. Berlino and Ángel have promised her.'

91

He stood up. 'They've no right to do that. I'm sorry, David, but every-thing here belongs to Juan!' He was furious. 'I know, but what can we do? They'll be here soon.' 'Well, they're not going to take him!' He immediately saddled Faraón up. 'Where are you going?' I asked. But I already knew. He was going to the woods. 'Wait a moment. I'll come with you.' Without exchanging another word, we saddled up Ava too. 'Steady, now, steady!' Lubis said to the horses, who were snorting rest-lessly, infected by our nervous excitement.

We rode into the woods. We startled the birds as we passed, for they weren't dead like the birds in the poem Teresa had copied out for me, they were very light and alive. They flew up above our heads, scattering in different directions.

I envied their freedom. I couldn't simply carry on, tirelessly riding; I couldn't hope to find some private place, hidden away from the world. The new term began the following morning. I had to go back to Villa Lecuona.

VII

I set off for school at seven o'clock on the dot, when it was still dark, and, with the first forty pedal strokes, I left behind me my parents' house and the site of the new sportsground, and, with another forty, the area where they were building the new houses. Soon, at the first crossroads, the turning for the Hotel Alaska, I was joined by Teresa and Martín, who used to wait for me there so that we could cycle the rest of the way together.

The three of us usually arrived at the train station at around a quarter to eight in the morning, at more or less the same time as the other students from Obaba: Adrián, Joseba, Susana and Victoria. They, however, went by taxi, because Adrián still couldn't do any physical exercise, and his father, the owner of the sawmill, preferred this option to sending him to a boarding school.

Martín and Teresa were annoyed by this and complained because

Berlino and Geneviève denied them the option of going by car. I didn't mind, though. I preferred cycling. The pedals turned; the wheels and the spokes turned; the dynamo lighting the lamp turned: it was really pleasant riding along. It was even nicer, cosier, when rain or hail meant we had to wear a cape. Usually, I used the journey to go over in my head what the teachers had taught us in class, not just so as to do well in the various subjects, but because, by concentrating on something else, I didn't notice the effort.

The wheels of the train turned too, like those on my bike, but they made much more noise. At the same time – noise upon noise – we students travelling to San Sebastián, all crammed into the last carriage, with the girls on one side and the boys on the other, made our own tremendous racket too. Normally, if there was no delay, the De La Salle students – Adrián, Martín and me from Obaba, and about ten others from various different villages – reached our destination in half an hour, when the clock in the station showed eight twenty-five. The other students, Joseba, Susana, Victoria and Teresa continued on to the city centre.

From the station to the college it was exactly 'eight hundred and seventy steps', according to Carmelo, a member of our group who obsessively measured everything, and we walked that distance, passing first, a barracks – 140 steps – then an area of rather run-down houses – 600 – until we reached, after the hardest 130 steps of the whole route, the top of the hill on which the school was perched. Finally, we walked panting down the long gallery on the first floor, where the doors of the classroom were lined up 'just like soldiers', as the same Carmelo liked to say. By then, it would be twenty minutes to nine, and the prefect of studies, a monk we used to call Hippo or Hippopotamus, would always come in uttering the same reproach: 'Late again! Aguiriano, of course, has been sitting at his desk for ages.'

Aguiriano, who lived in a small village near Obaba, was a member of the school athletics team. He caught the same train as us and, when he got off, ran all the way to school, because, he said, he needed the training. 'Yes, but we're not athletes, we're normal,' Martín said to the prefect one day. It was a double-edged riposte, because, at school, Aguiriano was said to be not quite right in the head. For once, the prefect smiled.

I found the year from 1964 to 1965, when I was in the sixth form, harder than all the previous years. I didn't even manage to enjoy the bike ride. After spending the summer in Iruain, the corridors and class-rooms seemed dark, my classmates more alien than ever, and our disputes – for there was intense rivalry between the students from the villages and those from the city – insignificant and banal. I still couldn't free myself from the filthy cave revealed to me by my Second Eyes.

The weeks passed, dull and monotonous. On Mondays, we had a Maths test – 'the composition' in the language of De La Salle – on Tuesdays, a Physics and Chemistry test, on Wednesdays, Philosophy, on Thursdays, Literature and Art History, and on Fridays, they gave out the week's marks, and we filed up on to the stage, the best students at the front and the worst behind. On Saturdays, we arrived slightly later, and there was mass in the chapel, where I played the harmonium. On Sundays, after again playing the harmonium – this time in the church in Obaba – I either went to the cinema with Adrián, Martín and Joseba, or, on sunny days, I stayed in Obaba and went to Iruain to spend some time with Lubis. That was my life, week after week: a wheel that turned more slowly than the wheels on my bicycle or on the train. It was a very heavy wheel indeed, more like a grindstone, which trapped the tiny fragments of time and ground them up.

Nothing changed, especially not inside me. That slow turning led me nowhere. I wanted to talk to Susana and have her tell me more about the men who were shot. And I had it in mind to write to Uncle Juan with the same question. But these were plans without substance.

Gradually, the atmosphere at school began to improve for the students like us who travelled in by train. In our ancient conflict with the city boys, we were starting to get the upper hand, and, as Hippo, the prefect of studies, said, when the marks were given out, we were always the best at everything. Adrián, Carmelo, myself, and a few other *morroskos* who were boarders – *morroskos* or 'bruisers' was what the city boys called us – were all good students and always at the head of the queue when it came to getting top marks. Indeed, Adrián, who, because of his disability, was far from being a *morrosko*, became our official artist when, at Christmas time, he presented the school with some wooden carvings he'd made: a crib, complete with Holy Child, Mother and Father and animals. The chaplain of the school, Don Ramón, announced that we had a new Berruguete in our midst, and the monk who taught us Art History wrote an article in the school magazine praising the carvings. The other artist was me, because I played the harmonium and, at the occasional party, the accordion. Lastly, there was Martín, who confirmed the superiority of the village boys, although for rather different reasons. His popularity at school was constantly on the up.

Martín always got pretty bad marks and he had no particular skill, but he inspired a certain degree of fear and respect for the courage he showed both in playground fights and with the teachers. It was known amongst the students, too, that all the contraband cigarettes and alcohol circulating in the college passed through his hands.

Sometimes when we got off the train, Martín would tell us to go on without him, because he had some 'business' to do at a local bar. Then, when we were already climbing the hill to school, he'd catch us up and show Adrián and myself what he was carrying in his bag instead of books: usually miniatures of Martel cognac and a dozen packs of Philip Morris cigarettes arranged in neat rows. He had his distribution system organised too. At the door of the school, before we met Hippo, he would hand everything over to a boy who worked in the kitchen and who would be waiting for him. 'Where's your bag?' Hippo asked Martín once. 'I left it at home,' Martín said, without batting an eye.

On one of those days when he stayed behind to deal with this 'business' – it was May and the year was nearly over, and the grindstone was about to give one last heavy turn – Martín took longer than usual, and Adrián and I went into school without waiting for him. We told Hippo that he'd missed the train. 'A lie, I'm sure,' he said. We stood there, thinking he'd ask further questions, but, instead, he strode off down the gallery, whistling and jingling his keys. He was in a good mood, as if he, too, were infected by the spring.

Martín didn't arrive in the classroom until after break. It was the Art History class, and the teacher, the monk who'd written the laudatory article about Adrián's carvings, was explaining to us the composition of Velázquez's *Las hilanderas* with the help of a slide-projector. At one point, I noticed a commotion amongst the students sitting near Martín. None of them was paying any attention to the screen.

My eyes met Martín's. He was grinning broadly. I smiled back and gave him an interrogative look. Then he passed a magazine along the row of students separating us. I opened it and saw something in it that left me speechless: a man was having sex with a woman *zakurrak zakurrari bezala*, as Ubanbe, Opin and Pancho would have said – like a dog and a bitch. The woman had enormous breasts which hung down and touched the red carpeted floor.

I still hadn't recovered when Hippo appeared at the door of the classroom. 'All stand!' shouted the Art History teacher, and we obeyed instantly. Hippo told us to sit down again. The fluorescent lights on the ceiling, which had been turned off during the slide projection, suddenly flickered on, and the garish colours of the pornographic magazine glowed in my hands. I slid it down towards my knees, intending to slip it inside the desk. 'What are you hiding, David?' asked Hippo, coming over to me. He called me 'David' and not by my surname, as was the custom in the school. This display of trust made me blush still more deeply.

At the time – I was sixteen – I was already nearly five foot eight and weighed fourteen stone. However, this didn't prevent Hippo's punch from hurling me against the back wall of the classroom, because Hippo, as well as being extremely strong, caught me completely off guard. At first, he pretended to be going over to the window, as if he were about to throw the magazine out, but when he was standing sideways on to me, he suddenly turned and struck me on the left cheek, catching my eye.

When I got up, he was standing in front of me, looking very pale. He wanted to say something, but couldn't get the words out. He had his right arm raised, threatening me with his fist, and his left arm hung by his side. He was holding the magazine by one corner between forefinger and thumb, as if it were a filthy rag.

He would have blown his top at any of the students, but the fact that the *vile* perpetrator – that was the adjective he used when he finally recovered the power of speech – should be me, a *morrosko*, 'a noble lad' brought up in the pure, innocent surroundings of the country, and who played the harmonium in church, was unbearable to him.

'Go to the chapel and wait there. I have to speak to the headmaster. If he shares my view, you'll never set foot in this school again.' I wanted to protest, to proclaim my innocence, but I couldn't think clearly; the blow had left me stunned. My left eye was hurting.

As soon as I went into the chapel, I remembered the church in Obaba, and the time I was shut up there with Lubis and the other 'happy peasants' because of the fight on Palm Sunday. Unfortunately, after the incident with the pornographic magazine, I wasn't going to get off so lightly. And it was all Martín's fault. Suddenly – the pain in my eye was bothering me a lot – I hated him. What he'd done was despicable: remaining silent and not owning up; letting me take the punishment.

That initial reaction was followed by a moment of calm. When I thought about it, I could see why Martín had chosen not to explain the misunderstanding there in the classroom, when Hippo was still beside himself with rage, but he would doubtless clarify the situation later. Perhaps he was, at that very moment, explaining the matter to Hippo and the headmaster, in that characteristic way of speaking he had, barely opening his mouth: 'It's true the vile magazine was in my friend's hands, but ten seconds before that, it was in mine, and twenty seconds before that, in another classmate's hands. I've no idea who brought it in, but it certainly wasn't my friend. He doesn't deserve to be punished.' And given the headmaster's respect for Adrián as an artist, he would probably have gone with Martín too.

The pain in my eye was still there, but otherwise, I felt quite relaxed about things. I kept imagining that my two friends would turn up along with Hippo, and that the latter would declare as he came into the chapel: 'It's all been cleared up.' Instead, what I heard on the other side of the door was Ángel's voice. He seemed very agitated. 'Where are you?' he bawled as he entered the chapel. I hurried towards him. I'd long since removed him from my list of favourites, and suspicion was growing inside me – not as fast as the demons predicted by the parish priest in Obaba, but like the mustard seed of the parable, slowly, silently, unstoppably – yet, despite everything, affection won through. I wanted to tell him the truth about what had happened; I wanted him to see my painful, swollen eye – proof of the injustice of which I'd been the victim.

As soon as I was within reach, he slapped my face. It wasn't a particularly hard blow, but it caught the same side of my face, the left side, as Hippo's punch, and it hurt. 'Have you no shame, you disgusting creature!' he boomed, angrily shoving me away.

The headmaster raised one finger to his lips. Unlike the prefect, he was a short man with gentle manners. He didn't want people shouting in the chapel. 'As I'm sure you'll understand, we cannot allow him to stay here. There would be protests from the parents of other students,' he said. 'Naturally,' blustered Ángel, 'no one wants a rotten apple in the barrel.' Perhaps he was trying to curry favour with the headmaster, or perhaps he was remembering what had happened when Colonel Degrela's daughter had wanted to buy Faraón and was therefore glad to see me humiliated. 'Anyway, we'll say he's passed the year, and that way he'll be able to take his final exam,' said the headmaster. 'After all, the year is nearly over, and up until now, he's been an excellent student.'

This was a great favour on his part. At the time, students at private schools like De La Salle had to appear before a tribunal and pass a test that signalled the end of our secondary education and allowed us to go on to the pre-university course. The test was known as the *reválida*. If you didn't pass it, you couldn't continue with your studies.

'The headmaster is being very generous and you should be grateful to him for giving you this opportunity,' said Hippo, who had still not recovered himself. 'If it had been up to me, you'd have had to repeat

98

year six! And you would have failed Philosophy or, rather, Ethics.' The headmaster looked up at Hippo, who was nearly a foot taller than him. 'One must always avoid too great a disparity between the crime and the punishment. It's quite enough that he's being expelled from school,' he said. 'I must confess, moreover, that I particularly regret having to make this decision. We are losing not only a hard-working student, but an excellent harmonium-player as well.' He seemed genuinely upset. 'Thank you very much,' said Ángel. 'Thank you very much,' I said. And I meant it, because the headmaster seemed to me, then, a very decent man.

My eye was hurting and I found it hard to disguise this fact. 'You should have sent him immediately to the kitchen, so that they could put some ice on that eye,' the headmaster said to Hippo. I thought of the boy who worked there, Martín's distributor. 'When I saw the magazine, I just wasn't thinking clearly,' said Hippo, by way of an excuse.

VIII

My eye took ten days to heal, and during that time I stayed at Iruain. I wanted to keep a certain distance from Ángel, and even more than that, I wanted to be alone. Solitude, however, was hard to achieve. Despite the rain and the mud, a lot of people set out for Iruain and came to knock at my door.

The first to appear were some of the apprentice seamstresses from my mother's workshop. Despite their drenched shoes and despite having made it clear that they were 'just out for a walk', they made no attempt to conceal their interest in my black eye. I wasn't surprised, or, rather, it doesn't surprise me now when I remember it.

Liz, Sara, don't misjudge them: bear in mind that this was 1965 and we were living in Obaba, only a few miles from France but, at the same time, we were its antipodes. Many of these girls weren't even allowed to dance with boys; they didn't even know, or at least only very vaguely, what the word 'pornography' meant. They would probably see in my bruised eye what their parents saw in the stigmata on the hands of saints, namely, proof that life had a hidden side, and that the dreams which occasionally troubled them at night were not so very unusual. 'Would you care to have a look at one of those obscene magazines?' I asked them, inviting them in. It took them about ten seconds to realise I was joking. Meanwhile, they remained there in suspense, like figures turned to salt.

That was the first group of girls to visit. More came later, all of them in the rain, all of them 'just out for a walk'. 'You can't be that bad, David. The girls look at you as if you were a saint,' remarked Lubis after saying goodbye to the third or fourth group of visitors. A few boys came too, of course – Ubanbe, Opin, Joseba – but they did so in order to make fun and to laugh at me.

The rain was succeeded by the sun, the sun by clouds, and the clouds, once more, by rain. It was the wheel of the days and inside that wheel I had my own rhythm: I got up very early in the morning and studied for the *reválida*; at midday, I went to Adela's house for lunch; then, after lying down on the bed and studying some more, I would join Lubis and help him with his chores.

Sometimes it seemed as if the wheel were turning in the opposite direction, as if it were going back to the past. I'd look up from my book and there, outside the window, I'd see the horses grazing in the paddock, and the smoke from the chimneys of the houses in the valley, and the trees in the woods, already green – just like the year before, just as it had always been. Nevertheless, my eye was slowly healing, and it looked better every day. The wheel was following its course, and there was no going back.

One day, at dusk, I was with Lubis in the stable when we heard the noise of a car engine. 'It sounds like the Land-rover from the hotel,' he said, after stopping to listen. He may have been one of the 'happy peasants', but he had a knack for identifying the engine noise of different vehicles. 'I bet you it's Martín. He hasn't got a licence yet, but he drives better than a lot of people who have,' he added. 'I'm not talking to him at the moment,' I said, 'I don't want to see him.' Lubis was holding a bag of feed at about chest height, and he hesitated between going over to the horse's stall and waiting to hear my explanation. 'The day they expelled me from school, he betrayed me.' Lubis put the bag of feed down. 'Yes, I know. According to Pancho, Ubanbe went to talk to him to find out what happened and to ask him what he thought he was doing when you got punched. He said that if he'd been there, he'd have knocked out every tooth in that priest's head,' Lubis smiled. 'You know what Ubanbe's like, he thinks you can solve anything with a few well-aimed punches.'

The Land-rover was approaching fast; it was just passing Adela's house. I opened the stable door. 'What shall I tell him, David?' Lubis asked, seeing that I was about to leave. 'I don't know.' 'I'll tell him the truth, that you've been here all afternoon and must be around some-where.' That seemed to me like a good idea, and I raced over to the back door of the house. I went up to my bedroom and scrambled down into the hiding-place that Uncle Juan had shown me.

The horn of the Land-rover sounded insistently outside the house, as loudly as if it were right there in the room, between the bed and the wardrobe. There was a silence, and after a few minutes, I heard someone coming up the stairs – two people. I huddled in one corner of the hiding-place, clutching the J.B. Hotson hat. The soft felt calmed me and lessened the sense I had of being buried in a hole.

The footsteps passed immediately overhead. 'Well, he's not here either. I thought perhaps he'd come upstairs for a rest, but obviously not,' I heard Lubis say. I felt a sharp twinge in my eye, as if the pain from Hippo's punch had been reawakened. 'He's probably in the toilet, reading one of those dirty magazines,' said Martín. He was walking up and down, and I could hear the sound of his heels clearly. 'David! What are you up to in the toilet?' he yelled. 'No, you're wrong. He's not in the house,' Lubis said to him.

Martín kept calling, but not for very long. I heard him going down-stairs, and then the horn on the Land-rover. He was saying goodbye to Lubis. I climbed out of the hiding-place and went over to the window.

The Land-rover was disappearing off down the road, in the direction of the chestnut wood.

When I returned to the stables, I found Pancho sitting in Ava's stall. Beside him, Lubis was grooming the mare. 'Martín brought this brother of mine back in the Land-rover,' he said. Pancho was laughing to himself. 'He wanted to talk to you, but he was in a hurry and left.' Pancho's laughter grew louder, and Ava pricked up her ears. 'What a pair of tits, eh, David!' Pancho exclaimed at last. He used the word *errape*, a very coarse way of referring to women's breasts. Lubis made a resigned gesture: 'As you see, David, he's seen the magazines too.'

'How do you fancy having supper at Adela's house tonight? On me,' I said, changing the subject. I felt like talking. 'I'd rather see more tits,' said Pancho with another raucous guffaw. 'Sounds fine to me, David,' said Lubis. 'But I warn you, you're going to have to put up with a lot more stupid comments before you go to bed.' 'I don't mind. After hearing what Martín said, I'm unlikely to be shocked.'

When he left the stable, Pancho slapped Ava hard on her underbelly. 'What is it with you?' Lubis said angrily, pushing him out into the yard.

Adela's kitchen was large and spacious and, as well as the iron range, it still had the low fireplace that was usual in older houses. She had three long wooden tables covered with oilcloth, each one with its respective benches, and the whole thing was more reminiscent of kitchens in the days when people travelled on foot or on horseback. The only thing out of place was the fridge that Adela had bought on Juan's advice.

Adela received us with whoops of delight, as if she hadn't seen us for ages and our visit gave her especial pleasure. 'Of course! Come in! I'll rustle you up some fried eggs, potatoes and ham,' she said, ushering us over to the table by the door. She picked up one of the bottles of cider she had left to cool in a bucket and gave it to Lubis to uncork. 'The fridge is fine for meat and suchlike,' she said, selecting three glasses, 'but when it comes to cider, cold water is best, no doubt about it.' It was odd to hear a word like 'fridge' emerging from Adela's mouth. She was a plump, pink-cheeked woman. With her black-and-white headscarf, she, too, seemed to belong to the days when people travelled on foot or on horseback. 'I want wine. Get me a bottle, will you?' Pancho said. Lubis indicated to Adela that she should do no such thing. 'You're better off drinking cider, otherwise you'll just get drunk straight away.' 'Leave me alone!' shouted Pancho and took a bottle of wine from a wooden crate on the floor.

Sebastián appeared at the kitchen door and came straight over to me: 'Your mother told me to tell you that she'll be here tomorrow morning.' Adela ticked him off: 'Why are you telling him now? Why didn't you go to Iruain right away?' 'I did when Martín came, but he wasn't there,' explained Sebastián shyly. 'And what about the twins? Where have they got to? It's getting dark!' Adela said, speaking in the same scolding tone. 'I saw them down by the river a while ago; they were catching trout.' At that moment, Sebastián looked the very image of a Murillo angel. 'Well, go and tell them to come home at once, and that if they don't, I'll be after them with a stick.' Sebastián scuttled out of the kitchen.

Adela went from anger to smiles and, addressing me, said: 'Well, you certainly can't complain that nobody visits you, David. You've had loads of visitors lately.' She probably knew about what had happened at school, but I had no idea what she might think about it. 'Although, of course, it's perfectly normal that Carmen should come,' she went on. 'She's your mother, after all, and born and brought up here. Tell her tomorrow not to leave without popping in to see me so that I can give her some cheese. Don't forget, David.' 'I won't,' I promised.

My mother was driving slowly so as to avoid jolting too much as she drove through puddles and over potholes, and she parked with equal care too, advancing inch by inch. She was accompanied by four girls from the workshop. 'Here we are,' she said, giving me a kiss. She sat down on the stone bench, as if she'd walked all the way and needed a rest, and for a moment – no longer than that – she looked at the woods opposite. 'Everything's still here,' she said. 'So is Adela, the shepherd's wife,' I commented. 'She told me to tell you not to leave without

103

dropping in to see her.' 'I'll pop in for a moment to say hello.' Contrary to my expectations, my mother seemed quite cheerful.

Lubis appeared at the stable door, and the girls who had come with my mother in the car started calling out to him that they wanted to have a look at 'the horses with the long legs', and that this time they wouldn't leave without seeing them. 'You just wanted a peek at my black eye,' I said. 'But, it's no big deal. There's hardly a mark left now.' There were a few titters. 'Let's go and put the curtains up first,' my mother told them. Then, turning to me: 'I promised Juan that I'd make him some new curtains, because the ones he's got now are older than Methuselah.' We all looked up at the house, as if wanting to check that the curtains really were that bad.

'Is it my imagination or are you feeling happy?' I asked her. 'Yes, as it happens, I am happy,' she agreed, once the girls had gone into the house and we were left alone. 'Because I've been expelled from school?' 'It might be for the best,' she said. 'Next year you won't have to set off so early. I was always worried you'd have an accident, or that you'd catch pneumonia while you were waiting for the train, all sweaty after you'd been cycling for miles.' She really was happy. And I couldn't understand it. I would have expected her to be upset about that business with the porn magazine. As a woman who smoked and knew how to drive, she might be considered quite modern in the Obaba of the time, but my mother still clung to religion and accepted no morality but the Catholic one.

'I was at the sawmill yesterday, talking to Adrián's father,' she went on. She was wearing a blue cashmere sweater and a pearl necklace. Her brother, when he was there, used to wear a checked shirt; Lubis wore a cotton shirt and trousers; and I always wore my oldest clothes. She was standing outside the house where she'd been born, but she seemed to be from somewhere else entirely. 'After the *reválida*, Adrián's going to have another operation,' she told me. 'Apparently, it'll be more complicated than others he's had, and the doctors say he won't be able to move very much at all for a while and certainly won't be going on any train journeys.' 'I had no idea.' It was a rule with Adrián never to talk about his illness. I almost always got any news about him from my mother, because in the workshop 'everyone knew everything'. 'Anyway, Isidro has come to a decision,' she continued. Isidro was Adrián's father. 'Next year, he's going to have two teachers come to the house, one for literature and one for science. And guess who else is going to attend those classes?' 'Me?' 'Yes, David. But not only you,' and she began counting the names off on her fingers. 'Joseba, the son of the sawmill manager; Victoria, the daughter of the engineer at Kramer's; and Susana, the doctor's daughter. Apparently they're sick to death of all that coming and going and would prefer to stay in the village.'

'So, there'll be five of us,' I said to my mother. I liked the new plan too. 'Sometimes six. You know Paulina, don't you?' She was one of the girls who had come with my mother. I knew her more from seeing her at church than in the workshop. When she went back to her seat after taking communion, she used to walk past the harmonium, like Teresa and Virginia. 'She's that slightly plump girl who's gone upstairs to hang the curtains, isn't she?' 'Well, I wouldn't say she was plump,' protested my mother. She always defended the girls who worked with her. 'She used to be, but she's grown into a very pretty girl. Besides, she's going to be an excellent dressmaker. Anyway, what I'm trying to say is that Adrián's father wants you to study one other subject, technical drawing. And I've asked if Paulina can come too. If she wants to be a professional dressmaker, she'll find it really useful.'

As if at the mention of her name, Paulina appeared at the window. 'The curtains look great, Carmen.' 'Let's go and see them,' said my mother, taking my arm.

My mother was talking non-stop about the classes at the sawmill and was utterly indifferent to the walls and rooms of the house where she'd been born. She informed me that they were going to do up the workshop where Adrián currently did his carving and had already ordered desks and a blackboard, as well as a new stove for the winter. As for the teachers, the literature teacher would probably be Monsieur Nestor, the same one who taught us French, and the science teacher would be a young man called César who used to give classes at the university.

105

She concluded her exposition by urging me to study hard, because if I passed the *reválida*, I'd be able to do my pre-university course in comfort, without having to leave Obaba.

'What did you think of the curtains?' Paulina asked when we came downstairs to the kitchen. 'Fine,' replied my mother, but she hadn't even looked at them.

Everyone started making their way over to the stables so that the four girls could see 'the horses with the long legs', but my mother turned back and sat down again on the stone bench. 'I've got a message for you from Don Hipólito,' she said, 'just to say how sorry he was that you weren't there last Sunday to play the harmonium. He wants you to go this Sunday. He knows about the whole affair.' 'What did our parish priest tell you, Mama?' I asked, sitting down beside her. 'He says that Martín has got into some very bad company,' she said, lowering her voice. 'And that if this business with the magazine serves to distance you from him, then he's glad about what happened at school, even though you weren't to blame at all.' 'So I wasn't to blame?' I said. 'No, of course not, Don Hipólito explained everything.' I thought of my mother's feelings of despair when she heard Ángel's version of events, and how the parish priest's words must have brought her enormous relief, or more than that, euphoria. 'How did Don Hipólito find out?' 'He talked to the chaplain at the school, and he told him the whole truth. I think the chaplain's really sorry not to have anyone to play the harmonium.' 'The school chaplain's name is Don Ramón.' 'That's it, Don Ramón, well, he told Don Hipólito everything.' 'I'm glad one member of my family has such confidence in me,' I said. However, she ignored my words and continued regaling me with details of our new plan of study until Lubis and the four girls returned from the stables.

Paulina came over to me. 'Teresa sends her regards. And she gave me this to give to you,' she said, handing me an envelope. I took it and put it in my pocket. 'Oh, that's right, I almost forgot,' exclaimed my mother. 'Virginia asked me to send her regards too.' A shiver ran through me. Virginia was the country girl who always looked at me when she walked past the harmonium. 'Where did you see her? At church?' 'No, she's started coming to the workshop,' replied my mother. 'She's getting married next year, to her sailor friend, and she wants to have everything ready.' The happiness I'd just felt instantly dissolved. 'So she's marrying a sailor,' I said. Now I understood why Virginia was always either alone or with other girls, why I'd never seen her with any boys: sailors tend to spend long periods away from home. 'He's usually somewhere off the coast of Newfoundland in a trawler. That's the bad thing, of course, that he spends most of his life at sea and sometimes doesn't come home for months at a time,' said my mother, guessing my thoughts.

I noticed that Paulina was still looking at me. 'Apparently we're going to be studying together next term,' I said. 'Yes, I'll do my best,' she said and blushed. My mother kissed me. 'I'll be going then, David.' To her apprentices she said: 'You go on ahead. I'll catch you up. I just want to say hello to Adela.' She got into the car and manoeuvred it out on to the road. 'Study hard, David! You've got to pass that exam!' Paulina and the other girls had already crossed the bridge and were waving to me.

I sat down on the stone bench to read Teresa's letter. It was a postcard of a goldfinch that stared out at me with the hard eyes of a bird of prey. It stared out at me then as it does now because I kept the postcard and still have it amongst my papers. It said: 'On Sunday, the church harmonium was silent, and two of the people who went up to take communion realised something was missing and searched every corner to see if they could spot you. The other person – you know who I mean, *la paysanne* – has someone to console her. I do not.'

'Not another letter, David,' Lubis said when I joined him. 'Yes, from Teresa,' I said. Without meaning to, I pronounced her name in a weary tone. 'There's nothing wrong, is there?' asked Lubis. I told him I was feeling tired, that was all. In fact, I was thinking about *la paysanne*. 'She has someone to console her.' The words were painful to me.

On one of those afternoons, after studying for my exam, I took a notebook and drew up a new list of favourites. Martín could no longer be included. And, after our last encounter at Mandaska spring, neither could Ubanbe and Pancho. The little scream the mouse had made was

107

engraved on my memory. And I had my doubts about Adrián, too, because, since the incident at school, he hadn't even bothered to visit me. And it would have been dishonest to include Virginia since there was no real relationship between us. On the list there remained only Lubis.

IX

In my hands I have the first photograph of our pre-university study group, taken, according to the date on the back, on 27 October 1965. Victoria, Joseba and Susana are standing on the left, arm-in-arm; in the middle, sitting down, are the two teachers, Redin – Monsieur Nestor – and César; on the right are Adrián, also sitting down, with me behind him, standing up. Paulina should have completed the group, but however much Joseba's father begged her – for he was taking the photo – she refused to pose with us. She said she wasn't a student, just an apprentice at my mother's sewing school. Paulina was very shy in those days. She found our company inhibiting.

We're all smiling, and no one more so than Redin. He confessed that this was one of the best times of his life, finally liberated from the burden of private language classes and allowed to devote himself to teaching History and Philosophy, his preferred subjects. At the opposite pole, César's face reveals only the faintest flicker of a smile while he stares straight ahead at the camera through his black-framed glasses with their thick lenses. And yet he, too, was pleased to have this job, because, as he put it, there amongst the planks of the sawmill, he felt 'as if he were in a fort in the Wild West', safe from his enemies – 'Although, in my case, it's not the Indians I'm afraid of, but the White men.' César's words betrayed a genuine anxiety. Expelled from the university after some incident of a political nature, he was afraid, now he had a record, that the police could come for him at any moment.

The students' happy, smiling faces weren't a mere pose either. For the first time in our lives, we were free from the harsh discipline of school. You could still see, as with the dog in the fable, the mark of the chain we'd worn around our neck, and we didn't as yet move with total freedom, but the difference was nonetheless immense. We moved more easily. César would smoke a cigarette while he explained the minutiae of integral calculus or the structure of carbon molecules, and Redin would sit down before us with the thermos flask of coffee that the restaurant in the square in Obaba always prepared for him. Adrián expressed in his own way what we were all feeling: 'It's a shame I didn't get my back straightened out before, then we could have escaped from the penguins sooner.' The 'penguins' were the monks of De La Salle. We called them that because of the habit they wore – a black cassock with a white 'bib'.

After a while – and this always happens with things we leave behind us, it would happen with hell itself – we came to miss school life; and the girls, especially the girls, and Susana most of all, began to think nostalgically about 'the good times they used to have' and to go off to San Sebastián on Sundays to see the boys they'd met at student parties. Yet, despite this, we never really regretted the change.

There were a lot of photographs taken that year. Now, having put down that first one, I have in my hand the photo we took five months later, which is the one that most interests me, or, rather, that best fits this story I'm writing in Stoneham. It's dated 3 May 1966, the day of the inauguration of Adrián's new studio – about a mile upstream from the sawmill. As well as the people who appeared in the first photo, Lubis, Ubanbe, Opin and Pancho are there too: Lubis because I invited him; Ubanbe, Opin and Pancho because they were the ones who built the studio – a wooden cabin very similar to the one we used for our classes. In one corner of the photo you can see a barbecue still smoking, and behind it, in the background, a pool in the river known as Samson's Bath, because of its particular characteristics – its oval shape and the rock out of which flowed a miniature waterfall.

Once the meal celebrating the studio's inauguration was over, Lubis, Pancho and Ubanbe walked through the woods to their houses. 'We country people have to work harder than students,' said Lubis – while the rest of us strolled back to the village, intending to have a drink at the restaurant in the square; we did so cheerfully, laughing at Redin's comical comments about the difficulties involved in walking. 'One should only drink in civilised places, where one has but to raise one's hand to hail a taxi,' our teacher kept saying every hundred yards, vehemently expostulating on the 'the nexus between alcohol and wisdom' or 'the venerable custom in ancient Rome of carrying teachers on a litter'.

The loudest laughter came from Victoria and Adrián, who were also slightly tipsy, and the only exception was César, who was listening to his colleague with an even more serious expression on his face than usual. 'You scientists ought to drink more,' Redin said reproachfully, when we were nearly back at the sawmill, where stacks of planks lined the path. 'Oh, I drink enough,' retorted César, 'it's just that alcohol makes me sad.'

There was a rumour going around – it was Victoria who started it – that he'd been married to a fellow student, but that she'd left him when his political problems started and he was expelled from the university. According to Victoria, this was what lay behind the tension and anxiety that made him smoke cigarette after cigarette. I didn't set much store by my classmate's views. As César himself had once told her, she tended to confuse arithmetic with literature.

The sawmill had two entrances, one that led to the houses where Adrián and Joseba lived, and the one used by the trucks transporting the wood. In the latter, the name of the sawmill was framed in a bricked-off square in the concrete road surface: *Maderas de Obaba* – Obaba Wood Company. I saw Martín inside that frame, walking to and fro over the letters.

I felt uneasy. We hadn't exchanged a single word since the incident with the magazine. Besides, I'd seen Martín pacing up and down like this before, and I knew something was wrong. As we approached, he stopped in the middle of the frame. He had his fists clenched, as if he were spoiling for a fight. 'Look, there's our boxer in the ring, ready for action,' said Adrián drily, and nearly everyone laughed.

When we stopped laughing, there was – quite literally – silence. It

110

was Sunday: there were no cars on the road, no dogs were barking; the sawmill machinery had been switched off. The workers were resting in their houses. 'Why didn't you come to the meal, Martín? I left a note for you at the hotel,' Adrián said, going over to him. Martín backed into one corner of the frame, as if avoiding contact, and from there he looked at us. 'Teresa's seriously ill. The headmistress phoned us. She might die.' He finally opened his fists and put his hands to his face. 'What's wrong with her, Martín?' asked Joseba. Victoria covered her face too.

I caught sight of Moro, the donkey Pancho used when he took the woodcutters' lunch to them. He was in the field on the other side of the road, between two piles of planks. He was looking up as if he, too, wanted to know. But Martín said nothing. He kept walking back and forth inside the frame, like a prisoner in a cell.

'She hasn't caught polio, has she?' cried Susana. 'I heard my father saying that there's an epidemic in San Sebastián.' She and the rest of us formed a line running parallel to one side of the frame. 'Your father's very well informed,' said Martín bitterly. 'Perhaps, he should have given her a vaccination before it was too late. In France, they vaccinate all the children and all the young people too. A cousin of my mother's said so.' 'Teresa's got polio, poliomyelitis,' said Joseba absently. 'It's your father's fault!' shouted Martín, confronting Susana. 'A fat lot of use he is as a doctor!' His fists were once more clenched.

Susana was standing closest to Martín, then came the others: Adrián, Paulina, Joseba, Victoria, Redin, myself and César. 'Calm down,' César said from the far end of the line. All eyes turned to him. 'A doctor can only administer a vaccine if he has it. And in Spain that isn't the case. In France it is, but not here. We're more backward.' Martín took some time to respond. He went slowly over to César while he thought of a response. 'You're a communist, aren't you?' he said at last. 'Oh, don't talk nonsense,' replied César. 'The whole village knows,' insisted Martín. 'Look, don't start in on that. This is hardly the moment!' said Joseba, stepping forward into the frame. Adrián, Paulina and Victoria did the same, and the four of them surrounded Martín. Joseba yelled: 'Why

111

did you say Teresa might die?' 'Didn't you hear me?' Martín shouted back: 'The headmistress phoned.' 'But what did she say exactly?' asked Paulina. 'She said Teresa's got a very high fever and is delirious.' *Delirious.* Martín repeated the word twice. That day it sounded very new to us; it shocked us. 'How can she possibly die? She's too young!' cried Victoria, bursting into tears.

Her sobbing sounded strange in a place where normally one heard only the noise of saws. 'She won't die. Don't worry,' said César confidently. 'She'll probably be left with some paralysis, like my wife, but she won't die.'

Like my wife. These words proved decisive and changed the whole tone of the conversation. 'Your wife had poliomyelitis?' asked Martín. 'Yes. She has a slight limp now. One leg is marginally thinner than the other, that's all,' said César. 'So being left lame is nothing, is it? Well, some people would prefer to die!' Martín remained stubbornly unpleasant. 'Oh, please, don't talk such rubbish!' César threw his cigarette down on the ground. It came to a halt, still smoking, a couple of yards outside the frame.

Martín sat down on the concrete surface of the road. He seemed exhausted. 'Let's go to my house. We can talk more calmly there,' said Adrián. Martín shook his head. '*Myelitis*,' Redin suddenly said, pronouncing each syllable. '*My-e-li-tis.* The root of the word, you know, doesn't derive from *mel-mellis*; it has nothing to do with the honey made by bees. It comes from the Greek, *myelós*: meaning medulla.' His hair was dishevelled, and he was talking like a sleepwalker.

'What brand of cigarettes are you smoking?' Martín asked César, looking at the cigarette burning out on the ground, as if he'd suddenly forgotten all about his sister's state of health. 'He smokes Jean. All scientists smoke black tobacco, and my colleague here is no exception,' Redin told him. 'On the other hand, we literature teachers incline towards Virginia tobacco. Lately, I've gone over to Dunhill. Have one, if you like.' Martín declined. He got up and went and planted himself in front of César. 'I've never tried your brand before. I'll have one of yours, if you don't mind.'

César held out the pack to Martín. It was very pretty, red and black with a frieze along the bottom, imitating the squares on a chessboard. 'All you communists look the same. You're all skinny and wear thick glasses,' said Martín. 'Isn't that so, commie?' he said, patting César's cheek.

I could contain myself no longer. I hurled myself at Martín and pushed him out of the frame. 'Why can't you leave people alone!' I shouted, raising my fist. I wanted to hit him, to break his jaw. 'It's all right, David,' said César, putting his hands around my waist and trying to draw me back.

Martín flung wide his arms. 'You're not going to hit me here, are you? I'm outside the ring,' he said, indicating the lines of the frame. Joseba came over and stood between us. 'We don't need any fighting right now. There's Teresa at death's door, and here we are brawling!' I gave in and allowed César and Joseba to separate me from Martín. I felt no anger now, I simply felt like crying. Susana whispered in my ear: 'They're right, it really isn't worth it, David, but it's exactly what I felt like doing too.'

Adrián started walking over to the other entrance, towards his house. 'There's a football match on television tonight. Arsenal–Barcelona. If anyone wants to watch it, come with me,' he said. 'Shall we, César?' asked Redin. César agreed: 'Not a bad idea. Come and watch the game with us, David.' 'Yeah, let's all go,' said Joseba.

Martín put his hand on my shoulder: 'You still haven't forgiven me for that business with the magazine, then?' I looked away towards the field where Moro was watching us. 'Obviously not,' concluded Martín. 'Me, I'm like Teresa. I forgive everything, even that shove you just gave me.' Joseba joined us. 'When are you going to see Teresa?' he asked Martín. 'Right now.' 'Well, give her our love. Tell her we'll come and see her as soon as we can.' Martín turned to me. 'Does that include you?' he asked. 'Will you go too?' 'Of course I will,' I said. Martín said to Joseba: 'Good, that'll really cheer her up. You see how things are, Joseba. You're her friend, but David here is her little love.'

Everyone else had reached the steps up to Adrián's house, and I made to join them. Martín grabbed my arm: 'Why are you in such a hurry to leave? Don't you want to come to the hospital with me? Teresa would be thrilled. Look, my scooter's over there. I got my licence a month ago.' A Lambretta was parked at the roadside. It belonged to one of the hotel employees, but it wasn't the first time Martín had been seen riding it. 'There's no point going today,' Joseba said. 'They wouldn't even let him in.' Martín shot him a furious glance. He threw down the cigarette César had given him. 'Don't be such a smart-arse, Joseba. I was only testing him.' He swore and went to get his Lambretta.

X

Joseba brought me a letter from Teresa shortly after she'd returned from hospital. Inside, I found a piece of rough cardboard, the sort you use for packaging. *Ô triste, triste était mon âme* – 'Oh, sad, sad was my soul' – it said in letters written with a pale blue felt-tip pen. 'You really should go and see her, David,' Joseba said. I assured him that I would – soon. 'We've all been, even Adrián, who hates anything to do with illness. You're the only one who hasn't.'

I didn't keep my promise. Instead, I opted for replying to Teresa with another letter, telling her that I was still angry with her brother over the incident of the porn magazine, and that I didn't want to risk meeting him at the coffee shop or anywhere else in the hotel. And that, I said, was the reason for postponing my visit. But I would go and see her soon.

The truth, of course, was quite different. Martín wasn't the reason. Nor was his father, Berlino. The reason was Virginia, *la paysanne*. She was the reason I didn't go up to the hotel. As my mother had told me, Virginia was learning to sew, and she attended the workshop at Villa Lecuona at exactly the time Geneviève had set for people to visit Teresa, at six in the evening. Faced by this dilemma – a moment with Virginia, two long hours of conversation with Teresa – I always chose Virginia.

The grindstone of time couldn't undo that affection, on the contrary, the grain – the seed of love – was growing ever stronger.

Virginia, *la paysanne*, lived near the sawmill, on the other side of the river. Each evening, just before six o'clock, she would cross the bridge opposite her house and make her way to Villa Lecuona via the construction site where the new sportsground was being erected. As soon as they spotted her, the workmen would stop what they were doing and call out to her, offering her cigarettes; she, however, would keep walking and not even look at them.

I could see her from my bedroom window. This was my observatory. I enjoyed watching her progress past the containers and the cranes, nimbly avoiding all obstacles, barely touching the ground, like a butterfly. 'Hi, how are you?' I would say shortly afterwards, as I opened the front door to her, or 'There you are!' or 'You weren't put off by the rain, then.' She would smile in that way she had of smiling only with her eyes. 'I'm fine. How about you?' she would reply, or 'Yes, I'm a bit late today' or 'What awful weather, my hair's all over the place'. I always thought she looked lovely, even more so with her hair slightly windswept.

She was aware that I waited for her, just as I did in church, when she returned to her seat after taking communion, and she seemed to approve of my behaviour, my timid attempt to get closer. I found it hard to accept that she was planning to marry a man who spent most of his life at sea.

One day, I sensed that the narrow margin she had set for our relationship was growing slightly wider, and I dared to address her by name: 'How are things with you, Virginia?' 'Pretty good, David,' she replied perfectly naturally. It was a marvellous moment. *Presi tanta dolcezza*, I should say, stealing a line from one of the old poets . . . Indeed, such was the overwhelming sense of sweetness I felt when I received her greeting that I would retreat to the solitude of my bedroom in order to continue thinking about her.

Sweeter still was the first time we went for a walk together. We met on the stairs in Villa Lecuona. She was on her way home and I was off to Samson's Bath, to Adrián's new studio. It was a warm afternoon in

115

late spring; a south wind was blowing. 'I've got plenty of time. If you like, I can walk you home,' I said. The idea came to me suddenly. Had I planned it beforehand, I wouldn't perhaps have dared. 'Why don't we go the long way round?' she suggested. She meant that we could follow the road as far as the area where they were building the new houses and then walk back along the other side of the river to her house. As my classmate, Carmelo, would have said, she was inviting me to go for a walk of about 3000 steps, which was four or five times longer than the walk I'd had in mind.

The closer I became to Virginia, the stronger my desire. It wasn't enough to see her at six every evening, flitting like a butterfly past the cranes and containers; it wasn't enough to go for walks of 3000 steps: I wanted to see her all the time and to take 30,000, 300,000, 400,000 steps by her side. My desire, alas, was never satisfied. The fact that she was slightly older than me – she must have been nineteen at the time – inhibited me. And I was inhibited most of all by the absence of the sailor. I never saw him. Virginia never spoke to me about him. Only my mother occasionally mentioned him. I filled in that empty space myself and imagined him as having many fine qualities: a handsome fellow with a strong personality, endowed with all the wit that the sea bestows on the best of men.

Sometimes I rebelled against myself. Virginia – I thought – must have many admirers and I, fool that I was, was probably just one of many. I should try to distance myself from her, even if only for an evening, and go up to the hotel to visit Teresa, and not be so selfish, not be such a bad friend. However, six o'clock would arrive, and instead of going down to the garage to fetch my bike, I would run to my bedroom window.

During the first week in June, I finally got up the courage to go and see Teresa. I phoned her the evening before. 'This morning I walked round the mirador three times. What do you think?' she said, as soon as she answered. Not a word about my silence during all those weeks. 'Great,' I said. 'Believe me, it is. You know how far it is from one end to the other, don't you? Well, it took me half an hour to go round it three times.'

The mirador was an esplanade covering an area of about 6,500 square feet in front of the hotel. On the evenings when they held dances there, Ángel would perform a very slow passacaglia while walking round the edge, and that usually took him about three or four minutes. Three or four minutes, carrying the accordion and having to thread his way through the crowd. And it took Teresa half an hour to walk three times round that same area. She must, I thought, limp very badly indeed, or else be very weak.

'We'll go down to the garden tomorrow, Teresa. We'll go for a walk there,' I promised her. 'Like old times,' she said. The hotel garden was below the mirador, forming the next level down on the steep hillside. For both of us, it was the place where we'd played as children. 'Or we could go to the wood,' she suggested. 'Where shall we meet, then? In the garden?' I asked. 'I prefer the mirador.' 'All right, then, the mirador.' 'You remember where the coffee shop is, don't you, David? You come into the car park, and it's on the right immediately after the mirador.' This was the first reproachful comment she'd made. 'Please, Teresa, it hasn't been that long,' I said. 'They've put the tables out now,' she went on. 'And there's a new awning. A yellow-and-white striped one.' 'OK, then, underneath the new awning.' She hung up.

There were some foreigners sitting in the shade of the yellow-and-white awning, the first summer visitors of the year. Teresa, however, wasn't there. Geneviève immediately came out to greet me. 'She's upstairs,' she said, 'in her room. I think she's expecting you.' She was normally a rather distant woman, but that morning she seemed quite different – humbler, friendlier, smaller. 'Have you seen Martín?' she asked when we went inside, after she'd accompanied me to the stairs. No, I said, I hadn't. I'd heard that he was heavily into San Sebastián night-life and was going around with people much older than himself. I preferred to say nothing though. 'Thank you for coming,' she said, before going off to the kitchen.

Teresa was waiting for me on the landing. She was wearing a sleeveless white dress, and on her head, a wide black hairband. Without bothering to say hello, she immediately started talking about her brother as if our meeting were a normal part of her everyday life and she wanted to add a comment to a conversation we'd begun only a few moments before: 'My mother's really worried because, some nights, Martín doesn't even come home to sleep. He says he's staying with schoolfriends, preparing for his exams,' she pronounced these last words with utter scorn. 'What a crass lie, eh? But that's Martín, he'll never change.' I reached the landing. 'How are you, Teresa?' I said, kissing her on the cheek. She smiled as if my question pleased her, but didn't answer. 'Geneviève is obsessed with that son of hers,' she went on. 'It's a bit depressing, really. She behaves just like any other Obaba mother.' 'And her a Frenchwoman with Russian roots!' I exclaimed, just to say something.

We went up to the next floor. She leaned on the banister to climb each stair. 'What a shock yesterday!' she said. 'Who for?' I asked, thinking she'd finally decided to touch on the subject of her illness and was going to relay something her doctor had told her. 'For Geneviève,' she explained. 'Like any other Obaba mother, she went to pick up her son's clothes to take them to be washed, and the smell left her speechless.' She stopped to catch her breath. '*Le parfum n'etait pas très chic, vous me comprenez?*' she added.

When she reached the corridor on the second floor, she grabbed my arm. Her left foot lagged behind, but only slightly. 'Where are we going, Teresa?' I said, when I saw her walking past her bedroom. For two or three years now she had occupied the last room in the hotel, number 27. 'Up to the roof?' I asked. We were standing by some steps half hidden at the end of the corridor. She started to go up. 'There are some little rooms upstairs even I didn't know about, and in one of them, as you'll see, I've found some very interesting things.' She became breathless again, and, for a moment, had to lean against the wall. 'Ready to go on?' she asked five seconds later, turning her head. Her eyes the colour of olive oil looked straight at me.

On the topmost floor of the hotel, the ceiling was so low you had to duck your head. To the left and right of a corridor were a series of small, padlocked doors. Teresa took a key out of her pocket and opened one of them, the one marked '2'. 'Go in, David, but take your shoes off first,' she said. As I went in, I felt the softness of a blanket beneath my feet.

Teresa turned on the light, a bare bulb, and I found myself in a room of no more than sixteen or perhaps twenty square feet; the blanket covered nearly the whole floor. In one corner, leaning against the wall, I saw a rifle, and, beside it, a soldier's helmet and a pair of binoculars. Scattered about the room were various cardboard boxes stuffed with papers, as well as other detritus: a chair with a small leather bag on it, a suitcase.

Very gingerly, Teresa made as if to sit down, feeling with her hand for some support; however, before she could do this, she lost her balance and fell, leaving her legs and thighs exposed. Her legs, I thought, looked very strong and shapely. The only small difference I could see was in her ankles, the right one being slightly thinner.

In such a restricted space, her body seemed larger. I could see her ankles, her knees, her arms, the black ribbon she wore on her wrist, the equally black hairband, her eyes the colour of olive oil, her lips, her slightly open mouth. Her lips moved, her mouth closed and then opened again. 'You've behaved really badly towards me, and I must take my revenge. I have no option,' she said. Suddenly, we were in a different place: the game we'd been playing up until then was over.

Had it been high summer, July or August, we would have heard the voices of hotel guests or the honking of car horns. That day, though, the room was like an isolation tank. 'How are you going to take your revenge? With this rifle?' I reached out to pick it up. It was very heavy. 'I wouldn't be strong enough to hold it,' said Teresa. She put her black hairband down on the blanket and picked up the leather bag from the chair. 'But, don't worry, I have lighter weapons,' she said. She was holding a small pistol in her hand now. It was made of silver and very

119

pretty. Lubis would have described this action as 'imaginative', alluding again to Teresa's rich imagination – *pantasi aundia*. The silver pistol and the black ribbon round her wrist were very theatrical.

'Have I been that bad?' I asked. She wasn't pointing the pistol at me, but at the ceiling. 'Yes, very bad indeed. But without meaning to, the way children are. What is it that you like about *les paysannes*? No one knows. And why do I like a tall boy with a broad face like you? Again, no one knows.' 'I'm innocent then,' I said. 'Exactly,' she said, with a brief nod of the head, as if she preferred not to think any more about it, and then she handed me the pistol.

'It's very pretty,' I said. 'All these things have been here since the war,' she told me. 'I think the only things from a later date are the binoculars. They're very good quality too. German.' 'Everything's so clean. This pistol's positively gleaming,' I said. 'Gregorio's very meticulous. In fact, I only found out about this place thanks to him. He's in love with me, you see. But he's out of luck too. I just ignore him.' Gregorio was known as *Baria* – Slug – because he belonged to a family with that nickname, and he worked as a waiter in the hotel coffee shop. He was always very off-hand with me, and whenever we passed in the street, he pretended not to see me.

I put down the pistol and picked up the soldier's helmet. It, too, gleamed. 'When Gregorio first showed all this to me, I went and talked to my father, without mentioning Gregorio, of course. I didn't want them slitting my suitor's throat. So I went and told him that I wanted to keep the pistol.' She knelt down and put the pistol back in the bag. 'My father was angry at first, but ended up promising it to me for my eighteenth birthday.' I felt uncomfortable. All these weapons harked back to recent history, to the civil war. I was in Berlino's house, and all these things were his.

'What are the papers in the box? Letters?' I asked. 'Yes. They're letters belonging to our family. They're all here. The letters my father wrote to his brothers and those his brothers wrote to him.' She fell silent for a moment, then added: 'Do you understand? The letters that my father wrote. Do you see what that means?' 'That they were returned

120

to him?' I said idiotically. 'It means that his two brothers died at the front, and we were left with their personal effects.' She pointed to the cardboard box: 'Shove that over to me, will you?' I did as she asked and she took from it a crumpled blue envelope. 'This is from my Uncle Antonio. He sent it from the front at Jarama on 21 March 1937.' 'The first day of spring,' I said, equally idiotically.

Teresa removed a single sheet of paper from the envelope. 'You're right. He wrote it on the first day of spring.' She put her hairband back on to keep her hair out of her eyes, and started to read. Her uncle's writing – I'm looking at it now: I have the piece of paper on my desk in Stoneham – was very small. Teresa screwed up her eyes slightly as she read:

My dear brother,

I received your letter on St Joseph's day. So far, thank God, I've been very well.

I was beginning to think you'd forgotten about me or else that you must be feeling very frightened by this war.

The war there was nothing compared to the war here, it's really tough here, to get those reds out of a trench, you have to go in with a knife, ask anyone and they'll tell you what it's like, the hill where we are now is called Olivar, the reds have got themselves tanks and every-thing, maybe you know the sort they've got, the other day they started attacking, trying to advance with the tanks, we took out four of them, one is still usable, but the other three we set fire to with bottles of petrol and hand grenades, I tell you, though, those Russian tanks are really enormous, they've got a gun turret and two machine-guns and each tank can carry four people and they can get up really steep hills and they fire well too.

Some of the men here were in the army in Africa with Gregorio, Gregorio from the village, and I asked one of them what Gregorio was up to, and he told me that the guys who are no good for anything else do the cooking and that because Gregorio doesn't speak Spanish, he often gets excused duties. How's our friend Ángel? Tell him we could really do with him and his accordion, he should ask Captain Degrela to let him come down, even if it's only for a short visit. Your brother, Antonio.

Teresa put the letter back in the box and chose a white envelope edged in black. 'That man Gregorio, the one who was only any good as a farmhand, was, of course, my suitor's father,' she said. 'And,' I added, 'the accordionist called Ángel, mentioned at the end, was my father.' 'Now I'm going to read you this other letter. It's very short, just a note,' she said and burst out laughing. 'Have you seen the colours? Black and white. When I got dressed this morning, I had no idea I'd be holding it in my hands. But look how well it goes.' She held the small envelope to her chest, at the same time showing me the black ribbon on her wrist. 'You're mad, Teresa,' I said. 'Quite possibly, David.' She started reading the typed note.

My dear friend Marcelino Gabirondo and family. I have just found out about the great misfortune that has befallen you, losing another brother in action in this war for God and for Spain. First it was Jesús María. On 25 March, the day of San Ireneo, it was Antonio. It's very hard for me to find any words of consolation . . .

'That's enough, Teresa, please!' I broke in. 'Yes, you're right, that's enough,' she said, returning the letter to the box. Then she reached into a plastic bag and took out a pack of Dunhill cigarettes. 'That's the brand Monsieur Nestor is smoking now,' I said. 'My uncle died on 25 March, four days after writing that first letter,' Teresa went on. 'He had a very short spring.' She lit a cigarette. 'Why don't we go down to the garden?' I suggested. 'We'll be more comfortable there. We can get some air.' She didn't respond, but took a saucer from the plastic bag and started using it as an ashtray. 'I've often thought about it,' she went on. Now it was as if she were talking to herself. 'I imagine my uncle's hand moving over the paper, letter by letter. And then I imagine that hand dead. On 25 March, it would have been no use at all putting a pencil in his hand.' 'Please, Teresa, let's get out of this room.' It felt to me as if her words were whirling ever more furiously above my head, becoming ever more entangled. 'We can't leave, David. My mother gets annoyed if she sees me smoking. Martín can smoke and drink, and nothing happens, but I'm not allowed to. *Elle m'importune!*' She pushed the door open to let in some air.

We could hear the sound of cars from the hotel car park now. I thought it must be lunchtime, but I didn't dare glance at my watch. Teresa was studying me. For a moment, her eyes shone and a tear formed. 'You're right, it isn't really the best place for smoking. Look at this great cloud of smoke,' she said. She stubbed out the cigarette on the saucer.

She rummaged around in the cardboard box and produced a notebook. 'Look at this,' she said, handing it to me. It was like the notebooks people used to use at school, orange and with a picture of a gorilla on the front. At the bottom of the cover, inside a border were the words: 'This notebook belongs to' and underneath, a name: 'Ángel'. 'Do you recognise the handwriting?' she asked. 'It looks like my father's.' 'Yes, I agree.' I looked harder at the writing. 'His writing won't be exactly like that now,' she said. 'Bear in mind that this notebook must be nearly twenty-five years old.' 'Twenty-five?' 'Or a bit more.' Teresa showed me a page containing a list of names. 'What do you think of this.' The notebook was damp, and its pages made no sound when turned.

The writing was appalling, as if the author of the list had written it in great haste, and some of the names were hard to make out. On the first line was 'Humberto'. Then – it took me some time to decipher these – came the names 'Goena Senior' and 'Goena Junior'. On the fourth line was what looked like 'Eusebio'. On the fifth 'Otero'. On the sixth, in capitals, 'Portaburu'. On the next line 'the teachers'. And lastly, in a hasty scrawl and underlined 'the American'.

'It's the list of people who were shot in Obaba. The work of our two fathers, I believe,' said Teresa. Her eyes again filled with tears. 'You'll hate me now, won't you?' Her lips were quivering. She was crying. 'When I got ill at school, my one hope was that you'd come running to see me. And when I realised that you weren't going to, I started telling myself lies, making excuses . . .' She couldn't go on, and she lay down, hiding her face. 'Teresa, don't,' I said, taking her hand. It was a purely reflex reaction. I wasn't thinking about her, but about the list in the notebook.

XI

After the classes at the sawmill, we would all go down to the square and sit in the shade of the horse chestnut trees drinking the beer or lemonade we bought from the restaurant. On one such day, César said: 'I don't know why, but David is worried about something. You can see it in his face.' Susana and I had sat down with him on a bench and were studying the monument they were erecting on the other side of the square in honour of those who'd died in the civil war. 'Well,' I said, 'it is only three weeks to the exams.' This was a white lie. The cause of my anxiety was the notebook with the gorilla on the cover that Teresa had shown me. I could think of nothing else. 'I can understand why Victoria might be worried, but not you,' said Susana.

'David has his doubts and so, apparently, does "our artist",' said César. He pointed at the monument with his lit cigarette. 'In the end, he's gone for a truncated pyramid. First he made a cylinder, with the idea of having all the names inscribed on its surface. Then, he opted for a pyramid. And now, as you see, he's decided to lop the top off.' He inhaled deeply on his cigarette.

We all sat looking at the truncated pyramid. 'If they really were going to include the names of all those who died in the war, I wouldn't mind,' Susana declared. 'But the disgusting thing is, they're only going to include the names of the dead from one of the two sides.' She was wearing an orange-coloured summer dress and a pair of simple white alpargatas. Anyone who didn't know her would have thought she was a girl without a care in the world, someone who was concerned solely with her appearance; but, as Martín would have said, she was the daughter of 'someone

124

who had lost the war', and it showed. 'Susana's absolutely right,' I said. 'They should at least put the names of the people who were shot in Obaba.' As soon as I spoke these words, I saw the list in the notebook, as if it were there before my eyes: *Humberto, Goena Senior, Goena Junior, Eusebio, Otero, Portaburu, 'the teachers', 'the American'*.

On the truncated pyramid, only the names of the 'fallen' would appear, engraved in gold letters on the black marble: José Iturrino and Jesús María Gabirondo, one of Berlino's brothers. The name of the other brother, the one who wrote the letter that Teresa had read out to me, was yet to be engraved.

'What do you know about the people who were shot in Obaba?' César asked me. 'Not much, but I'd like to know more,' I said. Susana burst out laughing: 'He's changing. All he's cared about up until now is the accordion.' She was holding the fruit from a horse-chestnut by the stem and she hit me on the head with it, laughing. César spoke to me in the same jovial tone: 'So that's why he's been so preoccupied lately. He's finally opened his eyes and started looking at the world.'

Redin came over and suggested we go to the restaurant on the ground floor of the town hall. He and César usually had lunch there because it was quieter than the restaurant in the square. 'I fancy a vermouth,' he said. 'They say it's a dreadful drink and that even the owner of Cinzano loathes it, but I feel a sudden nostalgia for its taste.' César looked at him over the top of his glasses: 'I don't like it either, but I had no idea the owner of Cinzano felt the same. Are you sure, Javier?' He called Redin by his real name: Javier. 'Hemingway told me. He was invited once to a party held by the owner of Cinzano, and, as a way of honouring his host, he asked for a vermouth. The owner came over to him and said: "What are you doing drinking that rubbish?" And he led him off and poured him a whisky.' Redin laughed, and we laughed with him. 'Let's go to the town hall, then,' said César, getting up from the bench. 'If I may express myself in the manner of the literati, I feel a sudden nostalgia for the salad they serve in that restaurant.' We beckoned to our class-mates who were still standing by the monument.

In the town hall arcade was a large rectangular plaque with about thirty names engraved on it in black. There, too, the first names were José Iturrino and Jesús María Gabirondo. Antonio Gabirondo was the twelfth name. 'You see? Half the letters have become blurred. That's why they're building a new monument,' César said. There were five letters missing from Antonio Gabirondo's name, so that it read: 'nio abirondo'. 'They could just have touched up the lettering,' said Joseba. 'It would have worked out a lot cheaper for the village.' Adrián grabbed his hand and held it up, as the referee does with the winner of a boxing match: 'Thus spake the son of the manager of the Obaba sawmill.' 'Fascists have hearts too, you know,' declared César. 'They don't want their colleagues to be forgotten. Besides, that truncated pyramid in the square captures what happened much more accurately. He's cut off the top, just as one cuts off a head, just as one takes away a life . . . That artist knows what he's doing.' We all expected him to conclude with a wry laugh, but he remained serious.

Two men coming out of the restaurant stopped and stared at us. Redin went over to César and said: 'Try to speak more quietly. Otherwise, things might turn nasty.' 'They haven't stopped to listen to us,' put in Adrián, 'they're just admiring Susana's orange dress. Our classmate looks like a sun.' 'I name you Miss Obaba, Susana,' said Redin. After spending a whole term together, we were all good friends.

The list of those who'd been shot in Obaba reappeared in my mind: *Humberto, Goena Senior, Goena Junior, Eusebio, Otero, Portaburu, 'the teachers', 'the American'*. Although I was doing my best to forget — stuffing that notebook back in amongst other old papers in a box or immersing myself in my studies — I felt as if those names were always just beneath the surface of my thoughts, ready to rise to the top. They had remained engraved on my memory as precisely as the names of José Iturrino and Jesús María Gabirondo on the marble of the new monument.

The restaurant on the ground floor of the town hall had a covered terrace at the back which gave on to the area that was being transformed into a sportsground. We put two tables together and sat out there. Redin was the first to speak: 'This weary teacher would be deeply grateful if someone were to bring him a vermouth. With olives, if possible.' Susana and I both stood up at the same time. 'Two waiters at your service, Javier. Why, not even the tribunes of Rome could expect as much!' exclaimed César. 'Olives, vermouth, four beers and whatever you're drinking yourselves,' said Adrián, having asked everyone else what they wanted. 'Nothing for me,' said Susana.

At the bar there was only the female owner of the restaurant and the two of us. 'Susana, I wanted to ask you something,' I said, once I'd ordered the drinks. She stood looking at me. Her eyes were a very pale greenish-blue. 'I don't know if you remember, but we talked once about the innocent people from the village who were shot. Do you happen to know their names? I'm writing a story about the war, and I'd like to use real names.' I was speaking as lightly as possible. 'Do you want glasses too?' asked the owner, putting five beers down on the counter. 'Just three,' we said. Adrián and Victoria drank '*a gollete*', to use Redin's expression – 'straight from the bottle'. 'My father's sure to know,' Susana answered.

César suddenly appeared by our side. 'And what is it that your father, the good doctor of Obaba, is sure to know?' he asked. Susana started to explain to him while I went and paid for the drinks. 'So you're writing little stories, are you, on the eve of your university entrance exams? I ought to tell you off,' said César when I came back. He was holding a beer in each hand. 'I've only just started, and, besides, it doesn't take up much of my time,' I said in my defence. I picked up the three remaining beers from the counter. 'The glasses and the vermouth are already on the table. Is there anything else?' asked Susana when she returned from the terrace where our friends were sitting. 'The olives,' César and I replied in unison. 'If I were to write a story, I'd choose her as the protagonist,' added César loud enough for Susana to hear. 'Most teachers are mad, David,' she warned me, as we went back out on to the terrace. Her white alpargatas moved briskly across the restaurant floor.

'I'm lunching alone today,' César told me before we rejoined the group. 'Javier's going up to the hotel to visit that French lady.' 'Geneviève?' 'I don't know her name, but it seems that now and again she's assailed by the need to speak French, and, as you know, Javier is permanently assailed by the need to eat a good meal.' He looked at me hard from behind the lenses of his glasses.

There was something about César that didn't quite fit. He spoke animatedly, but there was no joy in his eyes. Perhaps – I thought – it's because they're not his First Eyes, but his Second Eyes. 'Why don't you stay and have lunch with me?' he said. 'It won't be a banquet like the one Redin will enjoy at the hotel, but at least it will be good clean food. Roast meat and salad. On me.' Most of his words were normal, spoken by his First Tongue, but that business about 'good clean food' left a more bitter after-taste, as if, at that moment, his Second Tongue had intervened.

Redin came over to us with the dish of olives. 'If you're exchanging confidences, you'd better go to a private room, if not, come and sit down with the rest of us.' 'I'll phone my mother and tell her I'm having lunch here,' I said to César. 'Good,' he said, sitting down next to Redin.

The pack of Jean cigarettes was on the table. Before us were two cups of coffee. 'Do you know why I started smoking this brand?' César asked me, lighting a cigarette and leaving aside the subject of my studies that had been occupying us until then. 'Because of the colour of the packet, because it's red and black. You may not know this, but those are the anarchist colours. But don't worry, I'm not an anarchist.' I said nothing. 'It was when I was fourteen. Imagine that, I've been a smoker ever since,' he went on. 'I did it for my father, because he was an anarchist. And, like you and Joseba, he wrote poems.'

I watched him stirring his coffee. With his glasses, his thin face and his cigarette, he seemed to be the man I was used to seeing, our science teacher. But beneath that appearance, I was beginning to glimpse a second César, who was looking with his Second Eyes and speaking with his Second Tongue.

All of a sudden he said: 'My father was shot here in Obaba.' He sat staring at the coffee in his cup, as if he no longer wanted to drink it. A shock ran through me. 'What was his name?' My question seemed to surprise him, but he replied at once: 'Bernardino.'

128

I felt as if I'd become weightless and was floating in the air, eight inches above the chair I was sitting in. I almost felt like laughing. *Humberto, Goena Senior, Goena Junior, Eusebio, Otero, Portaburu, 'the teachers', 'the American'.* There was no Bernardino in the notebook with the gorilla cover. 'When war broke out, my father was a teacher in Obaba,' added César. I felt exactly the opposite of what I'd felt a moment before, as if my body had suddenly sunk into my chair. On the seventh line of the list in the notebook was written: 'the teachers'. Now I knew that one of them was Bernardino, the father of the man sitting opposite me. 'So you lived in Obaba,' I said dully. 'Not for very long. As soon as the war started, they sent me to Zaragoza, to an aunt's house. I was only three.'

The doubt that had lodged in my heart vanished. What Teresa had told me was true: the list in the notebook corresponded with the names of those shot in Obaba. I could have wept.

César raised his cup to his lips and looked out at the landscape beyond the terrace, at the sportsground being built. Three garish yellow cranes rose up before us; further off, the alder trees near Urtza formed a line in front of the chestnut wood. 'An uncle of yours saved a friend of my father's. He was the owner of the Hotel Alaska, and was known as "the American". But my father didn't manage to get to . . . what's the name of that house of yours?' He pointed to somewhere on the other side of the alder trees. 'Iruain,' I said. 'That's right. Iruain. My father didn't make it. They killed him first.' 'In the woods?' I asked. 'I'm not sure where exactly.' César lit another cigarette. 'Your uncle's name is Juan, isn't it?' he said softly. 'Yes,' I replied. 'He'll be back soon to spend the summer here. He says it gets too hot on his ranch in California.' 'Perhaps I'll go and see him one day. Susana's father has often spoken to me about him.' I was beginning to see clearly now the Second Space in which certain people in my life were gradually coming into focus: César, Susana's father, my Uncle Juan.

I wondered how much he would know about Ángel. 'You're looking worried again,' he said. He was putting the money for the bill on the table. I could have said to him then, just as I could have said to Don Hipólito before: 'I've been given a notebook containing a list of all the

129

people who were shot in Obaba. Your father's name doesn't appear, there's no one called Bernardino, but on the seventh line it says "the teachers". I'm worried about what degree of responsibility Ángel may have had in the murder of your father and in that of the other men too. His name, you see, is written on the front cover of the notebook, underneath where it says "This book belongs to". It makes me feel physically sick to think that I might be the son of a man who has blood on his hands.' But I didn't have the courage. 'I'll get over it,' I said. 'Writing will help, and playing the accordion, of course,' he said. 'No, not the accordion,' I thought.

César finished his coffee. 'I have to go to Victoria's house. As you know, she's worried too.' He stood up. 'She's only scraping by in Chemistry at the moment. I don't know if we can make up much ground in the few days that are left.' He was the usual César, the teacher. He was looking at me with his First Eyes and speaking to me with his First Lips.

XII

The notebook Teresa gave me in that attic room in the Hotel Alaska is now on my desk, resting on a small pile of other notebooks and photographs. The gorilla looks out at me from the orange cover and follows me with his gaze when I lean to one side or the other in my chair. This doesn't bother me though. It's not like when I spoke to César on the terrace of the restaurant twenty or more years ago. I know the notebook's days are numbered, that soon I'll throw it in the trash so that the truck can take it to the dump in Three Rivers or Visalia. I laugh and feel real joy to imagine its pages, stained with bits of pizza and sauce, being devoured by the teeth of a machine, consumed by fire. *Finis coronat opus*: this piece of writing, this confession, will, in the end, have its reward.

It's been a hard road. At first, I thought it would be enough to remove the notebook from view in order for me to forget about it, by leaving

130

it, for example, in the hiding-place in Iruain 'so that Good, in the form of the Hotson hat, would neutralise Evil', as I thought one day; so that the symbol of my Uncle Juan's beneficent labours would compensate for the crimes possibly committed by Ángel. However, as soon as I did so, the memory of the notebook took such a hold on my mind that it almost drove me mad. Then I had no option but to rush off and retrieve it and put it where I could easily lay hold of it, on my bedside table or in my accordion case, until, once again, like a dog who doesn't know quite where to hide the bit of offal he can't manage to eat at one sitting, I felt an urgent need to remove it from my sight. *Humberto, Goena Senior, Goena Junior, Eusebio, Otero, Portaburu, 'the teachers', 'the American'*. The list went with me everywhere.

Of all the names, only four suggested any actual image. I could imagine Humberto in a dark suit, with no tie, and a white shirt buttoned up to the neck; when I thought of his face – perhaps because of the way he was dressed – the insurance salesman came to mind, the man who, when I was a child, gave me that piece of cord, 'the tool for remembering things'. Eusebio, for his part, I imagined as tall and thin, although for no real reason, merely because his name coincided with that of a farmworker I'd known in Iruain and who combined both characteristics. As for the teachers, two of them remained very indistinct, while the third, Bernardino, was identical to his son, César – skinny and with thick glasses. Lastly, I imagined 'the American' exactly as my Uncle Juan had described him to me, very fat and wearing his Hotson hat.

Night after night, when I stared with my Second Eyes into that filthy cave, those four figures took on more substance – on a par with the figures of Ángel and Berlino – and ceased to be mere shadows. My doubts gradually melted away. That recent history needed no messengers. Those images and the gaze of the gorilla on the cover of the notebook were enough. That look was saying: 'What do you make of all this, David? Was your father a murderer?' The gorilla seemed prepared to continue repeating those questions for a hundred years.

In the days leading up to the university entrance exam, I devoted myself to study and, in particular, to solving maths problems. Just as happened before with Lizardi's book, difficulty distracted me. That's why, when the results arrived in Obaba, and César told me the news – 'A distinction in maths, David!' – my response was both spontaneous and sincere: 'I owe half of that distinction to you and the other half to Bernardino, Humberto and all the other men who were shot.' César patted me on the back, but said nothing. It wasn't the right moment to talk about that. He was very pleased with our results – even Victoria had passed in everything – and he wanted to savour that success.

I, too, savoured my success, but the joy my exam marks brought me didn't last. By mid-July, the words that the 'happy peasants' applied to anyone who chose to shut himself up alone in his house and to speak to no one could well have applied to me: *bere buruari ekinda dago*, 'he has become his own enemy'. I felt utterly indifferent to everything. It didn't matter whether I was sitting with Lubis on the stone bench outside Iruain or watching Virginia making her way past the cranes and the trucks on the sportsground – nothing left any mark. I could only see with my Second Eyes; I could only think and remember with my Second Mind; I could only feel with my Second Heart.

I stopped going to Iruain, mainly because of Uncle Juan. I was afraid to be with him. I feared he might tell me some painful fact, that he might dredge up from recent history some new object, as he had with the Hotson hat, and which I might not be able to bear. In this state of mind, I spent nearly all my time at Villa Lecuona, lying on my bed reading a fat volume entitled *One Hundred Best Detective Stories* or watching the television Ángel had just brought into the house.

Fortunately, Ángel himself was hardly ever home. 'I sometimes think he bought the television so that we wouldn't notice he's never here,' my mother said one night when we were watching a film together. 'One day, it's the building work, the next, it's politics; the fact of the matter is he's always out.' 'That's fine by me,' I said. My mother sighed: 'Don't say that, David. I know he sometimes nags you about the accordion, but that's only because he cares. He thinks you love music as much as he does.' I said nothing. 'You've been a bit down lately, haven't you?'

she went on. 'This summer you haven't even been to see your friends at Urtza. You'll forget how to swim.' 'So what if I do!' I said. 'I hate it when you talk like that, David.' She wanted me to go out and enjoy myself.

One afternoon, towards the end of July, I decided to go to Samson's Bath, not to swim, as I told my mother, but to see Adrián. I thought that someone like him, who, although he never spoke about it, had suffered so much because of his twisted spine, might be able to help me. I got on my bike and set off.

I didn't reach my goal, at least not immediately. On the way, as I was passing the sawmill, I saw Virginia standing in the entrance, framed in the brick-edged area that surrounded the name of the company: *Maderas de Obaba*. She didn't, of course, remain trapped inside it, as Martín had on the day he came to tell us about Teresa's illness. She walked across it and kept walking. 'Hello!' she cried, when I drew up alongside her. Her whole face was smiling, not just her eyes. 'I haven't seen you for ages!' She was right. I no longer waited for her to knock at the door of Villa Lecuona.

I left the bike leaning against a tree. 'Ages!' she said again. 'It must be three or four weeks,' I said. 'I thought perhaps you were angry with me, David.' In the sawmill I could hear the sound of a machine, someone working overtime. I went up to her and I could smell the roses of her perfume. 'How are you, Virginia?' Unexpectedly, she placed one hand on my arm and kissed me on the cheek.

That kiss broke the spell. My First Eyes opened, and once again I felt the nearness of things. I noticed the brilliant gleam of the bicycle bell and the patch of moss on the bark of the tree. Suddenly, a butterfly – *mitxirrika, inguma* – fluttered past and alighted on the moss; the donkey, Moro, started trotting towards us across the grass; and a plane traversed the sky, leaving a trail behind it. It was evening. The sun would soon be setting.

'You look very pretty,' I said. She was wearing her hair shorter than usual, and I could see her ears. They were small and round; I felt like pinching the lobes between my fingers. She responded to my compliment with a smile: 'It's the outfit I'm wearing. Your mother said it would suit me.' 'Then I'll have to congratulate my mother.'

She was wearing a black shirt printed with lilac and gold apples; her skirt was made of a soft material in the same lilac colour as the apples on her shirt. Her moccasins were lilac too.

'I thought perhaps I'd come too late,' she said, 'but Isidro's still working. I've ordered a table from him. You know what lovely tables he makes.' People used to say of Isidro, Adrián's father, that he liked work more than he liked money. Despite his position – my mother said he was the richest man in Obaba – his life was no different from that of the lowliest employee at the sawmill. 'Do you need a table, then?' I asked. She smiled scornfully: 'People have to eat somewhere.' I didn't realise she was about to get married and was buying furniture for her new home.

'Why don't you walk me back to my house?' she said. 'If you like I can take you on my bike,' I said, joking. 'If we go via the sawmill, it'll be quicker to walk.' She spoke with great aplomb, as if she'd grown in confidence during the last few weeks. She took my arm. 'Let me show you the way.'

I was feeling emotionally drained, worn out by the days and weeks of thinking about the list in the notebook, finding rest only when I slept or read detective stories. As soon as I felt her hand on my arm, my knees went weak. Just as they had the first time she asked me to walk her home.

We went into the yard. We passed Adrián's house, then Joseba's. 'They'll all be in San Sebastián. They love the beach,' I said when I saw that both houses were in darkness. It was a foolish remark, and completely untrue, at least as far as Adrián was concerned. But I was feeling so nervous I hardly knew what I was saying. 'I think Paulina's really enjoyed herself,' she said. When we reached the cabin where we used to have our classes, she let go of my arm and peered in through the window.

Then we continued along, side by side. I talked to her about Paulina, about the progress she'd made in technical drawing, and about how my mother was sure Paulina would one day become a professional dressmaker, and that this was why she went to Villa Lecuona, not just to learn a bit about sewing before she got married.

It was then, when I pronounced the word 'married', that the penny dropped and I understood about the table Virginia had ordered. I understood, too, about her new-found confidence: the kiss she'd given me when we met and the fact that she'd taken my arm. Virginia was to be married, she was about to set up house with her sailor, and her attitude, far from being a step towards a more intimate relationship with me, indicated the end of our little friendship. 'Where are you and your fiancé going to live?' I asked after a pause. My knees had grown weak again. 'We've bought an apartment on the new estate,' she said. So it was true. There was nothing to be done about it.

Beyond the sawmill, the river formed a long curve, hugging the piece of land filled by those forty or fifty stacks of planks. Virginia and I walked amongst the stacks, trying to guess the right direction to take. 'Once, when I was little, I got lost in this maze and spent nearly an hour going round and round in circles. I just couldn't find the way out,' she said.

I could clearly hear the song of the toads on the river bank. It was always like this in summer as dusk fell. During the hottest hours of the day, the toads swelled up in the heat and, later, as the temperature fell, they began to deflate, making a sound rather like a hiccup. Contrary to what one might think, given their monstrous appearance, this hiccup, this song, was sweet, delicate, slightly child-like, and sometimes the notes sounded like words. On some days, we could hear them from the terrace of Villa Lecuona, and, if my mother was to be believed, what they were saying was: '*i-ku-si-e-ta-i-ka-si-i-ku-si-e-ta-i-ka-si*': 'look and learn, look and learn'.

'We used to come here to pick wild strawberries,' said Virginia, starting to look for them. It was hard to see, though; all the light was above the stacks of wood, in the sky, a sky in which, as chance would have it, the predominant colours were the same as those on Virginia's blouse. On one side, it was black, on the other, where the sun had just set, it was lilac and gold.

The toads continued their singing. I had the feeling they were saying 'take a seat' – 'take-a-seat-take-a-seat-take-a-seat' – as if advising me to rest. But I remained standing, waiting for Virginia to find a strawberry, watching her every move. She moved quickly, like a little girl, crouching down again and again to comb through the grass; in the half-darkness, though, her body seemed stronger, fuller.

'There are loads over here,' she said, and picked a flower in order to thread the tiny strawberries on to its stem like beads. 'When it's full, we'll go and sit by the river and eat them. Would you like to sit with me, David?' 'Of course,' I replied and went over to help in her hunt for strawberries. 'Why are you smiling?' she asked. I thought of saying: 'Because you're not the only one asking me to sit down. The toads are doing it too.' But I didn't dare. 'I don't know. I wasn't aware that I was.'

By the river was a building we knew as 'the old carpenter's workshop'. 'Adrián's father inherited it from his family when he was twenty,' I said. 'At the time, he only had one worker.' She smiled: 'Yes, my father.' 'I'm sorry?' 'That one worker was my father. But he'd already been working there for some time, since the days of Adrián's grandfather.' 'I didn't know that.' 'We have the use of it now. My father keeps the grass and the straw for the cattle there, although we're down to two cows these days. My parents are getting on a bit.' Two cows. She was, as Teresa said, *la paysanne*.

The water in the river flowed more gently on the curve, and the sound it made was fainter, a murmur that also formed into words: '*Isidro, Isidro, Isidro*'. And then there was the counterpoint of the toads: '*Take-a-seat-take-a-seat-take-a-seat*'. We went into the cabin, and I lay down on one of the bundles of straw piled up inside. I closed my eyes. 'Don't go to sleep,' said Virginia. 'Come and join me,' I said. 'No, come with me,' she replied firmly. She walked over to the river bank. 'When I was little, I used to come here with my strawberries.' She sat down on a stone. 'Would you like one?' I said 'No' and stood up.

When I was little. The stacks of planks were all around us; the river cut us off from the world; the gloom protected us; the old carpenter's workshop offered us the bed we needed; and yet she was behaving as

136

if she were a child. 'If you don't want them, I'll throw them in the water,' she threatened, waving the strawberries about. 'Don't be silly.' And I spoke to her as if she really were a child of seven. 'Yes, you're right, it would be silly. I'll take them home to my mother,' she said, getting to her feet.

I started to hear the sounds around me very clearly, as you do when your ears suddenly unblock. On the main road into Obaba, a truck honked its horn; on another road, a car accelerated furiously and then, suddenly, perhaps when it reached a tight bend, decelerated again until it was almost inaudible. And Adrián's father was still working at his machine. And the water in the river was making a sound, a kind of murmur, but it was no longer saying that name: '*Isidro, Isidro, Isidro*'. Nor were the toads repeating: '*Take-a-seat-take-a-seat-take-a-seat*'.

We left behind us the area filled by the stacked wood and, walking along the river bank, reached the bridge that led to Virginia's house. 'Your mother's like Isidro. She does nothing but work,' she said, pointing with her string of strawberries in the direction of Villa Lecuona. Beyond the cranes and the trucks on the sportsground, about seven hundred paces away, the windows in the sewing workshop were lit.

Your mother. I felt angry. I'd had enough of this childish talk. 'Oh, she doesn't work that hard. Sometimes she goes out on to the terrace to smoke a cigarette,' I said. I wanted to leave. 'Well, she tells us we mustn't smoke in the workshop, because, if we do, the clothes will stink of cigarettes.' 'Hm.' The indifferent tone in which I spoke made it clear that this was goodbye.

Two paths led away from the door of her house: the main path, towards the bridge we were standing on, and a smaller track that followed the river and disappeared somewhere towards Urtza. Unexpectedly, a little terrier came racing along that track, barking. When it reached the bridge, it stopped and stood next to Virginia, whining.

'Who did you think it was, Oki?' she asked the dog, stroking its head. 'I have to go,' I said, but she didn't hear me. 'Oki will have to stay here. I can't take him with me to the flat.' A light went on in the house, the kitchen light. 'Your parents will take good care of him,' I said. 'My parents are going to live with my brother. Oki will stay here alone. I'll have to come every day to feed him if I don't want him to starve to death.' The dog was wagging its tail, never taking its eyes off Virginia. 'I've got to go,' I said again. She looked straight at me: 'Don't be angry, David.' She hesitated for a moment over what to do with the strawberries, and finally put them down on the parapet of the bridge. 'Oki, in your kennel!' she said to the dog, and the dog ran over to its kennel on the other side of the river.

The light was growing ever dimmer, and on her shirt I could see only the golden apples now. She was suddenly very serious. 'It makes me really sad to have to leave my house, especially when I know it's going to be empty.' The house had only two windows on the top storey and one, belonging to the kitchen, down below. The front door was equally plain and, unlike many of the farmhouses in Obaba, it had no arch. 'It may not be Villa Lecuona, but I've lived here since I was born, and however poor it is, I really love it.' 'Of course,' I said. 'What I mean is that when you gain something, you always lose something too. Do you understand?' Something inside my chest unknotted. I gave a relieved sigh. 'I know you're not going to be like the house, you're not going to be left empty, it's just a manner of speaking,' she added in a tone of voice that reminded me of Lubis.

She went over to the bridge and picked up her strawberries. 'We need an accordionist for the wedding, and, at first, I thought of asking you. But, in the end, I felt it best to get someone else.' 'What day is the wedding?' 'The first of August.' 'That's really soon.' 'I hope we can still be friends in the future.' 'So do I.' She walked a little further off, to the middle of the bridge. 'See you, then,' I said. I turned and started walking towards the sportsground, following the same path she always took to Villa Lecuona.

'David!' she called. 'Aren't you going to get your bicycle? You left it leaning against that tree by the sawmill.' 'So I did!' I exclaimed. I would have to retrace my steps through the stacks of wood, past our 'schoolhouse', past the houses of Joseba and Adrián. The journey back to my bike seemed suddenly very long. Virginia came over to me: 'Give me a kiss before you say goodbye.' I felt the warmth of her kiss on my cheek. Then I watched her run towards her house, clutching the strawberries.

As I passed the old carpenter's workshop, it seemed to me that the toads were saying something which, at first, I didn't understand: '*Winni-peg-win-ni-peg-win-ni-peg*. Then I remembered: I'd seen that name on the Hotson hat in the hiding-place in Iruain, or, more precisely, on its label. *Darryl Barrett Store. Winnipeg. Canada*. It must be some city visited by the 'American' who only escaped with his life thanks to my Uncle Juan.

My thoughts went back to recent history, to the notebook with the gorilla on the cover. The kiss with which Virginia had greeted me had broken the spell, erasing what my Second Eyes insisted on showing me; its effect, however, had been only brief.

It was a clear, starry night. And yet I didn't once glance up from the yellow stain made by my bicycle light on the road, and I pedalled hard as far as Samson's Bath.

Adrián was bent over his carpentry bench, by the light of an oil lamp. 'What are you doing?' I asked. 'I'm making a toad.' 'Really?' 'Can't you hear them? They're my neighbours.' In the silence of the night, the song of the toads could be heard very clearly. 'What are they saying?' I asked. 'They're asking me for a beer. *Give-me-a-beer-give-me-a-beer*. But I won't. It doesn't agree with them at all.' 'And where is this dangerous stuff?' 'In the usual place, cooling.' I went outside and took two bottles from the river.

XIII

In the book of one hundred detective stories, I'd read a story by Edgar Allan Poe in which the mystery lay precisely in the lack of mystery, since the object being sought, a letter, was found at last in the most visible of places, on the desk in an office. Perhaps influenced by that story, I started to think about things in a different way, and I began,

139

like the characters in the book, to consider a new hypothesis. 'The list in the notebook wasn't written by Ángel,' I said to myself one night when I couldn't sleep. Immediately, as if I were standing before a judge, I offered the irrefutable proof: 'It isn't his handwriting.' No sooner had I spoken these words than I felt a great excitement welling up inside me. What if I was wrong, I thought, and the key to the matter lay there, in that very notebook. Perhaps the gorilla's eyes weren't saying: 'Do you believe your father was a murderer?' but 'Calm down, don't put yourself through any more unnecessary suffering. If you analyse carefully what's in the notebook, you'll recover your peace of mind.' I took the notebook out of the drawer in my bedside table and placed it under the reading lamp.

The look in the gorilla's eyes was just the same, the look of someone asking a question and waiting for an answer. But it was impossible to know what the question was. I opened the book and found the list: *Humberto, Goena Senior, Goena Junior, Eusebio, Otero, Portaburu, 'the teachers', 'the American'*. At first sight, it didn't look like Ángel's handwriting. But, of course, as Teresa had pointed out, there was a gap of twenty-five years between how he wrote now and how he'd written then on this sheet of paper. If I was going to compare, I should study how he'd formed the letters that made up the name that followed the words 'This notebook belongs to'. I copied it on to a strip of paper, trying to reproduce it identically. Then I compared it with each of the names on the list, sliding the strip down the page. This, however, got me nowhere. The name 'Ángel' wasn't enough to go on. It gave me hardly any clues at all.

I started looking around the house for something my father might have written during the war. Again, I had no luck. All I found was a letter my mother had written to him in 1943: 'Dear Angelito, I don't know how I could bear the work in this restaurant if it weren't for the lovely things you say to me . . .' The image of Ángel evoked by this letter was of a kind, tender man, who took pains to cheer his girlfriend up. This still didn't dispel my doubts about his guilt. I went back to the notebook, examined the writing and reached a provisional conclusion:

140

the names Portaburu and Eusebio might have been written by him, but not the others. Nevertheless, as the characters in the detective stories said, I needed more solid proof. Acquiring this proof appeared to be difficult.

The hours and the days passed. As during my last year at school, I had the feeling time was turning very slowly, that it was, once more, a heavy, clumsy grindstone, incapable of undoing anything, and incapable, of course, of undoing my anxieties. In reality, it was my own mind that was really moving with such ponderous slowness.

One morning, I heard the sound of bells and fireworks and went into the sewing workshop to ask what was going on. There was no one there. I found my mother in her room, looking very elegant. 'Is there some kind of celebration today?' I asked. 'Don't you know? It's the first of August. Virginia's getting married! Aren't you dressed yet?' I said I had no intention of attending the service. 'But who's going to play the harmonium?' I lost my temper: 'How should I know?'

An hour later, the phone started ringing, and I thought it would be my mother or even Don Hipólito himself, phoning to say that the person who should be playing the harmonium at Virginia's wedding had been unable to make it, and could I please hurry over to take his place. That was probably what I wanted. My First Eyes wanted to be there, they wanted to see *la paysanne* wearing her white dress.

As soon as I picked up the phone, I heard Martín yell: 'Hotel Alaska here!' I was dumbstruck. 'What is it?' I asked after a few seconds. He adopted a calm, confidential tone: 'First, you have to tell me something, David. Do you want to be my friend? That's the most important thing.' I had no idea what he meant by this, and I remained silent. 'Yes or no, David. It's very important!' he insisted.

I couldn't bring myself to say 'no'. It was best just to let things happen. 'I'm glad, David,' he said. His tone changed again: 'I guess you'll have heard already that I failed all my exams – sciences *and* arts.' He didn't sound particularly concerned. 'Geneviève won't leave me in peace. Ever since I got my marks, she's been nagging me to phone you. She wants to know if you'll be my tutor until the resits in September.

You'd be well paid, of course. She's sorted out the room where we used to have our French classes, just in case you agree.'

I mentally took a step back. If I started going to the hotel, I would see Berlino with my First Eyes. Going there would be like climbing back down into the filthy cave. 'What do *you* want? To work as little as possible, I imagine,' I said. Martín spoke more slowly, less confidently than he had up until then: 'Do you want to know the truth? I need your help. If I don't pass the exam, Geneviève won't loan me the money I need. That's her one condition.' He waited for me to ask the obvious question. 'Why do you need the money?' I asked, giving in to his little game. He chuckled: 'I'm going into business. A club on the coast. A really nice place. You'll have to come and see it.' 'Pornographic, I assume.' He laughed more loudly. 'Why haven't you asked César or Redin?' I asked. 'We don't like César, David. As Berlino says, he's a bastard who's mixed up in politics. As for Redin, he's in Greece. You lot paid him so well for those classes at the sawmill that he's gone off on holiday. Geneviève got a postcard from him a few days ago. Do you know what he said? That Greece was his true homeland.'

While I was talking on the phone, I could see the notebook on the bedside table. *Humberto, Goena Senior, Goena Junior, Eusebio, Otero, Portaburu, 'the teachers', 'the American'*. I remembered that the letters Berlino had written to the two brothers who had died at the front were kept in the attic at the hotel, and it occurred to me that if I could compare the writing on the letters with the writing in the notebook, I'd be able to determine both how far Berlino was implicated and also, by a process of elimination, the degree to which Ángel had been responsible.

Suddenly, it seemed to me of vital importance to accept Martín's proposal. 'I could come in the mornings,' I said. 'You'll do it? Oh, you don't know how happy that makes me. OK, in the mornings it is, then. Geneviève will probably prefer that.' 'But you don't.' 'Waiters at night-clubs tend to go to bed very late. But I'll make the effort. I can stand it for a month. Business is business.' We agreed to start the following day.

I took him through the science subjects in the same room where we used to have our French classes; then, at about eleven, we'd order coffee

142

and sit under the awning on the terrace or walk up and down the mirador while I taught him art or philosophy. Sometimes, when it was very hot, we'd go down into the garden and lie in the shade.

On the fifth or sixth day, one of the summer visitors came over to us. She was known as Signora Sonia, and she and her husband were, according to Martín, old clients of the hotel. She said she envied us looking at all those art books, because she was fascinated by art. 'We've no option. I've got an exam at the beginning of September, and David's reputation as a teacher is at stake,' explained Martín, winking at me. Signora Sonia didn't quite understand. She thought we both had to sit an exam and offered to be our teacher. '*Io amo l'arte. Io poi explicare tutto il Rinascimento in cinque ore.*' She spoke a mixture of Italian and Spanish.

Martín offered her a cigarette, which Signora Sonia accepted without hesitation. 'If you like art so much, why come to the hills of Obaba?' Martín asked. 'Why don't you go to Greece to visit the Parthenon, like our French teacher?' Signora Sonia turned to the hills of which Martín had spoken. '*Dio è il miglior artista*' – 'God is the best artist' – she exclaimed, flinging wide her arms as if to embrace the hills. 'Don't try telling Teresa that,' Martín warned her. 'She's very angry with God for leaving her lame.' Signora Sonia sighed: '*Ah, Teresa, poverina mia.*' Martín placed one hand on the woman's shoulder: 'Poor little Teresa? I don't think so. Do you know what she said the other day over lunch, when I was telling my parents about a club I want to set up on the coast?' Signora Sonia took a puff on her cigarette and shook her head. 'She looked straight at me and said: "How many whores are you thinking of employing at this club?" In those very words. Geneviève nearly fell off her chair, and Berlino choked on his soup. But no one dared say anything. When my sister's angry, you'd better watch out. There's nothing *poverina* about her.'

It had rained a lot while I was spending my time reading detective stories in my room at Villa Lecuona, and the hills we could see from the hotel mirador were intensely green. In the distance, over towards France, the colour changed, the hills became blue or grey. *Teresa, poverina mia.* The Italian woman's sigh engraved itself on my mind.

Martín brought an ashtray over from one of the tables on the terrace and held it out so that Signora Sonia could stub out her cigarette. 'So what's it to be, then? Are you going to help us with our art?' he asked her. 'I'd love to. Besides, the days are awfully long. As you know, my husband and his friends do nothing but attend official functions.' 'Why's that?' I asked. 'Don't be silly, David. Surely you know that these Italians fought in the war with our fathers? They're comrades.' '*Io odio la guerra*,' said Signora Sonia. Martín winked at me again. 'But it must have had its good side. Your husband in Spain, you all alone in Rome and only thirty, with all those men around, eyeing you up in the street . . .' Signora Sonia burst out laughing. '*Martin è pazzo!*' – 'Martín's crazy!' – she said as she walked away. 'You have to give these older ladies a bit of a boost, David.' Martín said. 'That's my next project. A club where ladies of a certain age can have a good time looking at handsome waiters. Not here, of course, David. Not yet anyway. But in Biarritz or Arcachon, you could, I'm sure of it.' I'd known Martín since he was a child, and he was still capable of surprising me.

The expression on his face changed. 'Teresa's furious with me. Since she can't tell God off, she takes it out on me. As if her being lame was my fault. She's really messed things up for me. Ever since she made that comment about whores, Geneviève is very suspicious. She says she's not lending me money so that I can set up a brothel.' I suggested we continue with the class. The September exams were getting ever closer. 'You're right. If I pass, Geneviève won't be able to refuse me anything.' We went back to the fundamentals of existentialism. There were rumours that the subject would come up in the philosophy exam.

Teresa. I never saw her at the hotel, and I was beginning to fear that she might be angry with everyone, and not just with God and with her brother Martín, but angry, above all, with me, because I hadn't been to see her since my one visit in the summer. I even considered using an excuse to get hold of Berlino's letters through Martín, by telling him, for example, that I was studying graphology and that I needed access to lots of different people's handwriting in order to practise; in the end, though, I didn't dare. I was just about to give up altogether, when, one morning, I met Teresa in the hotel car park.

She was wearing a very short black-and-white dress. She covered the few yards that separated us with painful slowness, step by step. The effects of her illness were more obvious now; her right leg was much thinner than her left.

We greeted each other with a kiss on the cheek. 'You have no teaching duties this morning. The gentlemen have gone off to Madrid, and Geneviève has gone to Pau,' she announced. 'No one told me,' I said. 'No? Well, your father's gone too. They're all preparing for the inauguration of the sportsground and the unveiling of the monument.' 'I don't talk much to my parents lately,' I admitted. Teresa pulled a face. 'Like me. Naturally, I hardly talk to Geneviève at all.' 'Martín didn't tell me he was thinking of going.' 'My father invited him at the last minute. I guess that's why he didn't warn you.' Teresa burst out laughing. 'David, do you realise how absurd this conversation is? We haven't seen each other for days and days, and here we are wasting precious time talking about all these completely worthless people.'

The mirador was packed with summer visitors, and so Teresa suggested we go to the garden, which, at that hour, was emptier. Walking by her side, I was keenly aware not only of distance but also of each and every dip and depression in the ground; when we reached the stone steps that led down to the garden, the steps seemed much steeper than usual. At one point, I held out my hand to help her, but she pushed it away and continued on alone.

Teresa was talking about what she'd been reading. She had, she said, a pile of books on her bedside table, but ever since she'd discovered the novels of Hermann Hesse, she'd been unable to read anything else. 'Why is everything that I need in order to be happy so far away from me?' she said. 'Oh, don't worry, David, don't look like that. It's just a sentence I read in one of Hesse's books.' 'Don't look like what?' 'Like a teacher about to get annoyed.' 'Oh, please!' I protested. 'You see, you're already starting to get angry with me, David,' she said, 'you always do.' 'That's not true, Teresa.' 'Yes, it is. On the day you came to see me, you got angry too. Just because I showed you that notebook of your father's.' I made a gesture intended to silence her, but she continued talking: 'I know I shouldn't have done it, but I needed revenge. I had to pay you back for the hurt you caused me. Otherwise, you would have lost all respect for me. That's why I did it, to gain your respect.' She was gabbling now, barely pausing for breath. 'Please, calm down.' 'Let's not get angry with each other, David,' she said in a whisper.

The garden had circular beds full of red flowers, walls adorned with climbing roses, and magnolia trees, which, compared with the beech trees in the forests, seemed effete and decadent. At the far end, there was a second mirador, smaller than the one above, furnished with three wooden benches. Teresa and I sat down on the one in the middle. Before us lay the whole valley of Obaba and the hills and mountains that separated us from France.

'My limp is very noticeable, isn't it?' she said. 'Not really,' I replied. 'Do you remember, David? When you were little, you boys used to play football here, and when the ball went rolling down the slope, I'd be the one to go and fetch it.' Two sparrows alighted on the fence opposite us. 'They come for the crumbs,' explained Teresa. 'The cook keeps any bits of bread left on the tables, and the sparrows wait for him outside the kitchen door.' As if wishing to prove her right, the two sparrows flew off towards the hotel as soon as Teresa had finished speaking. 'Don't worry,' I said, 'in a month or two, when you're better, we'll have another match and, if we lose the ball, we'll send you off to look for it.' Teresa stretched out her legs: 'You see? The left one looks as if it had been sort of filed down. I'd say it was almost half an inch thinner.' She had nice legs, slender and shapely, but they didn't look as if they belonged to the same person. She drew closer and leaned her head on my arm. 'It was a very hard blow, David,' she said very quietly.

We stayed for a while like that, not moving. 'I know, Teresa, but it will pass. Cheer up,' I said at last. In the circumstances, it was better and more honest to resort to clichés. 'The odd thing is I wasn't even aware of my misfortune,' she said. She got up from the bench and went over to the fence, which was made of wood, like the benches. Standing there, against the fenceposts, with the valley of Obaba and the hills of France in the background, she looked like someone posing for a photograph. 'But, you know, there's always some disinterested person ready to help you keep your feet firmly planted on the ground – appropriately enough!' She laughed, as if the double meaning of the phrase had taken her by surprise. 'Is that why you're angry with Martín?' I asked. 'I'm not angry with Martín. He's just a common lout. *Un garçon grossier*, as Geneviève would say, if she were clear-sighted enough.' It occurred to me to wonder then if *I'd* been the first to make her aware of her misfortune, but she mentioned the wife of Lieutenant Amiani. 'You know the one I mean. She was with you on the terrace the other day.' 'You mean Signora Sonia?' Teresa nodded. She was standing opposite me, her arms hooked over the fence behind her. 'She's a kind person in her way, but a bit of a pest at times.' She left the fence and went over to one of the other benches. The sun fell full on her. 'I'd got bored sitting in my room and so I thought I'd go downstairs to the coffee shop and have a cup of tea on the terrace.' And that woman was there. She came running up to me and said "*Teresa, poverina mia!*" She looked so sad and her words were so deeply felt that I suddenly understood what had happened to me. Up until then, like a fool, I'd believed the consoling words of Joseba and the others. She was the person chosen by truth to reveal itself.'

I could add nothing to this confession. Teresa came over to me. 'Do you want to come upstairs to my room?' she said. She had tears in her eyes. I got up and took her arm.

Teresa opened the door of room number 27. '*Ma tanière!*' she cried, allowing me to pass. 'What does *tanière* mean?' I asked. I couldn't remember. 'The lair of a wild animal, of a wolf, for example.' She laughed and picked up the book by Hermann Hesse that was lying on her bedside table and showed it to me. It was a Spanish edition. The

147

title of the book *El lobo estepario* – *Steppenwolf* – was written in yellow letters.

It was a large room, with two windows. Outside the windows, the hillside took much of the light from the rear of the hotel. Inside, as well as books, there were a lot of magazines scattered about, but, in general, order reigned. The bed was made, and there were no clothes left draped over the chairs.

Teresa went to the window. 'Do you see that target?' 'Where?' 'On that big tree, down below.' I could see it. It was just near the hill. 'It's a shooting target, isn't it?' 'I use it to practise with my pistol.' 'You don't shoot the birds, do you?' I said. Just as she had described, there were crowds of sparrows on that side of the hotel. They fluttered and hopped about near the rubbish bins, never straying far from the back door of the kitchen. 'No, I've nothing against the birds,' said Teresa. 'I only target certain extremely elusive boys.' Laughing, she pushed me so as to make me lose my balance and fall on to the bed, but she didn't push quite hard enough. 'I'm a very big tree, Teresa. I won't be felled that easily,' I said.

She took the little silver pistol out of the drawer of her bedside table. 'I didn't think it would work, but Gregorio had kept it primed and ready for shooting,' she said. 'I told you, didn't I? My father's employee is determined to sleep with me. Some nights, he comes and knocks at my door and asks: "Would you like a glass of milk?" A glass of milk! Who in their right mind would ask such a thing!' She took off her shoes and lay down on the bed. 'Sit here, next to me,' she said, patting the bedspread. 'I suppose I'll have to take my shoes off too.' She nodded. I pointed at the gun: 'I thought your father was only going to give that to you on your eighteenth birthday, and not before. That's what you told me the day we went up to the attic.' I sat down beside her. 'You're right, David. But then when Lieutenant Amiani's wife said that thing about *poverina mia*, I went upstairs to get it. I wanted to shoot myself. Cripples can't be happy. I'll never be happy, just as Adrián won't ever be happy either.' 'Do you know what I'm going to do the next time we go up there?' I commented frivolously. 'I'm going to take

148

the helmet we saw up there and put it on your head. Just in case.' She placed one foot on my belly and pushed. I grabbed her foot. 'We'll have to go up there again one day,' I said. 'Why? This room is just as private. No one can come in here without my permission.' I stroked her leg. 'I'm thinking of writing a story,' I said, 'about the war. It would be really useful for me to have a look at the letters in that box.' 'They're over there in the wardrobe. I didn't bring the helmet down, but I brought the papers, although I don't know why. I shouldn't think I'll read them again.' 'No, you're going to devote yourself exclusively to the books of Hermann Hesse,' I said mockingly. 'You'd like them too, David.' She leaned over to the bedside table. She put down the pistol and picked up *Steppenwolf*.

The clock on the bedside table said half past twelve. It was a grey day. The green grass looked dark. 'It's going to rain,' said Teresa, getting up from the bed. 'Shall I put some music on?' The record-player was on a shelf next to the door, and there were records to the right and left. The record-player was red and white. 'It's a Telefunken. My father bought it in France,' she told me. 'And when I asked him, he bought me this record too. He's very good to me really.' Suddenly her voice sounded different, slightly hoarse.

The turntable began to spin, and the arm bearing the needle lifted automatically from its support. A woman's voice emerged from the loudspeakers. It was a very slow, rather melancholy tune. 'Who is it?' I asked. Teresa was still standing by the record-player. 'Marie Laforêt.' She threw the record sleeve over to me on the bed. *La plage. La vie s'en va*. Those were the titles of the first two songs. Something fell to the floor, and I looked up. 'I had a coin in my pocket,' Teresa said, her voice choked with emotion. She was naked. 'I love you so much,' she said. These words robbed her of all her breath. 'Come here,' I said, lying down on the bed.

'How much happier I would be if I could always live like this!' sighed Teresa. We were lying next to each other; she was smoking a cigarette and I was leafing through the Hermann Hesse book and reading the

149

various sentences and passages she'd underlined. 'Alone, you mean? Without any family?' I was struggling to make my voice sound natural. 'Yes, far from Geneviève and Martín especially. As I've told you before, I get on better with my father. I know you don't like him much, but that's just because of his eyes.' I denied this. She exhaled the smoke from her cigarette. 'Actually, he may be able to do something about his eyes. In France we were told that there was a long-term cure for chronic conjunctivitis. The other day, he phoned a hospital in Bordeaux, and they confirmed that they've been doing the operation there for a couple of years now.'

The underlined passages in the Hermann Hesse book were very dramatic. Far from identifying with them, as Teresa or Adrián did, I found them repellent. I turned towards the bedside table and placed the book between the ashtray and the pistol. When I lay down again, Teresa sat up, and we kissed. Her lips tasted of tobacco. 'What did our respective relatives go to Madrid for?' I asked. 'They've gone to talk to that famous boxer of theirs. They want him to come and lend lustre to the inauguration of the sportsground and, of course, to the unveiling of the monument.' 'Do you mean Uzcudun?' I'd seen him several times on TV. He was often interviewed. 'Yes, I think that's his name. There's going to be a big party.' She sat down and stubbed out her cigarette in the ashtray. For a moment, her face was like the face she'd had before she was taken ill, as if she'd removed a mask. She burst out laughing. 'You're kidding, aren't you, David? Are you really so very badly informed?' 'Yes I am. I don't know anything, Teresa, honestly. Except that the inauguration is going to take place during the village fiesta.' She climbed on top of me, on all fours. She had very round breasts. 'Everyone will be there. Your father will give a speech; you'll play the accordion; and Geneviève will be in charge of the banquet to be given in honour of all the VIPs. And at night, there'll be an exhibition boxing match right here, on the mirador, and they'll present Uzcudun with a medal. They're going to make him a freeman of Obaba.' After each statement, she gave me a kiss that was more like a blow. I stroked her breasts. 'How come you know so much?' 'I'm interested in everything to do with you.' I put my arms around her. 'Are you feeling strong enough to do it again?' I asked. 'I suppose so.' 'This time it will be easier.' I stuck my tongue in her ear.

Teresa picked up the phone. 'I'm going to call Gregorio,' she said. 'What for?' 'It's three o'clock. We should eat something. Do you like salad sandwiches? In the kitchen they make them with *salsa rosa*. They're delicious.' 'I don't want Gregorio coming up here, Teresa.' 'He won't come in, David. He'll leave the tray outside the door. He's a waiter.' She was smiling, but was once more wearing her post-illness face. Her olive-oil eyes showed not a glimmer of happiness; on the contrary, they made her smile seem cruel.

I insisted that I didn't want Gregorio to come to the room. I didn't trust Teresa. One way or another, she would let slip to him what had happened between us, so as to humiliate him in my presence. 'Well, I don't know what we're going to do then. As I told you, the other waiter's gone to Madrid with his father.' She meant her brother. Martín helped out at the hotel from time to time. 'I suppose I'll just have to go myself,' she said at last.

As soon as she placed her feet on the floor, she grimaced and put her hand to her back. 'It hurts me a bit if I make any sudden movement. My body hasn't got used to being lame yet, and now and then it protests.' She sat there like a statue, her eyes closed, waiting for the pain to abate, silhouetted against the light coming in through the window: from neck to knee, her body was a series of harmonious lines. I wondered if Virginia's body would be as lovely as the one I was looking at now. Possibly not. Besides — as Teresa had repeated over and over again as she kissed me — she was ready and willing to give me everything. For a moment, I even thought that perhaps we could start going out together.

She went into the bathroom and emerged a few minutes later wearing jeans and an emerald green blouse. 'How do I look? It's known as *prêt-à-porter*, and the French are wild about it. Not Geneviève, of course. She only likes the classic look.' 'It really suits you. I've never seen you looking so pretty.' She came over and kissed me. 'Oh, you are being

151

good today! I'm amazed!' This time, her smile also reached her eyes. She opened the bedroom door. 'I'll phone you from the kitchen to tell you what's on the menu. There may be something better than salad sandwiches.'

'Teresa,' I said, getting up from the bed. 'Would you mind if I had a look at those letters from your father?' She stopped for a moment. 'Oh, right,' she said at last, 'you mean the stuff from the war!' She opened the wardrobe and took out the cardboard box I'd first seen in the attic room. 'If I were you, I wouldn't write stories about the war. The subjects Hermann Hesse chooses are much more interesting. Not to mention love-songs. Yes, why don't you write love-songs? Listen to this, it's really lovely.' She took out a record and put it on the turntable. 'It's called "To you, my love." It's by an English group – The Hollies.' And it seemed to me that she pronounced the name correctly in English. 'Do you know them?' I said that I didn't. 'In matters of music, you're very *démodé*, David.' The song was rather sad, but very haunting.

Teresa stood at the door, thinking, murmuring the words in English and repeating the refrain: *to you, my love, to you, my love.* 'It's my fault,' she said in the same resigned tone as the song. 'Why do you say that?' 'You've become obsessed with these stories about the war. I should never have shown you that wretched notebook of your father's. Now you're all disoriented. A story about the war! What an idea!' She walked over to me and struck my forehead with the flat of her hand. I put my arm around her waist and led her out into the corridor. 'That's what they're going to say to you in the kitchen. What an idea – eating lunch at gone three in the afternoon!' I kissed her on the cheek. She pushed me back into the room. 'Don't stand there. I don't like people watching me from behind.' She closed the door. 'I'll phone to tell you what's on the menu,' she said from the other side.

Humberto, Goena Senior, Goena Junior, Eusebio, Otero, Portaburu, 'the teachers', *'the American'.* I'd memorised how each of these names was written and could recreate them much as a botanist could recreate the leaf of the

152

most common plant. From the box I took an envelope bearing these words: *Antonio Gabirondo, the Front at Jarama*, and removed the letter. At the bottom of the letter, was the clear signature: *Martxel*.

I was quite taken aback. I found it hard to accept that Berlino – or Marcelino – should sign himself 'Martxel', the affectionate diminutive of Marcelino, a name suited to a decent man. Above the signature, in a backward-sloping hand, were these words of farewell: *'Zuek eutsi or tinko guk eutsiko zioagu emen eta'* – 'Stand firm there, and we will stand firm here'. Despite myself, those words echoed inside me in the intonation of Ubanbe and Opin, in the accent of the 'happy peasants', and that wasn't easy to accept either. As far as I recalled, Berlino always spoke in Spanish.

Humberto, Goena Senior, Goena Junior, 'the teachers', 'the American'. There was no doubt about it, it was the same handwriting. Those names had been written by Berlino, by Martxel. And 'Otero' had almost certainly been written by him as well. Then again, he had clearly not written 'Eusebio' and 'Portaburu'. They – and the matter was much clearer now – had been written by his close friend Ángel.

My initial relief didn't last long. Berlino seemed to have been the instigator, but Ángel was still a murderer and not just an innocent who, in the confusion of war, had found himself caught in a compromising situation; nor was he a coward forced by circumstances to become an accomplice. No, alas, he had been more than that.

The phone rang loudly enough to frighten the birds nearby, and before I knew it, I was sitting up in bed, with the receiver in my hand. When I sat up, I knocked over the box Teresa had given me, and the letters and other papers fell on to the floor. 'So what would you recommend from the kitchen?' I asked. The person on the other end of the line said nothing. 'Hello,' I said. 'I wanted to talk to Teresa,' said Geneviève cautiously, as if she were afraid to speak. 'Oh, hi, it's David here. I just dropped in to see Teresa.' 'Ah, I didn't recognise your voice,' she said, but without sounding particularly reassured. She was doubtless wondering what I was doing in her daughter's bedroom now that Teresa was better. 'She's not here. She's gone down to the kitchen to get something to eat. I stayed up here reading that Hermann Hesse book.' I sat on the edge of the bed. I had the feeling Geneviève must be able to see me down the telephone line, and that her reserve was due to my nakedness. I was sweating. 'Would you mind giving her a message? Tell her I phoned from Pau and that she's been accepted at the school here.' 'She's been accepted at the school,' I repeated. 'As you know, she couldn't finish the year because she was ill, but here she'll be able to catch up without missing a year.' 'Can't she go to her old school in San Sebastián?' 'No, she'll have to come here.' 'Well, I suppose it's not that far,' I said. 'Yes, it is. The road is dreadful. This morning it took us nearly four hours to get here. But there's no alternative.' She hung up, having first reminded me to pass the message on to Teresa.

When Teresa finally stopped crying, she repeated Hermann Hesse's words: 'Why is everything that I need in order to be happy so far away from me?' She was curled up beside me, her head half buried beneath the sheet. 'I hate Geneviève,' she said. 'It's perfectly normal to hate your parents,' I told her. 'Which of yours do you hate most, your father or your mother?' she asked. 'Oh, I don't hate my mother at all, on the contrary, but I absolutely loathe my father!' I pronounced these last words so vehemently that she looked up from beneath the sheet to see my face. 'I've been at home these last few weeks,' I went on, 'and I'm not exaggerating, I mean it. I'm going to leave for Iruain as soon as I can.' I'd made this decision while I was talking.

The curtain didn't cover the whole window, and two birds had alighted on the piece of window-sill still visible; they were perhaps, I thought, the same two I'd seen a few hours earlier on the fence in the garden. They were looking inside at the sandwich Teresa had left on the bedside table. 'You haven't eaten anything,' I said. 'I'm too sad to eat.' 'Do you want to go downstairs to the coffee shop to have something to drink? It would do you good to get out of here.' 'Do you know Pau?' she asked. No, I said, I didn't. 'I do. The nuns took us there on a trip once. Half of the girls were sick on the bus.' 'But it's a nice town, isn't it?' 'The best thing about it are the shoes. They make really beautiful shoes. When I go there, I'll buy twenty pairs. Orthopaedic ones, of course. Special shoes for people who've had polio.' 'Why stop at twenty pairs, buy forty!' I joked. 'You're happy, aren't you, David?' 'Well, yes and no,' I said cautiously. 'I'm going far away, that's why you're happy.' 'That's not true.' 'Isn't it?' 'No.' The birds had vanished from the window-sill.

Silent and still, room number 27 at the Hotel Alaska was beginning to seem like a place outside of the world. 'But don't think you're going to escape, David,' said Teresa, putting her knee between my thighs. 'I'll come every Saturday to fetch you. Or you'll come to Pau.' 'On my new VeloSolex,' I said. My mother had told Ángel that he should buy me one of those small motorised bikes that didn't require a driving licence, so that I could cycle to the station in more comfort. 'They're not going to buy you a VeloSolex, but a big motorbike, a Guzzi, I think. A red one.' 'How do you know all this?' 'As I said, I'm always interested in anything other people have to say about you. That's how I found out that they're relying on you to provide the music for the party on the day they unveil the monument. And that's how I found out about the Guzzi. It was Signora Sonia, the wife of Lieutenant Amiani, who gave your father the idea.'

In another tone of voice entirely, Teresa said. 'David, I want you to promise me something.' 'That I'll visit you in Pau,' I said. 'I'd love you to do that, you know I would, but I have another favour to ask.' 'Go on,' I said. I felt as if room number 27 were moving further and further away from the world, that it was a spaceship circling the Earth on some very distant orbit. I could hear Teresa's breathing, nothing else. 'I want you to agree to play the accordion at the unveiling cere-mony. Do it for me, David, not for my father or for that Uzcudun guy or whatever his name is.' 'Why is it so important to you?' 'I'll be there on the day, and I'll take loads of photos of you, and then I'll put them up in my bedroom at the students' residence in Pau. I'll fill a whole wall with photos of you.' 'You're joking.' 'No, I'm serious. Do you know when I fell in love with you?' She sat up in bed and gave me a very pretty smile. 'The first time you played the accordion

155

at that dance at the hotel. I went out on to the mirador and saw you on stage playing that accordion you had then, the one with the iridescent bodywork. And you've been in my heart ever since.' I said nothing. 'It's not just a whim of mine, David, it's deeper than that.' 'I suppose I can't refuse.' 'No, you can't.' 'All right, then, I'll play at the inauguration and you can take photos of me.' She kissed me. 'I'll do all kinds of things for you. Everyone will realise what's going on between us.' Room number 27 was travelling through space, heading for Earth. It was not an easy re-entry.

Teresa started to laugh. 'Now what's wrong?' I said, pulling away from her. 'Do you know what Martín is going to do at university? Media Studies.' She could barely speak for laughing. 'And do you know why he's chosen that course?' 'So that he can go to Madrid?' 'No, because it's a phantom course. It isn't a real course at all. Apparently, they're having so many problems that they're not even giving any classes, so they just pass everyone. And the really funny part is that Geneviève has no idea. She's utterly delighted with her son. She thinks he's taking a very modern degree. Anyone would think she was stupid. She's a great disappointment to me.'

Her words dissolved in the air. Silence wrapped about the hotel. 'Don't you fancy going down to the coffee shop?' I asked again. 'Yes, but I can't go down there naked, and I want to lie here naked by your side.' She turned to the bedside table to get a cigarette. Before lighting it, she removed the small pistol from its position on top of the book and replaced it with the ashtray.

I looked at the clock. It was a quarter to six. Geneviève would be somewhere on the road from Pau to Bayonne. Berlino, Ángel and Martín would not yet have left Madrid. 'I don't know if he's told you or not,' said Teresa, 'but Martín's involved in a business deal. He met the owners of a club and now he's an associate. He brought them back to the hotel a few months ago. Awful people.' Another bird alighted on the windowsill. It, too, fixed its gaze on the sandwich on the bedside table. 'The birds are hungry,' I said. 'They should take up smoking, like me. Tobacco

156

suppresses hunger pangs.' Teresa blew out the smoke from her cigarette, and the bird at the window flew off.

We lay for a few moments in silence. 'Joseba says he doesn't understand why you stay in Obaba.' This remark caught me unawares. 'Do you know what Adrián calls Joseba?' I said. 'No.' 'The personnel manager, because he likes organising other people's lives.' Teresa ignored my remark. She put down her cigarette on the ashtray and picked up the Hermann Hesse book that was on the bedside table. She started leafing through it. 'You'll be the only one,' she said. 'Everyone else is going away to study.' It was true. Susana and Victoria were thinking of studying Medicine at the University of Zaragoza; Joseba and Adrián would be going to Bilbao, one to study Law and the other Engineering. 'What's your course called again, David? I can't remember.' She was still turning over the pages of the book, looking for something.

I was going to do a new degree devised by the Jesuits. It was known as ESTE – which stood for Estudios Superiores Técnicos de Economía – and my mother loved reminding me that any student with this degree would qualify as both a lawyer and an economist. Teresa found the page she was looking for and started to read: 'No prospect was more hateful and distasteful to him than that he should have to go to an office and conform to daily and yearly routine and obey others. He hated all kinds of offices, governmental and commercial, as he hated death . . .'

The smoke from her cigarette drew undulating lines across the ceiling, and the area of sky not covered by the curtains was the same grey colour as when I'd arrived. 'Shall I put some music on?' I said. I needed to move. 'David, you've been a bit of a disappointment to me as well. Would you like to know why?' 'Yes, tell me.' 'I thought you were like Harry, the protagonist of this book, but now I'm not so sure. You get the chance to leave home and go to university, and you decide, instead, not to detach yourself from your mother's apron-strings. And to top it all, you choose that degree. What possible interest is there in being a lawyer and an economist? What do you want? To spend your whole life working in a bank?' I found this topic of conversation unbearable, insufferable. 'I'm doing it for the Guzzi,' I said. 'I really fancy having a motorbike.' I freed myself from her embrace and started the record-player. *To you, my love.* I began to get dressed. 'Leave your clothes where they were,' she said. She was holding the pistol and pointing it straight at me. 'Point it somewhere else, please,' I said. 'The safety catch is on. Look.' She squeezed the trigger, but I didn't hear a sound. I imagined that such a small pistol was sure to be very quiet and that even if it did go off, the explosion would barely be heard above the music. 'Do you know what I think, David? That we should go around like Bonnie and Clyde. Have you seen the film? I saw it the other day with Adrián and Joseba and really loved it. It's about a couple who spend their time robbing banks.'

I went over to the window and opened the curtains. There were the grey sky, the green hill, the black-and-white target, the brown sparrows at the kitchen door. Just as it was before, entirely unchanged. It was pointless, time had stopped. The wheels on the car bringing Geneviève from Pau had stopped. So had the Mercedes that Ángel was driving.

The record-player fell silent. I started it up again. 'To you, my love.' As it turned, the record carried the world with it, but only for a moment. My watch showed six twenty.

'You're not telling me that staying in this village for the rest of your life seems a better idea than becoming a bank robber,' Teresa said. She had rested the barrel of the pistol between her breasts. I sat down on the edge of the bed. 'I'll spend the first three or four years in San Sebastián, and then I'll go to Bilbao. And I'll finish my degree in Deusto.' Deusto also belonged to the Jesuits, and it was the university held in highest esteem by my Uncle Juan. I would have enrolled there right from the start if my mother hadn't asked me to spend my first few terms in San Sebastián. I loved my mother, and it seemed wrong to leave her all alone in Villa Lecuona.

'All right, if you're not convinced that you want to take up a life of crime, we could do something else,' Teresa said, taking my hand. I took the pistol from her and put it back on the bedside table. She had just extinguished the cigarette that was still burning out in the ashtray. 'We could travel round all the cities in Spain. My father says that street artists earn more money in Spain than they do in France. You can play the accordion and I'll dance.' 'What will our stage name be?' Teresa put her arms about my neck. 'Pirpo and the lame ballerina', she said. 'Pirpo's a nice name,' I remarked. 'I think it's the name of a friend of that boxer, Uzcudun. I've heard my father mention it.' 'You obviously talk to your father a lot.' She climbed on top of me again. 'David, were you frightened when I pointed the pistol at you?' 'No.' 'Yes, you were. And you were right to be. You know very well that I'm capable of exacting my revenge. Like when I handed you that notebook with the gorilla on the cover. But this time it would be much worse. You would be left incapacitated.' 'Incapacitated for what, may I ask?' She was trying to grab the pistol again, but I caught her hand. 'Stop it. It's a fantastic idea. That way, I'd be your only wife.' Laughing, she tried to reach the bedside table with her other hand.

I put the pistol in the drawer and locked it. For a moment, I hesitated, not knowing what to do with the key. 'That's a bit of a problem, you haven't any pockets,' said Teresa, laughing still louder. I opened the window and flung the key out. Five or six sparrows took flight. 'Come here, David.' Teresa was lying on the bed with her legs spread wide. 'If you want to hit me, go ahead,' she said. 'When are we going to go outside and get a bit of fresh air?' I asked, lying down beside her. 'In a while. If you like, we can go and do some target practice with the pistol.' 'But I've thrown away the key to the drawer.' 'I have another key. You see, I've thought of everything.' She gave me a kiss, an unpleasantly moist kiss. 'I really am a very naughty girl. You ought to beat me,' she said. She smelled of sweat and tobacco. 'I'll beat you to a pulp,' I said. She licked my face.

The bird fell dead beside the target. I tried to go back to the moment before I'd fired, but the bullet wouldn't return, and my finger was still squeezing the trigger. 'Oh God, what have I done!' I yelled. Teresa crouched down beside the bird. 'It's still got its little eyes open. You'll have to finish it off,' she said. I didn't move. 'Look, it's opening its eyes,' she insisted. 'Quick, David. It's better to kill it than leave it to suffer.' I couldn't say a word. I was drenched in sweat. 'It hardly weighs a thing,' she said, with the bird in the palm of her hand. 'It's still warm.' She came over to me. 'Go on, take it. Finish what you've begun.'

Suddenly, she hurled it at me as if it were a stone. I felt it hit my chest. 'Stop it!' I cried. I made as if to throw down the pistol. 'No, don't do that! You've got to finish the bird off, remember.' Teresa was laughing. 'What are you talking about? It's dead already!' I looked more closely: the bird's tiny head was hanging limply to one side; its eyes were two tiny puckered slits. I hurled the pistol down at the foot of the tree. Teresa went to pick it up.

She returned looking angry, examining the pistol. 'I don't know why you're so upset. The boys in Obaba kill twenty birds in a single day with their pellet guns.' 'But how did it happen?' I just couldn't grasp what I'd done. 'How do you think it happened?' said Teresa, losing patience with me now. 'You fired at the target, but it's not that easy to hit. This silly bird got in the way. It wasn't your fault.' I felt that it was and that I should have been home hours ago. It must have been about eight o'clock. Geneviève wouldn't be back for another two hours at least. Berlino, Martín and my father would be back even later. The sky was a still darker grey.

Teresa dropped the bird in a rubbish bin. When she returned, her olive-oil eyes were full of tears. 'That was our first argument, David. So soon too, on the day we made love for the first time.' She walked back over to the rubbish bin. 'What are you going to do?' I asked. But I knew already; she was going to rescue the dead bird. 'I'll find a nice piece of cloth and bury him wrapped up in that. I don't know how I could have just tossed him in that disgusting rubbish bin. It was very cruel of me.' She was stroking the bird. 'I'm about to suffer the same fate as this bird. I'll write to you from Pau, and you'll throw my letters in the bin.' 'I thought you preferred to identify yourself with Hermann Hesse's wolf,' I said. I wasn't about to let myself get sucked into one of her rapid mood changes.

From one of the windows upstairs came the sound of music. 'It's our

160

song,' said Teresa. I listened. *To you, my love.* She was right. It was coming from her record-player. 'Who's in your room?' It occurred to me that it might be Geneviève, but that was impossible. Even if she had gone into her daughter's room, she'd be unlikely to play that record by the Hollies. 'It's the dog,' said Teresa scornfully, 'he's probably been sniffing the sheets.' 'Gregorio?' 'I had an idea he'd made a copy of the key to my room. Now I know it's true.'

I noticed a boy running across the car park. 'Sebastián!' I called. I couldn't have felt happier than if it had been Lubis himself. '*Ire bila nitxabilen, David.*' – 'I was looking for you, David' – he said, coming over to us. 'What's wrong?' 'The motorbike's arrived. Your mother told me. And she said you should go straight home now so that the mechanic can explain to you how it works.' I gave a sigh of relief. Sebastián looked at Teresa. 'What's that in your hand?' he asked. 'A dead bird.' 'No, in your other hand.' 'A very beautiful pistol. Do you want to try it?' Teresa held out the gun to him and he grabbed it. 'It's rubbish! Give me a cartridge gun any time,' he exclaimed, handing it back to her.

Teresa and I kissed goodbye. 'It's been the happiest day of my life,' she said. 'I'm glad.' 'But you're gladder still that I'm going to Pau.' 'That's not true,' I protested. 'Besides, you haven't gone yet.' 'That's what you think. You don't know Geneviève. I'll be sleeping there tomorrow night, you wait.' Sebastián gestured to me to say that he'd wait for me in the car park. 'You'll keep your promise, won't you?' said Teresa, 'On the 16th, I'll play the accordion and you'll take photos of me,' I assured her. 'Then we'll be together again,' she said and held out her hand to me. 'I'll see you then,' she added, and started walking back to the hotel. 'Will you write to me?' 'No, David.' 'No?' 'You never answer, or if you do, you always lie. After what happened today, I really wouldn't like that.' I could think of nothing to say in response. 'Leave the bird out here,' I said, seeing that she was still holding it in her hand. 'I want to give it to Gregorio as a present,' she said, without turning round.

Sebastián was scrutinising a car in the car park. 'Anything wrong?' 'Not that I can see, but I want to be a mechanic and I've got to start

161

learning somewhere.' 'A mechanic? Really?' 'You don't expect me to be a shepherd like my father, do you? I don't want to spend the rest of my life in the Navarra hills!' We both got on my bike, with Sebastián behind me, his feet resting on the butterfly nuts on the rear wheel, and we set off downhill. 'It's a fantastic motorbike. A red one. You'll have to let me ride it,' he shouted. 'Do you know how to?' 'Of course I do. It's a lot easier than riding a horse.' I promised to let him have a go. It was finally getting dark. In the few houses by the roadside the lights were lit.

XIV

At the end of August, it began to rain, and the hills and woods surrounding Iruain became lost in the mist. Nearer the house, the leaves on the solitary trees hung heavy and wet; they looked like drawings of leaves, as if they'd been cut out and stuck on a page. Nearer still, Faraón, Ava and the other horses were quietly cropping the grass. The grass was very green; the muddy road along the valley was yellow; the roof of Lubis' house was red, dark red; and the sky was a murky white, like the mist.

I spent hours and hours never leaving the house, staring at the rain and practising my accordion. I didn't feel like practising, and, worse still, it really bothered me having to perform at the party being held for the inauguration of the sportsground, but I felt obliged to do so because of the promise I'd made to Teresa. 'Your taking part has been the best news we've had in a long time,' Martín said to me with a solemnity I'd never have imagined him capable of. He spoke, he said, on behalf of Berlino and Geneviève. Then he handed me a note from my father: a list of the tunes I'd have to play.

Uncle Juan eyed me sadly whenever he saw me playing the accordion. One afternoon, I started rehearsing the Spanish national anthem in the kitchen, and he could contain himself no longer: 'I don't want to hear that music in this house!' I felt really embarrassed. 'I have to

162

play it at the inauguration, Uncle. And I still haven't got it quite right,' I said, trying to justify myself. 'And why exactly have you got to play for the benefit of those fascists?' 'I promised, Uncle, and I can't go back on my word.' 'What could you have been thinking of when you made such a promise?' He was so angry that he left the kitchen, slamming the door.

During the next few days, I didn't touch the accordion, and most of that time passed idly by, while I did nothing but lie on my bed or sit by the kitchen window. Sometimes, I forced myself to pick up a book in order to read something, a poem by Lizardi or another of the one hundred detective stories; however, I soon lost concentration and returned to staring out of the window at the mist and the rain. Then the gorilla on the notebook would make its presence felt again, and I understood, more clearly than ever, what its eyes were saying. Not what I'd originally thought: 'Do you think your father was a murderer?' No, not a question, but a statement: 'David, it's time you accepted it. Your father played an active role in the deaths of those people, especially in the deaths of Portaburu and Eusebio.' This thought made me breathless, and I would have to leave the house and go for a walk in the rain. Then I'd lie down. And in bed, trying to calm myself, I would search my memory for an image of Virginia. 'One day, we'll take that same walk through the piles of planks at the sawmill,' I thought, 'and that day I'll be happy.'

The last few days of August came and went. I was almost always alone, because Juan spent most of his time away, in Biarritz or in San Sebastián, and because Lubis was obliged to do not only his own work, but also that of his brother Pancho, who was in a state of high excitement as he always was when fiesta time approached. It fell to Lubis now both to look after the horses and to go up into the woods with Moro to take the woodcutters their food. He had no time to come and see me and talk for a while.

One morning, from the kitchen window, I saw Sebastián's twin brothers playing on the other side of the paddock with what looked like a large stone. The stone did seem unnaturally white, and the twins

163

appeared to have no trouble moving it, but I gave it no further thought. Nor did I stop to wonder why they were so intent on this game despite the rain. They were, after all, tough little boys, who lived according to ancient laws. They were, perhaps, fearful of thunder, but not of the rain.

At midday, Juan came into the house to change his clothes after a ride on Faraón. He was washing his hands in the sink when he looked up and exclaimed: 'What are those boys doing? What have they got hold of?' But he knew already; he understood the moment he opened his mouth. He muttered something I didn't quite catch and went outside.

He headed straight for the stable, calling to Lubis. 'He's not here, Uncle. He had to go to the sawmill,' I said, running after him. Then he strode towards the bridge and into the paddock. I followed him. 'Not now, Faraón,' he shouted to his horse, when it trotted over to him. 'Where did you say Lubis had gone?' he asked, frowning. 'He has to do his brother's work as well now. He's in the woods, delivering lunch to the workers from the sawmill.' 'That Pancho gets lazier by the day. He's going to end up making himself thoroughly unpopular,' he declared loudly. As soon as they saw us, the twins fled.

What I'd taken to be a white stone was, in fact, the skull of a horse. It was lying next to a stake, and the eye sockets were plugged with mud. About five yards away, in the middle of a rectangle of lime, lay a row of ribs. There were also some clods of earth on the wet grass surrounding the rectangle. 'Oh, God, how disgusting!' my uncle exclaimed, pulling a face. 'What is it?' I said. 'Ask them up there!' he replied. Two crows were flying off into the mist.

My uncle carefully picked up the skull and placed it at the top of the ribs, inside the lime rectangle. 'His name was Paul,' he said, 'and he was a really wonderful horse.' Then he fell silent, absorbed, as if praying. 'A hunter killed him. He must have been in a bad mood because he hadn't managed to kill anything out hunting, and so he decided to get his own back. He saw Paul in the field and shot him, like big game.'

He strode off again, keeping close to the fence. 'We'd better tell Lubis, and Ubanbe too. We'll have to bury the horse again.' We passed Ava, Blaky, Zizpa and Mizpa. Faraón was grazing on his own, some yards away, apart from the group. 'He was an Arab horse, like Faraón,' added Uncle Juan. He was walking faster and faster now. 'He was worth 5000 dollars at the time. And he was killed stone dead with a single shot.' 'Where was the hunter from? From Obaba?' We were still a few yards from the road, and he didn't answer my question until we'd covered that distance. 'It's not certain that the person who did it was a hunter. Some said it was the civil guard who were out patrolling in search of a thief in weather much like today's, and that they confused the thief with Paul. But we never found out exactly what happened. If I'd been here, we would have.'

I didn't doubt it. He was a very energetic person. You only had to see the deep tracks left by his feet in the mud. 'Did no one tell you about it?' No, I said it was the first I'd heard anything about the dead horse. 'Didn't Lubis tell you?' No, I said again. 'And Ubanbe and Pancho said nothing either?' A third time I said 'No'. 'Your questions always catch me off guard, Uncle,' I said. I was starting to get annoyed. 'You, David, live in cloud-cuckoo land!'

Lubis' dog came out on to the road and stood watching us, wagging its tail. As he did with the horses, my uncle used to give sugar lumps to all the local dogs: 'Not because I'm fond of them,' he said, 'but just so that they don't bark at me.' Addressing the dog, he said: 'I've got empty pockets today. I came out in a hurry.' He took a few steps towards the front door of the house, then stopped short. 'There was another version of events,' he said. 'It was rumoured that Ángel was the one who shot Paul.' 'My father?' I asked.

The dog had sat down beside us, as if wanting to take part in the conversation. 'He was the person who broke the news to me,' my uncle went on, lowering his voice. 'He phoned me at Stoneham, absolutely beside himself. "Why are *you* in such a state about it?" I asked. "How do you think *I* feel? That horse was worth 5000 dollars." Anyway, he finally calmed down enough to tell me what was wrong. He'd been slandered; people were blaming him for the horse's death. And that's how I left it. On my next visit from America, Lubis told me the rest of the story.'

When he heard Lubis' name, the dog walked over to the road, waiting for his master to appear, but no one came. 'The rumour went that Ángel had come to Iruain with a woman,' Juan went on, 'and something must have happened with the horse, who knows what. Anyway, he hit the roof when this rumour started doing the rounds, and it's hardly surprising really, because it was a very serious allegation indeed. In the end, Lubis paid the price.' 'Lubis? Why Lubis? I don't get it, Uncle.' Again the dog shifted about nervously. 'Ángel thought Lubis had started the rumour, which was totally ridiculous, but, as you know . . . or, rather, as you probably don't know, given that you live in cloud-cuckoo land, Ángel has always been at loggerheads with Lubis' family. Anyway, the upshot was that Ángel gave Lubis a real thrashing.'

My uncle set off again, and the dog rose imploringly on to its hind legs. 'I've told you before, I haven't got any sugar lumps!' Juan told him, pushing him away with his hand. 'If you want my opinion,' he went on, 'Ángel had nothing to do with the death of that horse, and there was no truth in the story about the woman either. But that's what happens to politicians who collaborate with the dictatorship. People are always looking for a chance to throw mud at them. And now that the subject has come up, I'm going to say something very important,' and he pointed at me with his finger. 'The same thing will happen to you if you play the national anthem at the inauguration. Believe me, you'll be marked for life!' He rapped on the door. '*Etxean al azaude, Beatriz!*' – 'Are you there, Beatriz?' – he said.

Beatriz, the mother of Lubis and Pancho, was a small woman of about sixty. Her eyes, large and calm like Lubis' eyes, remained fixed on Juan while he explained to her what we'd just seen.

'As you know, Juan, I was already quite old when my sons were born,' she said, while she prepared us some coffee. 'I was really frightened, and Don Hipólito, the priest, was always talking to me about Sarah in the Bible, and about how when she gave birth to Isaac she was even older than me, ninety, if I remember rightly. And when Lubis was born, I saw at once that everything was fine. But then along came Pancho and, what can I say, I mean, I know a mother shouldn't say these things, but it would have been better if he'd never been born. He's been in such a state of excitement lately, he's hardly been home at all. And Lubis has to do everything. That's why he's gone up to take the woodcutters their lunch.' 'It's not that I'm in that much of a hurry, Beatriz, but it would be best if the horse's remains could be buried sooner rather than later,' said my uncle. 'Of course,' she agreed, 'the sooner the better. Don't worry, Juan, as soon as Lubis gets back, I'll ask him to call Ubanbe so that they can start digging.'

On the table she placed three small green, gold-rimmed cups and poured out the coffee she'd heated up in the saucepan. The smell of chicory was more pungent than that of the coffee. 'How many lumps?' she asked. We put two in each cup, and Uncle Juan put one in his pocket. 'I don't know if you'll manage to persuade Ubanbe, Beatriz. He's all over the place as well. With Uzcudun coming, there are sure to be boxing matches during the fiestas, and the young people want Ubanbe to have a go.' Beatriz sat down opposite us. 'Is Ubanbe thinking of fighting?' she asked. 'He certainly is, and with a professional boxer too. He's in training apparently.' 'Well, he should try doing a bit of training with the hoe,' said Beatriz.

We were standing in the kitchen, ready to leave. 'So Paul's risen up from his grave, has he?' sighed Beatriz, looking out of the window up towards the paddock. 'The trouble is his remains are scattered all over,' said Juan. Beatriz sighed again: 'I'm obviously not thinking clearly at the moment. I saw the crows hanging around over there, but didn't put two and two together. As if crows would ever be interested in grass!' 'It was the same with me. I'd noticed the crows, too, but took no notice.' Beatriz accompanied us to the door. 'The thing is, Eusebio was getting on a bit when there was that business with the horse,' she explained. 'He probably didn't dig deep enough. Or maybe he put in less quicklime than was needed.' 'No, no, Eusebio did a good job,' said my uncle. 'But it rains a lot here and the earth gets very soft. Besides, the woods are so close. It could have been some animal sniffing around, possibly a boar.' 'I reckon it was dogs, Juan.' 'Yes, you're right.' My uncle opened the door: 'It looks like it might be clearing up.'

We went outside, and Beatriz said to me with a smile: 'You're very quiet, David.' I replied as best I could with some banal comment. I was thinking about the phrase I'd just heard in the kitchen: *Eusebio was getting on a bit when there was that business with the horse.*

In places like Obaba, where the link between the generations was kept up through names – when someone died, he might leave behind him several godchildren all named after him – it was normal that someone called 'Eusebio' would be related in some way to all the other 'Eusebios'. I was sure that the former owner of that house – Beatriz's husband, Lubis' father – would be related to the Eusebio on the list in the notebook. He might even be the same person.

Beatriz spoke affectionately to me: 'You don't know how pleased I am that you and Lubis get on so well. My son may be a country boy, but he's got manners. He feels more comfortable with you than he does with Ubanbe and all those other troublemakers.' 'I've just thought of something, Beatriz,' said my uncle, interrupting and coming to join us. 'I'll talk to the manager of the sawmill. I'll ask him to give Ubanbe and that other lad, Opin, the day off. If we all work together, we'll soon get the job done.'

When we set off back to Iruain, the dog followed us. 'Catch!' cried Uncle Juan, taking the sugar lump from his pocket and tossing it into the air. 'Hey, you're quite the acrobat!' he cried when, in one smooth movement, the dog leaped and snapped up the sugar lump.

I followed the various stages of the reburial from the stone bench outside Iruain: Lubis, Opin and my uncle dug the earth and threw it in; Ubanbe pounded the earth flat with a crowbar; Pancho and Sebastián carried something that looked like sand in a basket we called a *kopa*. When they'd finished, the entire group went down to the river to wash. Then, with my uncle at their head, they all walked over to Adela's house, laughing, satisfied with the work they'd done, and knowing that a good meal awaited them. I waved to them and stayed where I was on the stone bench.

Lubis came to ask how I was, if I still had a fever. This was the excuse

I'd given for not joining the group, and I really did feel ill. 'Do you want me to call the doctor, David?' he said. No, I didn't. It wasn't necessary.

The doctor. I remembered that his daughter, Susana, had been the first to tell me about the men who'd been shot. Suddenly, that name – Susana – sounded completely odd to me. Susana, Joseba, Adrián, Victoria, César, Redin. They seemed like people from another age.

'The best thing you can do is go to bed,' said Lubis. 'Just what I was thinking,' I replied. We went into the house. 'Ubanbe told me to bring the accordion over, because he knows how to play as well. But I'll tell him I forgot. I don't think that instrument was made for his great paws.' The accordion was on the kitchen table. 'Whatever you think best, Lubis.' I couldn't look him in the face.

When I went up to my room, I removed the trapdoor from the hiding-place and picked up the J.B. Hotson hat. I lay down on the bed, covered my face with the hat, and went to sleep.

When I woke up, Juan was sitting beside me. He was holding the hat. 'I see you've taken to behaving strangely,' he said. He wasn't angry, but he frowned as if he was. 'There was a lot of light coming in through the window, and I put it on to shade my eyes,' I said by way of an excuse. 'I don't mean because of the hat, but because you didn't join us for lunch.' 'I wasn't feeling well.' 'You're not ill either. You don't appear to have a fever.'

He got up and went over to the window. 'We had a good time,' he said. 'After the fifth bottle of wine, Ubanbe put on a boxing display for us. He landed some really impressive punches on Tony García. It's just a shame Tony García was only there in spirit in Adela's kitchen.' My uncle chuckled to himself. He'd had too much to drink as well. 'Who's Tony García?' I asked. 'Spain's middleweight champion. As you know, they're going to put on a special event in honour of Uzcudun, who's coming to unveil the monument. There are going to be four fights, and, at the end, Ubanbe will come on to do a bit of sparring with García.' My uncle imitated Ubanbe's accent: *a hazer goantesh con Gartzia.*

I looked out of the window. The group in charge of Paul's burial were now in a field near the stables, in an angle formed by the fence. All of them, with the exception of Lubis, were bare-chested. On the other side of the stream, the horses were still cropping the grass, and only the donkey, Moro, seemed interested in what was going on around him. He had his head on one side and was looking at the group.

Ubanbe and Opin started fighting, imitating the way boxers move, but then Sebastián came over bearing two pairs of gloves. 'Fancy Sebastián thinking of that!' exclaimed my uncle. They were gloves from America, padded and fingerless. 'If he'd only apply his mind to doing something useful, he'd be a rich man.' Ubanbe and Opin resumed the fight. Now and again, they looked like real boxers. 'If he manages to land a single punch on Tony García, he'll knock him out. He's really strong, our Ubanbe!'

He took a piece of paper from his shirt pocket. 'Before I forget, the doctor asked me to give you this.' On the piece of paper was a list. 'As I understand it, you asked his daughter for a list of the people who were shot in Obaba.' 'Yes, I was talking to her in the restaurant and I mentioned something about it,' I replied. The feeling of distance was growing still stronger. It really did seem like a conversation from the remote past.

I read the names on the list: Bernardino, Mauricio, Humberto, Goena Senior, Goena Junior, Otero, Portaburu. 'The first two were teachers. The rest were farmers and shepherds,' Uncle Juan told me. He was reading through the list with me and commenting on the names. 'And what about Eusebio? Why doesn't his name appear here? I thought he'd been shot too,' I said. My question surprised Juan. 'What has Lubis told you?' 'Lubis hasn't told me anything. I found out from Teresa.' 'Well, if you want to know, they didn't kill Eusebio. He escaped before they could catch him. He spent some time here, in the hiding-place, and then made it across country into France.' 'I didn't know Lubis' father had survived,' I ventured. 'Well, he did. He escaped,' said Juan. 'As the American did later on.' I had the confirmation I wanted. The Eusebio on the list and Lubis' father were one and the same person.

The notebook with the gorilla on the cover was on a shelf in that room, and although it occurred to me to show it to my uncle, I didn't move. 'Who's this Teresa person who spoke to you about Eusebio?' 'The girl from the hotel.' 'Berlino's daughter, the one who's been ill?' He frowned. 'She's in Pau at the moment. Her parents sent her there.' I didn't know what else to say. My uncle went to the window and looked over towards the village. 'If you've spoken to her, then you know everything there is to know,' he said, without turning round. He gestured with his hand in the direction he was looking. 'In a few days' time, they're going to unveil that monument in the centre of Obaba, and then they'll hold a banquet in honour of Uzcudun. And they'll pose for a photograph which will be published in the papers the following day. And they'll all be wearing suits and ties, like real gentlemen. But I'll tell you something: that photograph will be full of criminals. Colonel Degrela – a murderer. Berlino – another murderer. And the others the same, or most of them. Forgive me for saying so, but they're all fascists.' My uncle folded his arms. He was waiting for my question. 'You mean Ángel as well?' I finally asked. He replied sharply: 'Everyone knows he was on the side of the fascists. Carmen says that, even before the war, he was friendly with Berlino and his brothers, which is why he got involved in politics. But she says he didn't do what Berlino did. Apparently, he lacked conviction.' 'And what do you think?' 'Carmen rarely lies.' 'Well, I'm convinced that he wanted to kill Eusebio, and Portaburu too.'

I took the notebook down from the shelf and placed it in his hands. 'This is the list of people to be killed in Obaba,' I said. He read it slowly, stopping at each name. 'Where did you get this?' he asked. 'From an attic room in the hotel. I reckon my father wrote the names "Eusebio" and "Portaburu".' He re-read the list. 'Maybe, but I still don't think Ángel took part in the executions. Portaburu, for example, was picked up on the street in San Sebastián and killed by a group of gunmen.' But he wasn't sure either. The notebook had taken him unawares. 'He may not have participated directly, but he was surrounded by murderers. That much is undeniable,' I said. 'Yes, it is undeniable,' he replied, 'but

171

you could say the same of so many people. As I said, some of the "gentlemen" who'll be attending the banquet for Uzcudun are real criminals.'

He grabbed my arm. 'You mustn't appear at the unveiling of the monument, David!' Suddenly, he was giving me an order. 'As I said before, if you play the national anthem at the unveiling, you'll be marked for ever! Besides, those people have no future. They're going to have problems even on the day of the inauguration. People are going to boycott it.' 'But it would be very difficult for me not to play, Uncle. They'll come looking for me, you'll see,' I said. 'No, I won't see. I'm leaving for America tomorrow. I've told your mother that this year we won't be getting together for the fiesta. Your mother would like the family to be above politics, but sometimes that's just not possible.'

I took the notebook from him and returned it to its shelf. 'Well, if you're not here, I don't know how I'm going to manage,' I said. 'You go down into the hiding-place at midday on the 15th and don't come out for twenty-four hours. The celebrations will have finished by then.' 'Put like that, it sounds pretty easy.' 'It won't be easy, David. It will be very hard to shut yourself up in the dark for twenty-four hours. You'd better get used to it gradually.'

When I walked towards the stable, dusk was falling, and everyone who'd helped with Paul's second burial was sitting on the ground, most of them smoking cigarettes. They were discussing who would have won the fight, Cassius Clay or Uzcudun, had the two boxers been active at the same time. Ubanbe was saying: 'You've got to bear in mind that the night before a fight, Uzcudun and company used to sleep with three or four women apiece, and of course, being normal filthy swine like you and me, they fucked until they dropped, and the following day, they'd stagger into the ring and not even have the strength to fight a paper bag. Nowadays, though, boxers are better prepared, and there's no comparison . . .' Ubanbe interrupted his explanation when he noticed my presence. 'Haven't you slept long enough, David?' he asked. 'You look like a right daydream!' Everyone burst out laughing, and Pancho

172

continued shrieking for some time afterwards, imitating the neighing of the horses. 'He got drunk during the lunch your uncle treated us to, and now he thinks he's a horse,' Ubanbe explained. Opin slapped Pancho on the back. 'We should put him up to fight Tony García. He could kick him into submission,' he said. Lubis came over to me: 'I'm going home. I'm fed up with listening to them.' 'I'll come with you,' I said. 'Goodbye, Mr Half-asleep!' said Ubanbe, and they all roared with laughter again.

'Are you going to the woods tomorrow, Lubis?' I asked, as we walked past the paddock. 'I haven't much option. You've seen the state my brother's in. He's completely out of it. He says this will be the best fiesta ever in Obaba, and that's all he can think about.' 'Could we go together?' 'Of course. I'll drop by Adela's house at nine to pick up the food, and we'll be back by midday. There are only three groups working in the woods at the moment.' 'Great, that way we'll be in time to say goodbye to Juan. You know he's decided not to wait for Uzcudun before returning to America.' 'Yes, he told me.' I was relieved to find that I was still capable of talking to Lubis.

XV

We collected the food that Adela had prepared and set off into the woods at nine o'clock on the dot. Unlike the times when we used to go riding on Ava and Faraón, we rode in almost a straight line, with no diversions, no looking for the gentler inclines, but trying to gain height as quickly as possible. We found ourselves in areas of dense forest where the light didn't penetrate, and with slopes made slippery by rain; but by dint of constant tugging at Moro, who didn't know the route and kept resisting, we managed to advance step by step, not saying a word, concentrating all our efforts on getting past any obstacles, and we only stopped when we reached the first of the cabins.

'Why didn't you come up the centipede track?' one of the wood-cutters from the sawmill asked us. The 'centipedes' were the trucks used for transporting the tree trunks. 'We didn't come from the village today,' Lubis explained. 'We came from Iruain, and Adela, the shepherd's wife, prepared the food.' The woodcutter had curly hair, and when he smiled it was as if his lips curled too. He turned his attention to me. 'Lubis, look at the state of your friend here. He's drenched in sweat.' It was true. My shirt collar was wet through. 'It'll do me good,' I said. 'They say that sweating gets rid of toxins.' The man grabbed an axe lying on a felled tree and offered it to me: 'If you want to sweat, come and work with us.' The blade of the axe reflected the morning light like a mirror.

Lubis took a saucepan out of Moro's basket. The woodcutter lifted the lid to see what it contained. 'Stewed meat and tomatoes. It's not roast chicken, but we'll eat it anyway.' He was in a good mood and was soon smiling again. Suddenly, he threw the axe as if it were a machete, and it stuck fast in a tree about five yards away.

'What are the people in the village saying about the woodcutter, then?' he asked me. I didn't understand. 'What woodcutter?' 'Uzcudun! Didn't you know that before he became a boxer, he used to work with an axe, just like us?' This, I told him, was news to me. 'Where are you from?' 'From here. I'm Juan Imaz's nephew.' He hesitated, then said: 'The accordionist's son?'

Lubis rejoined us once he'd left the contents of the saucepan in the cabin. 'How many loaves of bread do you need?' 'Eight will do.' They were large loaves. 'So Uzcudun's coming to the village fiesta,' the man said to Lubis, clutching the loaves in his arms. 'I'd come too for 15,000 pesetas!' replied Lubis. That was a considerable sum of money in the Obaba of 1966. 'Me too!' exclaimed the man. 'Not many people get to eat their bread without having to work for it.' 'Don't complain,' said Lubis, 'some people have no bread to eat at all.' He patted Moro's back, and the donkey set off unhesitatingly along the path going into the wood. 'He knows the way from here,' said Lubis, 'so we won't have to keep dragging him along. You'll see, David, he'll lead the way.'

The woodcutter with the curly hair waved goodbye from the door of the cabin. He must have been about fifty, and I couldn't imagine him either older or younger. It seemed to me that he would always be the

174

same, standing at the door of that cabin, clutching those eight loaves of bread.

It was delightful to plunge into the depths of the forest, with nothing to worry about apart from the route picked out for us by Moro. The simple act of breathing was pleasurable, and to this was added – pleasure upon pleasure – the peace I felt at finding myself in that particular world: not the world of Ángel or of Berlino, nor that of Adrián, Joseba and my other fellow students, but in the forest, where it was still possible to find people from the past. And there was another flame burning in my mind – a third cause for pleasure. After my conversation with Juan, I'd decided not to play the accordion at the fiesta over which Uzcudun would preside.

Now and then, as we crossed the darkest areas of the wood, I felt as I had years before, again with Lubis and his brother Pancho, when I'd first encountered the pool in the cave. I saw the drops of water hanging from the edges of the ferns, and they looked to me like crystal, like the drops that used to spring up when we struck the surface of the water in the cave. During those moments, my First Eyes and my Second Eyes were seeing the same landscape.

It was, alas, not a very stable feeling. As with those cheap holograms you can buy in souvenir shops, in which the same person appears one minute clothed from neck to ankles and the next stark naked, so the forest was constantly being transformed before my eyes. I took a step and I was suddenly in that other cave full of shadows. My Second Eyes would impose themselves then on my First Eyes, and I would see, parading before me, Berlino, Ángel, the American, the good mayor Humberto, César's father – Bernardino, Lubis' father – Eusebio, Goena Senior, Goena Junior and all the others. And for the first time, these shadows spoke to me: 'Why did they kill me? I never harmed anyone,' said Humberto. And the American: 'So you want to wear my hat, do you, the grey Hotson hat I bought in Winnipeg?' And Eusebio: 'Are we always going to go on like this, killing each other?' And Berlino: 'We know you spent the whole day in Teresa's room. Gregorio told us.

175

Geneviève and I are waiting for you in the hotel to clear the matter up. There'll be hell to pay if you did get up to mischief.' And Ángel: 'I know you're not practising. You'll make a fool of yourself on the day of the inauguration. You'll shame me in front of all those important people.' These voices made me so nervous that Lubis would occasionally glance at me anxiously. 'Are you feeling faint, David? Have some water.' But I didn't need water. I only needed to hear Lubis speak in order to escape the filthy cave. His voice swept away those murmuring shadows and returned me to the forest of Obaba.

One morning, we heard rockets being let off. 'It's only four days to the fiesta, and they've already started celebrating,' said Lubis. 'There'll be masses of people there this year,' I replied. 'Everyone will want to see Uzcudun. You heard the woodcutters. They talk of nothing else.' It was true. The woodcutters felt a special sympathy for the boxer who, as the man with the curly hair had put it, 'also used to work with an axe'. 'And I've seen Ubanbe and company training by the stables,' I added. 'This whole business has really gone to their heads.' Lubis smiled: 'Well, it doesn't take much.'

When we reached the edge of the forest, the little hamlet of Iruain opened up before us. It was a beautiful day, and the place seemed larger than normal, as if it had grown. The sky was very high, and the sun too. The stream, made muddy by the rains, now ran with water so clear it seemed to be made of tiny fragments of mirror. The houses – Uncle Juan's, Lubis', Adela's, Ubanbe's, the mill – all appeared to be sleeping. And the horses, dogs, sheep and chickens we could see next to the houses appeared to be sleeping too.

In the sky, a tiny cloud formed: the explosion of yet another of the morning's rockets. 'I want to tell you something, Lubis.' He stopped. So did Moro. 'I'm not going to play at the inauguration.' 'No, I'm not going either,' he replied. I felt like walking over to the stream and sitting down on a stone on the bank, but I didn't move. What would have been perfectly normal with Adrián or Teresa, taking them aside in order to share a confidence, didn't feel right with Lubis. 'Although I don't know if you can get out if it that easily, David,' he went on. 'Your name's in

176

the programme.' 'I haven't even seen it,' I said with some amazement. 'Along with a photo.' 'Really?' Teresa, I thought, had probably asked her father to include it. 'Adela's got a copy, you can see for yourself.' 'I wanted to ask you something,' I said. He stood waiting. The stream flowed past in silence. 'I've noticed that you always avoid Ángel. And I wondered if it's because he and your father were enemies during the war.' I found it hard to talk, but forced myself to continue: 'I suppose you know that they, Ángel, Berlino and the others, but especially Ángel, wanted to shoot your father. Ángel actually pursued him.' My confession was over. 'Your Uncle Juan saved him,' said Lubis. 'He hid my father when the patrols were out looking for him.'

Moro had started cropping the grass on the bank of the stream, but Lubis gave him a couple of slaps to get him moving again. 'It's nearly thirty years since the war ended, David, and nearly seven since my father died. To be perfectly honest, I've forgotten all those stories.' He started walking again. 'I don't believe you. I can't.' He beckoned me to follow. 'Come on. We've got to take the empty saucepans back to Adela. She likes to have them washed in time for the evening.'

I felt furious with Moro. He was advancing ever more quickly towards Adela's house and seemed to be dragging Lubis with him, as if they were joined by some invisible thread. It was difficult to hold a conversation at that pace.

We reached the bridge, opposite Iruain. Suddenly, the thread joining the donkey and my friend broke. Moro trotted over to Adela's house, and Lubis sat down on the bridge parapet. 'Do you know why Moro is in such a hurry?' he said. 'Because Adela gives him the coffee grounds to eat. And as far as he's concerned, there's no better treat in the whole world.'

He picked up a twig from the ground and threw it into the stream. 'Your father and mine had a serious falling-out,' he said. 'Before the war, certain people used to come here in a truck. They'd round up a few men and take them off to various houses of ill repute in San Sebastián. They paid a kind of all-in fee.' 'And my father was involved in this, was he?' I asked. Lubis threw another twig in the water. 'I wouldn't go that far, but the truck used to go to all the village fiestas, and sometimes your father went too. With his accordion, of course. But – I don't know – my father may have been wrong. He was very Christian. Too Christian, I think. And he couldn't stand that business with the truck. It seemed to him shameful to treat people like animals. And in the end he reported them.' Lubis stood up. 'The owners of the truck had to appear before the bishop. And the bishop threatened them with excommunication. That's why your father hated mine so much. And then, when the war came, well, they killed whoever they could.'

The twins appeared on the path, leading Moro by a rope. When they reached the paddock, they opened the gate and ushered him in. Faraón, Zizpa, Ava, Blaky and Mizpa were standing by the fence, but didn't even deign to look at Moro.

Opposite Adela's house there were some smooth stones in the stream that acted as stepping-stones. 'You're worrying yourself about ancient history, David,' Lubis said when we crossed to the other side. We were about twenty yards from Adela's kitchen; I only had that distance in which to bring up the other subject that interested me. 'What stories *do* worry you, Lubis? Why do you avoid meeting my father? Because of what happened when Paul was killed? I've heard certain things . . .'

Adela came out to greet us 'I've given the twins their lunch, so today we can eat in peace,' she called to us. When Lubis and I took the wood-cutters their lunch, we all ate together. 'What about Sebastián?' asked Lubis. 'I've got him cleaning out the chicken-run,' said Adela. 'Lately, I can't get him to stay home at all. But he'll learn. I'm not as kind-hearted as you, Lubis. If Pancho were my brother, I'd give him a good hiding and take him down a peg or two.' She waved her arm about as if she had a stick in her hand. 'If Pancho was your brother, Adela, you'd have to take the woodcutters their food yourself,' retorted Lubis. Adela gave a loud sigh and ushered us into the house. Once we were in the kitchen, she showed me the programme for the fiesta and said: 'It's a really good photo of you, David!' It was a photo taken some years before, one I didn't recognise. I assumed Teresa must have supplied it.

178

We sat down at the table. 'Nothing out of the ordinary happened when the horse died, David,' Lubis said to me softly. 'You should forget about all these stories and work out how you're going to get out of playing at the inauguration. It won't be easy, especially now you're in the programme. They'll come looking for you.'

'It's true! Someone did come looking for you!' cried Adela, who had caught Lubis' last remark. 'Martín from the hotel came to see you! And he brought a crate of champagne too! It's over there!' Then she started complaining loudly that her children were driving her half-demented, especially Sebastián, which is why everything slipped her mind. 'And what did he say?' 'Well, apparently he passed his exam, and it's all thanks to you. That's why he brought the champagne. He wanted to celebrate. He left about a quarter of an hour before you got back. Honestly, how could I have forgotten!'

The crate was next to the hearth and contained six very flashy bottles of French champagne. 'Oh, and he said something else.' She raised her hand to her head, as if trying to concentrate. 'He'll come and fetch you on Friday. They want to have a rehearsal at the hotel before the inauguration. Teresa will be travelling back from France that day.' She sighed again and picked up the crate, still complaining about her bad memory. 'I'll put a few bottles in the fridge for when you need them,' she said.

Adela removed the earthenware pot from the stove and placed it on the table. 'It's fiesta time, so today we're having roast chicken!' she announced. She started serving us pieces of chicken. 'That Martín is a bit of a performer too,' she said. 'He picked up a few bottles of wine and you should have seen him juggle them, just like they do at the circus. He says he's going to amaze everyone at the banquet for Uzcudun.' 'Not us,' replied Lubis, and he winked at me. 'No, really, he's very good. The trouble is that now Sebastián is trying to do the same thing. He's smashed two bottles already. That son of mine will be the death of me, I mean it.' 'Sebastián wants to learn too many things, that's his problem,' said Lubis. 'Which is why I sent him to the chicken-run,' declared Adela, 'so that he can learn how to clean up chicken poop.

179

Let him sweat a little, while we eat like kings.' She raised the first bit of chicken to her mouth with a smile of satisfaction.

XVI

I heard laughter outside, cheerful whooping and the tinkle of glass, and when I looked out of my bedroom window, I saw Ubanbe and Opin wearing shorts and boxing gloves. They were in the same place as before, in the corner formed by the fence, and for spectators they had Lubis, Pancho, the twins, Sebastián and three of the woodcutters from the sawmill. Sebastián was holding an empty bottle which he occasionally banged with a spoon. One strike announced the beginning or the end of a round; a series of rapid strikes indicated some irregularity.

When I went over to join the group, I saw that the fight between Ubanbe and Opin was not just play; both had red marks on their faces. 'I'm out of breath!' said Ubanbe after a while. His chest was running with sweat. 'You've got no stamina, Ubanbe!' said Sebastián. 'You've only fought seven rounds, and you're shattered already. At the fiesta, Tony García will beat the living daylights out of you.' The three wood-cutters burst out laughing. 'What do you mean "beat the living daylights out of me"? It's going to be an exhibition match, idiot,' replied Ubanbe. 'You're the one who's going to get the living daylights beaten out of him if you're not careful!' 'To hell with Tony García!' cried Pancho. And again the woodcutters guffawed loudly.

Ubanbe pointed at Sebastián: 'This little squirt here says someone brought you some bottles of champagne. What are you planning to do with them, David? Drink them all yourself? Just in case you're inter-ested, I'm dying of thirst.' 'Me too,' added Pancho. 'Take no notice of them,' said Lubis. 'Let them drink water from the river.' 'No, Lubis, it's a good idea. Let's all go and have supper at Adela's place. And we can drink the champagne together.' 'Now you're talking!' cried Ubanbe. The woodcutters indicated that they wouldn't be able to join us, and left after a brief goodbye. Ubanbe watched them leave with a look of scorn on his face: 'We're better off without those dimwits anyway. More champagne for us!'

Everyone laughed again. But I did not. It wasn't any feeling of happiness that had prompted me to invite them to supper, but a desire to finish what I'd begun. There was quite a lot of light in the filthy cave, and I could already make out fairly clearly the features of each of the shadows, those of the murderers and those of the victims. Only one question remained unanswered: what exactly happened when the horse Paul had been found dead? I was convinced that Ubanbe and Pancho would tell me what Lubis had preferred not to, especially if there was plenty of champagne to loosen their tongues.

There were five empty bottles in the kitchen sink, and only the sixth remained on the table. Pancho had fallen asleep in a rocking chair; Lubis and I were drinking coffee; Adela and Ubanbe were sipping champagne from ordinary glasses. 'I'll finish my coffee and then I'll go home,' said Lubis. 'What's the hurry?' asked Ubanbe. 'You haven't got to go to the forest tomorrow. Isidro has given us a week's holiday. He says he's going to work on his own at the sawmill until the festivities are over.' He shook the bottle to see if there was any fizz left in the champagne. 'He's going to work? Surely not, Andrés,' said Adela, addressing him by his real name. 'Even Isidro stops working sometimes.' 'Oh, right, like this fellow here,' and he pointed at Lubis. He moved his whole body with every gesture he made. 'You heard what he just said. He's going home. He doesn't have to get up early tomorrow, but he's perfectly capable of working, even during a fiesta. Just like Isidro.' 'Well, I'm not,' said Pancho, rousing himself slightly from his torpor. 'Come off it, Pancho, you never do any work at all,' retorted Ubanbe, emptying into his glass what little champagne remained in the bottle.

Ubanbe's cigar had burned out in the ashtray, and he was trying to re-light it. 'I have to clean out the horses,' said Lubis. 'Not the one we buried the other day,' said Ubanbe. 'He was as clean as a whistle!' The cigar refused to light. 'Do you mean Paul?' I asked. 'Ah, Paul! God, he was a beautiful horse!' said Adela. 'Why do they say that my father killed him?' I asked loudly. Lubis and Adela both stared at me. 'You know how people like to talk . . .' Adela couldn't finish her sentence. Ubanbe interrupted her. 'Who else could it have been, David?' he exclaimed with an interrogative lift of his chin. 'A hunter? But what hunter? Who's ever seen a hunter round here?' He was sitting leaning with his back against the wall. 'Some people said it was the civil guard,' suggested Adela. 'The civil guard? They never come around here either. The only person anyone saw was the accordionist, and no one else. Ask him.' He pointed at Lubis. 'You talk too much, Ubanbe,' Lubis said, getting up from the table. 'You talked too much then and you talk too much now.' Ubanbe got up too, clumsy and unsteady on his feet. 'You listen to me, Lubis,' he shouted. 'I didn't say a word at the time. You know perfectly well who screwed things up.' This time he pointed at Pancho. 'Your brother!'

Pancho tried to stand. Lubis grabbed his arm and shoved him unceremoniously in the direction of the door. He turned to Ubanbe, stern-faced. 'Don't speak so loudly,' he said, controlling his voice, 'and calm down.' Ubanbe was almost eighteen inches taller than Lubis, but looking at them both, one had the feeling that, if it came to a fight, Lubis would prove the more difficult opponent for Tony García to beat. 'He's right,' said Adela. 'You'll wake the twins up shouting like that.' 'We're going,' said Lubis, and he left, taking his brother with him.

The kitchen seemed suddenly empty. Outside, the south wind was beating against the windows. Further off, in the forest, on the hills, in the mountains, it would be blowing hard, stripping the trees of their dry leaves.

'So what happened, then? Can *you* tell me?' I asked Adela. I couldn't go back now. 'What can I say, David?' Adela folded her hands in her lap. 'At first, when the horse was found dead, we thought perhaps it had been struck by lightning, but then we saw that someone had shot it in the head. I saw it myself. They'd shot him right here.' Adela placed her hand next to her ear. 'No, not there, Adela. That's *your* ear,' said Ubanbe in a slurred voice. He had finally managed to re-light what remained of his cigar and kept taking long drags on it. 'Then, of course, the rumours started flying,' Adela went on. 'For a long time, it was all anyone talked about. And, how can I put it . . . certain people, especially certain kids, started putting it around that it could have been your father . . .' Ubanbe thumped the table with his fist. 'Pancho saw him! And so did Lubis! Ángel came to Iruain with one of those *señoritas*, thinking that no one would notice, and as soon as he tried to get stuck in, what do you know, the horse started neighing, and so he kept trying and the horse kept neighing. Anyway, the horse wouldn't let him fuck in peace, and suddenly, because, as we all know, Ángel has a very short fuse, he picked up his pistol and shot the horse through the head, which silenced the horse for good. What we don't know is whether or not he continued screwing after he'd killed the horse. You'd have to ask Pancho that.'

Ubanbe was about to go on, but the smoke from his cigar made him cough. 'Whether Pancho really did see all this or not, nobody knows,' said Adela. 'The one thing we do know is that some of you believed it and the story spread.' 'In Obaba, *everyone* believed it!' Ubanbe again thumped the table. Adela shook her head. 'Your mother came to talk to Lubis,' she said, turning to me. 'Carmen is from Iruain and knows us well. And naturally, she wanted to talk to Lubis. Not to Ubanbe or to Pancho. Lubis could only have been twelve at the time, but he had a better head on his shoulders than either of them. And he explained the whole thing to her very clearly. He said that Pancho wasn't to be trusted, that he was always coming up with dirty stories and that he was quite capable of inventing anything. And Carmen went away quite happy.' 'You *do* know a lot, Adela!' exclaimed Ubanbe. His eyes were closed. 'Go home before you fall asleep, and leave us in peace,' ordered Adela.

Ubanbe finally got up and tucked his white shirt into his trousers. He had his cigar gripped in the corner of his mouth. 'How come you know so much, Adela? You still haven't said.' Adela answered me, not him: 'Beatriz told me.' Ubanbe was standing at the kitchen door. 'Well, if you know so much, tell him the state we found Lubis in just two days later.' 'What do you mean?' I asked. 'He was covered in blood, his face, his chest, everything. He was crouching by the stream, trying to wash away the bloodstains. Didn't you know?' I shook my head. 'Hm, I thought you were brighter than that,' said Ubanbe scornfully.

Adela and I remained alone in the kitchen. 'Who beat him up? My father?' I asked. 'Ángel was like a mad thing because of that rumour. And it wasn't surprising really. Everyone was pointing the finger at him. And he thought Lubis must have been to blame, because he'd spoken to Carmen. And that was the result. Lubis' whole face swelled up. And do you know who looked after him until he was better? Carmen. Carmen was so upset that she begged Beatriz to let her take care of him. We'd all be there, waiting outside the house. Don Hipólito too. And Lubis got better much more quickly than anyone could ever have expected.'

'They should have reported my father!' I cried. 'My mother should have brought charges against him!' I loathed them both, my mother as much as my father. Adela took a while before responding: 'That's what the doctor wanted, but Beatriz wouldn't let him. Beatriz is a real Christian. Like your mother. She knows how to forgive.' 'But it was Lubis who got beaten up, not his mother.' My hatred extended to Beatriz as well. 'Lubis is ashamed of the whole episode. He doesn't want to remember the beating he was given. You know what he's like, he doesn't let anyone push him around.' 'No one would dare to try it now,' I said. 'No, of course not. Now, everyone respects him. You saw Ubanbe's reaction. He's twice as big as Lubis, but even so, he backed down.'

I felt like hugging Lubis, but he might not have liked that. He was angry when he left. 'There's only one thing that saddens me, David,' Adela said. 'That my sons are going to turn out like Ubanbe and the others. They're certainly nothing like Lubis.' I went over to the door. 'Put tonight's supper on my account,' I said. 'We've been remembering a lot of sad things tonight,' Adela said, 'but we'd better cheer up now. It's almost time for the fiesta.' 'Yes,' I replied, 'the day after tomorrow.' 'The mistake you made, David, was not bringing your accordion with you. If you had, we'd have spent the whole evening dancing and singing, and there'd have been no time for quarrels.' 'Next time,' I replied and waved goodbye.

When I went outside, the south wind was blowing hard enough not

184

only to carry off the dry leaves or the moths that had come out that
night, but even the birds. I walked back to Iruain feeling shrunk in upon
myself, barely able to walk.

XVII

I have before me a photograph of the day the monument was unveiled.
It wasn't taken in the square in Obaba or on the sportsground, but on
the mirador of the Hotel Alaska. There are more than twenty people
there, and right in the middle, elegantly dressed, is the guest of honour,
the ex-boxer Uzcudun, the man whom the Americans, thinking he was
Italian, used to call Paolino. Beside him, to left and right, are Berlino,
Colonel Degrela, the colonel's daughter, Ángel and a young man who
looks like a boxer and who must be none other than Tony García; Ángel
has his accordion with him. Behind that first group, as if forming two
wings, are another fifteen or so men, all smiling and all dressed as
elegantly as Uzcudun himself. Amongst them are the owner of a well-
known Madrid bar, the civil governors of the Basque provinces, the
minister for sport, a few local businessmen and a dozen or so journalists. In one corner are Martín, Gregorio, Sebastián, Ubanbe and
Geneviève. The first three are wearing the black jackets of waiters;
Geneviève is wearing a chef's hat; and Ubanbe is frowning and in shirt-
sleeves, with his right eye slightly swollen.

Teresa and I aren't in the photo. Teresa, because, according to
Sebastián, she stayed in her room throughout the fiesta; I, because I hid
at Iruain. Just as I'd planned and just as I'd promised Juan and Lubis.

I stayed in the hiding-place for thirty hours. When Lubis lifted the trapdoor, he found me with the Hotson hat on my head. 'What are you up
to, David?' he asked, smiling. His anger of the previous evening had
apparently been forgotten. 'I didn't think you knew about this place,' I
said. 'Of course I do. This is where my father hid!' He gave me his hand
and helped me up the steps. 'Well, you concealed the fact very well,'

185

I said. 'I had no option.' 'Juan assured me that no one else knew about it, and that I must keep it a secret.' He laughed: 'You see, I'm not the only one who has to pretend.'

The window in the room was closed and the curtains drawn, and yet even so, the light bothered me. Lubis sat down on the bed, and I started doing some exercises, pacing from one side to the other, as if I were measuring the room. 'You've had loads of visitors, David.' 'I know,' I replied, 'I was terrified. Especially when Berlino turned up. I think he and my father must have stood right here, next to the wardrobe. Do you know what he said to Ángel? "Your son's a real escape artist. Do you remember that time we wanted to give the colonel's daughter that horse? He gave us the slip then as well."' We both laughed. 'They couldn't enjoy the fiesta, and they're really angry. There was a boycott and people distributed propaganda. Look at this.'

He took a flyer out of his pocket. I went over to the window and read: 'Boycott fascism. Boycott Uzcudun and all the other fascists. *Gora Euskadi Askatuta*. We want a free Basque Country.' It was the first time I'd come across such language. 'Who else came?' I asked, while I opened the window a crack. In the distance, I saw that the forests had grown red, as if they'd suddenly changed colour. 'I only know what Adela told me: that Martín and Gregorio came yesterday, then Berlino and your father. And this morning, very early, Teresa. I think she's angry too.' 'I'm not surprised. I'll have to write to her in Pau.'

'Now don't be frightened by what I'm about to tell you, David.' Lubis said, looking very serious. 'The civil guard came as well, in two Land-rovers.' I found it hard to grasp what he was saying. 'Looking for me?' I asked at last. He nodded. 'They came a couple of hours ago. I was in the stables with the horses. They surrounded me. "Here he is, Lieutenant," one of them said. "Are you David?" the Lieutenant asked me. When I told him I wasn't, he said: "Do you know where he is?" I told him you'd be at the fiesta, that everyone had gone to the banquet. And then they left, and that was that.' I said nothing. It made no sense at all. 'Don't get frightened.' 'But I haven't done anything. Why would they come looking for me?' 'You were supposed to play the accordion and you didn't. But they can hardly put you in prison for that.'

I opened the window wide. Everything was quiet. There was a sweetness in the air, as always when autumn comes. 'Juan said you should phone Don Hipólito and that the two of you should present yourself at the barracks as soon as possible.' 'You've spoken to my uncle?' 'No, your mother phoned him.' My heart was beating fast, and the palms of my hands were sweating. 'Hurry up. Your mother and Don Hipólito will be waiting for you.' 'But how am I going to get there?' The civil guards' barracks were next to the station. At that moment, the distance seemed insuperable. 'I brought your new Guzzi motorbike. It's outside.' He took the flyer from me. 'You'd better not take that with you,' he added with a smile. 'Don't worry, David. We'll be having coffee together tonight in the restaurant in the square.' 'I don't know if I'll be able to keep my nerve,' I said. We went downstairs and left the house.

'I don't like denunciations,' said the Lieutenant. He was very young and wore very small glasses that gave him an intellectual air. 'The war's been over for nearly thirty years, and there are certain police procedures which are, in my view, outmoded,' he went on. 'I try to keep to the Christian law.' It was clear from his accent that he was Spanish not Basque. 'I'm glad to hear you say that,' said Don Hipólito, the priest. 'Besides, in this case, there's no basis for the denunciation at all. To say that this young man is responsible for yesterday's incidents is ridiculous – a nonsense.' My mother spoke next: 'I know he didn't turn up to play the accordion. But so what? He didn't do that as part of a boycott, but simply because he doesn't like being an accordionist. And that's his father's fault. He's forced him to play ever since he was a child, and, of course, now the boy's seventeen, he's starting to rebel.'

The Lieutenant had a piece of paper before him. He glanced at it before he began speaking again. 'Maybe so, but there's another matter I'd like to clear up too,' he said. We all stood looking at him. 'It seems that David was mixed up in some business involving pornographic magazines, and that he was expelled from school because of that.' I noticed that beside the piece of paper was a flyer like the one Lubis had shown me. The priest burst out laughing. He even clapped his hands before exclaiming: 'Oh, really!' He then went on – in a Spanish as correct as the Lieutenant's – to explain the incident with the magazine, and concluded by naming my many good qualities. 'I'll make no bones about it, Lieutenant: David is an exemplary young man,' he concluded.

The Lieutenant smiled discreetly. 'There's one other matter. The boy's uncle, Juan Imaz.' He was holding another piece of paper. 'Apparently, when he's here, he often goes to France. Almost every week. There are suggestions that he meets people there who are intent on attacking the State.' Don Hipólito sprang to his feet: 'Oh really, what rubbish! You have, if I may say so, been very badly informed. That's not the reason Juan goes to Biarritz. May I speak to you privately?'

For a few moments, they stood in one corner of the room talking. When they returned, the Lieutenant was smiling a rather grave smile. 'You were very wise to marry young,' Don Hipólito said to him. 'I'm most grateful for your collaboration,' said the Lieutenant, bringing the interview to a close. 'You may leave now.'

I set off on my new Guzzi, and as I drove, I had only one thought in my head – who could have denounced me? I was surprised when I realised how long the list of suspects was. Berlino was one of them, of course. And Teresa, above all, Teresa. Anyone capable of giving me the notebook with the gorilla on the cover could easily have decided to denounce me when I stood her up. But there was also Gregorio, who, ever since he found out about my relationship with Teresa, had doubt-less loathed me and longed for revenge. And what about Martín, whom I'd let down on what was, for him, a very important occasion? It was disheartening: the wheel of time presented me with ever sadder reali-ties. Lists of the executed and of informers, instead of lists of people I loved.

I was nearing Obaba. Despite the noise of the motorcycle engine, I heard the sound of a rocket exploding. And of another immediately afterwards. And of a third seconds later. For the first time in ages, those three explosions found an echo inside me. They cheered me up. I told myself that I mustn't be overwhelmed by sombre thoughts, that the wheel of time would eventually bring me happier days. Several other rockets exploded in the sky, and I squeezed the accelerator on the handle of my bike.

'I've been talking to Don Hipólito,' my mother said to me once I was home. I'd showered and put on clean clothes. 'You've been through a very bad patch lately, and you could do with the help of a psychologist before you start university. I can call the one you saw at school, if you like.' 'How do I look?' I asked her, studying my reflection in the workshop mirror. 'Very handsome,' she said. 'I need the hat, though. I'll bring it tomorrow from Iruain.' 'What hat? Juan's? The cowboy hat?' 'You'll see tomorrow.' My mother went over to the door: 'So what do you think about the psychologist, then? Will you go?' 'Certainly not. I've never felt better.' And I meant it. 'As you wish,' she said, 'and don't worry about your father. I've spoken to him on the phone. He won't nag you about the accordion any more.' 'I want to leave, Mama,' I said. 'I'll find a student flat in San Sebastián and I'll stay there while I'm studying. I'll come back often. And you can come and see me too.' She said nothing at first, then repeated what she had said before: 'As you wish, David.'

In the square, a band had started up. 'What are you going to do, do you want to eat here or go to the fiesta?' my mother asked with a touch of sadness in her voice. It wasn't easy for her to accept my decision. 'I'm on my own tonight,' she went on. 'Ángel will be staying up at the hotel. You know how it is, he's with Uzcudun morning, noon and night.' I said that I'd have supper with her, and then we could go out together.

I had a sense that I loved her in a different way. In part, I felt sorry for her because at a given moment, in her youth, her heart had deceived her, propelling her into the arms of a man capable of killing and betraying his fellow man, but, at the same time, I admired her for not having been carried along with him. She remained her own mistress.

We began setting the table for supper. 'Is it true what Don Hipólito told the Lieutenant?' I asked. 'What did he tell him?' 'I think you know.'

She said she didn't. 'What does Uncle Juan go to Biarritz to do? To dance with tourists from Paris?' 'Juan has never liked dancing,' she responded very gravely. 'Are you sure?' 'Ask him yourself. I have to phone him to say that you're home.' 'I will! I'll ask him myself!'

I didn't ask him. As soon as I heard his voice on the phone, so pleased to know that they'd let me go, I was too overcome by emotion to say a single word.

Obaba's first American

When he returned from Alaska and set about getting the hotel built, Don Pedro was a very fat man who, it was said, used to weigh himself each day on a modern set of scales he'd brought with him from France. 'Apparently, it's the first thing he does every morning,' said the people of Obaba, unfamiliar with such customs. 'After he's weighed himself, he picks up a pencil and writes whatever the scales say on the wall.' These remarks were quite accurate. When civil war broke out in 1936, the soldiers who searched the hotel found his bathroom walls covered in numbers that all hovered around the 265 pound mark: 266; 262; 270 . . . On some sections of the wall there were so many numbers that they were nothing but a grey blur.

Don Pedro did not watch his weight for reasons of health, although he knew that losing twenty or thirty pounds would relieve the occasional breathing difficulties he experienced, nor was he driven to do so by concern for his physical appearance, given that in the years before the war – 1933, 1934 – the shadow cast by tuberculosis was hardly an encouragement to be thin. In fact, this weighing-in ritual was merely a hobby. At the weekly *tertulias*, or get-togethers, at the coffee shop in the hotel or out on the hotel mirador, he would make a point of introducing, right at the start of the conversation, some reference to how much weight he had lost or gained, and his words had a way of setting an appropriately cheerful note. 'I've lost half a pound already this week,' or 'I've put on three pounds,' Don Pedro would say, and the friends gathered there with him, especially Obaba's three schoolteachers, would give free rein to their laughter and their jokes.

On some occasions – for fear that repetition might lead to boredom – he would forget about his weight and take as his subject the grey J.B. Hotson hat he had brought back from America. The theme of his story was, in this case, the hat's extraordinary ability to elude its owner and to disappear. 'Do you know where I found it this morning?' Don Pedro would exclaim. 'In the bread oven! How can a hat made in Canada possibly feel the cold?' It was this brand of humour that pleased his friends most.

Almost everyone in Obaba and in the surrounding area referred to him as 'Don Pedro' or 'the American', but there were other people, less well-disposed toward him, who preferred a third name: the Bear. This had nothing to do with his heavy build or with any other aspect of his physical appearance – he was plump and gently rounded, like Oliver Hardy – but was intended as a calumny, to give credence to one of the versions, the most contemptible of all, of how his brother had died. The story went that his brother, who always joined him when he went prospecting for silver, had died in a forest in Alaska, killed by a bear, 'which attacked him while he was out hunting', as Don Pedro himself had told the few relatives he still had in Obaba, but this story was twisted by certain malicious people, who said: 'The only bear in that forest was him. He killed his own brother so as not to have to share the profits from the silver mine they were working. That's how come he owns the hotel and drives around in that big car.' The car, a beige-and-brown Chevrolet, was the only one of its kind in Obaba at the time. It made even more of an impression than the hotel.

No crueller calumny could have been invented than the one about that hypothetical murder. In the first place, because Don Pedro was in Vancouver on the day of the disaster, renewing some documents to do with the mine, but, above all, because, police evidence aside, the two brothers really loved each other: they were Abel and Abel, and certainly not Cain and Abel. Unfortunately, as the Bible so rightly says, slander is sweet to the ears, and the slander that the malicious tongues of Obaba had put around soon spread.

Those who worked hardest at spreading the slander were also the most fiercely Catholic, those who should have paid most attention to the Bible. They hated Don Pedro because he never set foot in church and because, or so they believed, his favourite topic of conversation was sex. 'The jokes he tells,' they said, 'are invariably *blue*. And the dirtier the better.' At a time when traditionalists would lock up the rooster as soon as Good Friday arrived, this was an even graver sin than killing his brother.

'Where have certain members of this village been, in America or in Sodom?' roared a preacher called Brother Víctor on Good Friday in 1935. He was an athletically-built young man, famous throughout the region for the virulence of his sermons. Whenever he got angry – whenever he climbed into the pulpit armed with *evil reports* – one vein in his neck would swell up so much it was visible even to those of the faithful watching him from the pews. He was crazy, although not entirely. His madness would only reach its peak the following year, when the civil war began.

One of the teachers who was a regular at the *tertulias* was Bernardino, whose hobby was writing poetry. After the banquet held for Don Pedro's sixtieth birthday, he recited a long dithyramb in which he referred to the defamation of which Don Pedro had been the object: '"Bear" they call you, and while the resemblance is not complete, it is true that from your mouth flows honey sweet'. He meant that Don Pedro's words were beautiful and never aggressive. Another of the teachers, Mauricio, told him then, as he often had before: 'Too much sweetness is a bad thing, Don Pedro.' Sometimes it pays to be a bit nasty. Why didn't he have them hauled up before the judge? That's what he should do; he should confront these slanderers.

Don Pedro paid no attention. He would reply with a joke or change the subject or talk to his friends about his life in North America. He would list the names of the places he had lived in – Alice Arm, Prince Rupert, Vancouver, Seattle – and he would tell them some curious anecdote, one of the many he told about his life in that continent: 'One day, there was a big strike in Seattle, and ten or so of us boys from Obaba, who always went around together, found ourselves without a cent to our names. We didn't even have anything to eat. In the end, we decided to go to a Chinese restaurant in King Street. We didn't much care for the food, but, since we couldn't pay for it, all that really mattered was that the restaurant staff were small and docile . . .'

The names of the places, people and objects that emerged from Don Pedro's memory jingled like bells in the ears of those who attended the *tertulias* at the Hotel Alaska. Most of the *tertulia* members were educated folk, who believed in progress. They liked having someone remind them that there were other countries in the world, and that not all countries were like the one they could see from the hotel's mirador, so green without, so dark within: a black province under the yoke of an equally black religion.

Of these members, it was the schoolteachers who most appreciated hearing the jingle of those distant names. Bernardino even wrote a poem entitled 'America', which, like the Unamuno poem naming the villages of Spain, listed one after the other the North American cities that Don Pedro had known: 'Seattle, Vancouver, Old Manett, New Manett; Alice Arm, Prince Rupert, Nairn Harbour . . .' They needed to be able to dream about a far-off world, because in the world they knew, in Obaba, they had to live with narrow minds and 'evil reports'. In his Holy Week sermons, some of Brother Víctor's invective was always directed at them: 'And what about these schools corrupting the souls of our children!' he would cry, and the list of accusations went on and on. At the root of it all were the voting choices made by the schoolteachers in the elections of 1934. All three had voted for the Republic. 'Why do you stay here?' Don Pedro would say to them, whenever the teachers complained. 'You're still young! Pack your bags and leave! I'll write letters of recommendation that you can present to the great and the good in Vancouver.' The teachers all shook their heads. They weren't as bold as he was. Besides, they were married. And their wives were Obaba women, of the kind who attended all the church services. Don Pedro understood his friends and continued recounting his stories and listing those names: Seattle, Vancouver, Old Manett, New Manett . . .

Time passed, and what began as a game, another way of amusing his friends, took an unexpected turn for Don Pedro. The places, people and objects from his past began to gain in volume and clarity, to grow in his mind, although not the ones you might expect, not those – like the silver mine and the miners who had worked with him – most closely related to the anecdotes he told his friends, but entirely random places, people and objects which drifted into his thoughts by chance. For example, he recalled over and over, the piece of amber containing a trapped bee that he had found in a forest near Old Manett. Or the look he got from the daughter of the Indian chief Jolinshua of Winnipeg. Or the shy black bears in Alice Arm that used to gather round the fire that he and his brother lit to make tea. Because it was true, the bears were as shy and as innocent as lambs of God; they never attacked anyone unless they were wounded.

The bears. So inoffensive, so innocent. So beautiful. But Don Pedro did not want to remember them, because from that memory he would jump to the memory of his brother and the circumstances surrounding his brother's death, far sadder than those he had described. For his brother had not been killed by a bear, even though the animal had attacked him after he had fired six shots at it. In fact, it hadn't even wounded him. Unfortunately – as Dr Corgean explained to Don Pedro when he returned from Vancouver – the incident had left such a strong impression on his brother that he had lost his mind. One night, he had escaped from the hospital and jumped into the icy waters of a lake. 'If I may, I'm going to give you a little friendly advice,' Dr Corgean said to him. 'You must watch yourself. You might have the same propensity.' 'A propensity to what?' 'To commit suicide.' He tried to explain to Dr Corgean that no such propensity had ever existed in his family, but the doctor interrupted him with a gesture: 'You'll see. I have merely given you my opinion.' Don Pedro had said nothing more, and kept his protests to himself.

He understood one day, when the places of the past began to grow in his mind, that there was perhaps a bit of truth in what Dr Corgean had said to him. On occasions, alone in his room, he would suddenly feel a great sadness, and his eyes would fill with tears. In a private conversation with Bernardino, Don Pedro confessed the reasons for his disquiet: 'When I came back from America to Obaba, I thought I was leaving exile behind me and returning home. Now, I'm not so sure. Sometimes I wonder if I'm not doing the exact opposite. Perhaps America is my real home, and this is exile.' For someone, like him, who, shortly before turning sixty, had come back to the village where he was born, this thought was very worrying indeed.

One summer night, he heard the toads singing. He was sitting out on the hotel mirador, smoking his last cigar of the day, when he had the impression that he could understand what the toads were saying – as if he were at a fantasy-theatre in Vancouver and not looking out at the hills around Obaba. *Winnipeg*, the toads were saying. *Win-ni-peg-win-ni-peg-win-ni-peg*. As night fell, when there were more stars in the sky and the south wind had dropped, when the woods around the hotel were darker, Don Pedro understood: these far-off names and the memories associated with them were having the same effect on him as the amber had had on the bee. If he didn't confront them, they would end up suffocating him.

The toads continued singing in the woods of Obaba, more delicately and charmingly than ever: *Win-ni-peg-win-ni-peg-win-ni-peg*, they repeated. They were like bells, but sadly tolling bells. He would not, he decided, give those names and memories any further opportunities to suffocate him. He would no longer talk about his life in Canada.

The other members of the Saturday *tertulias* noticed that Don Pedro now spoke about other things, but assumed this was due to the changed political situation, which, in that year of 1936, after the elections, was bad and getting steadily worse. Instead of those far-off, unknown Canadian names, the names mentioned in the conversations on the mirador were now those of the politicians of the day: Alcalá Zamora, Prieto, Maura, Aguirre, Azaña, Largo Caballero. When, in the dusk of a hot mid-July day, the toads started singing, Don Pedro sat down with his cigar on the bench on the mirador and listened uneasily. What were they saying to him after that period without memories? *Win-ni-peg! Win-ni-peg! Win-ni-peg!* replied the toads stubbornly. The song seemed to Don Pedro more urgent than ever, and, filled with sombre thoughts, he withdrew to his apartment in the hotel.

A few days later – 18th July – the bathroom scales registered 258 pounds, his lowest weight for a long time, and, as he wrote the figure on the wall, he decided that next Saturday, he would take up his old joke. He would sit out on the mirador with his friends and say to them: '258! I've lost six and a half pounds! If I carry on like this, I'll have to buy some new clothes.' He had just made this decision, when, from the mirador, he heard someone shouting and went over to the window. It was Don Miguel, one of the teachers. Despite having cycled all the way up to the hotel, he was looking deathly pale. 'Don Pedro, the army has rebelled!' he shouted. Don Pedro did not, at first, understand what these words meant. 'War has broken out in Spain, Don Pedro!' Don Miguel shouted again. 'What should we do?' Don Pedro exclaimed, taken aback. 'We must leave as soon as possible. We Republicans are in danger!' 'What, here too, Don Miguel?' The teacher pointed to a hill at the far end of the valley. 'The rebels are over there. A whole battalion is advancing on us from Navarra.'

During his life, Don Pedro had found himself in many difficult situations. On one occasion, while travelling to Prince Rupert with an Asturian friend, he had nearly frozen to death in a blizzard, and he would never forget the happy moment when they spotted a cabin in the snow, nor what they found when they went inside: a group of men sitting round a stove, listening attentively to an old man reading to them from the Bible. However, on that day, 18 July 1936, after the teacher had pedalled off on his bike, he was gripped by an unfamiliar feeling of dread. In the wilderness surrounding Prince Rupert, he had had a picture in his mind of a cabin, a warm refuge full of friends – exactly what he had found – and that image represented the whole world, or more precisely, all that was good in the world. On the other hand, the images that came into his head now were the product of fear, especially one image: the banquet held at the hotel after the Republicans won the elections; *a banquet arranged and paid for by him*, as his inner voice was at pains to remind him. This trivial fact placed him clearly on one of the two sides.

There were moments when he examined his situation and it seemed to him that it would be easy to flee to Bilbao, but, at the beginning of August, the front moved closer to Obaba, and some stretches of road became dangerous. Besides, the radio broadcasts put out by the forces opposed to the Republic never tired of repeating that anyone caught fleeing their place of residence would be deemed a criminal and summarily shot. In the end, both he and the teachers Bernardino and Mauricio decided to stay. 'We haven't harmed anyone. We'll be all right,' said Bernardino when they met to discuss the matter. As for Don Miguel, who was a more prominent figure in local politics, he had stuck with his initial plan. He would take a chance and try to reach Bilbao. His wife should be there already. 'We've got family in the city, and so we'll have a decent house to stay in,' he told his friends. Don Pedro slapped him on the back: 'You see? A man should marry! Not like me! I wouldn't have anywhere to go even if I did manage to get to Bilbao.' 'Would you like to come to *our* house, Don Pedro?' Bernardino said. 'We've sent our César to my sister's house in Zaragoza, so there's a spare room.' Don Pedro replied vehemently: 'The miner cannot abandon the mine, Bernardino.' He considered adding a joke: 'He cannot abandon the mine, still less the bathroom scales.' But he didn't feel up to it, and so said nothing.

These were long days. Don Pedro would fall into bed exhausted. He would lie there thinking, and say to himself: 'This is like a bad joke.' For the war went completely counter to everything he had imagined while in Canada. From that distance, he had dreamed of a welcoming land of small rivers and green hills, just like the land he had known as a child. In its place, he was offered the boom of cannon and the buzz of German aeroplanes coming to bomb Bilbao.

Don Pedro wished for an even greater miracle than the one called for by Joshua: to stop the Sun and the Moon and to make them go back, back to 17 July, or at least to the 18th. Because the 18th, the day on which war broke out, would have been all right too. He could have crossed over to France. France was so close! Even on foot, crossing the frontier was only a matter of hours. He regretted not having set off along the road to the frontier immediately after Don Miguel had brought him the news.

*   *   *

The first thing the forces opposed to the Republic did when they 'liberated' a village was to bring in a priest to celebrate mass in the church, as if they were afraid that, under the Republicans, the devil had established himself there. That is what they wanted to do in Obaba too, once they had forced their way into the town hall and changed the flag. However, the battalion of Navarrese *integristas* – right-wing Catholic extremists – arrived on 10 August at eleven o'clock in the morning, only hours after a few escaping militiamen had gunned down, right outside the town hall, both the old village priest and the villager who had been designated the new mayor. Captain Degrela, who was in charge of the battalion, decided to delay the mass and take reprisals. Twenty-four hours later, another seven men, chosen by the village fascists, were lying dead outside the town hall.

'You don't seem to have much fear of God,' said Captain Degrela to the young man at the head of the Obaba fascists. He had seen him finish off two of the executed men with his own gun. 'God's the only thing I *do* fear,' replied the young man. 'Who are you with? The Falangists?' asked the captain, noticing that the man wore his wavy hair slicked back with brilliantine. 'I support the army, that's all.' The young man's way of speaking indicated a certain level of education, and Captain Degrela thought that he had probably been to the seminary, the only 'higher school' to which village boys had access. 'I don't like flattery. If you really respected the army, you'd be wearing a soldier's uniform,' he said curtly. 'If I hadn't been born to a poor family in Obaba, I might be a better soldier than you are,' retorted the young man, holding the captain's gaze.

The captain stood for a moment in silence, his hands behind his back. 'What's your name?' he asked the young man. 'Marcelino.' The captain learned later on that, in the village, they called him Berlino because he had visited the German capital after seeing a cinema newsreel about the National Socialist Party. 'All right, Marcelino, I'd like you to do me a favour. Find me a priest, will you? We have to celebrate mass.' 'There's one,' said Marcelino, pointing at Brother Víctor. With a pistol stuck in the belt of his cassock, Brother Víctor was striding around inspecting the bodies of the executed men and shouting: 'They're not all here!' 'His name is Brother Víctor,' Marcelino explained. 'Bring him to me,' said the captain.

The priest was very hot and agitated, and his cassock stank of sweat. 'Brother Víctor,' said the captain quietly. 'I don't want to see you carrying a gun. I know that some members of the army allow it, but I do not. The priests should be in the church and the soldiers in the trenches. That is how God wants it, I'm sure. Kindly hand your weapon over to Marcelino and go and celebrate mass.' Brother Víctor replied in surly fashion: 'I'd be happier if you could assure me that you're going to finish what you've started.' Marcelino removed the pistol from the priest's belt. 'What do you mean?' asked the captain. 'They're not all here! The worst of them are still missing!' yelled the priest. Then he mentioned Don Pedro's name. 'He's a mason, by the way.' 'Do you know this Don Pedro?' the captain asked Marcelino. The young man nodded. 'Try to make it a beautiful mass,' the captain told Brother Víctor. This was his way of dismissing him.

'I've got a friend who's an accordionist,' Marcelino said to the captain. 'He's not bad on the organ either. I'll go and get him, if you like.' 'Who is this Don Pedro?' asked the captain, ignoring Marcelino's suggestion. 'A fat fellow who spent a few years in Canada. In the village they say that every morning he makes a note of his weight on his bathroom wall,' answered Marcelino. 'Is he a queer?' 'I wouldn't be surprised.' 'Do you agree with what the priest said?' 'There's no doubt that he voted for the Republicans. When they won the municipal elections, they celebrated at his hotel. They were all there.' Marcelino glanced across at the bodies of the executed men. A group of soldiers were piling the corpses into a truck. 'You're very well-informed. I congratulate you.' For the first time since the conversation began, Marcelino smiled. He appreciated the captain's compliment. 'Like I said, I have a friend who plays the accordion. He played at that party too.' 'If I understand you rightly, then, the queer American owns a hotel,' the captain went on. 'Yes, it's newly built and very classy. It's a couple of miles outside the village, on the side of that hill. I don't know exactly how many rooms it has, but at least thirty. And a coffee shop. He calls it Hotel Alaska.' 'And if he's a queer, then presumably he has no family?' 'Not that I know of.'

There were now two women outside the town hall, equipped with buckets of water and rags to clean up the pools of blood on the ground. 'Hey, you!' yelled the captain. 'We haven't done anything, sir!' exclaimed one of them, kneeling down. 'Who told you to do that! I don't want anything cleaned up.' He was planning to give a speech to all the boys in Obaba to encourage them to enlist in his battalion. Standing in the blood of seven village men would be a good baptism for the new soldiers.

Don Pedro met every day at the hotel with the two teachers who had decided to stay in the village, and when it came to the moment to say goodbye, he always tried discreetly to make them stay a little longer with him. 'Are you sure you don't want another coffee?' Bernardino and Mauricio would tell him that they really shouldn't stay and would then begin the descent down to the village, taking the paths through the forest. Every bend in the road could conceal a patrol. And the patrols always asked questions.

When his friends left, Don Pedro felt helpless, especially during the days that followed the initial deployment of troops, when the hotel staff, including the older ones, decided to abandon their posts – 'What's the point of us being here, Don Pedro, if there are no guests?' With the bedrooms, kitchen, lounge, coffee bar and mirador all empty, with the hills empty too – not even the toads could be heard – his mind was transported beyond his solitude, as if the Hotel Alaska were now merely an ante-room to somewhere else. To the kingdom of death? Possibly. Don Pedro tried to use his natural good humour to reassure himself, telling himself to leave all thoughts of death until he had turned eighty – but in vain. He had just heard about the men who had been shot outside the town hall. When the south wind rattled the shutters, he imagined that it was Death itself knocking on his door.

On 15 August, the Feast of the Assumption of the Blessed Virgin

Mary, Don Pedro assumed that all the soldiers would be in church, and so he decided to go down to the village. He wanted to study the situation at first hand, to seek out the people who had done work at the hotel and whom he suspected of being fascist sympathisers, and to see how they reacted. However, when he was walking across the mirador to get his car, he found himself confronted by a patrol of soldiers pointing their guns at him: some were kneeling down and those behind them were standing up, as if they were a firing squad. From their red berets, he knew they were *requetés*; not fascists exactly, but right-wing Catholics. The man in charge, a swarthy fellow in his fifties, walked towards him and said scornfully: 'So, how much did your scales say you weighed today?' '258 pounds,' replied Don Pedro as if it were a perfectly normal question. Some of the soldiers tittered. Compared with their chief, they looked like adolescents. 'The same weight as the pig we killed the other day. Except that, unlike you, everything on a pig is good to eat.' The swarthy man stuck his pistol in Don Pedro's ribs and pushed him. 'Just as I thought! He smells of perfume!' he said. More titters from the soldiers. 'Two of you stay here with me. The others, search the hotel,' he ordered.

Don Pedro had heard Don Miguel say that the Navarrese battalion was made up of ignorant country people whose main interest when they took a village was to steal the furniture and mirrors from all the houses; however, those who went into the hotel took only the weapon he kept in his bedroom, a six-shot Winchester rifle he had bought in Winnipeg. 'Where the hell did you get this?' asked the swarthy man, examining the weapon. It was a beautiful rifle, inlaid with mother-of-pearl; next to it, the weapons carried by the soldiers looked like so much junk. 'I brought it from Canada.' 'I'm going to try it,' said the swarthy man, and he walked over to the balustrade around the mirador and stared out at the trees in the woods on the hillside. He was looking for a bird. 'There's a thrush over there, Don Jaime. Just beyond the trees, in the meadow,' said one of the soldiers. The man raised the gun to his cheek and squeezed the trigger. Nothing happened. The rifle had no bullets in it. 'So our pansy's a bit of a joker, is he? You knew the rifle wasn't loaded, didn't you, but you preferred not to say anything so that I would look ridiculous in front of my men.' He hurled himself on Don Pedro and struck him in the ribs with the butt of the gun, a violent blow that shifted even Don Pedro's 258 pounds and made him stumble. His grey J.B. Hotson hat fell off and rolled towards the soldiers' feet.

That blow with the rifle butt penetrated his whole body and reached his soul. Then, like Lazarus on the day of his resurrection in Bethany, he heard a voice saying: 'Get out of here, Pedro! You've been trapped for far too long in this tomb in which your fears and doubts have kept you buried; it's time to wake up.' These words were followed by various images, and he saw himself in Winnipeg, drinking coffee with the Indian chief Jolinshua; he saw himself in the depths of the mine in Alice Arm, examining a vein of reddish silver that the miners called 'ruglar silver'; he saw himself in Prince Rupert, after walking all day, lost in the snow. And he thought: 'I'm not going to be cowed by these murderers.' That was his decision.

'Here's your hat,' said one young soldier, handing it to him. 'I'm glad to see you're not all the same,' answered Don Pedro, after thanking him. 'What are the rest of us like, then?' The swarthy man, Don Jaime, still had the Winchester in his hand. 'Given that you're all devout Catholics, I'm sure you often read the Bible,' Don Pedro said, looking at him. He was sure they did nothing of the sort. They were not like the Protestants he had known in Canada, who used to read the good book for entertainment. 'Of course, I do,' said Don Jaime. 'Then you'll know what the Bible says about people like you. "They are like unclean beasts," that's what the Bible says.' The rifle fell to the ground, and a pistol appeared in the hand of the man with the swarthy complexion. 'Don Jaime!' shouted the young soldier who had picked up the hat, 'remember our orders. The captain said we should take the American alive.' Like a true unclean beast, Don Jaime started cursing and raging. 'Get in the truck!' he ordered at last, panting. 'This queer presumably has some useful information, which is why they want him alive,' he said, going over to Don Pedro and jabbing at him with his finger. 'But we'll find ourselves alone again one day, you can be sure of that.'

As they walked to the car park, the young soldier who had been kind to him asked: 'What part of North America were you in?' He was tall and strong, and looked like a woodsman. 'I spent most of my time in Canada,' replied Don Pedro. 'Is it a good place? I've got an uncle who lives over there, and he's always telling me to go and join him. I might do that when the war's over.' 'Where does your uncle live?' 'On Vancouver Island.' He pronounced the name exactly as it is written. 'Oh, it's a wonderful place. And the people there are a lot more charitable than they are here.' 'I'll think about it then.' They had reached the truck. The young man asked a colleague to help him, and, between them, they lifted him into the back.

On the ground floor of the town hall, between the porch and the tavern, there was a room with just one window, which the people in the village used to call 'the prison', and which, 'since all the thieves had disappeared from Obaba', had been used as a storeroom for food and drink. Shut up in the dark – the one window had been planked over – Don Pedro lay down on some wineskins and considered what to do, how to make the most of what time was left to him. 'Reflect upon your journey through this world. That's what everyone does in their final hours,' advised his inner voice.

As on so many occasions, Don Pedro tried to concentrate on those far-off names: Seattle, Vancouver, Old Manett, New Manett; Alice Arm, Prince Rupert, Nairn Harbour . . . But the names disappeared into the void and he couldn't remember a single fragment of his life. He felt like a large, foolish animal and decided, in order to buck himself up and keep his mind occupied, to make an inventory of all the foodstuffs in the storeroom. At first, he restricted himself to recognising and memorising the various products by smell; then, as luck would have it, he found a small notebook and pencil – and he was as overjoyed by this find as if his salvation depended upon it! – and he started writing a list.

He was just examining some conserves, having nearly completed his inventory, when the door opened and the storeroom was filled with light. His eyes soon grew used to the brightness, and he recognised the swarthy man whom the others called Don Jaime. He was accompanied by a group of soldiers. 'Just as I thought,' Don Pedro said, holding up one of the tins of conserves, 'sardines'. He felt suddenly exhausted and sat down on a box. 'This is no time to sit down,' warned Don Jaime in a hoarse voice. He seemed tired. 'I'm ready,' replied Don Pedro, standing up and putting on his hat. 'It's time to die,' said his inner voice. Again he tried to think about his life, his parents, his brother, about the friends he had made in Canada. But his brain insisted foolishly on remembering the inventory he had just carried out: *five wineskins and five of oil, sixteen boxes of biscuits, three cans of tuna of ten kilos each* . . .

They led him out on to the porch and immediately stood him with his face to the wall. He could see, however, that the village square and streets were deserted, and that the sun had withdrawn to the other side of the mountains. The 15th of August was coming to a close. 'The day of your death,' said his inner voice. A soldier came over to him. 'Would you like to go to the toilet before the truck comes?' he asked. It was the young man with the uncle in Vancouver. 'Good idea,' Don Pedro replied. 'Don't lose hope, sir,' the soldier said, as he led him into the tavern on the ground floor of the town hall. 'I heard this morning that the captain wants you alive. That's a good sign.'

As he went into the toilet, Don Pedro gave himself a slap round the face. The contents of the inventory — *five wineskins and five of oil, sixteen boxes of biscuits* — were still buzzing in his head. He couldn't get rid of them. Not even by slapping himself.

'Don Jaime looks exhausted,' he said to the soldier as they walked back out on to the porch. 'He's upset because he's lost his pistol. Captain Degrela doesn't like that kind of thing,' explained the soldier with a smirk. 'Besides, it's been a hard day. He's not as young as he was, and going back and forth all day is really tiring.' These words made Don Pedro think. He could guess at the reason that lay behind all that going back and forth by the young man and his colleagues, and his own situation seemed distinctly odd. They had kept him in isolation; he had seen no one else all day. Where were the other detainees? Had they taken them straight to the forest?

The truck, the same one he had ridden in that morning, was waiting with its engine running. 'What took you so long? Were you giving him one up the arse?' Don Jaime tried to shout, but his throat would not let him. The soldiers laughed surreptitiously, but not only at his remark. It was clear that the loss of his pistol had undermined his authority. One soldier – who looked like a heavy drinker – muttered snidely: 'Don Jaime's got the voice of an old man now!' 'Come on, come on, we haven't got all day!' said Don Jaime, climbing into the cabin of the truck. The young soldier asked another colleague for his help and together, as they had that morning, they hoisted Don Pedro into the back. Then they got in as well, along with the other soldiers.

They set off towards the main road. 'So Vancouver Island is nice, is it?' asked the soldier. '*Ailand*, not *Issland*. *Vancuva ailand*.' 'That's what worries me most – the language,' said the soldier, smiling. 'That's why I've never got up the courage to go. Otherwise, I'd be there right now.' 'You learn because you need to. You'll learn,' said Don Pedro.

It was a beautiful summer evening. A south wind was blowing, and the remnants of light left behind by the sunset softened the sky; in one part, full of light cloud and patches of blue, the sky looked like a child's bedspread. Don Pedro breathed in the air. For the first time since that morning, he could see something, a scene from his life; he saw his parents standing by a cradle, and his brother sleeping in it. How could they possibly have imagined the fate of that baby? How could they possibly have imagined that he would find death in a lake on the other side of the world, over 5500 miles away? He felt he was losing control, growing dizzy; he felt like crying.

'How do you say *chica* in their language?' asked the soldier. '*He* won't have a clue,' commented the soldier who looked like a drinker, 'you'd be better off asking him how to say *chico*!' 'Why don't you shut up?' said another man. '*Girl*,' replied Don Pedro. '*Girl*? Is that all?' said the soldier, surprised. The truck slowed almost to a halt, then headed off up the hill. 'Where are we going? To the hotel?' asked Don Pedro. 'It looks like it,' said the soldier. He didn't tell Don Pedro that, since that morning, Captain Degrela had made the hotel his headquarters.

They were on the terrace of the hotel's coffee bar, with the captain seated at a table next to a young man who looked like a Falangist, and with Don Pedro standing opposite them. It was getting dark, and all the lights were out. It was hard to see. 'Take that hat off and show a little respect for the captain!' ordered Don Jaime, who was next to him. He obeyed. 'Tell me, Don Pedro, what sentence would a man who kills his own brother deserve, do you think?' asked Captain Degrela, dispensing with any introductions or greetings. Don Pedro was about to answer, but Don Jaime said: 'Before I withdraw, sir, I wish to inform you that I have lost my pistol, and that I am at your orders, sir.' 'I wasn't talking to you, Don Jaime,' said the captain in a barely audible voice. Then he turned to Don Pedro. 'I will tell you. He deserves the death penalty.'

Don Pedro's heart was beating fast. Even under cover of darkness, even though he knew the place – his own house! – escape seemed to him impossible. 'What are you doing in my hotel? That's what I'd like to know,' he said. 'Don't get angry, Don Pedro. The hotel now belongs to the Spanish National Army.' 'I haven't done anything, and your duty is to set me free,' protested Don Pedro. 'That's what I'm trying to do,' said the captain, getting up from his chair. He walked past Don Jaime without even deigning to look at him and took a turn about the table.

Don Pedro's eyes were growing accustomed to the dark. He reckoned the captain was about thirty-five. As for the young Falangist, he couldn't have been more than twenty-five. He thought he had seen his face before. 'You're a man of the world, Don Pedro, and I hope we can reach an agreement quickly,' said the captain. 'We are, as you know, living through the very beginnings of a major political movement. We hope to extend throughout the world what has happened in Germany and in Italy, and what is happening here, right now. That is to say that, while this particular war will eventually end, our revolution will continue.'

Don Pedro had managed to remember the name of the young man sitting at the table. People called him Berlino. He had heard it said that he had spent some time in the seminary and had emerged from there transformed into a great admirer of Hitler. He was going out with a French girl who had worked as a pastry cook in the hotel kitchen. 'So I'm sure it will be easy for you to understand our offer,' the captain went on. 'You will sell us the hotel for an amount of money we have already fixed upon. As you will see, given the circumstances, the price is not at all bad. In any case, we need the hotel. As your Communist friends would say, we require some winter quarters.' The young man called Berlino put a file on the table. 'Sit down and read through the contract,' said the captain. 'We want to do things properly.' 'It's too dark,' said Don Pedro. 'That's easily remedied.' Captain Degrela looked at Don Jaime for the first time. 'Bring us a lantern.' Don Jaime scuttled off. Suddenly he resembled a waiter.

The document was dated April of that year, as if it had been drawn up before the war began. Moreover, the buyer was Captain Degrela himself. It was not, therefore, a requisition; the hotel would not become the property of the army, but of a private individual: Carlos Degrela Villabaso. 'I certainly wouldn't put my name to this contract if I was in Canada,' said Don Pedro, 'but I realise that this is a special situation, and so if I have to sign, I will.' He put his hat on the table and picked up the fountain pen offered him by the young Falangist. 'In fact, bearing in mind the unusual nature of the situation, I'd like to make a proposal,' added Don Pedro. 'I'll hand the hotel over to you without receiving a penny piece in exchange; it will be a donation. I could also make a financial contribution; if you're agreeable, of course.' It was blindingly obvious; he needed no lantern to see it: if he wanted to offset the weight of death and get out of there alive, he had to put everything he could in the other pan on the scales.

The captain rubbed his cheek, as if to check how much his beard had grown. He didn't know quite how to interpret what he had just heard. 'I have money put away in foreign banks,' Don Pedro explained. 'In dollars, francs and pounds sterling. If you allow me to leave for

France, I will donate part of my wealth to your revolution. If I do this, I will, of course, require help. Give me a safe-conduct pass and take me to the other side of the frontier. I'll keep my word.' The captain hesitated. 'What do you think?' he asked Berlino. 'How much money are we talking about?' asked the latter. 'Ten thousand dollars.' Berlino took a while to make the calculation. 'That's a lot!' he exclaimed in surprise. It was more than his girlfriend could have earned in her entire life working as a pastry cook. He addressed the captain: 'If you like, I could go with him to France.' 'We'll see. I'll have to think about it. Meanwhile, sign the contract.' The captain got up from the table. 'When he's finished, take Don Pedro to his room,' he told Don Jaime. 'And then, please, look for your pistol. Don't go to bed until you've found it. Such negligence in a person in command is disgraceful.' Don Jaime remained at attention until the captain had gone inside to the coffee bar. 'Sign here! And here!' Berlino said to Don Pedro.

Don Pedro's bedroom had been turned upside down, with all the clothes from the wardrobes scattered on the floor. He did not stop to look, but sought refuge in the bathroom: the mirror had been cracked and the scales lay face downwards in a corner, as if someone had kicked them, but otherwise, the soaps were in their usual place, as were the bath salts and shampoos he usually brought from Biarritz. He turned on the tap; the water flowed as it always had.

Before getting into the bath, he turned the scales over and stood on them: 254 pounds – his lowest weight for years. Four pounds less than that same morning. He realised then that he hadn't eaten all day, and decided to go and find something to keep hunger at bay. However, what he wanted most of all, more than food, was a smoke, and when he started searching the room and found, not only a box of biscuits, but also the case in which he kept his cigars, he felt that this small success could well be a good omen, and he got into the bath in better spirits.

Half an hour later, he was sitting at the window, smoking a cigar. It was a clear, moonlit night, and he could see the shadows of the soldiers patrolling the area. Everything lay in silence, though, and it was as if even the cars parked on the mirador had gone to sleep. Don Pedro saw his beige-and-brown Chevrolet and felt sad to think that they had impounded it. Then, to shake off this feeling, he looked across at the valley of Obaba.

'I drink in the valley with my eyes,' he heard inside him. It was the voice of Bernardino, the teacher. His friend had written a poem which began like that: 'I drink in the valley with my eyes, in the golden summer sunset, and my thirst is never quenched . . .' What would have become of him? And what about Mauricio? 'The hills and mountains, and the small white houses, which seem, in the distance, like a scattered flock of sheep . . .' Would they have managed to hide? Would they have been more prudent than he had been in these dreadful times? He was not so worried about Mauricio, because he was older and more resilient; Bernardino, on the other hand, despite his intelligence, was hopeless. Even in ordinary life, he got into difficulties: the children at school played cruel tricks on him, knowing how he hated to dole out punishments. And if he was like that in ordinary life, how would he manage now that murderers were on the loose? *Agnus Dei*! Like a lamb amongst wolves.

The red tip of the cigar he was smoking burned brighter or died down, at the mercy of the breeze blowing in through the window. And his thoughts followed the same rhythm: they alternated between burning brighter and dying down. But they led him nowhere. What had Jesus thought about in the garden of Gethsemane? He had no way of knowing. It was stupid even to ask such a question. But he did, for the to and fro of his thoughts was not under the control of his will. A question was followed by an answer, and that answer by another question, but nothing that passed through his mind made any sense.

He listened. After many days of silence, the toads were singing again, but they sounded fainter now, further off. *Win-ni-peg-win-ni-peg-win-ni-peg-win-ni-peg*, they were saying. It occurred to him that they might be baby toads, the children of the toads who used to sing there, and that was why they sang so feebly. He extinguished his cigar under the tap in the sink and lay down on the bed. *Win-ni-peg-win-ni-peg-win-ni-peg-*

210

win-ni-peg. However faintly they sang, their song still reached his room. Gradually, he fell asleep.

He had the feeling, as he dozed, that German planes kept flying over the hotel and that, from time to time, judging by the noise of the engine, one of them landed on the terrace itself. When he woke up properly and realised that this was impossible, he leaned out of the window and saw passing by, immediately below, three trucks like the one that had brought him from the town hall. They stopped at one corner of the hotel, next to the door that gave access to the cellars.

Alarmed, he stepped back: the three trucks were packed with men. He heard moans, shouted commands, sobs. One soldier started hitting those who protested in order to silence them. 'But I haven't done anything!' someone shouted. Then, silence. Only for a short time, though. The noise of engines again filled the night. Three cars were approaching, one after the other, with his Chevrolet in the middle. He noticed that there was a dent on one side of the front mudguard and that the headlight on that side wasn't working. He looked at his fob watch. It was half past four in the morning, and dawn was not far off.

He took his time getting dressed. From amongst the clothes scattered about the room, he chose a light grey summer suit with a matching hat, and some new suede shoes he hadn't worn before. He put in his pocket the small notebook and pencil he had found in the storeroom, hoping, however faintly – as if his heart, too, had grown smaller and almost lost its voice – that it would bring him good luck. When he felt he was ready, he took another cigar out of the case and sat down on one corner of the bed to smoke it. Out on the mirador, there was a constant noise of cars coming and going.

Just before five o'clock, Don Jaime came to fetch him. His eyes looked bruised from lack of sleep, and a thin layer of sweat covered his face. 'You've made yourself very elegant for the trip to France,' said Don Jaime. He tried to laugh, but started coughing instead. 'Put out that cigar!' And as he shouted these words, he slapped Don Pedro and the cigar ended up on the floor. 'If you don't find that pistol of yours soon, you'll have a nervous breakdown,' replied Don Pedro.

211

It was a real effort to get up from the edge of the bed, as if his weight had suddenly increased from 254 pounds to 295 or even 320. 'We're going to France!' said Don Jaime to the men who came with him, and two of them grabbed Don Pedro's arms. They were all in plain clothes, and they were older than the soldiers of the previous night. They all had their hair slicked back with brilliantine. 'You're not fussy who you mix with, are you? Yesterday it was the *requetés*, today it's the Falangists,' said Don Pedro.

He was trying hard not to succumb to despair, but it was difficult to keep calm and to think of a way out. The truth of the matter was, there *was* no hope for him. Don Miguel, the schoolteacher, used to say that of all the extreme right-wing groups in Spain, the Falangists were the ones with most poets and artists in their ranks, and that when they started killing, they would show no mercy, 'it's what always happens when you mix idealists up with the military'. Barely a month had passed since the war began, but that much was already clear. Now it was his turn.

'We could go in your car, but it's only got one headlight, and we need plenty of light. The road to France is very dark,' one of the men holding his arms said when they went outside, adopting the same tone as Don Jaime. Don Pedro ignored him and continued scrutinising the interior of the car before him. He thought he could see someone in there. A thin man, with glasses. 'Bernardino!' he cried, as he was shoved inside. The two friends embraced as best they could in the back seat. 'They've killed Mauricio, Don Pedro. And now they're going to kill us.' 'Don't give up hope, Bernardino. We're still alive.' These were no mere empty words of encouragement. As he embraced Bernardino, he had noticed a sharp pain in his side. There was a hard object on the seat. *Win-ni-peg-win-ni-peg-win-ni-peg!* screamed the toads from the forest. He righted himself and sat further back in the seat. He felt the same pain, this time in his thigh. He had an immediate image — his suit was made of very fine cloth — of a cylinder.

Bernardino could not stop crying, and the Falangists guarding the

212

car told him bluntly to shut up. 'Where's Don Jaime gone?' asked one of the group. 'I think he's gone to get a drink. He'll be back,' replied the driver. 'It's nearly six. It'll be dawn soon,' his companion said in a complaining voice. Don Pedro was gently patting Bernardino. 'Courage, Bernardino, courage. We're still alive.' He took off his hat and placed it on his knees. Then he reached one hand back and picked up the hard object. It was a pistol.

Don Jaime sat down next to the driver, and the other two men occupied small drop-down seats opposite Don Pedro and his friend. The car started with a jolt and headed off down the narrow road from the hotel to the village. The car was travelling so fast that, on the tightest bends, they could barely stay in their seats. 'Slow down, will you, we're not in that much of a hurry,' said the Falangist sitting opposite Don Pedro, after he was thrown against the door when the car swerved. The woods on either side of the road were brilliantly lit by headlights. They could see trees heavy with leaves, the intense green of the beeches.

When they reached the crossroads, they drove down the valley, away from Obaba. The driver had not reduced his speed, but now they were following a mainly straight stretch of road. 'If that bloody pistol isn't there, I don't know what I'm going to do,' said Don Jaime. 'It'll be there,' said the driver soothingly. 'I've looked everywhere. That hill is the one place I haven't looked.' 'What do you mean? I thought we were going to France,' said the Falangist sitting opposite Don Pedro, laughing. 'Don't you want to go to France? Why are you so sad, then?' he asked Bernardino, lighting up the interior of the car with a lantern. 'Follow the example of your queer friend here. Look how calm he is.' 'Here!' yelled Don Jaime, spotting a rough track off to the right of the road. 'Slow down!' he yelled again when the car started bumping wildly over the potholes and stones. 'God, the road to France is really terrible!' said the Falangist, directing the light from his lantern at the window and peering out. Don Pedro put his hand under his hat and gripped the pistol. 'Watch out, Bernardino!' 'Watch out for what?' asked the

Falangist, swinging round. Don Pedro raised his hand and shot him in the head.

He ran up the hill, while, all around him, the toads were shouting *Win-ni-peg! Win-ni-peg! Win-ni-peg! Win-ni-peg!* four or five times faster than their normal rate. He was running clumsily, but as fast or faster than any other man of his age and weight. The desire to avoid certain death lent wings to his feet.

The first light of dawn was beginning to appear, and one area of the sky was becoming tinged with orange. He had reached the highest part of the woods and could make out below a small valley in which lay a rural settlement. He counted the houses: there were five in total, and all faced on to a stream, on to a stream and a road. Four of them were painted white and, despite the still-dim light, he could make out their shapes quite clearly; the first house, nearest to him, was at the entrance to the valley, and was made of dark stone.

He went carefully down the slope, because he knew, from his days in Canada, that it was best not to rush, that now was the time when one was most likely to stumble and sprain an ankle. Once he had reached the bottom, he hid behind some bushes growing on the banks of the stream and studied the stone house. It did not appear to be inhabited. He took the gun out of his trouser pocket and crossed the stream.

The house had a millstone on the ground floor, but there was no flour dust around or any tools. It must have been a disused mill. It was, in any case, not a good place to hide. The patrols always searched the uninhabited houses first. 'All your efforts will be in vain,' his inner voice told him. 'You're not going to find a warm cabin full of friends as you did when you got lost in the snowbound wilderness of Prince Rupert.' He felt suddenly faint and sat down on the mill-stone. When he had recovered, he put the gun in his jacket pocket and went outside.

The dawn light was gradually filling the little valley, and the walls of the houses were now glowing orange, like the sky. 'It isn't some remote settlement in the hills, as you thought,' his inner voice said, 'it's part

214

of Obaba. It won't take long for the patrols to find their colleagues' bodies and then they'll be after you like dogs.'

He scrambled down to the stream bed, and started walking towards the houses down the beaten track that had formed beside the stream. When it seemed to him that he had drawn level with the first of them, he peered over the top of the bank and studied the house for some moments. Then, still advancing, he repeated the operation with the remaining houses. He wondered which of them would provide him with a refuge; which one concealed an Abel and which a Cain; which concealed the brave, compassionate man, and which the scoundrel. However, he reached the far end of the valley with his doubts unresolved. There were no signs. God had said to no one in that place: 'Kill a lamb and paint the posts and lintel of your door with its blood, and the angel, seeing the blood on the door, will pass over.' With no signs, with such minimal certainty, all doors were dangerous. 'And even if there were a sign, what difference would that make?' he thought glumly. The patrols that came after him would be more implacable than the exterminating angel himself, and would leave no house unsearched. Besides, given that he had spilled the blood of his fellow man, God might not be willing to help him. The man who killed Abel was called Cain, but the man who killed Cain, what name did he deserve? He splashed water from the stream on his face. His thoughts were whirling feverishly inside his head.

When he reached the last house, the ground began to rise. The slope was gentle at first, meadowland; then it became more pronounced, and the grass gave way to trees, to forest and to mountain. Don Pedro headed in that direction, determined to get as far away as possible. However, he wanted to take one last look at the valley, at the path that had brought him that far. As soon as he turned his head, however, he understood the truth: he was not going to walk any further, he didn't want to.

He sat down on a rock and continued looking. The five houses lay in silence, peace reigned. Three of them had kennels, but these appeared to be unoccupied. In the house closest to the old mill, a few hens were

215

scratching about in the earth. In the fields belonging to the next two houses were some sheep; next to the last house, about a hundred metres from where he was sitting, two horses were cropping the grass. The horses were chestnut brown. And the grass was green. Just as the maize-fields, the vegetable plots, the apple orchards, the woods and the distant hills were green too. Although on the distant hills, the green turned to blue, dark blue. Like the sky. Because the sky, at that early dawn hour, was dark blue with streaks of orange and yellow. From the chimney of one house, the third one, smoke began to emerge. The smoke dispersed slowly in the air. The sun was moving slowly too. It was still lingering behind the mountains, but was about to appear.

Don Pedro checked his gun chamber to make sure that the last two bullets were still there. He suddenly remembered the conversation he had had with Dr Corgean at the Prince Rupert hospital: 'You might have the same propensity.' 'A propensity to what?' 'To commit suicide.' Now, though, he knew that he had no such propensity. He would commit suicide as soon as the sun came up over the mountains, but he would do so out of fear, under the threat of something far worse than death. He didn't even want to think about what the dead Falangists' compan-ions would do to him if they caught him. He knew about the tortures these criminals inflicted; he had heard that they gouged out people's eyes with spoons or hurled people on to red-hot sheets of iron. Compared with that, dying with a bullet through your brain was a blessing. Besides, there was a certain justice in his death. Inside the car lay three men whose lives he had taken. He must pay for it.

A boy emerged from the last house. Don Pedro followed him with his gaze and saw, somewhat indifferently – as if he had already shot himself in the head and only his spirit was witnessing the scene – that the boy was heading towards the horses, that he was talking to them and stroking them, and that he was leading them out of the enclosure down to the stream. Don Pedro stood up, his despondency forgotten. 'Juan!' he shouted. The boy did not hear him. 'Juan!' he called again, hurrying down the hill.

When the road to the hotel had still been under construction, Don

Pedro used to ride up there on horseback, always accompanied by a boy. That was five years ago, and there was that same boy. He had grown into a fair-haired young man, not very tall, but strong. 'Go to the bridge and hide underneath it,' the young man said, without so much as blinking. Don Pedro remembered that he had always been a very serious boy. Once, he had addressed him as 'Juanito', as he would a child. 'My name isn't Juanito, Don Pedro,' he had retorted. 'My name is Juan.'

The bridge was a little further down, level with the house, and Don Pedro hurried over there. Memories stirred in his mind. The boy was an orphan and lived with his sister, who was younger than him. The name of the house was Iruain, which is why the boy would often be referred to both as Juan and as Iruain. When Don Pedro was hidden underneath the bridge, he remembered another detail, a very important one. The boy was always asking him about North America, just like the soldier who had an uncle in Vancouver, and with equal longing: 'Is it true that in America there are ranches as big as our village? Have you seen them?'

Juan came over with the two horses. 'I recognised you because of the horses,' Don Pedro said. 'Did you know you've got blood all over your jacket?' asked Juan. No, he didn't. 'There were three of them and two of us,' he replied. 'I was the only one to get out alive.' He relived the pain of that moment. If he had used his second shot to kill the driver, rather than the ridiculous Don Jaime, Bernardino would be with him now.

The sun was climbing in the sky. Captain Degrela and his men would have noticed by now that the car was missing. 'Years ago, you told me that you dreamed of going to America. Have you changed your mind?' 'No. I'd leave right now,' said Juan without a moment's hesitation. He didn't move, as if he were made of stone. 'I need your help to save me, and you need me in order to start a new life in America. We could make a deal.' A dog barked, and the young man scanned the length of the valley. The dog fell silent. 'What's your idea?' Juan asked. Now he seemed somewhat shy. 'With those horses, we could be in France in seven or eight hours,' said Don Pedro. Juan said nothing. 'Is there somewhere in your house I could hide?' Don Pedro added.

Don Pedro was pretty sure the answer would be in the affirmative, because many of the buildings in Obaba still had the hiding-places they had been fitted out with during the wars of the nineteenth century; but when he saw Juan nod, he nearly fainted from pure excitement. For the first time since his arrest, his hopes had some basis in reality.

'Hide me in your house and then, when it's convenient, take me to France. In exchange, I'll give you 3000 dollars. That's enough to get to America *and* buy a ranch.' Juan grabbed the horses' reins. 'It seems to me that you could easily afford 5000,' he said. 'Fine, 5000 dollars,' Don Pedro answered at once, and the two men shook hands. 'Stand between the two horses and we'll go slowly up to the house. Once we're inside, follow me, but don't make a sound; we don't want to wake my sister.' He appeared to feel no fear. 'Where's your hat? You always used to wear a hat,' he said suddenly. Don Pedro made a gesture of irritation. 'I don't know, to be honest. I suppose I must have lost it during the shooting.' 'Where was that?' Don Pedro carefully described at which crossroads the car had left the road, but could not describe in detail how he had got from there to the valley. 'I think I came through a wood, of chestnut trees not beeches,' he said. The young man thought for a moment, then, 'Let's go!' he said, tugging at the horses' reins.

The darkness inside the hiding-place was total, and he adapted to the new situation as a blind man would have done. He first of all determined that he was in a kind of short passageway, six paces long and barely two paces wide; then, once he had overcome the anxiety he felt at being so enclosed, he examined the contents of the cooking pots that Juan had handed down to him through the opening above. There were four pots in all, three large ones and one smaller, wider one: the first contained water, the second apples, the third carrots. The fourth, the wider one, was empty and from it hung pieces of newspaper strung together on a piece of wire. He slowly arranged the pots, moving them as quietly as he could, putting the one that would serve as a latrine on one side, the three larger pots on the other. Once he had got himself organised, he sat down with his back against the wall and started to eat. '3 apples, 3 carrots', he wrote in the notebook which he carried in his jacket pocket, taking great care to write neatly despite the darkness.

He was assailed by a terrible unease. If he had left his hat in the car, it wouldn't matter, but if he had lost it during his escape or nearby, and a patrol found it, the house would cease to be safe. Many of the soldiers were country people and knew about the existence of these hiding-places. However, his disquiet did not last. It had been a very long day, and he was very tired. He fell asleep.

When he woke, the hat was lying on his chest, as if it had landed there as gently as a snowflake. He clasped it in his hands and wept silently. He recalled how little faith he had had when he arrived in the settlement and saw no sign on the doors of the houses. Far from abandoning him, God had chosen to send him a protecting angel, brave and decent, in every way like the angel Raphael who had helped Tobias. He started eating apples and did not stop until he was incapable of swallowing another mouthful. 'Apples: 7', he wrote in his notebook. Then he lay down and went to sleep again.

A few days passed, three or four, possibly more, and there came a moment, when the pots were already half empty, when Don Pedro felt safe. 'It seems I may have escaped the search,' he said to himself one morning – or one afternoon, for he had no way of knowing which it was. At that precise instant, he heard noises inside the house. He knew at once that it was his pursuers. It seemed to him that he himself had summoned them, that he had been wrong to make baseless assumptions.

He reacted by lying face down and covering his head with his hands. However, the loud beating of his heart made this position too uncomfortable, and so he turned over and resumed his normal posture, sitting with his back to the wall. His pursuers came up the stairs fairly quietly, and, a few seconds later, he heard a young female voice explaining: 'This is our mother's room. It's exactly the way it was the day she died. It seems incredible really, but it's nearly ten years now. My brother Juan still refuses to change anything, though. He's two years older than me, and as you know, two years is a lot when you're a child. He says he can remember my mother clearly. I can't, or at least not very well.' The girl chattered on, and the men accompanying her, doubtless soldiers, kept grunting their agreement. Don Pedro assumed she must be pretty and that the soldiers felt sorry for her. 'This was her wardrobe and these were her dresses,' the girl went on. A drawer opened and was closed again, and the noise sounded immediately above the hiding-place. It was, it occurred to him, that piece of furniture which was blocking the small amount of light that might reach him, the light that should illuminate the cracks in the trapdoor that formed his ceiling. 'And when did you lose your father?' he heard someone ask. The soldiers were leaving the room. 'When I was four,' said the girl. 'That's terrible. It must be miserable being an orphan,' said a soldier. The girl changed the subject: 'Are you going into the village? I work at the sewing workshop there and it would be really helpful if you could give me a lift in your truck.' The soldiers said they were sorry, but they couldn't. They had orders to continue the search.

The steps of the soldiers echoed on the stairs. Once outside – Don Pedro regarded the scene as if it were there before his eyes – they would see Juan in the paddock, grooming one of the horses. He would lift the brush for a moment by way of saying goodbye, and the search would be over.

Don Pedro had finished the apples and nearly all of the carrots, and was beginning to get worried. Juan was leaving it longer than usual between visits; he didn't even come to fetch the wide pot, which he normally changed fairly regularly. Then Don Pedro's anxiety ebbed away, and he got it into his head that Juan was only late because he was thinking about how to provide him with a better and more varied diet, and that the next time he came, he would leave him some beautiful round bread rolls made from maize flour, and that he would be kind enough to bring him a good slice of cured meat or ham; not bacon, obviously, because bacon had to be eaten straight from the frying pan,

220

still dripping grease. Then, as these food-related images became more detailed, he thought how easy it would be for Juan to roast a chicken in the oven while his sister was at the workshop, and if, as a side dish, he threw in some fried potatoes and red peppers, all the better. Not forgetting the cheese. They were sure to make cheese locally and, with any luck, there would be some quince jelly as well. Yes, he would ask Juan for a bit of cheese and quince jelly. He remembered, too, the cans of tuna he had seen in the 'prison' at the town hall. Canned tuna, with a bit of finely chopped onion, was delicious. And with the addition of some green olives, it was a delicacy!

The carrots finally ran out too, and while his fast continued, he did nothing but stare up at the ceiling, like a hungry dog waiting for his master to come. There were even moments when he despaired and felt sure that Juan would leave him there to die of hunger; however, he would grow calm again when he considered the situation – the risk Juan was running, the agreed sum of 5000 dollars – and he continued to wait. Until, at last, his protecting angel returned.

Using the rope, Juan lowered down two pots, as well as the one containing water. Don Pedro put a hand inside: nothing but apples and carrots. He couldn't contain his anger, and, for a moment, his voice took on the authoritarian tones of the hotelier: 'Is there no bread in this wretched house? Is there no cheese? Is there no meat? Are there no eggs?' A long list of various food items completed his protest. 'Have you finished?' said Juan sharply. 'They're still looking for you everywhere. We mustn't lose our heads now.' Don Pedro sighed: 'Tobias caught a fish with the help of the archangel Raphael. Then they removed its gall-bladder, liver and heart, and cooked and ate it.' He was talking to himself now, aware that he was being unreasonable. 'When we get to France, I'll treat you to a lobster,' said Juan from above. He was closing the trapdoor. 'French pâté's not bad either,' said Don Pedro. 'I've never tried it.' 'May I ask you a favour?' 'Look, I'm not bringing you any more food, Don Pedro, so don't ask,' replied Juan in his severest tones. 'All right, but how about a little light? If you draw the curtains at the window and move that piece of furniture a smidgen, the light will reach me here.' 'The room has two windows,' said Juan. 'Even better.' 'Don't worry, and try to move around as much as you can and do some exercises, otherwise you'll seize up.' 'One other thing,' said Don Pedro. 'Couldn't you bring me a razor and a bit of soap. My beard is making me itch.' 'You can shave in France, just before we eat that lobster,' replied Juan, closing the trapdoor. Moments later, Don Pedro heard the sound of curtains being drawn. In the ceiling of his hiding-place, four lines of light appeared.

The lines of light were a great help during the days that followed. He got into the habit of examining them and calculating, according to their intensity, not just the hour of the day – an easy enough thing to do, as he realised at once – but also what the weather was like, if it was a sunny day or a cloudy one, and if the latter, how cloudy, and with what likelihood of rain. He noted his observations down in his note-book. 'Today, drizzle. The gaps on the outside of the trapdoor almost invisible, and those in the middle very faint.' 'Today, sunshine and showers. When it cleared up, very intense light. I can see the shape of my hat on top of the pot.' 'Today, blue skies, a lovely summer's day.' As long as he kept himself occupied, time seemed to weigh less heavily.

He began to take as his focal point the moment when the sun was at its highest, and to organise everything around that moment: meals, rest, sleep and the physical exercises Juan had recommended. What he enjoyed most were the exercises, and he ended up doing them almost continu-ously, morning and evening. As well as the exercises themselves, he walked tirelessly up and down the hiding-place, from one end to the other, five paces in one direction and five paces back, over and over. He enthusiastically noted down the number of steps taken: 'Morning 475. Afternoon 350.' The figures for the meals, on the other hand, drove him to despair: 'Breakfast: 1 apple, 2 carrots. Lunch: 3, 4. Supper: 2, 4.' When the pots were almost empty, he could stand it no longer and decided to eat nothing more until Juan returned. 'Breakfast: 0 apples, 0 carrots. Lunch: 0, 0. Supper: 0, 0'. He wrote these zeros with real spite, almost as if the apples and carrots were capable of feeling his scorn.

When Juan reappeared with the new pots of food, Don Pedro could not hold back a groan. He wanted to carry his thoughts beyond the hiding-place, to escape spiritually from that hole and persuade himself that he was on the way to salvation, but his mind would not obey him, and kept insinuating that it might perhaps have been better to have shot himself. Now he did not even have that option, since Juan had taken the gun and hidden it, or so he said, in a hollow tree in the woods. He could not understand Juan's stubbornness. How could he expect him to eat more apples and more carrots? It was impossible. They smelled to him now like the excrement in the pot that served as his latrine. Or like the pestilential stubble of his beard, once stiff and rough, and now growing steadily longer and limper. It made him feel like throwing up. Juan saw his distress. 'We'll be leaving for France soon,' he told him. 'Be brave, it won't be for much longer.'

He said nothing. He had the feeling that the floor of the hiding-place had given way and that he was once more underground, as he had been as a young man. Except that there was no silver or gold in that wretched hole, only apples and carrots. Now – just as had happened a few days before with varieties of food – names and people began to whirl around inside his head, people from another age, people who had died: his brother, the Indian chief Jolinshua from Winnipeg, the schoolteachers Mauricio and Bernardino, especially Bernardino, his unfortunate friend, whose only crime had been to write poetry and who had been murdered for that crime, right in front of his eyes. 'Another week in here, and I'll go crazy,' he told Juan. 'Three more days, and we'll be off,' Juan promised him.

Juan came with a ladder and helped him out of the hiding-place. Then, by the light of a candle, they went downstairs. Juan prepared him a good hot soup made from maize, and he settled down to eat it, very slowly, with a wooden spoon. 'I've received orders to take twenty cows to the area near the front line, and they've given me two safe-conduct passes. One for me and the other for the cowherd. You're the cowherd. But don't worry, you'll be able to make most of the journey on horse-back.'

Don Pedro nodded his agreement, and moved the candle on the table a little farther off, because the light bothered him. He continued eating the soup. 'I reckon that with the cows and all it will take us about ten hours to get to the place they've asked me to go to,' Juan explained. 'So if we leave early, we'll be free by nightfall. And the French frontier will be just a step away. The next day, you can shave your beard off and we'll go and eat that lobster.' 'Not forgetting the visit to the bank,' he added. 'Now finish that soup, we have to get ready.' 'Wait a moment, I'm still eating.' 'It struck four o'clock some time ago, and there's a lot to do.' Outside a cow mooed. 'I'm not getting out of this chair until I've finished my soup,' Don Pedro insisted.

Once outside, Juan made Don Pedro take a turn around the cattle pen to see if he could walk. Then he led him to a bend in the stream. 'The water will come up to your waist here, so have a good wash,' he said, handing him a piece of rough soap and a towel. 'You'll make a lot of money when you go to America. You're *very* organised.' 'That's what my sister says.' 'Where is she?' 'She's staying with a great-aunt until I get back. She's got a job in a sewing workshop. She's going to be a dressmaker.'

'Won't the water be cold?' asked Don Pedro, looking at the stream. 'Of course it will, uncle, but if you're quick, you won't even notice.' Juan seemed very calm and unconcerned. 'Uncle? So, from now on, I'm going to be your uncle, am I?' Juan nodded. He was laughing. 'Yes, my uncle and my cow-man,' he added. 'Tell me, nephew, what exactly is it that you find so very amusing?' asked Don Pedro. He was gradually returning to his old self. 'Forgive me for saying so, but it's just your whole appearance. You'll see for yourself when you look in the mirror.'

Don Pedro scrubbed his body repeatedly with the soap and plunged again and again into the water. When he emerged from the stream, he felt like a new man and started striding back up to the house almost naked. He stopped after taking only a few steps: for the first time in ages, for the first time since the attempt on his life, his ears were open. He could hear the south wind murmuring in the leaves in the woods, and accompanying that murmur, peppering it with sound, was the song of the toads. *Win-ni-peg-win-ni-peg-win-ni-peg*, they were repeating, but this time with brio, with feeling. There was no doubt about it, life was beautiful.

Juan trimmed Don Pedro's beard and cut his hair with a pair of his sister's scissors. Then he asked for the clothes he was wearing so that he could burn them 'straight away', and, in their place, he gave him some work clothes, suitable for a farm labourer. 'It's my hat I find hardest to part with,' said Don Pedro. 'A cow-man would be more likely to wear a black beret, I'm afraid. But don't worry. I'll leave it in the hiding-place as a souvenir,' replied Juan. Then, putting on a serious face, he added: 'Right, Don Pedro, the moment has come to look in the mirror. There's enough light now.' It was dawn.

Don Pedro didn't recognise himself. In the mirror he saw a man, neither fat nor thin, with a weary face and a white beard, and who looked much older than him. 'The patrols are looking for a fat man elegantly dressed, but that man doesn't exist any more,' said Juan, smiling. Don Pedro kept staring at his reflection in the mirror, trying to take in what he saw. 'Now I understand about all those apples and carrots. *Very* clever. But you're absolutely pitiless, you know. The odd treat wouldn't have made me put on weight.' He again examined the old man before him. 'Have you got any scales?' he asked. 'There are some old-fashioned ones next to the stable. I think they still work.'

While Juan was preparing more maize soup, Don Pedro learned his new weight: 206 pounds. The same as when he was a young man, and 52 pounds less than when they had taken him from the hotel. 'Where's my notebook?' he asked Juan while he was having breakfast. 'I burned it along with the clothes. Remember, you're my uncle now, Uncle Manuel. And my Uncle Manuel can't even write his name. He's done nothing else all his life, but keep cows.' 'As I said before, you're going to make a lot of money in America. You're *very* intelligent. I'm sorry about the notebook, though. I would like to have known how many apples and carrots I ate during the time I was in that hole.' Juan pointed to the clock on the wall. It was seven o'clock. Time to round up the cattle and set off.

While they were riding along, Don Pedro noticed a few splashes of red amongst the trees in the woods. Autumn was coming. He would, he thought, stay in France that winter, and then return to Canada in the spring. He felt quite calm, confident that his plan would be successful.

   He had one last scare: a patrol stopped them as they were leaving the outskirts of Obaba, and he found himself face to face with the soldier who had an uncle in Vancouver. 'Fancy still having to work at your age, grandpa!' the young man said. Don Pedro gave a resigned shrug and continued on his way with a smile on his lips.

Burnt wood

I

'I assume you still play the accordion,' said Ángel, appearing at my bedroom door. I continued what I was doing, putting my summer clothes in a bag, without even looking at him. 'I'm in a hurry,' I said. It was the end of June 1970, and, having passed my fourth-year university exams, I could see stretching before me three whole months of vacation; but the minutes and hours I had to spend at Villa Lecuona seemed to me unbearable. I wanted to leave as soon as possible for the house in Iruain.

Ángel made an attempt at a smile. 'Yes, I can tell you're in a hurry. You haven't even had time to turn on the light.' 'Leave it!' I yelled, when he raised his hand to the switch. 'I can see fine with the light from the window.' 'You're in a bad mood,' he said, with a still more strained smile, 'just for a change.' He disappeared down the corridor and returned with the accordion. It was in its case, ready for the trip.

I closed the bag and stood there, arms folded. 'What do you want?' I said. 'The sooner we get this over with, the better.' I didn't want to talk to him; all I wanted was his confession: 'The gorilla on the cover of the notebook is telling the truth, my son. During the war, I was a murderer. And I deeply regret it.' Remorse could be a first step, the beginning of a better relationship between us. Or perhaps not. 'All hearts soften before the repentant sinner, even hearts of stone,' Obaba's parish priest, Don Hipólito, used to say. I wasn't so sure.

'I get really tired playing at the hotel dances now,' he said. 'It's a lot of hours. I want you to take my place.' I eyed him distrustfully. The hotel was his second home, and he hadn't missed a dance or a fiesta for years. The shirts and jackets he wore for these performances were still hanging in the wardrobe in his practice room, as impeccable as

227

ever. 'I've spoken to Marcelino, and he's happy for you to replace me.' 'And what about Geneviève? What does she think?' I said. According to my mother – she'd told me this on one of her visits to the student flat where I lived in San Sebastián – Geneviève was annoyed with me because of Teresa, who refused to come to Obaba and preferred to spend the vacation with her relatives in France. She thought her daughter's actions were motivated purely by rancour, and that it was my fault because I'd aroused 'false hopes' in her.

Ángel ignored the question and pointed to the accordion. 'If you want to work this summer, you'd better start practising. The sooner, the better.' I lit a cigarette and began putting some books into a smaller bag than the one containing my clothes. I'd been smoking since my second year at university. 'All Marcelino and Geneviève want are for the dances this summer to be a success,' Ángel said. 'A lot of disco-theques are opening, and people don't go to open-air dances so much any more. That's the only thing worrying us.'

'Worrying *us*,' he said, including himself in that phrase. But he was lying. I knew from Martín that the summer dances at the Hotel Alaska were still very profitable, thanks mainly to the drinks that had become fashionable, gin and tonics and Cuba libres. What they were really worried about was not, therefore, the way business was going, but the political situation in the Basque Country. It was becoming almost night-marish, with frequent strikes and violent attacks which the continual states of emergency imposed by the Madrid government did nothing to halt. Moreover – and worse still – they had the reminders of what was happening right there before them: on Easter Sunday of that year, a bomb had destroyed the marble monument unveiled four years earlier by Paulino Uzcudun; the ruined remains were still there in one corner of the square in Obaba; not far away, in the sportsground, huge letters announced from the wall of the pelota court 'Death to Spanish fascism' and demanded freedom for Euskadi, 'the one Basque homeland'. As a third reminder there were the pamphlets that had been handed out on 1 May in the new housing estate, in which they denigrated 'the peons working for the military dictatorship'. It was hard to believe, but it was true: the enemy, whom they had thought defeated, dead and buried, had risen up and were once more walking the Earth. It was only natural they should be worried. Worried and vigilant. The Mexicans at Stoneham Ranch would have described this situation by saying that all the snakes of Obaba had '*la cabeza levantadita*', 'their heads up'.

Ángel grew impatient: 'So what shall I tell Marcelino, then? Do you want the job or not?' 'How much will he pay me?' I asked. 'The same as he pays me.' 'How much is that?' The amount he named was very large indeed. I would, I calculated, only have to play at twenty dances to earn enough money for a whole year at university. Colonel Degrela obviously rewarded him well. Just as he rewarded Berlino by leaving the running of the hotel in his hands. In one way or another, both men remained at his service. The political graffiti and the pamphlets were telling the truth: they were peons working for the military dictatorship.

I reworked my calculations. No, I was right. If I played the accordion at the dances all summer, I wouldn't need any money from my mother in order to go to Bilbao and finish the studies I'd begun at ESTE. 'It's very well paid, so, yes, I'll do it,' I said. Ángel smiled again, this time mockingly. 'I thought you were an idealist, and that money mattered less to you than to other mere mortals. So you're not the Immaculate Virgin after all.'

He was about to leave the room, when he stopped at the door. 'When are you going to bring back the Guzzi?' 'Why do you want to know?' I asked. I'd lent the bike to one of my friends from ESTE and hadn't seen it for weeks. 'How are you going to get up to the hotel? On horseback?' 'It's in the repair shop,' I lied. 'It needed a service.' 'Use the old car then.' He'd just bought a grey Dodge Dart, but the Mercedes was still in the garage at Villa Lecuona. 'I won't need it. Joseba will take me,' I said. 'Who? Manson?' Ángel's smile changed again. This time it was disdainful.

Joseba, who had always been the best-behaved of my friends when we studied with Redin and César at the sawmill, now wore his hair halfway down his back, and his unkempt beard was long enough to cover his Adam's apple. He looked permanently rumpled and rolled his own aromatic herbal cigarettes. The nickname, Manson, was a reference to the hippie murderer who'd been much in the news over the last year.

'I don't call him that,' I said. I stuffed the books that still remained on the bed into the bag. 'Which car will he be driving, may I ask?' I pointed at the window: 'If you look out there, you'll see it.' Joseba's car, a yellow, second-hand Volkswagen, was parked outside the house. 'Why would anyone buy a car that colour!' exclaimed Ángel, still standing at the window. 'You have some very strange friends, David!' For a moment, his expression mirrored his words. He gave a truly heartfelt sigh.

My friends. The second was Adrián, whose outward appearance was even worse than Joseba's. He mostly wore baggy white shirts that came down almost to his knees, or else vast sweaters. However, in his case, people were more understanding. They put this eccentricity of dress down to his hunchback and his need to disguise his deformed spine.

'I assume Manson has a driving licence,' said Ángel, moving away from the window. 'If he doesn't, there's no way you're going up to the hotel in that yellow car. You can't be too careful on the roads nowadays.' Following the bomb that had wrecked the monument in the square, roadchecks had become frequent. Ángel was right: you couldn't be too careful on the roads. There were rifles and machine-guns watching; the police viewed with distrust any drivers travelling through places like Obaba, especially if they were young and looked like Joseba. 'He's had his licence since he was eighteen,' I said. 'Well, that's something, I suppose,' he muttered, leaving the room.

He returned at once. He wasn't happy, he wanted to have the final, emphatic word. 'I trust you'll behave like a real professional, always smartly turned out. You know where my jackets are. Try them on and see how they look.' 'I don't need your jackets,' I said, and his eyes immediately changed expression. I thought he was going to hit me or try to slap me. But he controlled himself. 'What are you going to wear, then? A hat?' he said.

230

I had two Hotson hats, one for winter and one for summer. Uncle Juan had sent them to me after a trip to Canada. 'Exactly. How did you guess?' I said. I went over to my wardrobe and took out one of the Hotson hats, the summer one. It was cream-coloured, and I thought it was wonderful. I put it on. 'The two of you will look like a carnival float,' he said. He was close to losing his temper. He picked up the accordion and put it down next to my bags. 'Start practising as soon as possible, if you don't want to make us all look like fools, especially me!' 'I'll be all right,' I said.

He left the room. I heard him go into the sewing workshop and start talking to my mother. I could imagine what he would be saying: 'You ask too much of me, Carmen. I do my best to rub along with him, but all I get in return is a lot of lip. If he wants to go and spend the summer in California, then he should forget about playing at the hotel dances and just get on a plane. It would certainly be a weight off my mind.'

The idea of a trip to California came up every year, especially now that Uncle Juan had stopped coming to Iruain each summer because of the political situation and the states of emergency, but the trip never happened. Nor would it that year either, 1970, even though Ángel would probably have liked me to go. My mother wanted me by her side. I'd be spending the next year in Bilbao, a city she didn't know, and which was ten times farther away than San Sebastián.

II

We were driving along the road to Iruain; we had the windows of the Volkswagen wound right down and were singing loudly, shrieking every time we hit a pothole and Joseba appeared to lose control of the car. All three of us were feeling very happy, especially me: the start of summer was delicious; the cool air beneath the dark leaves of the chestnut trees was delicious; and returning to Iruain after the year in San Sebastián was delicious too. As we drove down towards the little valley, I saw

Juan's horses in the distance. There it was, there it still was, the land of the happy peasants.

We passed a girl of about fifteen, and Joseba stuck his arm out of the window and waved to her. 'Who's she?' he asked. 'Ubanbe's sister,' I said. Joseba opened his eyes wide. 'That's incredible. Last time I saw her, she was a little girl.' 'Time flies,' I said. Adrián sat up in the back seat and leaned forward: 'It certainly goes a lot faster than this second-hand VW.' 'What do you mean? Are you saying we're going slowly?' 'No, Joseba, what I'm saying is that we're not going at all. We've stopped. Or hadn't you noticed?'

Joseba put his foot down hard on the accelerator and the car leaped forward, hurling Adrián backwards. 'Music!' cried Joseba, pushing in the tape that was poised and ready in the cassette-player. 'Creedence Clearwater Revival! The favourite of all the law students in Bilbao!' 'What song is this?' I asked. 'Susie Q!' he said, keeping time with the music by swaying about in his seat. It was a lovely song and had a trans-forming effect on the landscape: the melody seemed to make the maize fields, the apple trees, and the trees in the forest seem somehow happier and greener. At the hotel dances, I would be playing a different sort of song; sadder music from another era.

I saw Pancho standing in the river, with his trousers rolled up to the knee and his head bowed; I saw Adela's twin boys watching him from the shore. Joseba papped his hooter, and they responded with a wave. 'It really is amazing,' said Adrián from the back seat. 'Amazing? What's amazing?' we asked. We had to shout because the music of Creedence Clearwater Revival was blaring out at full volume. 'The fact that Ubanbe should have a sister,' said Adrián. 'I always thought there would be nothing in his house but oxen, lions, wild boar – that sort of thing.' 'As you see, you were wrong. There are no wild beasts, only a rather pretty girl,' said Joseba, braking. We were almost at the bridge that crossed the stream, just opposite Iruain. 'You think *all* girls are pretty, Joseba,' Adrián went on, 'but that's because of the crocodile. He's very, very hungry and often leads you astray. You see beauty where there's only flesh.'

232

Adrián referred to the male member as the crocodile. He'd given all his friends wooden penises in the form of a crocodile about to take a large bite out of something. Adrián said these were his finest works. And so did Martín, who, at his club on the coast, had a pile of replicas which he handed out to his best customers.

Joseba parked the car outside the house and turned off the music. The ensuing silence in the valley immediately imposed itself on us, and we started speaking softly and timidly, not daring to raise our voices. 'You artists have a very peculiar way of looking at things,' said Joseba. 'An excellent way,' Adrián corrected him. 'A dreadful way,' retorted Joseba. He got out of the car, and I followed. Adrián took a little longer. Despite all the operations on his back, he still found certain movements difficult. But no one was allowed to help him. If anyone so much as tried, he got furious.

I had a sense that the house at Iruain gave off a smell whose ineffable ingredients included Lubis and the horses, Uncle Juan and Adela, the book by Lizardi, the beer Redin had drunk one day in that very place, the birds in the forest and the trout in the stream. I felt it was my true home, and I closed my eyes to become more aware of my breathing and to capture that smell.

But, no, I was deceiving myself, I was allowing myself to be swept along by an illusion. Iruain, my true home! Experience showed exactly the opposite to be the case. I hadn't even thought about the place or the house for ages; the smells I was most familiar with now had changed: they were the butane gas we used in the student apartment in San Sebastián, as well as the petrol I filled the Guzzi with each week and the cigarettes I smoked each day. This seemed hard to believe on an evening like that, at the beginning of summer, as I sat on the stone bench and looked out at the maize fields, the apple trees and the green forest, beneath a pale blue sky announcing the approach of nightfall; but, as my teachers of economics at university used to say, those were the facts.

'Where's Lubis got to?' I said. The stables looked deserted. Adrián

233

pointed at the river, where we'd seen Pancho and the twins. 'He'll be in the river, keeping an eye on his brother. And quite right too, because Pancho is perfectly capable of eating those boys. You knew he was a cannibal, didn't you?' 'Oh, not again,' said Joseba, without looking up from the cigarette he'd started to roll. 'We've gone from Ubanbe's sister and the crocodile to Pancho and his cannibalistic tendencies. You're obviously trying to keep us awake at night.' 'It's astonishing!' exclaimed Adrián. 'It certainly is,' agreed Joseba, lighting his cigarette. His cigarettes had the honeyed smell of pipe tobacco: 'After all, it's not every day one sees a cannibal.' 'No, I don't mean that.' 'Then get to the point, please.' 'I mean, Joseba, that Pancho and Lubis are so different, you'd wouldn't think they'd come from the same crocodile.'

Adrián didn't know Beatriz, the mother of the two brothers; he felt no regard for peasants, be they happy or unhappy; he was, as usual, stuck in his own world. 'That's a really crass thing to say,' I said. 'Don't ever say that again, all right?' 'Don't get angry, David. White hands can do no harm, as they say.' He held out his hands, and they were, indeed, very white. They looked as if they were made of cream, and had tiny bluish threads running across them. 'Why don't you shut up?' said Joseba. 'I'd like to be able to enjoy the countryside in peace.' 'You see what these poets are like, David, always working.' This time, Adrián's words provoked no response.

Two of the horses, Ava and Mizpa, were grazing in the middle of the paddock, accompanied by three foals; farther off, by the fence higher up in the paddock, the donkey, Moro, appeared to be deep in thought. Then came occasional trees and, a short distance beyond that, the forest, growing up the sides of the hills and the mountains – the extraordinarily green forest of late June. In the pale blue sky there were a few small clouds which looked as if they'd been edged with silver glitter paint.

'Now I know why Lubis isn't here,' I said. Adrián put his hand to his eyes, like a visor, as if shading them from the sun. 'Of course. He has to watch Pancho, but he doesn't seem to be doing a very good job. I can only see one of the twins now. I bet you Pancho has eaten the other one.' 'Will you be quiet, Adrián,' said Joseba, blowing a mouthful of smoke into his face and making him cough. 'Forgive me for ruining your lungs, but I had to do something to shut that filthy mouth of yours.' 'He must be out riding Faraón,' I said. 'Faraón's not in the paddock, and as far as I know, my uncle hasn't sold him. He's sold Zizpa and Blaky, but not Faraón.' Joseba went over to the car to stub out his cigarette. 'When Lubis comes, I'll ask him to let me have a ride,' he said. 'I've never tried it.' 'You've never had a ride?' asked Adrián innocently. 'Oh, no, not again,' cried Joseba, covering his ears. 'I don't want to hear any more about crocodiles!' A rider and horse appeared on one of the paths leading out of the forest. The horse was white. 'There's Lubis,' I said. All three of us waved, and the rider waved back.

Joseba looked frightened when he first climbed on to Faraón. 'It makes me feel dizzy,' he said. 'It's just a matter of getting used to the height,' said Lubis. 'Everyone feels odd the first time.' 'You're right, the first time you feel dreadful,' put in Adrián, 'but in Joseba's case, there's a double problem. You've seen the cigarettes he smokes. They're pure drugs. It's hardly surprising he feels dizzy.' Lubis helped Joseba to dismount, and left us on the pretext of taking Faraón to rejoin the other horses. Our behaviour seemed odd to him, in particular, Adrián's jokey, over-excited way of speaking. Lubis had just come from the forest, from the silence, and needed time to get used to the brand of humour we brought with us from the city, from student apartments and bars.

'How are you doing, Lubis?' I asked shortly afterwards, when he helped me carry in my bags and my accordion. We were standing in my bedroom. 'I'm fine,' he said. I remembered that the last time we'd been together there, it had snowed. We hadn't seen each other for five or six months. 'How about you? How's life in San Sebastián?' 'Pretty good,' I replied. I didn't find it easy to start a conversation either.

In the end Lubis smiled and asked: 'How's that boy with hair like a hedgehog?' 'Komarov?' He was my best friend in San Sebastián. He took his nickname from a famous Russian astronaut. 'He's got some guts that boy,' Lubis went on. 'The time you came here when it had snowed, he shinned up the drainpipe on to the roof. He didn't look like a hedgehog then, more like a cat.' The memory of my friend made him smile broadly. 'He'll probably drop by at some point,' I said. 'He's got to give me back the Guzzi. I lent it to him weeks ago.'

I returned to the beginning of our conversation. 'So you're doing OK, then?' I said. 'Well, yes, although it's a shame Juan won't be coming and that Pancho isn't behaving himself.' 'Yes, I saw Pancho when I arrived.' I started putting the books I'd brought with me from Villa Lecuona on a shelf. 'What was he doing? Catching trout?' 'I think so,' I said. 'Pancho loves being in the water, but when it comes to drinking, he has different tastes.' He went over to the window and looked out. 'He was just a bit further down from your house,' I told him, 'with the twins.' 'I can't see anyone now. They've probably gone to Adela's,' he said. 'I don't know what it is about this place,' he went on, after a silence. 'Everyone drinks so much. My brother, Ubanbe, and even Sebastián. If they carry on like this, they're likely to come to a sticky end. Especially Pancho. He hasn't got much sense as it is.'

I opened the window. Ava, Mizpa and the foals were no longer standing in a group. Moro was still in the upper part of the paddock. 'Who takes the woodcutters their lunch now?' Lubis gave a resigned shrug. 'It's pointless asking Pancho to work at the sawmill. And he doesn't do much at home either.' 'So you're the one who has to go to the forest?' Lubis nodded.

Oh, Susie Q, oh Susie Q, oh Susie Q. Joseba turned the cassette-player in the car up to full volume, and the colts raised their heads and stood looking over at the house. One of them started frisking about. Underneath the window, Joseba wasn't frisking about exactly, but he was shaking his long hair and moving in time to the music. 'He's in a good mood,' said Lubis. Then he pointed over at the paddock. 'What do you think of the three colts? Beautiful, eh?' 'Yeah, cool,' I said. 'Juan phones me nearly every week to ask after them.' 'What have you called them?' 'The two chestnuts are Elko and Eder, and the white one is Paul.' 'Paul? Like the horse that got killed?' He nodded. 'He's mine. Juan gave him to me. He says that now he doesn't come here

236

any more, I've got more responsibility and that I deserve him.' 'He's right,' I said.

Joseba turned off the cassette-player. 'Are you coming down?' he shouted, looking up at the window: 'It's getting dark.' 'It won't be dark for another hour,' Lubis told him. The clouds were no longer edged with silver glitter, but it was still very light. Adrián gave Joseba a shove to get him moving. 'We'll be at the Ritz,' he said: 'Be sure to join us there before it's time to pay the bill.' They set off in the direction of Adela's house, waving wildly.

I closed the window and started making the bed with the clean sheets I found in the wardrobe. 'I promised them I'd treat them to supper. You come too, Lubis,' I said. He'd gone round to the other side of the bed to help me. 'I'll come if you want me to, but if Pancho is around, he'll want to join us. He won't go home to have supper with his mother, that's for sure.' 'Let him stay with us then.'

The bed was made, and we were about to go downstairs. Lubis stopped at the door of the room. 'Do you remember the day you spent in there?' he said, pointing to the hiding-place. 'It was pretty tough, wasn't it?' 'It did me good though. I learned a lot from it.'

'Why have you brought your accordion with you? Are you going to start playing again?' Lubis asked as we walked over to Adela's house. Conversation was becoming easier. 'They want me to play at the dances at the Hotel Alaska. I don't know now if I should have agreed to do it.' 'Well, everyone needs money.' I improvised a response: 'True enough, but there are times when I regret having said "Yes".' Suddenly, I felt ashamed. Lubis' presence only highlighted the contemptible nature of my decision. Going back to the Hotel Alaska was tantamount to surrendering, to bowing the knee.

'But the hotel isn't just Berlino's home,' said Lubis, sensing my unease. 'It's Martín and Teresa's too. And they're both friends of yours.' This argument wasn't exactly perfect, but I didn't want to give it any further thought. 'I have to go up to the hotel sometimes too,' Lubis went on. 'Pancho's always hanging around there because of the tourists. They drive him wild, especially the Frenchwomen. If I let him, he'd spend all summer there.' We were outside Adela's house. Lubis stopped. 'You go in. I'll go and tell my mother I'm eating here. I'll be right back.' He crossed the stream by the stepping-stones and strode along the path.

Adela greeted me warmly, saying how glad she was to see me again and that I was quite right to bring my friends with me. 'We don't get many students. You're doing us a great honour, David.' Adrián and Joseba were sitting at one of the long tables in the kitchen, eating bread and cheese. Before them stood an almost empty bottle of wine. Pancho was there too.

On another smaller table, one of the twins was eating in silence, his head down. 'Where's Sebastián?' Adela yelled at him. 'I saw him with Ubanbe this morning,' said the twin, without looking up. He was eating a fried egg and wiping his plate with a huge piece of bread. 'And Gabriel?' That was the name of the other twin. 'Dunno.' 'Well, finish eating and go and find him!' Adela sighed loudly. 'Those kids are enough to drive a person to drink, David.' 'I'm glad to see nothing's changed around here, Adela,' I said, 'I really am.'

Pancho started thumping the table. He seemed angry. 'Bring us some more cheese, Adela. They eat like horses, these students. They haven't left me a crumb.' Adrián pulled a face of mock astonishment. 'What, you mean you're still hungry?' 'What have I had to eat?' said Pancho, wounded. 'Just a little piece of meat at midday, that's all.' Adrián opened his eyes very wide. 'A little piece of meat, you say. So you *are* a cannibal, Pancho!' Joseba burst out laughing. 'I don't know about that,' said Pancho, not understanding the joke, 'but I'm certainly hungry.'

Lubis appeared at the kitchen door. 'I'm having supper here, too, Adela,' he said. 'Have you told Beatriz? The telephone's right there. You know how your mother worries.' A brand-new red phone was next to the fridge. Lubis made a gesture indicating that there was no need.

The kitchen door opened again, and Gabriel, the second twin, sidled over to join his brother. 'Oh, so there you are!' said his mother. Adrián raised his arms: 'Thank God,' he exclaimed, 'thank God!' Adela looked at him uncomprehendingly. 'The return of a child is always a reason for celebration,' explained Adrián. 'Don't give this student any more wine,

238

Señora,' said Joseba. 'When he drinks, he talks nothing but nonsense.' Adela's attention, however, was elsewhere. 'You're soaked to the skin!' she said to Gabriel. 'Where on earth have you been?' 'In the stream,' replied the boy. 'At this hour? But why?' 'I'll tell you why, Adela,' said Pancho. 'There's a very wily trout, and Gabriel wanted to catch it and bring it here for his mother and for everyone else too. But the wily trout refuses to be caught.' Gabriel nodded slowly.

III

A small stage with a microphone and a stool was usually set up for the accordionist on the hotel mirador, and when I began to play, I'd be alone there, isolated from everyone else – not in the hotel or on the mirador, in the middle of a dance, but in some other separate place. If I pulled my hat down low over my face, that feeling was even more pronounced, and I felt protected, hidden from the others. It was like going back to being a child and sitting crouched between the supports beneath the stage, eating peanuts and watching the movements of the various shoes – black shoes, brown shoes, white shoes – that belonged to the people dancing to Ángel's music.

People would start arriving at the hotel at about six o'clock. The boys would mainly hang around the balustrade surrounding the mirador or outside the coffee shop, on the terrace, smoking cigarettes and drinking Cuba libres or gin and tonics; as for the girls, they'd go down to the garden and stroll around amongst the rose-covered walls or the flower beds and then, at about seven o'clock, they'd come upstairs for the dance. That was my cue to start playing light, rhythmical tunes, and everyone, girls and boys, would start whirling round and jumping in their black shoes, their brown shoes, their white shoes. At half past eight there was a break, and afterwards it was the turn of the slower songs like 'Orfeu negro' or 'Petite fleur'. Then it seemed that the 200 or 250 people dancing on the mirador began to move closer together to form a clump, until little by little, as it grew dark, they became a single mass, one slowly moving body.

239

That mass gradually fell asleep, just as spinning tops do when they reach the moment of perfect equilibrium. The valley of Obaba seemed then quiet and serene, and the Hotel Alaska itself seemed quiet and serene. Half past ten would strike. I'd play a current hit song – that summer of 1970 it was 'Casatschok' – and bring the dance to a close. The mass, the one slow-moving body, would wake up and fragment. Some would rush off home; the rest would carry on to the last note, spinning and jumping in their black shoes, their brown shoes, their white shoes.

Sometimes, I, too, almost fell asleep, gazing out over the heads of the dancers, absorbed in my contemplation of the landscape. The valley of Obaba was, at first sight, cool and green, then, where the hills and mountains seemed to shelter the little villages and the solitary houses, it was sweet and soft, and finally, where it reached the mountains that looked towards France, it was as blue and ethereal as smoke.

In the darkness of night, the valley seemed a more intimate place. The lights went on in the houses and the villages; the valley filled up with yellow smudges. Still playing the accordion, I'd follow those yellow smudges with my eyes: first, those of Obaba, then those of the sawmill, and, at last, the lights of Virginia's house.

The sailor whom Virginia had married had been involved in an accident at sea, off Newfoundland, and she'd had no news of him for two years. She was living back in her house by the river, on the other side of the sportsground, and, according to my mother, was in very low spirits. 'His body's never been found, and so she can't really come out of mourning. That's why she always wears black or grey. A little while ago, I suggested making her a green dress, and she burst into tears.' My mother's eyes also filled with tears when she was telling me this.

Virginia worked now at a coffee shop on the new housing estate, and that was where I'd see her when I came to Obaba to spend the weekend or for some celebration. I usually dropped in at breakfast time, when the place filled up with customers, and I'd watch her as she came and went – with pastries and coffees – on the other side of the counter. When my turn came, she would stand in front of me and smile. In a

240

special way – or so it seemed to me – but from a great distance, as if the looks we'd exchanged in the church in Obaba were dried flowers, scenes from the past. She'd ask: 'How are things in San Sebastián, David?' And I'd give her some banal reply, and she'd bring me my coffee and whatever else I'd ordered.

Occasionally, she and I would find ourselves alone in the coffee shop. She wore her hair very short now, almost straight, so that it revealed more of her face: her forehead, her dark eyes, her ears, her small nose, her lips. The peasants of Obaba would have said: '*Virginia está muy bonita*' – 'Virginia is very pretty' – using the verb *estar* to indicate a temporary state 'rather than *ser*' indicating some permanent, inherent characteristic. In the same spirit, judging beauty to be a state that can improve or deteriorate, I would have added: 'It's true, Virginia. *Estás más bonita que hace cuatro años*.' – 'You're prettier than you were four years ago.' But I never did say that, or anything like it. The images in my mind stopped me: a boat was sinking; a woman was weeping in a room; the telephone was ringing and a voice was telling me: 'No body has yet been found.'

Sometimes this changed. These dramatic images faded in my mind and were replaced by others – simpler and stronger – fuelled by desire. I would imagine her naked and imagine myself touching her breasts, her belly, her thighs. I would feel afraid then, fearing that as soon as I opened my mouth, I would speak the words I should not say: 'Virginia, you're even prettier than you were four years ago. Please, come with me.' I would put my money down on the counter and leave the coffee shop. Adrián was quite right when he said: 'If that crocodile of yours doesn't give her a good bite, it'll go crazy.'

I'd look away from the yellow smudges, from the lights of Virginia's house and return to the dance. I'd see before me the people with their arms about each other; I'd see Ubanbe and Opin talking to a group of girls; I'd see Joseba and Adrián having a drink out on the terrace, and sometimes Lubis too. I envied them. It seemed to me that they were living in the pure present, in the summer of 1970, and that everything they'd experienced before had already dissolved in their hearts and their

241

minds; that, for them, the past was a fluid that flowed through their spirits unimpeded. My spirit, on the other hand, was like dough, like thick paste. The hatred I felt for Ángel clouded my relationship with my mother and sometimes still led me down into the filthy cave, as it had when I was fourteen or fifteen. On the other hand, my love for Virginia stopped me approaching other women. I no longer made lists of those I loved, but if I had, Virginia would have occupied first place. There were other women I felt attracted to – Susana, Victoria and Paulina, for example, or some of the girls I studied with at university – but they didn't belong on such lists. They belonged only on the crocodile's lists.

IV

Time flowed softly by, spinning like a top: one dance followed another; after Saturday came Sunday, and after Sunday came the Saturday of the following week. And it seemed everything was set to continue like that, as if time, too, like a spinning top, was falling asleep. However, at the beginning of August, there was a sudden strange movement, and I found myself involved in an altercation between Adrián and the girls who'd been our classmates at the school in the sawmill. It was nothing important, but it made it clear to me that peace and quiet are qualities to be found only among mountains or in the sky, but never in the minds and hearts of people. It was a sign: more strange movements would follow, more oscillations, and they'd get worse and worse, more and more serious. At a given moment, someone's life – some other spinning top – would fall to the ground.

It was Saturday. I'd finished my performance and gone to join Adrián, Joseba and Lubis on the terrace outside the coffee house. 'Why do you finish the dance with that tune, "Casatschok"?' Lubis asked me: 'It seems a bit out of place in Obaba.' He was looking at me with his large eyes. I didn't know what to say. I didn't understand what he meant. 'What Lubis means is that we're not in Russia,'

242

explained Joseba in a slightly ironic tone: 'In other words, you're a traitor for bringing that dance from the Volga to Obaba, and you deserve our utter scorn.'

He inhaled deeply on his cigarette, leaned towards me and blew out a mouthful of smoke. 'Do you mind!' protested Victoria, waving the smoke away with her hand. She was sitting just behind me, with Paulina, Niko – the daughter of the manager of a bank that had opened in Obaba – and four French boys who were holidaying at the hotel. Susana and her boyfriend – Martín called him Marquesito, 'the little Marquis' – were also nearby, at a table behind Adrián.

Victoria seemed annoyed. 'Forgive the grave offence I caused you,' Joseba said quietly. 'To ensure that you bear me no ill feeling I will now roll you a cigarette.' 'I don't want a cigarette!' retorted Victoria. 'You must tell me then what I must do to win your forgiveness. I am entirely at your disposal.' It was difficult to get angry with Joseba, as difficult as it was to know what he really felt.

'Lubis is right, David. This isn't Russia!' declared Adrián. 'At least I don't think it is. I see no snow, I see no Bolsheviks, and, above all, I see not a single bottle of vodka.' He stood up and pointed to the other tables on the terrace. 'Not a single one!' he shrilled. Then he raised his glass as if to make a toast. 'Not that I'm about to complain. This gin and tonic is delicious!' 'Well, I don't know about there being no Bolsheviks around,' said Joseba. Lubis leaned towards me: 'I was just giving you my opinion, David. If you want to play "Casatschok", you're perfectly at liberty to do so.' That expression 'perfectly at liberty to do so' sounded strange in Lubis' mouth. 'What would *you* play at the end of the dance?' 'I really like that tune "Pagotxueta". People always used to play it here.' He was talking about a passacaglia that was often played at the end of village fiestas. 'That's a good idea, Lubis. I'll practise it this week and include it in my repertoire.'

Adrián was standing up again. 'This isn't Russia, my friends. This is France!' he bawled, pointing to the table where Paulina, Victoria and Niko were talking to the French boys. Niko whispered some comment of which we heard only the words: 'gin and tonic'. 'Of course, I didn't realise,' Adrián bawled again. 'Gin and tonic! This isn't France, it's England!'

'You're giving us a real geography lesson,' said Marquesito, Susana's boyfriend. He was about twenty-five and the polar opposite of Joseba. He dressed impeccably and wore a neat beard. He looked at us with distaste. 'How ignoble of you, Marquis!' Adrián said reproachfully. 'Attacking from behind like that, like a rogue.' 'Oh, please, Adrián, don't get all stroppy,' said Susana. *Stroppy*. I found that word unexpected too. It didn't suit her, even though she was living in Madrid, finishing the medical degree she'd begun in Zaragoza. She was, after all, the daughter of Obaba's doctor, the man who had silently applauded me when he saw me reading a book by Lizardi. 'Forgive me, Marchioness,' replied Adrián, turning his gaze on her.

Adrián's eyes would sometimes suddenly go dull and dead, as if they were made of wood, like the figures he made in his workshop. Susana knew those eyes and knew what they meant – that Adrián might, at any moment, say something outrageous – and so she turned away instead and sat staring out at the valley. Finding nothing but darkness to look at, however, she shifted uneasily in her chair.

Joseba placed the accordion on my knees. 'What was the name of that tune you recommended, Lubis?' 'Pagotxueta,' Adrián said loudly. 'What new atrocity are you planning, Manson?' Joseba clapped his hands: 'Adrián, friends, pray silence. David is going to play "Pagotxueta".' 'If I can remember it,' I said. 'That doesn't matter, David,' smiled Joseba, 'the audience will applaud you anyway.' Susana and the Marquesito had stood up, ready to leave. 'I hope the Marquis and Marchioness sleep well!' said Adrián, by way of bidding them goodnight.

V

It was the custom for the accordionist to have supper out on the terrace once the dancers had gone to their beds. Ángel always used to, and, in that summer of 1970, I did as well, inviting my friends, Joseba and

Adrián, to join me and also, occasionally, Lubis, who would bring Pancho with him – 'So that he doesn't go off in search of Frenchwomen,' said Adrián. Martín was often there too, even though he worked until late at his club on the coast and only got back to the hotel when we were eating our desserts or drinking our coffee.

We used to stay out on the terrace until late into the night, because it was pleasant to sit there, listening to the truths and lies that the south wind brought us after a long day: 'It's best not to take life too seriously. It's best to enjoy yourself. It's best to eat and drink without a care in the world, to spout a lot of nonsense and puff away on your cigarettes with the sole aim of creating a lot of smoke.' We followed this advice – we ate fish and salad, drank beer and wine, smoked Joseba's honey-scented cigarettes or the American cigarettes Martín brought us, and we did everything very languidly, with the lights on the terrace turned right down so that the insects wouldn't come near.

One particularly hot August night – it must have been the third Sunday in the month – we suddenly found ourselves, despite the dim lights, surrounded by insects that looked like dragonflies, but which were so heavy and slow they appeared incapable of remaining airborne. When one of them landed on the table, Adrián would trap it under a large beer glass and hold it there for a long time, and then, just when it seemed about to die of suffocation, he'd lift the glass and set it free. Pancho immediately copied him, except that he prolonged their imprisonment, and the insects died inside the glass.

'Stop it, Pancho!' Lubis said. Like me, he felt the insect's suffering as keenly as if he himself were suffocating inside the glass. I thought I should invent some distraction and change the after-dinner mood at the table; if I didn't, Adrián and Pancho would continue their 'entertainment'. 'Who would you choose for the title of Miss Obaba?' I said, picking up a newspaper someone had left on a chair. On the back page, a banner headline declared: 'Soledad Errazuriz. Daughter of Basque family could be next Miss World'.

They all stared at me. 'It's not an easy decision to make. We'd have to discuss it,' said Joseba, realising what I was trying to do. 'Let the crocodiles decide,' said Adrián, picking up my Hotson hat and shooing away the insects that were still fluttering round the table. 'I know,' said Pancho. 'What do you know?' asked Adrián. 'I know that girls are good.' 'Good for what? To eat?' Lubis held up a hand to Adrián, telling him to stop. 'Why don't we just leave Pancho alone and then we'll be all right,' he said. Joseba looked suddenly weary and said: 'Lubis is right. You're starting to repeat yourself.' Adrián covered his face with the hat. 'Forgive me, my friends. As the saying goes, all humpbacks end up giving you the hump. It's as if it were in our blood.' 'Stop arguing for a moment,' I said, 'and let's discuss the matter of Miss Obaba.'

Gregorio came to ask if we wanted anything else, because it was late and they were getting ready to close. He didn't address me, but Joseba and Adrián, despite the fact that I was the accordionist and the person paying the bill. He still couldn't forgive me for the afternoon I'd spent with Teresa four years before, right there, in the hotel. 'Gin and tonics all round,' said Adrián. 'Make that two fruit juices for me and Pancho,' Lubis said. 'Pancho's taking medication at the moment and shouldn't be drinking any alcohol at all.' Gregorio went back inside. 'Can you bring us some paper and a biro as well, please,' Joseba called after him, just as Gregorio was about to disappear through the door.

The gin and tonics, the juices, the piece of paper and the biro were on the table. 'What about Paulina?' asked Joseba, taking a sip of his gin and tonic. The drink was in a tall glass and topped with a slice of lemon. 'That new dress she was wearing tonight showed her knees,' he added, 'and very nice knees they were, I thought.' We started discussing Paulina's qualities. 'Where would you put her on the list?' I asked at last. 'Twenty-third?' suggested Adrián, fanning himself with the hat. Joseba and I protested, and decided that she had to be among the ten prettiest girls in Obaba. 'Eighth?' I asked. 'Sixth,' said Joseba. Pancho raised his hand, the way children do at infant school. 'Ninth,' he said. 'What about you, Lubis? What do you think?' Lubis shrugged. He didn't want to say. 'I'm with Pancho. Let's put her ninth,' I said, settling the matter. Paulina's name and the appropriate number were set down on the piece of paper.

We continued the game, until we had a list of ten names, but Adrián complained that we were clearly prepared to consider any girl at all, 'even the ones,' he said, 'who are female versions of me', and he made us reduce the number of candidates. We reduced them down to eight, and then to five. The chosen girls were: Bruna, Niko, Victoria, Alberta and, ahead of them all, Miss Obaba, Susana.

After choosing the names, we had another idea: why didn't we write the list out? Why didn't we make loads of copies and distribute them during the dance, the way clandestine political groups did with their pamphlets? It was Joseba's suggestion. 'That's a great idea!' exclaimed Adrián. 'It could be fun. We'll be competing with the revolutionaries!' Lubis glanced at me: 'We should be careful, David. It's best not to mix things up.' 'All those in favour, raise your hand,' said Adrián. The only one who didn't was Lubis.

Pancho was half-asleep; his eyes were closing. 'We'd better get home,' said Lubis, addressing Joseba and me. 'If it was up to me, I'd head off alone, but you see what Pancho's like. It's the effect of the pills he's taking.' Joseba got up from the table. 'Don't worry. We're leaving too.'

'So who's going to write the report on Miss Obaba and her four ladies-in-waiting?' asked Adrián. 'I think the best person for the job is the group poet, Joseba, although he's been a bit slack lately.' 'Joseba and I will do it together,' I said. I could see that Lubis was getting impatient and I didn't want things to drag on any longer than they had to.

Adrián put on the hat. 'Do me a favour will you, and get a dig in at the Marquis. Just a couple of lines in the section devoted to Susana will do.' This, it seemed to me, was his main concern, the point he'd been wanting to reach from the moment we first discussed making the list. 'Where can we get copies made?' asked Joseba. 'On the photocopier at the sawmill?' Adrián said: 'No, not there. As Pancho's paragon of a brother said, we shouldn't mix things up.' '*He* could do with taking a few pills too, if you ask me,' Lubis whispered in my ear. 'He's such a stirrer.' 'Leave everything else in my hands,' said Adrián. 'I'll make sure we get maximum coverage.' *Coverage*. That was the word used at the time for distributing political pamphlets.

VI

MISS OBABA AND HER FOUR LADIES-IN-WAITING
THE PRETTIEST GIRLS IN OBABA
(Secret publication. Essential information.)

The fifth prettiest: Bruna, the forest warden's daughter. Twenty-three years old. There's no other girl in the whole region to match her athletic body. No man could fail to be entranced by her thighs and bum.

The fourth prettiest: Niko, twenty-one years old. She's slim and dresses like an English pop-singer. She has beautiful large, grey eyes. And a lovely mouth.

The third prettiest: Victoria, the daughter of the German engineer who runs the Kramer company. Twenty years old. Her body is softer and fleshier than any of the aforementioned bodies and, according to those who've seen her bathing naked in the swimming-pool at her house, she has the biggest tits in Obaba.

The second prettiest: Alberta, the assistant at the sports shop. She's very tall and muscular, as befits someone who has played in a handball team for years. She looks as if she could squeeze a man to death with her embrace. She likes to wear her hair short to show off her full lips. She's twenty-four.

The prettiest, Miss Obaba 1970: Susana, the doctor's daughter. Some will argue that she's too short, since she's barely five feet two inches tall. However, her body, from her head to her feet, is so delicately, softly curved, that one might say she resembles a piece of fine porcelain. Some people use words such as doll-like to describe her, but there's nothing feeble or silly about her. On the contrary, her body gives off a feeling of power, and her tits are almost as big as Victoria's. Her eyes are simultaneously green and blue. Her voice is husky, slightly throaty, and many a young man in Obaba has dreamed of hearing that voice in bed, close to his ear. For the moment, however, only the Marquis of Coldcock can claim this privilege. Twenty-one years old.

VII

On Uncle Juan's typewriter, Joseba and I typed out 100 copies of the list of Obaba's prettiest girls, making three carbon copies a time. On the last Saturday in August, we put the 300 sheets of paper in a file and took them to the hotel, where Adrián was waiting for us.

'How are you going to distribute it?' we asked, showing him one of the sheets. We were in a room downstairs that was sometimes used as a dressing-room. 'I know what I'm doing, don't you worry,' he replied, removing from his mouth a coca-cola-flavoured chupa-chups.

He sat down in front of a mirror to read the list. In his mirror image, his hunchback seemed larger. 'Special treatment for Niko, I see, as expected,' he remarked, without looking up. Then his face lit up: 'The Marquis of Coldcock! Oh, excellent! Excellent!' and he roared with laughter. 'Forgive me, Joseba, for doubting you. When it comes to inventing names, you're a true artist. The Marquis of Coldcock!' He started pacing up and down the dressing-room. He was very excited.

'What are you going to play just before the interval, David? I need to know,' he asked, having once again congratulated Joseba. 'How about "Padam Padam"?' It was a piece that Lubis really liked. 'What's that?' I picked up the accordion and played the refrain. 'No, that's too slow. Think of another one.' 'What exactly are you intending to do?' asked Joseba. Adrián responded not to us, but to our reflections in the mirror: 'None of your business. Leave it all in my hands.' The skin on his face was as white as the skin on his hands. 'You have to make a decision, David. Tell me what you're going to play.' 'How about "Casatschok"?' Adrián paused to think. 'Not bad. People always make a lot of noise when you play that.'

249

Someone knocked on the door, and Gregorio came in. 'It's time for the dance to start,' he said. Joseba pointed to his wristwatch: 'As the artist's agent, I must tell you that he has another three minutes.' 'Aren't you the funny one!' retorted Gregorio before turning on his heel and leaving. 'He's a nasty piece of work, that waiter,' remarked Joseba. 'In fact, they say he's a police informer.' 'I'll keep my eye on him,' said Adrián. 'The distribution will be over before he's noticed a thing.' He was talking as if our bits of paper really were political pamphlets.

I put on my hat and went over to the mirador. Adrián pointed at me with his chupa-chups: 'Remember. Before the interval, "Casatschok".' 'Don't you want to share your plans with us, General?' asked Joseba. 'No, you may leave.' 'Even if we give you another chupa-chups?' But Adrián was re-reading the list and didn't reply. 'Let's just hope he doesn't cause too much of a ruckus,' whispered Joseba as we left the room.

It was a very muggy evening, much hotter than the previous days, and the mist over the hills looked grubby, as if it had been sprinkled with lime. I took up my position on stage, feeling slightly nervous this time, no longer in a separate place, hidden beneath my hat, but exposed to the gaze of everyone who had come to the dance. I couldn't imagine how Adrián would go about distributing the sheets of paper, but his behaviour in the dressing-room didn't augur well. I felt we were taking the Miss Obaba joke too far, and that we should have heeded Lubis' advice when he warned us about mixing things up. Now, though, it was too late, and all I could do was carry on playing the accordion.

I put off the moment again and again, but, in the end, at about eight o'clock, I launched into the agreed tune – 'Casatschok'. By then, the temperature had fallen slightly, and out on the terrace there were more or less the usual number of people, around 200, some – the majority – dancing, and others – amongst them Paulina, Victoria, Susana, Marquesito and a few summer visitors – drinking and eating ice creams beneath the awning.

As soon as I played the first notes, all the dancers started making Russian-style leaps, and Ubanbe, who was right in the middle, leapt higher than anyone. He was wearing a huge pair of white tennis shoes and looked the part of the lead dancer, the person everyone would follow when it came to the moment to call out the chorus: *Casatschok! Casatschok! Casatschok!* I glanced over at the terrace. Marquesito was offering Susana a cigarette, but she was eating an ice cream and declined.

Then Marquesito's pack of cigarettes fell to the floor, and someone started shouting and screaming. Ubanbe immediately ran over to see what was wrong. And Marquesito ran too, but in the opposite direction to Ubanbe. I stopped playing. More shouts.

'It's a bull,' someone yelled. But the only animal to cross the terrace and emerge on to the mirador was a donkey jumping and kicking like a mad thing. It had its harness on, with a basket on either side of its back. The pieces of paper in the baskets floated up into the air and landed on the floor. The donkey was Moro. One person – Pancho – stood on a chair on the terrace to get a better view of what was going on.

Moro grew still more frenzied once people realised what was happening and tried to corral him, and I was terrified when I saw him galloping blindly towards the balustrade. If he fell into the garden, he would break his legs or his back. He was saved from this fate thanks to the strength of Ubanbe and several friends of his. They grabbed the mule round the neck and grappled him to his knees. Ubanbe shouted: 'Someone's put pepper up his arse! Bring some water!' Three bottles were brought and they used all three of them.

'God, we're stupid! Just the thought of it depresses me,' said Joseba in despairing tones. We'd eaten supper and were still sitting at the table with Adrián and Pancho. 'It really upset me to see Morito like that, especially when's he's normally so docile and quiet!' said Pancho. Joseba didn't even look at him.

Worried because Lubis hadn't come to fetch him, Pancho started offering explanations and excuses: 'I told Adrián he was sticking too much pepper up him, but he wouldn't listen, he used a whole packet. I said to him, there's no way we're going to get this donkey up the hill tomorrow morning, because I don't think we managed to wash all the pepper away, and what will we do if he starts leaping about and upsets the woodcutters' food?' 'Don't worry,' I said. 'Ubanbe has taken him to Iruain. Between him and Lubis they'll clean him up.' 'I don't know, David. I don't think that brother of mine is going to forgive us for this.'

Yawning ostentatiously, as if the conversation bored him, Adrián went into the coffee shop and returned with Gregorio. The waiter was carrying bottles of beer on a tray. 'I'd have brought them myself, but my hump's playing up tonight and I might lose my balance.' Not a muscle moved in Gregorio's face. 'That's what I'm here for,' he said. 'What did you think of the distribution of pamphlets today,' Adrián asked him. 'Marcelino has been informed,' replied Gregorio sharply.

Adrián placed two bottles of beer in front of each of us, including Pancho. 'Have a drink,' he said. 'Not drinking seems to make you stupid. Fancy calling a donkey *Morito*, for God's sake. *Morito*! In this village, we've always called a donkey a donkey.' He leaned back in his chair, looking up at the yellow-and-white awning. 'Honestly, I don't under-stand your reaction at all. It's as if your crocodiles were all like this,' he said, wiggling a limp index finger. 'A week ago you were all for it. And now you tell me you're depressed. Well, you're not depressed, you're just shit-scared. Your crocodiles are all limp.' Again he let his index finger dangle loosely.

Pancho was scratching his head. 'I really have got my tail between my legs!' he said: 'You heard what Ubanbe said. If he finds the person who put pepper up the donkey's bum, he'll pulverise him.' 'He wouldn't dare do that to the boss's son!' exclaimed Adrián. 'Or perhaps he would . . . The suspense is killing, isn't it, my friends!' He started clapping, but no one joined in. 'I just don't understand these long faces. You're a load of cowards, the lot of you!' He took a sip from his bottle of beer.

Martín appeared, having just come from the car park, his car keys still in his hand, and he stood watching us from the entrance to the terrace. 'I could hear you from the crossroads, Adrián. Can't you talk without bellowing?' He came over and, very formally, shook our hands.

252

Then he stroked Adrián's hump. 'The Romanian girl sends her love. She misses you and wants you to go and see her.' Without looking up from his bottle of beer, Joseba asked: 'The Romanian? Don't you mean the Moroccan? I'd heard that all the young ladies who offer their services at that club of yours are subjects of King Hassan.' 'You're a complete ignoramus, Joseba,' retorted Martín.

Adrián put a bottle of beer down in front of Martín, but he pushed it away. 'Sorry, but at this time of night, I drink only champagne.' 'I know all about the Romanian girl,' said Pancho. 'Adrián takes her to Samson's Bath to fuck her.' 'Don't be so crude, Pancho,' said Martín, pinching his arm.

Adrián told Martín what had happened, about how the donkey had appeared on the mirador, kicking and bucking, sending the French and all the other summer visitors fleeing to their rooms, convinced they were being chased by a bull. And that the little Marquis, equally terri-fied, had fled too, the coward, without a thought for Susana's safety. Paulina, for her part, had shown no fear whatsoever, but she was furious not to have been included on the list of the prettiest girls in Obaba. She'd torn up a whole pile of the leaflets and was thinking of taking steps. 'Apparently, next Sunday, she's going to turn up wearing a mini-skirt, to show off her thighs. I wonder if she'll get on the list after that.' 'You're drunk, Adrián, and you're still talking too loudly,' Martín said. 'Do you want Berli to hear you from his bedroom? If he finds out that you were the people behind tonight's "action", you'd better watch out. He didn't like it at all. I spoke to Geneviève on the phone, and she said that he very nearly called out the civil guard.' 'May I say something?' asked Adrián. 'Yes, as long as you stop shouting.' 'Like my companions here, I too have regrets. I just wish we'd taken a photo of Ubanbe and Co. washing the donkey's bottom. We should have called in Joseba's father; he's a good photographer! It would have made a lovely picture. We could have sent it to the newspapers to show them what we're like in Obaba. Newspapers love that kind of thing – local colour, they call it.'

I couldn't stand Adrián's chatter a moment longer, and I started picking up the bits of paper still scattered around the terrace. They bothered me. I hated the sight of them. 'Let me see,' Martín asked. Joseba had still not looked up from his bottle of beer. 'Oh, please, just throw them away!' he begged me. 'I'll put them in the accordion case,' I told him. I had about fifteen in my hand. 'I'll dispose of them.' I started walking in the direction of the dressing-room. 'Hey, prof!' Martín called. 'My mother's still around somewhere, in the kitchen, I think. Tell her to bring us a couple of bottles of champagne and a tray of cakes. Say it's for her beloved son.' He turned to Pancho: 'We have to fight against the long faces Joseba and David are wearing tonight. Don't you agree, my dear friend?' '¡Bien me parece!' agreed Pancho in his rudimentary Spanish.

When I came back, Martín was still holding the list of Miss Obabas. 'You *are* a lot of babies,' he said. 'And you're the biggest baby of the lot, Joseba. Fancy including your own little love on the list! Because Niko is your little love, isn't she? "She's slim and dresses like an English pop-singer. She has beautiful, large, grey eyes . . ." Oh, please, Joseba. That's so twee!' Adrián let out a guffaw. 'Be quiet, you drunk!' said Martín slapping him on the back. 'You're a baby too, but a nasty one. You've got no heart.'

'The list is worthless anyway,' concluded Martín, lighting a cigarette. He was wearing a ring I'd never seen before, with a round, red stone. 'For example, you haven't included Virginia, the waitress. When she gets dressed up, she looks like Claudia Cardinale. And she has a special way of breathing. She breathes like someone who's got a cold, do you know what I mean?' I knew what he meant. I felt a lump in my throat.

'Do you mean the way an owl breathes,' Pancho suggested. Martín stared at him. 'I know about women, my friend, but not about the beasts of the forest or the trout in the stream. How exactly does an owl breathe?' Pancho sat for a few moments with his eyes closed and then began to pant. It sounded to me like a death rattle. 'Incredible!' exclaimed Martín. 'Virginia's breathing is exactly like that. I would never have thought it!'

254

'She's certainly very attractive,' I said. 'We'd forgotten all about her.' I was trying to prevent the conversation from deteriorating. 'Oh, she's gorgeous,' agreed Martín. 'Alberta, on the other hand, the one who works in the sports shop, is a horse, but a carthorse, like the sort people used to use for ploughing. Not a thoroughbred like Virginia.' He kept putting his cigarette to his lips, each time revealing the ring with the red stone.

Martín seemed to notice my unease. 'What do you think, David? Do you know what that breathing means?' I was afraid he might be able to read my thoughts, or that he knew everything. Perhaps through Teresa, who, or so I was told, had still not forgiven me for letting her down four years previously, on the day the monument was unveiled. 'No, you tell me. You know more about women than I do,' I replied. 'Well it means: 'I'm all alone, I can find no one to quench my desire, I don't want to give myself to any of the men who try to tempt me, but my desire is getting stronger and stronger, and I can't hold out much longer, I can't.' Martín fell back in his chair, as if exhausted. 'A woman who breathes like that deserves to be number one on the list,' he said.

'When she gets frightened, she lets out a real screech, Martín,' said Pancho. 'Who does? I don't understand.' 'The owl.' With no further explanation, Pancho began imitating the bird. He made a sound like someone being stabbed. 'No, not like that,' said Martín mockingly. 'If someone, me, for example, got on top of her, she'd scream: "No, no, please, no, stop, stop, please, no, oh, come inside me, come inside me, more, more!"' As he spoke, Martín was panting and writhing about on his chair, his head back and his eyes closed. I thought he was about to start masturbating.

'Are you playing the fool again?' said Geneviève, putting the bottle of champagne and the tray of cakes down on the table. 'Hello, sweetheart, how are you?' Martín said, getting up and putting his arm about her waist. 'Get off! You stink. Where on earth do you get your colognes from?' 'The one I'm wearing now was given to me by a lady-friend who's very fond of me. If I didn't love my *maman* so much, I'd marry her.' He started kissing his mother. 'Will you stop it, please!' Geneviève

255

looked annoyed, but she was only pretending. As Teresa always used to say, she adored her son.

Then she became thoughtful. 'You weren't the ones who caused this evening's rumpus, were you?' she asked. 'You all seem a bit over-excited.' 'You can't mean Joseba. He doesn't look over-excited, he looks positively funereal,' said Martín. This wasn't entirely true. Joseba, with folded arms and attentive gaze, looked more like an observer now, someone outside the group. 'It's all this boy's fault, Geneviève,' said Martín, pointing at me. 'He's such a brilliant accordionist that he attracts all the donkeys in the area, the two-legged variety and the four-legged ones too.' His mother wagged her finger. She wouldn't allow any jokes on the subject. 'Will you be quiet. I've told you already how angry your father was. And now he's even angrier because the civil guard won't take his complaint seriously.' Martín put his arm around her shoulder. 'Do you know what you should say to Berli, *maman*? You should tell him that we're all sitting round the table here talking about love. And that, on a hot night like tonight, the civil guard will also be talking about love. They're in no mood to worry about donkeys.' Geneviève gave a heavy sigh. She didn't feel like talking after a long day's work. She was going to bed. 'It might not be a bad idea if you boys went to bed as well,' she said, as she left.

'What are you thinking about, David, if I may be so bold?' Martín asked, offering me a glass of champagne. I told him the truth, that I was thinking about Virginia. 'Good, David. I'm glad. You may be a baby, but you're a fast learner.' 'She's got very nice tits, too, very round and quite big,' commented Pancho. This time, we all looked at him, including Joseba. 'What did you say?' asked Martín. 'I said: that girl Virginia you're talking about has very round breasts. And hers don't hang down like Victoria, the German girl's do.' 'Do you mean you've seen them?' Martín raised his eyebrows. Pancho nodded. He was eating a *petit-suisse*. 'How?' 'With your father's binoculars.' 'I thought you wanted them to go bird-watching,' said Martín, 'that's why I got them off Berli. As an act of charity. But, when I think about it, what could be more normal? I prefer tits to birds any day.'

'Let me just get this straight,' Joseba said, emerging from his silence. 'Are you saying that you spend your time prowling round houses?' 'How did you manage to see Virginia's tits?' I asked. It was best not to beat around the bush with Pancho. 'It's summer, right, and really hot,' he began, somewhat embarrassed, 'and Virginia arrives at the coffee house really early, right? So later, she has an afternoon nap.' 'Such logic. I would never have thought of that!' broke in Adrián. Pancho finished his explanation: 'And if she gets all hot and sweaty, she goes into the kitchen to have a wash at the sink. Without her night-dress on sometimes.' He leaned towards the cakes. First, he picked up another *petit-suisse*, but then replaced it on the tray and put a mille-feuille in his mouth instead.

'Listen,' said Joseba. 'Going fishing for trout at night isn't the same as spying on women. The latter is a very serious offence.' 'You'd better listen to him. Joseba's almost a lawyer,' said Adrián, emphasising the 'almost'. 'Would your Honour like some more champagne?' asked Martín. Joseba shook his head. 'Well, I don't know how we're going to change this gentleman's mood,' Martín went on with a sigh. 'Where's your accordion, David?' 'In the dressing-room,' I said. 'Why don't you go and get it? Music works wonders. It might even cheer Joseba up. And Berli too, if he hears it from his bed.' I thought this might be a way of bringing the meeting to a close and so I agreed: 'A couple of tunes and then we go to bed, right? I'm exhausted.' 'That's fine by me. It's been a long, hard day,' said Joseba. 'Are there any more cakes in the hotel?' asked Pancho. These long, hard days had scarcely any effect on him at all.

As I came out of the dressing-room with my accordion, I noticed two figures walking along in the dark, at the far end of the mirador. At first, when I saw how cautiously they were moving, I thought they must be secret police. But one of them came towards me, saying gleefully: 'There you are, David!' 'I'm sorry, who are you?' My eyes were still getting used to the dark. 'Are you blind or something? It's me, Agustín!' 'Agustín or Komarov?' I said, recognising him at last. We embraced. 'Outside of university, it's best to forget all about my Russian name. It saves a lot of explaining.'

'So where have you sprung from?' I said, laughing. I was really pleased to see him. 'We came to Iruain to give you back the Guzzi. About time too, eh?' I asked if they'd seen Lubis. 'He has fond memories of that time we came when it snowed and you climbed on to the roof.' 'No, we only saw the twins.' 'And the horses,' added the person with Agustín. He was an athletic young man, dressed somewhat unusually for the time in a white polo shirt and red jeans. 'Very beautiful horses, by the way, not to mention the foals,' he said. The way he spoke reminded me a little of Lubis. Agustín introduced me to him: 'He's known as Bikandi.' We shook hands.

I suggested they come over to the terrace and meet my friends from Obaba. Bikandi said they couldn't stay. 'We have to get back to the friends we left behind in Iruain. To be honest, we only came to have a look at the political propaganda that was distributed today. We weren't expecting to find you here.' 'No, we assumed you'd be in Iruain,' said Agustín. 'I'll be going there shortly,' I said.

It was a rather awkward situation. Joseba and the others were expecting me. I had to play the tunes I'd promised to play. 'I'll see you later,' I said. Bikandi gestured to me to wait. 'Is it true they used a donkey to distribute the propaganda? I only ask because it seems so odd.' I explained that there hadn't been any political propaganda. I opened my accordion case and handed them a couple of sheets of paper.

'The prettiest, Miss Obaba 1970: Susana, the doctor's daughter!' Agustín read out loud. He roared with laughter. 'How stupid!' said Bikandi. He was not amused. And I had to agree with him that it was, indeed, stupid. 'Can I keep this, David?' Agustín asked. 'I'd like to show it to the friends waiting for us in Iruain.' 'You may have thought our curiosity somewhat excessive,' remarked Bikandi, 'but without curiosity one learns nothing.' He really did speak like Lubis, choosing his words carefully. I said that I was a curious person too, and that their curiosity was fine by me. 'Thank you. We'll see you later, then,' he said. 'We've parked the car behind the hotel,' Agustín told me. Then they vanished into the darkness of the mirador.

'It was a couple of lads wanting to see our list,' I explained when I returned to the terrace, and in response to Martín's stern expression. 'You took ages, and now there's no point. Look at the state these two are in.' Adrián and Pancho were both slumped in their chairs; Joseba had gone over to the balustrade of the mirador and was studying the lights in the valley. 'I'll play for you another night. I think we all need some rest,' I said. This wasn't entirely true. I did feel tired, but, above all, I wanted to go and meet Agustín and Bikandi in Iruain. 'I'll help you get these two into the car,' said Martín.

Joseba joined us. 'Next time, I'll ask Geneviève to bring us some marijuana,' said Martín. 'Perhaps that'll put a smile on your face. The champagne had no effect on you at all.' 'It's been a very long, hard day,' Joseba replied.

'Leave me alone! I want to sleep!' bawled Pancho, when we tried to get him to his feet. 'Well, stay here, then, if that's what you want,' said Martín, going into the hotel. 'Let us take you home,' said Joseba, struggling to help him. 'Just leave me in peace!' shouted Pancho. 'He'll wake everyone up in the hotel,' I said. 'Oh, let him sleep here. It's not cold.' Joseba agreed, and grabbed hold of Adrián instead. 'Now all we need is for him to kick up rough too.' But Adrián was incapable of any kind of reaction, and it was easy enough to escort him to the car.

VIII

The long, hard day took a further turn for the worse when we found Isidro waiting at the entrance to the sawmill. He looked like someone who's just received bad news, and we feared some mishap in the forest or at the workshop. However, we understood the real reason for his distress as soon as he took his son's arm to help him up the stairs, saying softly: 'Fancy letting yourself get in this state, Adrián, a boy with your talent.' 'I'm all right, Pa,' Adrián stammered. But he clearly wasn't. 'You boys should help him,' Isidro said, when Adrián had gone up to his bedroom. He said this humbly, without bitterness,

259

like someone asking a favour which he knows will be very hard to grant.

We set off for Iruain. 'Isidro looked so sad,' commented Joseba. I replied that *he* didn't seem very happy either. 'Oh, I don't feel sad, just ashamed,' he said. 'If you want to know, it made me feel quite sick, sitting there, eating cakes with our friend the pimp and that idiot Pancho! Enough is enough!' 'I think you're right,' I said. 'I don't know what we could have been thinking of when we wrote about the Marquis of Coldcock and all that other rubbish.'

We turned off the main road towards the forest of chestnut trees, and the VW started bumping about. 'Slow down,' I said. He did. 'I think we're drinking too much, David.' I didn't know what to say, and we drove on in silence until we could see the little valley before us. The houses there seemed to be floating in the air, because the single light-bulb illuminating each façade lit up the roofs, but left the ground floor in darkness. High above the houses and the hills hung the faintly shining stars.

As we approached Adela's house, we saw Sebastián sitting at the front door. He vanished into the dark and then reappeared on the road, standing in the car's headlights. 'I don't think today is ever going to end,' said Joseba as he slammed on the brakes. Sebastián came over to the passenger window. 'You might have come earlier. I'm really tired,' he said. 'What's wrong, Sebastián?' I asked. 'Your mother phoned, David. She says your father's away and she could do with a bit of a helping hand. She wants you to go to Villa Lecuona.'

A bit of a helping hand. I didn't think Carmen would have said that. The expression sounded more like Adela's way of speaking. 'And you stayed up just to tell him that? Couldn't it have waited until tomorrow morning?' Joseba asked him. 'That's what I said to my mother, but she wouldn't listen; she wanted a way of punishing me.' 'I suppose you've been up to some mischief again,' I said. 'It wasn't me, it was the twins!' Sebastián said in his defence.

The lightbulb above the door of Iruain meant that I could just make out three or four people sitting on the stone bench, as well as the shape

260

of a Renault. 'It's Komarov and his friends,' I told Joseba. He turned to me: 'What did you say?' 'At university in San Sebastián, my friend is known as Komarov.' 'Komarov! Hardly the most usual of nicknames!' 'Komarov was a Russian astronaut, I think. My friend's real name is Agustín. And the guy who came to the hotel with him is Bikandi.' 'Two very sensible men. They could tell what kind of people we were, eating cakes on the terrace, and very wisely chose not to join us.' As we crossed the bridge, the car headlights revealed five people sitting outside the house. As well as Agustín and Bikandi, there were two strangers and Lubis.

Agustín was sitting astride my Guzzi motorbike. He made the introductions from there. 'Jagoba and Isabel,' he said, pointing to the two strangers. We introduced ourselves as well, and Jagoba gravely shook our hands. He was a man of about thirty and wore round glasses that gave him a vaguely professorial air. 'He's an entomologist, but he earns his daily bread teaching in a school,' Bikandi told us, confirming my impression. 'Isabel, on the other hand, does educational research. Like me,' he said. 'We prepare teaching materials for schools.' The woman's appearance also chimed in with her profession. She was dressed very traditionally, in a grey pleated skirt. She was the image of the old-fashioned schoolteacher.

I went over to Lubis and asked how Moro was. 'He's recovered now, but I've left him in the stable just in case,' he said. He wasn't angry. When I told him that Pancho had stayed behind at the hotel, he merely shrugged and made no further comment. 'Jagoba has been telling us some really interesting things about insects,' he went on. I apologised profusely for what had happened at the hotel and described the dreadful state Adrián had been in by the end of the evening. 'As I said the other day, Adrián should be on medication, like my brother.' Lubis hesitated for a moment. 'Although, I don't know . . . I haven't noticed much of an improvement in Pancho. He's not too bad while he's taking the stuff, but as soon as he stops, he goes haywire again.'

We joined the rest of the group. Agustín was telling Joseba the story behind his nickname: 'Vladimir Mikhailovich Komarov was the first astronaut to die in space. The valve on his spaceship went wrong, and he orbited the Earth at least five times before he ran out of oxygen. I was so shocked by his death, that I used to talk about nothing else, and in the end, my friends started calling me Komarov.' Joseba looked up at the sky, as if searching amongst the stars for the Russian astronaut's fateful route. 'So he was going round and round up there,' he said.

He seemed interested in this accident in outer space, but when he spoke, it was to tell Bikandi and Isabel that once, on the first day of term, our teacher in Obaba had asked me to stand on her desk and play the accordion. 'Of course, you're talking about a time when the levels of attainment at schools left much to be desired. It was all pretty amateurish,' said Isabel.

'You'll be spending the night here, will you?' I asked, taking advantage of the silence that followed Isabel's response. It was Agustín who answered: 'Yes, if you don't mind. But don't worry, we've brought sleeping-bags and we'll sleep on the floor.' 'My uncle's room is free,' I suggested. 'We'll let the entomologist have the bed,' said Bikandi. 'He's the oldest member of the group.' 'I certainly am, and the only one who's going bald,' agreed Jagoba, lifting his fringe. He had fair, rather sparse hair.

We sat talking until three in the morning. About schools and insects, but also – it was Bikandi who introduced the subject – about the political situation in Spain and in the Basque Country. I had a sense of novelty. It seemed to me that some of the group members, especially Bikandi and Isabel, belonged to a country I knew nothing about, and that L.P. Hartley's words: 'They do things differently there' could easily be applied to them. Bikandi and Isabel interspersed their words with terms like 'the national problem', 'popular culture' and 'alienation' as naturally as Lubis, Ubanbe and the other country people from Obaba said *gezeta* or *domentxa* when they picked an apple, and *mitxirrika* or *inguma* when they pointed to a butterfly. At meetings held in the university, I'd heard students speaking in a similar way, but with one difference: Bikandi and Isabel mastered the lexicon, as if it were part of their mother tongue and came from deep within them.

'Wonderful! At last, a proper conversation!' exclaimed Joseba when I went with him to the Volkswagen to say goodbye. I agreed with him and said I hoped to have more opportunities to talk to Bikandi and his colleagues. In reality, though, I wanted to leave Iruain. I was thinking about Virginia. I couldn't get Pancho's words out of my head: 'She's got very nice tits, very round and quite big.' In Iruain, Virginia was a long way off; in Villa Lecuona, she was very close.

I was still in bed when Bikandi and Agustín came into my room and suggested I go with them on a butterfly hunt. 'A butterfly hunt?' I said. I didn't know what they were talking about. Bikandi brought a chair over to the bed, sat down and leaned towards me, like a doctor visiting a patient. He was wearing the same red trousers he'd worn the night before, but had changed his white polo shirt for a black one. He looked as if he'd just got out of the shower. 'I bathed in the pool by the bridge. That's why my hair's wet,' he said, smiling. Then he asked me a question that any real doctor would have asked: 'Did you sleep well?' 'I dreamed about a girl,' I replied.

This was not quite a lie. The list of the Miss Obabas was on my bedside table. On the other side of the sheet of paper I'd written a few lines before going to sleep: 'Virginia, I hope I'm not being presumptuous in taking advantage of our former friendship to write to you on this hot night of 27 August. I just want to ask you one question: Would you like to go for a walk with me? I look forward to hearing from you.' I intended to copy this note on to a postcard and send it to her.

'I didn't know you were that interested in girls, David,' said Agustín. 'I've never seen you chasing after them in San Sebastián.' He was dressed for the country, in walking boots, known as *chirucas*, and a green tracksuit. 'I only like girls from Obaba,' I replied.

'Well, I didn't sleep well,' said Bikandi. 'I never do when I'm worried about something.' I looked puzzled, and he leaned still closer. 'We've virtually colonised your house,' he explained. 'Four of us arrive on the pretext of returning the motorbike and then we move in. But this isn't

263

a student flat where people are always coming and going, it's your family home. Anyway, I'd like to apologise on behalf of us all for our lack of consideration. We should have asked your permission first.'

Suddenly he was speaking very modestly, with downcast eyes. 'I should apologise for receiving you in bed,' I joked. But he continued in the same tone. I sensed that he had something to confess to me. 'I'll explain to you about the butterfly hunt,' he said. 'As we were saying yesterday, Isabel and I are part of the Basque schools movement. One day, we realised that there were hardly any play materials in the Basque language, and so we decided to create packs of cards. At first, all we did was translate the Walt Disney ones available, but then we thought that, by doing so, we were building bridges with imperialism and denationalising our children, and so we decided to create our own autonomous products. To cut a long story short, we've made one pack of cards that illustrates all the different styles of Basque houses. And now we're working on another to be called *Butterflies of the Basque Country*. That's why we got in touch with Jagoba, who, as we told you, is an entomologist, which is why we're here, on the trail of our Basque butterflies. We've already got colour photos of sixteen different species, male and female, so that's thirty-two cards, but we need another three pairs. And Jagoba is convinced we'll find them in these woods. Forgive the rather long-winded explanation, David!'

Imperialism, *denationalise*: these are not particularly attractive words, but in the summer of 1970, I thought they were – new and attractive. Bikandi stood up and returned the chair to its place. 'If you've got sixteen pairs of butterflies, you need four more, not three. There are usually forty cards in a Spanish deck,' I said. 'David's right!' exclaimed Agustín gaily. 'You'd better watch it, my friend here is pretty bright.' 'He's right, but not entirely.' A flicker of a smile crossed Bikandi's face. 'Our pack will have forty-one cards. On the last card, we'll have a robin, an insectivorous bird.' Then, addressing me again, he went on: 'So, David, my question is this: can we stay in your family house until we find those missing four pairs of butterflies? Jagoba reckons it'll take us at most two weeks.' He stressed the word 'two'. 'Of course you can. I'm sure my uncle would very much approve of the work you're doing,'

I replied. He thanked me and shook my hand. Agustín did the same. They both seemed very pleased, and before they left the room, they asked me to join them downstairs with the others soon. The first butterfly hunt would start that very morning, at around ten o'clock.

I went over to the window to smoke my first cigarette of the day. Lubis, Joseba, Jagoba and Isabel were in the paddock on the other side of the stream, looking at the three foals, and when Bikandi and Agustín left the house they walked over in that direction too. Their car, a grey Renault, and Joseba's car were parked next to the bridge, and the Guzzi by the front door. On the stone bench there were three butterfly nets and a pair of binoculars in a case.

I looked again at all these things. I looked at the Guzzi. It was no longer red. It had been sprayed black.

'I didn't notice last night, but what's happened to the bike?' I asked Agustín when I joined him. He scratched his head. He didn't know what to say. 'Well, I just thought it looked nicer black,' he said at last. We were standing by the fence. The others – Lubis, Joseba, Jagoba, Isabel and Bikandi – were still with the foals. It seemed to me that Jagoba was explaining something to them.

Bikandi left the others and came over to us. 'What are you talking about? About the Guzzi?' he said. 'You ought to tell him the truth, Agustín.' 'It's all right, Komarov,' I said, patting him on the back. I could see he was upset. 'Joseba says people notice him more now because of his yellow VW,' Bikandi went on. 'And I take his point. Red and yellow are very Spanish colours.' 'We messed up with the bike, David,' Agustín said at last. Initially, I thought he was referring to some kind of mechanical problem. 'We were distributing pamphlets in favour of Basque-language schools, and the police realised we were taking the stuff out of the panniers on the back. They couldn't get the licence number, because we'd been careful to smear it with mud, but they could see it was a red Guzzi. That's why I had it resprayed. Next time we'll use a donkey, like last night at the hotel.' Agustín smiled. 'It looks quite good painted black. Unusual,' I said, as if I didn't mind.

265

The change in itself didn't bother me at all, what worried me was what it meant. I could see this clearly now. I was no longer the adolescent I'd been when Uncle Juan talked to me about the war. Bikandi and his friends – with the exception of the entomologist, I thought – weren't from another country or another world, they were, rather, people who led double lives, like my former teacher César, like Uncle Juan himself, they had two languages, two names, two territories. They were – they couldn't be anything else – underground activists. I remembered the monument in the square in Obaba, destroyed by a bomb, and the organisation that had claimed responsibility.

We were joined by the friends who'd been standing round the foals. 'Bikandi has just told me that we can stay at your house. Thank you very much,' Jagoba said to me. In the light of day, he looked younger than he had the previous night. 'Are there many species of butterfly in these forests?' I asked. 'I haven't had time to examine the area yet, but I'd estimate that there are at least ten. One of them, a moth, *Dasychira pudibunda*, will prove particularly difficult to catch. We may have to publish the pack without it.' 'Why is it so difficult?' I asked. He, too, seemed to come from another country. 'When it lands on a tree trunk, it's completely invisible,' he replied. 'You wouldn't be able to tell it apart from the trunk even at a distance of only seven or eight inches away. It'll be a real challenge.'

When we reached the forest, Jagoba, Lubis and Agustín went on ahead, each armed with a net, and they began the ascent, going from one tree to another, constantly straying off in different directions as if they were looking for mushrooms. Bikandi and Isabel followed about a hundred yards behind. Isabel was wearing jeans, which gave her a more youthful look than the pleated skirt she'd been wearing the previous evening.

At first, Joseba and I kept up with the first group, but then, at his request, we dropped back. He wanted to talk to me alone in order to tell me about certain decisions he'd taken that night. I slowed down and prepared to listen. The forest in late August wasn't a bad setting

266

for a confession: there was silence, there was shade, there was the soft earth beneath our feet.

'I'm not going up to the hotel any more,' he said. 'It just doesn't feel right. The way we sit on the terrace with Niko, Susana and the other girls at one table and us at another, like idiots. And our friends, David, I mean they're just not presentable. I don't mean Adrián. Adrián's a real bore with his crocodile jokes, plus he drinks too much and is a general disaster area, but he's a person in pain, who's finding it hard to come to terms with his problems, and it's up to us, his friends, to support him. Besides, my father told me this morning that Isidro is aware that his son needs help, and that he's gone to talk to the psychologist you saw at school.'

About a hundred yards further up the path, the atmosphere was quite different: we could see the butterfly nets sticking up amongst the nettles; we could hear the voices of Jagoba and Lubis, and, above that, the sound of Komarov laughing. 'I don't feel at all comfortable with Martín,' Joseba went on. He was walking faster now. 'I mean, let's not fool ourselves, he's a mafioso. Once, on our way back from Bilbao, we dropped in at that club of his, because Adrián wanted to see a girl there, and I met Martín's partner, an ex-policeman. To be perfectly honest, I want nothing to do with that world, absolutely nothing!' This final exclamation broke the otherwise rather depressed tone of his monologue. The thought of Martín's nightclub incensed him.

Amongst the trees, I could make out the red of a roof, but I didn't recognise the place until we got there: it was one of the woodcutters' cabins. 'You obviously did a lot of thinking last night,' I said to Joseba. 'Yes, I did. Didn't you?' I wanted to tell him the truth, that I'd thought only of Virginia, but that seemed too frivolous after his confession, and so I opted to remain silent.

'I wonder if they've caught one of the species we need,' said Bikandi, catching up with us. Outside the cabin, Jagoba, Lubis and Agustín were talking to a man wearing a check shirt. Jagoba was showing him something he had in his hand. Bikandi overtook us, as if spurred on by curiosity.

'I've made a decision too, although not as important as yours,' I said to Joseba. 'I'm going to go back home, to be with my mother. You heard the message she left with Sebastián yesterday.' 'Yeah, that sounds like a good idea.' But his mind was already somewhere else. He was looking back, searching for Isabel, who was lagging behind by some two hundred yards. 'What do you think of our new friends?' I asked. 'They seem like really interesting people.' He said this with such conviction that, again, I didn't dare to say what I was thinking, that they were perhaps people living double lives, with plans they weren't prepared to divulge and that being involved with them could bring us problems. I'd had one brush with the civil guard and I didn't want to repeat an experience which, this time – without the help of Don Hipólito and my mother – would be much worse. 'You're pleased too, aren't you, David?' 'Yes, very pleased.' It was true. My decision to go back to Villa Lecuona was a great relief.

Jagoba showed us the little box he was holding in his hand. Inside was a small blue butterfly with a pin through it. 'This is one of the butterflies we were looking for,' he said. 'It's a *Plebejus. Plebejus icarus*.' 'Lubis found it,' Agustín told me. 'With his help we'll be finished in no time.' Lubis laughed: 'You know who the clever one in the team is, don't you, David? The hedgehog who climbs on to the roof like a cat.' The man in the check shirt came over to me: 'How are you, Imaz? Still playing the accordion?' I didn't recognise him at first. He was the wood-cutter with the curly hair whom I'd last seen standing outside that same cabin, holding eight loaves of bread. '*Eta zu? Oraindik hemen!*' – 'And you? Still here?' – I cried. His face was lined, and he seemed much older than the day we first met. '*Gu basoan hilko gaituk!*' – 'We'll die in the forest!' – he said. His lips crinkled into a smile. His smile was still the same.

IX

The afternoon's work at the sewing school in Villa Lecuona had ended, and all the apprentice dressmakers set off briskly towards the square, as if they were in a hurry to get back to their houses. When they'd all disappeared, the whole village fell silent: no cars passed on the road; there were no bathers in the river; on the sportsground, two boys were standing chatting by the goal on the handball court; a little further off, in the playground, a woman was mechanically pushing a baby on a swing. Now and then, a little breeze would get up and make the leaves on the trees whisper and hiss.

My mother was standing, leaning on the balustrade of the terrace, and she was talking precisely about that hissing sound, saying that she knew perfectly well where it came from, but that, in her imagination, she preferred to attribute it to the river. She liked to think that the sound came from the water, because water – especially water that flowed over a bed of stones – seemed a happy sound, whereas the wind – wherever it blew – was always sad. 'If I ever go and live somewhere else,' she said, 'I'll choose a house on the banks of a river.' 'Villa Lecuona isn't far from a river.' 'But it's not right on the bank.' 'Perhaps it's because of the house where you were born. After all, Iruain is only a few yards from the river.' 'I hadn't thought of that, David.' While I was talking to her, I was looking over at Virginia's house. Its walls, newly painted for the fiesta, looked whiter than ever.

I brought my mother a wicker chair and a stool for her feet. As she sat down, she started talking to me about Juan: 'My brother's written me a long letter. He says he's bought a wonderful ranch. A house with I don't know how many acres of land and more than thirty horses. Thoroughbred horses, for riding. Things are going very well for our Juan, thank God. The ranch is near the border between Nevada and California, on the Californian side. And he says he's changed its name. He's going to call it Stoneham Ranch. Is that how you pronounce it?'

I wondered why Juan had chosen that name rather than 'Obaba Ranch' or something of the sort. What I couldn't have imagined then was that one day it would be my home and that I would sit in Stoneham Ranch remembering my life while I watched my daughters Liz and Sara playing on the porch, completely oblivious to the world of my past; so much so that if they ever do read these recollections of mine, they'll seem unrecognisable to them, from another galaxy.

My mother asked me: 'Is it true that someone distributed propaganda at yesterday's dance?' I said there hadn't been any propaganda. I still had in my pocket the piece of paper on which, the night before, I'd written my message to Virginia – 'Virginia, I hope I'm not being presumptuous in taking advantage of our former friendship to write to you on this hot night of 27 August . . .' – and I handed it to her, right side up. But she didn't have her glasses on and couldn't read it. I told her it was a list of the five prettiest girls in Obaba, and that it had all been a joke.

My mother lowered her voice: 'On Sunday afternoon, Marcelino phoned your father. He was furious apparently. He said a berserk donkey carrying propaganda had been let loose on the hotel terrace, and that they should speak to the governor and to Colonel Degrela about it.' 'Because of this?' I asked, pointing to the piece of paper. I said that I found it quite incredible, that they must both be mad. 'No, they're not mad, David, they're just frightened. They've been worried sick ever since that bomb destroyed the monument. Your father says that activists from France train the people in small villages to commit illegal acts, and that they have practice runs first. He says that the reason they handed out those bits of paper supposedly about Miss Obaba was because the police wouldn't be able to do anything even if they managed to arrest the people responsible. According to your father, they don't carry out any "real" actions until they're fully prepared.'

I knew all about Ángel's theories. I'd heard the same reasoning applied to the attack that had destroyed the monument in the square. 'I don't think it's that big a deal,' I said, although without much conviction. I'd suddenly remembered the group looking for moths and butterflies in Iruain. My mother may not have expressed it very clearly, but what she was saying could well be true. She went on: 'Someone recognised the donkey. They realised it belonged to Beatriz's son, to Lubis. I know he's a good boy, a very reliable boy and . . . I'll tell you something, David, I almost left your father once because, one day, for no reason at all, he got hold of Lubis and gave him the most terrible beating. But now they're saying Lubis is involved in politics and that *he* took the donkey there, not that poor unfortunate, his brother. They say Pancho's incapable of organising anything.'

She fell silent. She was trying hard not to cry: 'Don't get involved in politics, David. Politics is a dirty business, as our civil war made perfectly clear. Getting involved in politics would be the worst possible thing you could do. You've got a bright future ahead of you. Lubis might not, but you have. You're Uncle Juan's only nephew, almost a son to him. He'll help you any way he can . . .' 'Where's Ángel?' I said, interrupting her. I wanted to change the subject. 'They're all in Madrid. Didn't they tell you? They want to make that great strapping lad, Ubanbe, into a boxer.' 'No, I knew nothing about it.' 'That's odd, because the person who's behind it all is your friend Martín. He says Ubanbe could become a second Uzcudun, and that if he does, they'll make millions. Ángel and Marcelino offered to go with him to Madrid. Well, you know what they're like, any excuse to get out of Obaba.' 'What are they going to do? Organise a fight in Madrid?' I underestimated their plans. 'In Madrid, in San Sebastián, in Bilbao, all over,' my mother said with a shrug, 'your guess is as good as mine. Maybe your friend Martín is right!' she concluded.

The playground was empty and full of shadows, unlike the handball court, which was much livelier than before. Two teams of girls were playing, under instruction from a young man, presumably the trainer.

There was still a lot of light in the sky. I looked at the alders over towards Urtza: they looked as black as cypresses. I looked at Virginia's house; it was still white. The floodlights at the sportsground began to come on.

My mother was calmer now and started talking about everyday matters. She mentioned the workshop, the new hymns they'd learned in church; she asked me about the people who went to the dances at the Hotel Alaska. She suddenly remembered the list I'd shown her: 'By the way, who *are* the prettiest girls in Obaba, according to the people who drew up this list?' I unfolded the sheet of paper again and read

271

out the names as if I didn't already know them by heart: 'Bruna — the forest ranger's daughter, Niko, Victoria, Alberta — the one who works in the sports shop, and in first place, as Miss Obaba, Susana, the doctor's daughter.' 'What about our Paulina?' My mother used the possessive 'our' with all the girls who came to the workshop, but especially so with Paulina. She was no longer an apprentice, but a professional dress-maker. 'Do you think she should be on the list?' 'If it's true what they say in the workshop, she has no shortage of suitors. And your friend Adrián is one of them.' 'Adrián?' 'So the girls say.' 'I think I really do live in a world of my own. I thought he hated Paulina!' 'The girls say things about you too.' 'That I behaved badly with Teresa.' 'And that you like that thin young woman, Niko.' I burst out laughing. 'They couldn't be more wrong,' I said.

She gave me a conspiratorial look. She had another name in her head. 'Do you know who's missing from the list?' she said. 'Virginia. She's a very good-looking young woman. With a lovely figure and a very elegant bearing. Yes, she has a kind of natural elegance. It's not something she's learned.' 'I think a lot of people would agree with you,' I said cautiously. 'I've made her a dress,' my mother said. 'It's green. Not black or grey. She's ready now to start living again. I think she might even dance at the fiesta.'

A tall girl went over to the handball court and kissed the young man acting as trainer. It was Alberta, the girl from the sports shop, the second prettiest on our list. But she couldn't compare with Virginia.

Virginia. There must be ten, fifteen, twenty men thinking about her. Thinking about how to approach her, how to earn her embrace. And when she appeared at the fiesta in her green dress, the number of her admirers would multiply: there would no longer be just twenty men, but a hundred, two hundred, three hundred. All of them like dogs on the trail of a hunted animal, with, at their head, Martín, the best trained of all the dogs. '*If someone, me, for example, got on top of her, she'd scream: 'No, no, please, no, stop, stop, please, no, oh, come inside me, come inside me, more, more!'* The memory of Martín's words filled me with unease.

The floodlights were on full power now and lit up the swings, the goals, the lines marked on the ground. But everything was utterly empty. The girls from the two teams had left along with Alberta and the trainer, and now and then there came again the hissing of the wind amongst the leaves. '*No, no, no, please, no, no . . .*' The hissing leaves reproduced Virginia's voice. I looked at her house: it was just a whitish smudge to the right of the alder trees in Urtza.

We went into the house to have supper. 'I think Adela uses too much fat in her cooking, David,' my mother said. 'While you're here, you'll eat much more healthily. I don't want you putting on any more weight.' She started preparing a tomato salad. 'If it's fine tomorrow, I'll go for a swim at Urtza. I want to look my best for the fiesta too.' My mother opened the fridge. 'There's some cold hake. What shall I do, David? Shall I heat it up, or shall we eat it as it is?' I didn't mind eating it cold, and so we sat down at the table.

'What are you thinking about?' I asked her, when we'd eaten the salad. 'Are you still worried about something?' 'I didn't explain the situation to you before, at least, not properly,' she said. 'Ángel doesn't sleep at home now, in fact, he hardly ever comes here, and, if he does, he always comes at different times. That was the advice the police gave him. It's the same with Marcelino. They have to be very careful as long as there's a continuing risk of an attack. Anyway, as you see, when the girls from the sewing workshop aren't here, I'm all alone. It's not so bad now we've got a television, but even so, I don't feel comfortable. That's why I phoned Adela's house. I know you'd probably have much more fun at Iruain, but I'd prefer to have you here. At least at night.'

The fluorescent light in the kitchen was harsher than the light out on the terrace. It emphasised the bags under my mother's eyes, the little lines around her mouth, the red patches on one cheek. 'Don't worry. I'd decided to come home even before you called. I've spent the whole summer in Iruain and I'm dying to watch some telly.' My mother smiled. 'Well, you can watch telly here to your heart's content.' We started eating the fish. 'Oh, I forgot to say,' I said. 'Some friends of mine are going to be staying at Iruain for a couple of weeks. They're teachers.' My mother smiled again. 'Yes, Adela told me. She said they're looking for butterflies because they want to write a book about them. She's says they seem very responsible people.'

The book of detective stories was still on the shelf in my room, and I enjoyed myself reading until very late. Before switching off the light, I got out of bed and chose a postcard from a bundle Joseba had given me for my last birthday. They were reproductions of paintings published by the Museum of Fine Arts in Bilbao, and one of them showed naked women sunbathing or towelling themselves dry on the top of a cliff.

I copied on to the postcard the note I'd written in Iruain. 'Virginia, I hope I'm not being presumptuous in taking advantage of our former friendship to write to you on this hot night of 27 August. I just want to ask you one question: Would you like to go for a walk with me? I look forward to hearing from you.' The next day, while she was working at the coffee house, I would slip it under her front door.

Before going to sleep, I was seized by doubt. Perhaps it would seem rude, too bold a step, sending her that postcard of naked women. We'd hardly had anything to do with each other during the last few years. I tore up the postcard and wrote out the message again on the back of another card bearing the photograph of a rose.

X

There were red geraniums outside the windows of Virginia's house, and it occurred to me that they must have got in Pancho's way when he was trying to focus on her 'round, white breasts' with the binoculars lent him by Martín.

I was crossing the bridge when a dog came out of the gloom of the undergrowth and starting circling me, barking, but not daring to approach. It was old and lame. 'Go away, let me pass!' I said. As soon as it heard my voice, it came over to me, wagging its tail.

I recognised it too: it was Virginia's dog. 'Haven't you got old, Oki!' I exclaimed. When I looked at the hills, time seemed not to have passed;

when I looked at my mother or my face in the mirror, it seemed to be passing only slowly; but the message written on the dog left no room for illusions. Time was inflicting terrible damage, it was destroying life. Oki would soon be dead. And unlike the flowers, unlike the geraniums at the windows or the rose on the postcard, Oki would never come back just as he was. There would still be dogs, but none of them would be Oki.

I stroked his head. 'How are you?' He had cataracts. He could probably see very little. 'Next time, I'll be sure to bring you a sugar lump, but I'm in a hurry now,' I told him. I didn't want to delay. I slipped the postcard under the front door and set off towards Urtza along the river.

The river. If you listened to it from close to, the sound it made did resemble, as my mother would have it, the sound produced by the wind moving in the leaves, but as the river flowed down towards Urtza, there were certain very smooth sections where it fell completely silent and you could hear the screams and splashings of the bathers.

The sunlight made me screw up my eyes. Suddenly, I heard Ubanbe's voice: 'Catch it!' This was followed by a curse and an impatient exclamation: 'Oh, no, you've let it go again!' 'Steady, Pancho, it's yours for the taking!' exclaimed a second voice, that of Sebastián.

The trout was slipping swiftly from one stone to another, but the distance it swam was shorter each time. Pancho looked up at Ubanbe and said: 'Any minute now, it'll plop right into my hand.' He was standing in the water, his trousers rolled up to his thighs, and he kept moving from side to side, trying to corral the fish. He was walking very slowly, without looking up, like someone in the grip of a terrible inertia. 'What are *you* doing here?' Ubanbe asked, when he saw me watching. 'Why aren't you off hunting butterflies?'

Butterflies. He gave a sarcastic edge to the word, trying to imitate Jagoba's way of speaking. Sebastián burst out laughing: 'What fine nets your friends have, David! The sort nice young ladies would use.' Ubanbe again shouted: 'Pancho! You're going to let the trout escape. I thought you were brighter than that.' He winked at me. He was sitting on a stone beside the river and was wearing a white shirt and black patent leather

275

shoes. Sebastián was crouched down beside him, as if he were his page. His curly hair was very long and fell in ringlets over his forehead.

'You're looking very elegant, Ubanbe. Aren't you working?' I said. Usually, like most of the other sawmill employees, he wore blue cotton trousers and a shirt the same colour. 'And what about you? Where's your accordion? Didn't you bring it with you?' he retorted in the same tone he'd used with Pancho. He seemed slightly drunk. 'Hey, David,' said Sebastián, 'our friend Ubanbe here has been to a clinic in San Sebastián today and they did some tests on him to see if he could be a boxer. And they said, yes, of course he could, and that he'll earn loads of money when he's European champion. Much more than he does working with an axe in the forest.' So what my mother had told me out on the terrace was true.

Ubanbe was staring at the river as if the boy's words had dropped in there and he could just make them out amongst the twigs and leaves borne along on the current. 'Martín and some friends of his have prom-ised me a million, a million a year. Ten times what I earn in the forest,' he said. 'So what's the problem?' I asked. He was looking very serious; something was bothering him. 'It's his nose, David,' Sebastián explained. 'If he wants to be a boxer he has to have an operation on his nose. And he's afraid he'll end up looking ugly and then he won't be able to pull the women.' 'Shut up, you, what do you know?' Ubanbe said, giving him a clip round the ear. 'A nancy-boy could hit harder than that,' laughed Sebastián. 'Oh, yeah, would you like me to smash your head in?' Sebastián moved away from Ubanbe in order to continue his mocking remarks: 'I thought you were a heavyweight, but now I'm not so sure. I didn't even feel it.'

'Shut up, you lot! You're frightening the trout,' shouted Pancho, holding out his arms to us. 'You're too slow, Pancho. I'll have to catch it myself,' said Ubanbe, standing up. 'I'm going for a swim,' I said. 'OK, but come back here afterwards,' said Sebastián. 'Did you hear?' insisted Ubanbe. 'Be sure to come back. We're going hunting for butterflies.' They all laughed, and Sebastián laughed the loudest.

*　　*　　*

After swimming for a while in Urtza, I decided to take the long way home, away from Virginia's house and passing through the new estate, and so I started walking, ignoring the path, and going in and out of the forest of chestnut trees. The leaves were very green and gave a lot of shade.

'Where are you off to, David? Stay here with us,' I heard someone shout. It was Ubanbe, talking to me from beneath one of those trees. He and Sebastián were smoking; a bit further on, underneath another tree, Pancho appeared to be asleep. 'He finally managed to catch the trout, and we ate it,' Ubanbe told me. 'Well, you chose a nice spot to hold a banquet,' I said. They were about 500 paces from where I'd seen them before. 'Don't be daft, David. Do you really think we came here to eat that stupid trout? We're here because we want to catch butterflies.' 'And to smoke a cigarette,' added Sebastián. Ubanbe stubbed his cigarette out on the ground. 'What time is it? Five o'clock already? My watch has stopped.' Sebastián winked at me: 'He couldn't wait and he made a grab for the trout without taking his watch off first. He'll have to buck his ideas up if he's ever going to be European champion.' 'It's five twenty,' I told Ubanbe, taking my watch out of the pocket of my swimming trunks. 'Hey, Ubanbe, get a load of the cute shorts David is wearing,' Sebastián went on. 'They look like they're made out of panther skin. You should buy a pair of those when you start boxing. The girls will go wild.' My trunks were yellow with black splodges. Ubanbe put his hands to his ears: 'He won't stop talking, David. He gets unbearable when he's had a bit to drink.'

Pancho suddenly sprang to his feet. 'Are we going or not?' he said. He had his binoculars round his neck. 'Yes, we're going. Our little butterfly will have started to fly.' Ubanbe set off at a run into the woods, followed by Pancho and Sebastián. 'Come with us!' they shouted. Out of inertia, or perhaps simple curiosity, I followed behind.

We were soon deep in the forest, beneath the dense shade of the beech trees. The branches intersected and formed, leaf by leaf, a thick roof that reduced the daylight by half. The ground was wet, but its softness – my foot sunk in slightly when I stepped on the grass or the moss

— felt as if it were due not to the rain or to the lack of sun, but to some secretion from the earth itself. In some places, it was even softer, and the woods seemed made of the same substance as the slugs we encountered at every turn.

Pancho and Sebastián ran tirelessly ahead of me, driving themselves on, falling over and shouting, with the kind of joy that precedes a celebration, their bodies smeared with that soft, slimy mud. About a hundred yards ahead of us, Ubanbe was pushing his way through the nettles. He was bare-chested, and, now and then, he would wave his white shirt and call to us, not to tell us anything, but simply to show how strong he was.

The slope grew less steep, as if we were reaching a summit, and at the same time, the forest thickened. We went on and met a kind of barrier: the trees there grew as close together as reeds. Sebastián whistled Ubanbe over to us, and soon, silent and intent, we were following Pancho through an opening in the barrier, invisible at first sight. We were all of us intent and purposeful: Sebastián and Pancho appeared to have lost all desire to play; Ubanbe pressed on, indifferent to the brambles scratching his skin; and I went after them, not wanting to get left behind along that narrow passageway. Another forty paces, and we started to go down a track full of gnarled roots.

'Our butterfly's around here somewhere!' exclaimed Ubanbe suddenly, sniffing the air, and this time he didn't say 'little butterfly'. I could feel the heat of his body. 'Can't you smell it?' Like the others, I sniffed the air. I noticed a vague smell of cologne, a trace of lavender in the air. Ubanbe ran on, taking short steps, again waving his shirt, and Sebastián, Pancho and I ran after him. Another twenty paces and we'd reached the end of the track.

I looked up ahead. Surrounded by ivy and moss, there was a pool, doubtless an abandoned reservoir. The water was so still that it looked like a mirror with green leaves incrusted in its surface. I heard splashes, as of tiny bodies plunging into the water. 'The toads have heard us,' said Pancho. And it was true; the toads were leaping over the moss and ivy and heading for the water. 'Look what's landed on David's chest,'

278

said Sebastián laughing. I saw a stain the colour of blood on my polo shirt. It was a butterfly with red wings. Pancho reached out and caught it in his hand.

'I'll keep it for those friends of yours in Iruain,' he said. 'They might pay me for it.' He was holding it by the tip of one wing. 'You must be joking!' mocked Sebastián. 'When they come and eat at our house, they always order the cheapest thing on the menu. They haven't got a cent!' 'Well, sod that for a lark!' Disappointed, Pancho threw the insect up into the air. The dust on its wings had come off on his fingers, though, and the creature dropped into the water.

'Will you be quiet!' said Ubanbe in an agitated voice. 'Where's that girl got to?' 'I can see her towel, but not her,' said Sebastián, pointing to the other side of the pool. The towel was white and lay about sixty paces from us, in the one clearing in the wood where the sun managed to penetrate. 'Here she comes,' said Pancho, peering through his binoculars, and at that precise moment, a girl appeared from behind a tree. She was completely naked. 'Who's that?' I asked. 'Bruna, the forest warden's daughter,' Sebastián whispered gleefully. 'So it is!' I cried. I hadn't recognised her. Ubanbe breathed deeply: 'On that piece of paper the other night, she was given fifth place, but I reckon she deserves the title of Miss Obaba, or at least second place,' he declared.

'*Bruna, the forest warden's daughter. There's no other girl in the whole region to match her athletic body . . .*' Seeing her next to the towel, Joseba's description didn't seem quite accurate. She had long, sturdy legs, but she was too plump from the waist up; she was more like the nymphs in paintings from times past than like an athlete from the end of the twentieth century. Nevertheless, this was the century she belonged to. She was applying sun cream.

'Here I go!' said Ubanbe, and he started walking towards the girl. I heard a shriek, like that of some forest animal, and Bruna dropped the tube of sun cream and ran to hide behind a tree. Ubanbe paused by the white towel. He threw his shirt down on the ground and took off his trousers. 'Now he'll start to talk to her, David. Just wait,' said Sebastián, lightly tapping his fingers together in quiet applause. Ubanbe had his head turned in the direction of the girl's hiding-place, and seemed to be saying something to her. He was naked now as well and was holding the tube of sun cream in his hand. 'I know what he's saying. He's asking her if she wants him to put some sun cream on her,' explained Sebastián. Pancho put his binoculars to his eyes. 'She's coming,' he said, 'she's coming out of her hiding-place.' I was sure Bruna would emerge fully clothed or covering herself with something, but she wasn't wearing anything.

Now there were two naked figures in the sunny clearing. The larger figure gradually drew the smaller one over to the towel, holding her around the waist. When he lay down on top of her, they started moving up and down, first slowly and then vigorously. Sebastián and Pancho said nothing.

'Has he finished?' asked Sebastián after a while. 'They're still on top of each other, but they're not moving much,' said Pancho. 'Let's go then,' cried Sebastián, running over to the edge of the pool. 'Now she'll let anyone do it to her, David,' said Pancho. He was smiling, his mouth open, and he started to pant lasciviously. He was imitating the breathing of an owl.

I felt as if I were suffocating, as if I were in the pool, fighting to free myself from the mud and the roots on the bottom, seeing above me the leaves and the twigs on the surface, as well as the dead red butterfly. I started running up the track, through the barrier of trees and into the open forest. I kept walking and, a thousand paces further on, I glimpsed patches of blue sky amongst the trees and the light of the setting afternoon sun. Five thousand paces more and I was sitting on the terrace at Villa Lecuona, feeling furious with myself.

I was postponing making a decision, the very worst of my bad habits. Instead of going to the café where Virginia worked and asking her point-blank: 'Would you like to go out with me?', instead of meeting her face to face and knowing in that moment how she felt about me, I had opted for writing a postcard. I was biding my time, and wasting the hours and the days.

The others wouldn't wait, though, that much was sure. Pancho would say to Ubanbe: 'Go and see the waitress at the coffee shop and feel her tits. You'll see how white and round they are.' And Ubanbe wouldn't hesitate, because he knew, without having read it in any book, that time doesn't pass in vain, that we will not embrace in the grave those whom we failed to embrace in life. My head filled up with images. I saw Ubanbe on top of Virginia, and Pancho beside me, drooling: 'Now she'll let us all have a go, David. Ubanbe's worn her out a bit, but she's still breathing like an owl.' Then I saw Martín doing his juggling trick with bottles behind the counter of the coffee house where Virginia worked, and her standing smiling by his side. This wasn't mere fantasy. It could actually happen. Martín might well overtake me, as could any of the ten or twenty or forty men who eyed her surreptitiously at the coffee house.

I watched television until my mother called me for supper. Just then the phone rang. 'It's for you. A friend of yours.' My mother was smiling, and I thought it must be Joseba, calling me from Adela's kitchen. My mother was fond of him, despite his long hair and unkempt appearance. But it wasn't Joseba. It was Martín.

'I'm so happy, David,' he said at once, as soon as I picked up the phone. 'I'm on the 27th floor of a hotel in Madrid and from my room I can see all the lights of the city, the lights of the houses and of the cars driving down the Gran Vía. And I'm very happy.' I was confused, my imaginings while out on the terrace had left me feeling uneasy. I thought I knew the reason for his happiness, and I imagined that he was about to say to me: 'There's a girl with me here, a girl with round, white breasts, a girl you know. She's having a shower at the moment. I assume you know who I mean.' 'Why are you so happy?' I asked. 'Everything's worked out really well, David, really well. Couldn't be better. This evening we signed a contract for ten fights. And after those ten fights, Ubanbe will compete for the European heavyweight championship. Our Ubanbe, David! Do you understand what I'm saying? He'll be a new Uzcudun, and we'll be his promoters. You too, if you want.' 'That's great,' I said. In comparison with what I'd imagined, his words were like celestial music.

I told him that I'd met Ubanbe near Urtza and knew that the doctors had given him permission to take up boxing. 'It's all turned out really well,' he said again, 'very well indeed. In a year, he'll be European champion. I don't know if you're up to date on these things, but the standard of the current heavyweights is at an all-time low. Most of the boxers are like sacks of potatoes, and Ubanbe will knock 'em dead. And then we'll go to America and visit all the places that Uzcudun visited: Las Vegas, Chicago, Reno, Atlanta and then, finally, New York, Madison Square Garden, but we won't let what happened to Uzcudun happen to us. Do you know why Joe Louis beat Uzcudun? Because the night before, they brought three women to Uzcudun's hotel room, and the man was exhausted by the next day. The promoters sold him down the river.'

My mother appeared at the kitchen door to tell me that supper was on the table and that I shouldn't be much longer. But I couldn't hang up, Martín was still talking. He explained that Ubanbe's first opponent would be a French boxer called Philippe Lou. And that then he would face a German. 'Anyway, that's the way things stand, David. We're going out to supper in Madrid's finest restaurant now, my father, Angelcho, Señor Degrela, another gentleman from the board of Real Madrid and the biggest boxing promoter in the whole of Spain.' I found his way of referring to these people odd: he said 'my father' instead of 'Berli', he added a diminutive to Ángel's name, he called Degrela 'Señor'. 'Fine, great,' I said as a way of bringing the conversation to a close. 'Just a moment, David. Here's me going on and on and I haven't even told you the real reason for my call.' My mother appeared again at the kitchen door. 'Look, my soup's getting cold,' I said. 'Yes, yes, I'm in a hurry too. Let me tell you what it's all about. Next Saturday, you've got to come up to the hotel . . .' 'To play at the dance, I know,' I said. He paused. 'The dance? There won't be a dance, David. Hasn't Geneviève phoned you? We've cancelled all the dances. As you know, my father was furious about that business with the donkey. He thought it was political propaganda being handed out.' 'Yes my mother told me that they're both afraid of being the object of some attack.' 'Oh, now, let's

282

not talk about sad things. All that stuff about clandestine political groups will be sorted out soon enough, I'm sure. Besides, you should see the two old codgers. They're over the moon.'

He finally explained to me why they wanted me to go to the Hotel Alaska. Ubanbe had to be presented to the public, and Martín's idea was to put on a party for the journalists. The invitations had already gone out. 'We want you to play the accordion there. We could have hired a band, but we wanted to ask you first. We want to make it up with you. We were all upset by what happened at the supper in honour of Uzcudun, but resentment and long faces aren't going to get us anywhere. We must look to the future.' 'Well, I'll have to say "yes", I suppose, otherwise, you'll never shut up, and the soup will be too cold to eat,' I said. 'You've no idea how glad I am to hear you say that, David. See you at ten o'clock at the hotel, then. On Saturday.' He seemed quite a different Martín, more affectionate, more serious.

'I'm not surprised you think he's changed,' my mother said when we sat down to supper. 'I spoke to Ángel earlier, and I got the same impression from him. Apparently, this is a really major business deal. Do you know how much money they're going to earn with those first ten fights, David? Do you know how much money they reckon they'll earn?' I remembered that Ubanbe had said they were offering him a million a year. 'Ten million?' I guessed. 'And that's just for the first ten fights,' said my mother, raising a spoonful of soup to her mouth.

XI

I had to fetch my accordion so that I could play at the event put on to present Ubanbe to the press, and I set off, intending to drop in at Iruain. 'Why have you had the bike sprayed, David?' my mother asked me when we passed on the stairs. On her doctor's advice, she went for a walk every morning. 'I preferred it when it was red,' she added, turning to look at the Guzzi. 'Joseba says it looks more modern sprayed black,' I said. My mother pursed her lips to express her disagreement, but didn't pursue the matter. 'Will you be back for lunch?' she said. 'Of course,' I replied. I was in no mood for talking either about insects or politics.

I spotted Beatriz and Adela as soon I left the forest of chestnut trees behind me. They were standing by the road, talking. I drew up beside them. 'Have you come to see those people from San Sebastián?' Adela asked me above the noise of the engine. 'If so, you'll have to wait. There's no one in the house at the moment. They go into the forest at first light and don't come back until supper time.' Beatriz smiled. 'Who would think butterflies would be so much work! It's hard to credit,' she sighed. 'Lubis spends more time out with his butterfly net than looking after the foals.' *It's hard to credit*, she said: *Ez da sinistatzekoa*.

The yellow VW was parked outside Uncle Juan's house. 'It looks like Joseba is with them too.' 'Yes, they've become great friends,' said Adela. 'Joseba and that Jagoba fellow get on very well.' 'And Lubis gets on well with that very lively lad,' said Beatriz. 'You mean Agustín,' said Adela helpfully. 'He's like a little weasel, that one. A better-educated version of Sebastián.' 'I'll see them another day. I've just come for my accordion,' I told them.

I drove on to Iruain and went into the kitchen. The sleeping-bags were still on the floor, along with a dozen or so books, a transistor radio, a packet of biscuits, and a couple of hold-alls. On the table, in small cardboard boxes were two white butterflies, each transfixed by a pin. I had a glance at the books: apart from one about the 'new schools', they were all about entomology.

I felt ashamed of my suspicions. What I was seeing only proved what Bikandi had told me. The group had purely pedagogical aims. They were there to help the teacher, Jagoba. They wanted to make a pack of cards so that Basque children would learn about their country's butterflies. In their way, they were all intellectuals, including Agustín, or Komarov. As Adela had just said, he was like her son Sebastián, only better educated.

I still wasn't convinced, though, and I went upstairs to the bedroom to have a look at the hiding-place. Lubis knew where it was. If he was involved in politics, as my mother said, and had become such good friends with the group, he would have shown it to them so that they could hide any propaganda.

I lifted the trapdoor and all I saw was the J.B. Hotson hat belonging to Obaba's first American. I went back into the kitchen, picked up my accordion and went outside. One's worst expectations didn't always come true.

Adela was waiting for me outside Iruain, on the stone bench. 'I need to talk to you, David,' she said. 'Is something wrong?' 'Yes, I think there is, but I didn't want to say anything in front of Beatriz. Her kids give her a hard enough time as it is.' I sat down to listen. 'Have you known these people from San Sebastián long?' she asked. 'I know Agustín from university, but I only met the others the day they arrived here.'

'Listen, David,' Adela said, looking over towards the forest. 'Yesterday evening, the twins came home stinking of petrol. You know what they're like, they can't be still for a moment, and they always come back covered in mud or with a cut head or something. Anyway, yesterday, as I was saying, they both stank of petrol. And I thought that was odd because you don't find a lot of petrol around here. I asked them where they'd been to, coming home smelling like that, and they told me there were four pots of the stuff in the forest. They'd had a look inside thinking they might be full of milk. I knew at once that they were telling the truth. 'Who put those pots there?' I asked them. They assured me that it was something to do with Bikandi and Isabel, that they'd put the pots there while their friends were hunting butterflies. Imagine, David, four cooking pots full of petrol! It could put your uncle in a very awkward position indeed.'

Her last words took me by surprise. 'What do you mean, Adela?' 'You know how people like to talk, and some say that Juan is never going to come back, and that he's been trying to sell this house and the stables for ages now. If someone set fire to them, the gossips would all start saying that he did it to get the insurance money. Everyone knows Juan has the place insured for a fortune.'

I looked at the horses, at the foals: Ava and Mizpa were languidly flicking their tails; Elko, Eder and Paul were chasing each other from one side of the fence to the other. Off on his own, Moro was peacefully munching the grass. It was a picture of contentment.

'That's the most stupid thing I've heard in a long time!' I protested. It was unthinkable that my uncle would want to sell Iruain. True, he lived in America, but he'd been born and bred in Obaba and would never get rid of the house where he'd been brought up. 'Yes, you're quite right,' Adela said. 'Besides, Juan has never married, he's never had any children and I know he often still thinks about his parents. But not everyone is like him. They killed that beautiful horse of his, remember, and now, who knows, they might be plotting some new mischief: burning down his house and stables so that people will say it was him. And all out of envy, because he's managed to make something of himself. Just as your mother has too.' 'I find that difficult to believe,' I said. 'Look, David,' she went on, 'far be it from me to speak ill of anyone, but it might be that those young people are involved in something of the sort. Someone might have paid them to set fire to the house and stables. What could be easier! An insurance salesman in Obaba often used to say just that. The biggest fool in the world could light a fire that the one hundred cleverest people in the world couldn't put out!' 'I'll phone my uncle to see what he has to say.' 'You do what you think best, David. I've done what I can.'

I tied the accordion on to the carrier on the back of the Guzzi. 'Don't let the twins go blabbing about what they found. Let's be discreet,' I said to Adela. 'Don't worry, I'll make sure they are.' She stood looking at the accordion. 'It looks like you're going to be playing at that party they're putting on for Ubanbe,' she said. But her mind was elsewhere, and she set off towards her house without waiting for my reply.

XII

Ubanbe entered the dining-room wrapped in a red cape and, amidst a spattering of applause, stepped on to the little stage where I'd sat to

286

play the accordion. When the photographers approached, he took off his cape and revealed his body: *Ecce homo.* His skin was very white, and he cut a handsome figure in his red satin shorts and black gloves, even more so when he raised his arms to show off his chest and stomach muscles.

The camera flashlamps lit him up again and again. Ubanbe was trying hard to smile. Perhaps the same thoughts were going through his head as through mine: What would become of his milk-white skin in the months that followed? How many bruises would it suffer? Would he end up as battered as the ex-boxers who had come to the party? Was it worth being nailed to that cross just to earn ten times what he earned at the sawmill? But the decision had been made, and his nose – flattened now, with the scar from the operation still visible – was proof of that. The time for doubts was over.

There were about fifty people in the dining-room, most of them men, but only those around the stage applauded. A former boxer, who picked up the microphone and introduced himself as the 'new star's trainer', started calculating how long it would take that 'strong, agile' young man to become European champion, and stated categorically: 'Fifteen months will be more than enough.' Next to speak was a businessman, who said he was one of the promoters and who confirmed that there would be no shortage of resources. 'He'll start training tomorrow morning in the gymnasium we've set up for him here, at the hotel,' he explained to the journalists. 'We felt it best for Gorostiza to do his training close to home.' So Ubanbe was going to be known professionally by his surname: Gorostiza. 'Who's his first opponent going to be?' asked a journalist. 'Philippe Lou, the former French champion,' replied the promoter. Then he announced that he wouldn't be taking any more questions and gestured to the main table in the dining-room, where, amongst others, Berlino, my father and Colonel Degrela were sitting. 'And now, to continue the introductions, I'd like to ask a gentleman who has been of prime importance in our plan to say a few words. I refer, of course, to Señor José Antonio Degrela.' The colonel's hair was whiter than when I'd met him, but he was still an elegant man.

'My one hope is that Gorostiza does prove to be a second Uzcudun and creates a positive image of Spain around the world. That's all.' He sat down again.

The journalists applauded. 'What kind of purse are you getting for fighting Philippe Lou, Gorostiza?' asked one of them. 'How much are you getting paid for that article you're going to write tomorrow?' retorted Ubanbe. Later, these aggressive responses of his would prove very popular.

'And now a little champagne to lift people's hearts,' announced Martín, going over to the microphone, and he and Gregorio began moving amongst the guests, bearing trays. Ángel came over to me. He looked fatter. 'You should have stayed up there on stage. It would have been good to have a bit of music to accompany Ubanbe's entrance,' he said. He wanted to teach me a lesson, as he used to when he taught me music theory, to make it quite clear that he was the better accordionist. 'What did you expect. I was playing for more than an hour, and he happened to come on just when I'd stopped. You might have warned me.' 'A professional never abandons his post! You should have kept playing to the end.' 'I'm not a professional and I've no intention of ever becoming one,' I yelled. I found the tone he took with me unbearable.

Martín came over to us. He lifted up the tray and spun it round on the tip of one finger. 'That's what we young people are like nowadays, Angelcho – stubborn and rebellious,' he said. 'I'll bring you a glass of champagne to console you.' He was in the same glad mood as when he'd phoned me from Madrid, but he no longer seemed like a different Martín. 'I don't understand this boy! Now he says he's not a professional!' complained Ángel. Martín patted him on the back. 'But he doesn't mean it. After supper, we'll ask him to play a few nice tunes. And he'll play them like a true professional, you'll see, Angelcho.'

Martín plunged back in amongst the guests. 'Don't drink too much during the meal,' Ángel warned me. 'Remember you haven't finished your work yet.' He seemed determined to keep nagging me, but then a woman came over and interrupted him. 'Don't you remember me?'

the woman asked, addressing me. She was wearing a very striking red dress. I hesitated. 'Well, I remember *you*. You were the one who stopped me buying that horse I liked so much.' She was Colonel Degrela's daughter. 'But don't think I didn't understand. You did it because you wanted the horse to stay there in that paradise.' 'Exactly,' I replied, and she seemed pleased. Then she went off with Ángel to where Ubanbe was talking to the journalists. I put the accordion in its case and left.

On the way to the car park, I noticed a couple walking slowly about the garden. The girl had a slight limp, and the boy was hunched over, as if tilted forward by the hump on his back. It was Teresa and Adrián.

I was happy to see them, and especially glad to see them there, in the silent, solitary garden, surrounded by flowers, by the last roses. Ángel, Berlino, Degrela, Degrela's daughter, the promoter, none of them would venture down there. They would stay inside, in the suffocating dining-room, eating egg mayonnaise and fried mussels, their lips all greasy. Of all the participants in that party, the only one I could imagine in that garden was Ubanbe, strolling amongst the flower beds in his red cape, looking thoughtful and sad.

I left my accordion beside the Guzzi and called to them from the stone steps. Teresa responded at once, as if she'd been waiting for me to greet them. After a few seconds, Adrián also raised one arm.

Teresa was wearing a close-fitting cream dress and a straw hat adorned with pale blue ribbons. Her shoes, of uneven size, the right one normal and the left one with a sole about an inch thick, were also a very pretty pale blue, a pastel shade I'd never seen before. We exchanged kisses. Her lips were painted orange.

'Let's sit down over there,' she said, pointing to a bench next to some rose bushes. 'Welcome to our reunion, David. It's always a pleasure to bump into one's first love.' I told her that I was pleased too, that up until then it had been a dreadful day. I hated the celebrations and hated playing the accordion too. 'You see?' said Teresa, looking at Adrián. 'We're rather alike. We make mistakes. Even David. He believes the things that people like my brother tell him. And he continues to play the accordion instead of freeing himself once and for all from his father's influence.' 'It's true,' I said. 'But the business with the donkey was dreadful,' said Adrián. 'It was just lucky no one got hurt.' He seemed very low.

Teresa gave me a mischievous smile: 'What was the phrase of Hesse's I used to like so much and which I kept repeating ad nauseam to you that afternoon?' 'Why is everything that I need in order to be happy so far away from me?' I quoted from memory. 'I liked it too. In fact, I underlined it in the book,' said Adrián. 'Well, it stinks. It's hollow and pretentious,' said Teresa. 'You have to take life very seriously indeed. We think we've got thousands of opportunities, but it's not true. We're allowed to take a card or two from the table, but not twenty, or even three. That's why when you start to lose at cards, it's best to change games. That's what I did. I thought I'd go mad when they sent me off to study in Pau and I realised that our good friend David here didn't love me. Then I decided to tear that love out by the roots. Sometimes, I hear a Hollies song on the radio and I remember the feelings I had, but it doesn't hurt me any more. On the contrary, it's rather nice, like finding a dried flower between the pages of a book.'

In contrast to what I'd just heard at the party for Ubanbe, Teresa's words seemed to me very profound, even though I didn't entirely understand them. 'What were you talking about before I arrived?' I asked. Adrián answered: 'Tomorrow I'm going to Barcelona to spend a few months in a specialist clinic, not because of my back, but because of this.' He tapped his head. 'Really?' I said. 'Yes, if I carry on as I have been, I'm going to end up a real mess, that much is clear. And with the treatment, well, we'll see.' Teresa took his arm: 'At first, you'll find it hard to do without drink, but you'll get help and move on. And if you succeed, then you'll be dealt some really good cards, because you've got genuine talent. You just have to play the game seriously, that's all.' 'Teresa has really helped me,' confessed Adrián. 'We've talked a lot on the phone lately,' she said in a brighter tone than she had until then. 'But believe it or not, our favourite subject is business.'

Adrián grew more animated too: 'I don't know what you think,

David, but Teresa has suggested that I add a new section to the sawmill, get myself a French patent and start making wooden toys. My father thinks it's a good idea too.' 'In a few years' time the demand will be enormous,' she said. 'Wooden toys have been a huge success in France, and they're backed up by new trends in education.' 'It sounds great, Adrián, but what will become of the crocodiles?' I joked. He said sternly: 'I won't be carving any more crocodiles. That's all over.' 'And I have another piece of news for you, David,' said Teresa. 'You're making me quite dizzy with all these novelties.' 'I'm a Frenchwoman now. In a year's time I'm going to start working with a cousin of Geneviève's. She runs a small hotel near Biarritz. Adrián and I have some very interesting ideas for promoting it.'

Adrián, Teresa, Martín, Joseba: they were all making decisions, all going somewhere. I, on the other hand, was still at home, immobile, protected by my mother, doing nothing but wait, waiting to see what would come of my letter to Virginia or the pots full of petrol hidden in the forest. 'What are you thinking about, David?' asked Teresa. 'That I have no character,' I said, 'that's what I was thinking.'

The image of the pots full of petrol filled my mind. Why didn't I go back to Iruain and tell the group to leave? It was difficult. I didn't think I'd be capable of talking frankly to Bikandi. 'That's a negative thought, David. Get rid of it at once,' Teresa said. 'All right, then, I'll tell you something else I was thinking. You've both changed. You seem different. Martín seems different too. The other day he phoned me from Madrid and waxed positively lyrical describing the lights of the city.' Teresa smiled in a way I *did* recognise: it was her peculiarly scornful smile. 'He was probably high on cocaine! That's the only thing capable of changing that vulgar brother of mine.' 'And I'm taking pills,' said Adrián. 'That's probably why I seem different to you.' 'There's no comparison,' I said. But his low spirits were clearly the result of taking those pills.

It was time to say goodbye. Teresa left us for a moment and returned with two roses. One for Adrián and the other for me. 'They're the last ones. There won't be any more,' she said. 'That's one thing about you that hasn't changed, Teresa. You're still as theatrical as ever.' 'Yes, but

291

now I devote myself to the theatre of truth.' She said this in French: '*le théâtre de la vérité*'. She kissed me on the cheek. 'See you again, David.' 'Aren't you staying in Obaba?' 'No,' she said. 'I'm off to London. I can't get a job in a hotel in Biarritz unless I speak good English.' I gave Adrián a hug: 'We'll talk when you get back from Barcelona.' His eyes filled with tears.

There were even more cars in the car park than before. Ángel's grey Dodge Dart and Berlino's Peugeot were side by side. I wondered if the petrol in the pots would be used to set fire to them. Whatever happened, I had nothing to worry about. I was in no way involved. Agustín and Bikandi had deceived me, they had lied in order to be able to stay in Iruain. If anything did happen, I'd be quite safe. 'I thought they were preparing teaching materials,' I'd tell the civil guard.

I started driving slowly away from the hotel, with my accordion strapped to the carrier on the back of the Guzzi. As I went round a bend, the valley opened up before my eyes. There was a river there, and in the river a pool that we called Urtza. And slightly up from Urtza, beside a bridge, there was a house. And in the house, the postcard with a rose on it. And on the postcard, a message: 'Virginia, I hope I'm not being presumptuous in taking advantage of our former friendship and writing to you on this hot night of 27 August. I just want to ask you one question: Would you like to go for a walk with me? I look forward to hearing from you.' I had stuck the rose that Teresa had given to me – a real rose and not just a postcard – on the handlebars of the Guzzi. As soon as I got home, I would put it in a cup of water. I would wait for a letter from Virginia until the day it lost all its petals. No longer.

XIII

It had started drizzling, and so I stayed home watching the ice-hockey match being shown on TV. 'There's a letter for you,' my mother said, coming into the living-room, carrying a small envelope. There was no

292

return address, and both the name and the address had been written with great care in very neat handwriting. 'Oh, right,' I said.

My mother was tired. She took off her glasses and rubbed her eyes. 'I'm going back to the workshop,' she said. 'I can't stop. Everything has to be finished in time for the fiesta.' 'Will there be a lot of new dresses this year?' I asked. I found it hard to say this in a normal tone of voice and to conceal the excitement I was feeling. I was sure that the envelope I was holding contained Virginia's answer. 'Most of the dresses have been made already,' she said. 'Now we're working on the ribbons. The girls this year have taken it very seriously. The ones who come to the workshop are all embroidering their own.'

It was the custom for the girls in Obaba to make these silk ribbons as part of the competition that took place on the first day of the fiesta. 'Do you need anything?' my mother asked. No, I didn't need anything. I was fine. She closed the door very quietly, as if afraid she might wake someone up.

There was something bulky in the envelope: a small, hard object that filled it out. I felt the packet again and again and decided that what I could feel were wood shavings, which were used at the time, before plastic became the norm, to protect porcelain figures and other fragile objects. But what were they protecting? At first, my finger tips could make out only the smallness and hardness of the object, but I continued touching and squeezing it and reached the conclusion that it was a ring. Unable to contain myself any longer, I ripped open the envelope. Hidden amongst the wood shavings was a small ring made of bakelite.

I looked at the TV screen. A player in a red helmet was tearing across the ice towards the goal. He shot the puck, missed, and three players wearing black helmets surrounded him and pushed him towards the barrier.

The only piece of paper I found inside the envelope, a kind of wrapping for the shavings, was blank. Virginia's answer was the ring. I felt confused, incapable of interpreting the message.

I went over to the sewing workshop. 'Can you ask my mother to come outside for a moment,' I asked the girl who opened the door. I

293

saw Paulina sitting beside the window, tacking the hem of a blue dress.

'What's this? Do you know?' I asked my mother. She did, indeed, know, and she looked at me mischievously. She went back into the workshop and returned with a handful of rings. Unlike my white one, they were all different colours: red, green, yellow, blue, pink. 'You're forgetting the customs of your own village, David,' she said. Someone inside joked: 'He's a student, Carmen, and students soon forget the girls from their village. They like city girls, especially the girls from San Sebastián.' All her workmates laughed. 'The rings are for the ribbons, David,' my mother said.

I suddenly remembered the 'race', the game that was held on the first day of the fiesta. Mounted on bicycles, the boys from the village rode underneath an arch and tried to stick a kind of iron spike through one of the rings and win the ribbon that went with it. The most important prize came afterwards: the girl who'd embroidered the ribbon and the boy who'd managed to seize it became 'engaged for a day'. They began by having an 'official' photograph taken, then they went to a banquet – *the wedding* – and remained together until the clock on the church or on the town hall struck twelve.

My mother handed the ring back to me. 'It wasn't made in the workshop. No one here has embroidered a white ribbon. Besides, they tend to be quite rare. Most girls prefer a colour.' 'The ring came with the letter,' I said. 'Girls nowadays are real cheats,' she replied with a sigh. 'In my day, you didn't know who had made it until you read the name embroidered on the ribbon. Now, though, they give you all kinds of clues. You know beforehand which girl wants to be with you.' This was good news for me. Virginia was skewing things in my favour. 'By the way, who is she?' asked my mother. She seemed suddenly surprised. 'I'll tell you later,' I said.

The ice-hockey game was continuing, and the men in the red helmets had just got the puck in the goal. They were hugging each other and waving their sticks in the air.

I tried to calm myself, to analyse the situation without getting up from my position on the sofa, in front of the TV, but I couldn't. In my

294

mind, which was spinning round and round, there was room for only one idea: Virginia had said 'Yes'. 'Yes, I do,' her message was saying. 'I want to spend the fiesta, the first since the shipwreck and death of my husband, enjoying myself and dancing with you.' The idea was whirling faster and faster inside my head; I felt like leaping up, like moving. Only one small detail curbed my joy. I hadn't ridden my bicycle since I'd had the Guzzi. And that was four years ago. I needed to get in training if I was to be successful in the race of the ribbons. I had to play my part as well.

The one thing I couldn't understand, and which I found slightly troubling, was her chosen form of expression, the fact that she hadn't written a single word. Although, when I thought about it, what did I expect? That she would call me up and ask me over to her house where I would find her lying naked on the bed in her room? That was quite impossible. Virginia was from Obaba and belonged to the country world. She couldn't draw attention to herself, certainly not in her situation. She had to find some discreet way of approaching me.

I turned off the TV and went out on to the terrace. There was her house with its white walls, beside the river, on the other side of the bridge, surrounded by hills and green mountains.

I put Virginia's ring in the garage, hanging from a piece of string, and started training for the race of the ribbons. 'What *are* you up to, David?' I heard someone say. Joseba and Agustín were watching me. I got off the bike and dropped the spike, known as an *entenga* in Obaba. I didn't want witnesses to what I was doing.

Joseba had cut his hair and now looked like a perfectly ordinary student. Agustín was wearing a baseball cap. 'He wanted to put on a space suit so as to look more like Komarov, but we wouldn't let him. It's still too hot,' said Joseba, picking up the spike. They were both smiling and seemed to be in excellent spirits.

'Do my eyes deceive me or are you in training for the race of the ribbons?' asked Joseba, looking at the ring dangling from the string. 'No, your eyes are not deceiving you,' I replied. 'Well, forgive me for saying so, David, but you're clearly the victim of some form of mental regression. You're returning to the most deeply rooted of Obaba traditions. Now I understand why you weren't interested in coming with us to look for butterflies. Like Ubanbe and the other village traditionalists, you obviously consider that to be girls' stuff.' He was joking, but, at the same time, he believed what he was saying. 'The butterfly hunt is going fantastically well, David,' said Agustín. 'We've even found a female *Dasychira pudibunda*. Jagoba and the others have stayed behind to see if the male turns up.'

We went to the square to have a beer in the restaurant there, and Joseba, more serious now, began talking to me about Adrián. It was good news that our friend had agreed to be admitted to a clinic. He'd seen Adrián's father, Isidro, that very morning, and he seemed a different man, much happier than when we dropped off his son after a drunken night at the hotel. He even had plans for the future. 'My father and he are looking into the market for wooden toys. They say it could prove very profitable. They might open up a whole new department at the sawmill.' I told him that I knew all this already, that I'd seen Adrián and Teresa in the hotel garden. 'By the way, Teresa told me a surprising thing. She said Martín takes cocaine.' On Joseba's face appeared a smile as mischievous as Teresa's. 'Mafiosi follow their own path,' he said. Agustín smiled too.

We took our drinks from the restaurant bar and went and sat on one of the benches in the square under the horse chestnut trees, just as we used to in the days of Redin and César. 'When are they going to get rid of those bits of marble?' asked Agustín, looking at the remains of the monument destroyed by the bomb. 'They'll leave them there until they make a new one. They're still not quite ready to abandon the trenches,' said Joseba.

Looking at the monument, but seeing something else, Agustín said in a faint voice: 'You don't know this, but my grandfather, my grandmother and two of my aunts lost their lives in the bombing of Guernica thirty-three years ago. Later on, it transpired that the 1500 people who died there, amongst them my relatives, were the victims of an experiment. Apparently, the Germans wanted to try out their new Dornier and Heinkel planes, and Franco said: "There's a target for you. Go and burn Guernica to the ground." And do you know what I think? That we cannot hold up our heads until we've made them pay for that.'

We sat in silence, watching the people labouring away in the square, putting up the stage for the band or chalking up the area where the race of the ribbons was to take place. The intensity with which Agustín had spoken these words touched me. At the same time, it dispelled my few remaining doubts: he and his companions were going to make use of the petrol in the pots.

We had supper together in the restaurant under the town hall portico, and I told them about the conversation I'd had years before with César in that same place, and about the people from Obaba who were shot. There was a moment when it occurred to me to forget all about the race, because, compared with the subjects we discussed over supper, it seemed a silly, anachronistic, frivolous waste of time. However, when I went back home and saw the rose that Teresa had picked for me in the hotel garden, still fresh, still with all its perfume and its petals, my thoughts turned to Virginia, and once more everything was as it had been before.

XIV

The photograph they took of us on the day of the race of ribbons has remained all these years in a box, here at Stoneham. I have it on the desk in front of me. Virginia is looking very pretty in her new green dress; she has her head up and is laughing at some foolish comment I'm making to the photographer. I'm holding out my arms and showing off the ribbon I've just won. The remains of the monument form the back-drop to the image; in one corner, you can see the tricycle belonging to the ice-cream vendor who came that year for the fiesta.

All those who had found a partner in the race, some thirty young men and women, went to the restaurant to enjoy a banquet. Virginia and I sat at one end of the table, opposite each other. Whenever I handed her some bread or replied to some question from her, on any pretext at all, I would touch her fingers, her hand, her arm. When they brought us dessert, I offered her a cream cake in my hand and she took it with her mouth. I felt her wet lips on my finger tips.

A boy wearing his red ribbon around his neck came over to us and placed an accordion on the table. 'Whenever you're ready, David,' he said. Everyone around the table began to applaud. I asked if they were going to make me work on a day like that. 'We have to dance a little before our fiancées run off with someone else,' said the boy with the red ribbon. His comment provoked more applause. 'What do you want me to play?' 'Casatschok!' they all cried. 'Oh, if you must!' I groaned, taking up the accordion. 'We accordionists have to do as we're told,' I said to Virginia, 'but this really is a harsh punishment. We won't be able to dance together.' I felt euphoric, and I could see that Virginia was happy too. 'We'll dance later, to the band,' she said blithely.

Some of the boys were getting out of control, running up and down between the tables, pretending to be horses and carrying others on their shoulders. 'Don't play for too long,' the owner of the restaurant whispered in my ear, 'someone might fall and hurt themselves.' 'I'll lead them straight out into the street,' I told him. I played the first notes of 'Pagotxueta' and began walking towards the door. 'They're all following us!' said Virginia.

When I got as far as the horse chestnut trees, I took off the accordion and returned it to the boy with the red ribbon. I was free now to enjoy my own fiesta.

The trumpeter in the band announced over the microphone a classic song: 'And now, for everyone, "Five hundred miles".' 'Oh, I love this song, it's got a really pretty tune,' said Virginia. *Faborez?* – 'May I?' – I said in turn. That was how men in the country asked a woman for a dance. 'I can hardly refuse,' she replied. 'After all, you won my ribbon.' We started dancing. 'How long does the privilege last? Only until midnight?' 'Since it's fiesta time, the ribbon will be valid until at least one o'clock.' I put my arm about her waist and drew her to me. I felt the tips of her hair brush my cheek. I held her still closer.

Suddenly, the band stopped playing, and the music was replaced by a steadily growing murmur. 'They're handing out propaganda, David,' said a man who was dancing with his wife. We knew each other from the days when I played the harmonium in church and he used to sing in the choir. 'Look! Look!' he cried, pointing across at the town hall. On the balcony, the Spanish flag was in flames. 'Whoever did that is a lot more agile than I am!' the man said to his wife. The trumpeter spoke into the microphone: 'Keep calm, please!' They resumed their playing of 'Five hundred miles', but in vain. Everyone was leaving.

As the crowd dispersed, I noticed two Land-rovers and about six civil guards brandishing guns. 'Look at that!' the man exclaimed. A red, green and white flag was now waving from the roof of the town hall. I'd seen it before, especially at university, but only in pamphlets or painted on a wall. 'The Basque flag!' said the man. There was excitement in his voice, or perhaps it was fear.

The band members got down from the stage. 'The fiesta's over,' said Virginia. The man from the choir nodded. 'Look, more civil guards are arriving.' From where we were standing, we could see five Land-rovers now. 'There's not much they can do! The old duster's been burned to a frazzle,' said the man, looking at the two men struggling to extinguish the burning Spanish flag. I didn't know the first man, but the second man was Gregorio. 'Have you got one of these?' asked a young woman as she pushed past us. She, too, was a member of the church choir; she used to stand next to my mother. She gave us each a flyer and then moved on.

The murmuring again began to grow louder, and people started running out on to the road. 'What's going on now?' said the man. His wife read what was on the flyer: 'Basques, Euskadi needs you! Do your bit for freedom.' The man gestured to her to keep silent. The woman who had given us the flyer came by again: 'There's a fire!' 'Where?' 'At the Hotel Alaska! You can see the flames from the new estate.'

299

The man from the choir and his wife set off running. Virginia and I walked at normal speed to start with, but ended up running like everyone else. When we reached the new houses, those who had arrived first began explaining the situation to us: 'It looks like burning the flag was just a ruse. And while the civil guard were down in the village, they set fire to the hotel.' The man from the choir was again by our side. 'They're not stupid, are they!' he said. Where the hotel was, we could see a black cloud. Red flames occasionally rose up from its centre.

'It's frightening,' said Virginia. 'Yes, it is.' I couldn't take my eyes off the black cloud. Sometimes it formed coils in the air. 'If you like I could make you a special coffee,' she said. We were standing near the café where she worked. 'Given that I want to stay with you always, I'll always say "yes" to everything.' 'Me too,' she said. 'Meaning?' 'That I want to stay with you too.' 'Even after the clocks have struck midnight or one o'clock?' She laughed.

'Things are going to turn really nasty here,' said the man from the choir, looking at us. But we weren't listening and walked, instead, over to the coffee house. 'Hi, David,' someone said as he passed us. I turned towards him. Agustín had also turned his head. 'See you later!' he shouted. 'Yeah, see you later,' I replied. He and Isabel had their arms about each other's waists, like two lovers. 'Who's that?' asked Virginia. 'A friend from university. We call him Komarov.' 'But he isn't Russian.' 'No, he isn't.' Virginia laughed again.

XV

I slipped out of Virginia's house at about two o'clock in the morning, leaving her asleep, and I found it odd that, at Urtza, there should be lights and the sound of people shouting; however, it was only our third night together and I felt very happy – 'for the first time,' as I told Virginia – and so gave the matter no further thought. Shortly after-wards, when I was setting off in the direction of the sportsground, Sebastián overtook me. He was crying and he said something I didn't understand. 'What's wrong, Sebastián?' I asked. 'Lubis!' he cried, clutching his hands to his head. 'Lubis has drowned at Urtza.' He ran on another ten yards and shouted back to me: 'I'm going to find Ubanbe. Who else can go and tell poor Lubis' mother?' – '*Zeñ jungo'a Lubis gizaajuan amana bestela?*' That's what he said. I started running towards Urtza.

A Land-rover with its engine running had its headlights trained on three men in the water, casting a dim glow over the group of people watching the scene from the other bank of the river. The place was surrounded by civil guards. One of them, holding his rifle in one hand, blocked my path. 'If you've come to gawp, go over there or up into the woods,' he said. And when I looked, there were, indeed, people amongst the trees. The red points of lit cigarettes were moving about in the dark. 'If you don't mind, I'll stay here,' I said. I didn't have the strength to go any further. He made no attempt to move me on. 'At least you know how to behave. Not like some. A few moments ago, some fellow kicked up such a ruckus the captain had to detain him.' He pointed to a Land-rover parked about twenty-five yards away.

The movements of the three men in the water became more abrupt. They were tugging on a rope or a cable. 'The judge has to write his report, so I can't let you through,' the guard said. He was very young and had a babyish face. Had I seen him out of uniform, I would have said he was no more than seventeen. He obviously wanted to talk. 'Those are the witnesses,' he added, looking across at the Land-rover with its headlights on. I recognised Isidro. 'I don't understand why they don't just pull him out,' the guard went on. 'The longer these things go on, the worse it is. Did you know him?' I said that I did. 'According to what we've been told, he was a poacher and used to come fishing for trout at night. He must have slipped, hit his head on a rock, poor bloke, and then drowned.' I heard someone shout 'Pull!', and the men in the the water struggled up to the bank. Lubis' body was dragged on to the small pebble beach.

'Very sad indeed,' said the young guard. I didn't respond. I couldn't speak. 'If you want to see him, come with me,' he said suddenly. There

301

was more movement around Urtza, as if with the recovery of the body, normality had been resumed. Those who'd been sitting on the grass got up; those in the forest walked down to the path and started to wander off. I didn't realise that the civil guards were forcing people to leave.

I saw Joseba's father talking to an officer. He was gesticulating, protesting. 'He won't get anywhere, the captain won't release the detainee until tomorrow morning,' said the young guard. 'He claimed he was the village doctor, but he didn't have any identification on him, and so the captain wouldn't let him through.' He walked towards the river bank, and I followed.

Lubis' body was still lying on the pebbles. A man lit up his face with a torch. 'That was some blow! His eye's almost out of its socket!' said someone.

In the knot of people that had formed around the corpse, a discussion arose as to whether the real cause of death had been the blow or the fact of remaining under the water unconscious. The man with the torch kept moving it about, and the ring of light flickered over the dead face. Sometimes it seemed that it wasn't the light that was moving, but a part of the face, the lips or the eyes, and that we were all wrong, Lubis wasn't really dead. However, the torch finally stopped at the battered eye, and the triumph of death became clear.

'No one could ever say he was anything but a decent lad,' said Isidro. 'I wanted to take him on at the sawmill, but he was always more interested in horses.' There was a silence. No one had anything to say. Everyone was silent, apart from the man with the torch, who kept going over and over the question of whether Lubis had died from the blow or from drowning. 'Will you put that damn thing out!' shouted Isidro. Then he looked at me. 'Where's Pancho? Have you seen him?' I shook my head; no, I hadn't. 'I think he's coming now,' said the man with the torch, shining the light on the path. Sebastián, Pancho and Ubanbe appeared out of the darkness, running.

Ubanbe stopped short when he saw the body. He covered his face with his hands. He was wearing a white track suit, and that's how I imagined him: dressed in white, carrying Lubis' dead body in his arms through the forest, running from one cabin to another, telling the wood-

302

cutters: 'Bury him in some private place, so that when he wakes again he'll see his beloved beech trees. And bring from Iruain the foal that Juan gave him; it will give him joy to see it grazing near his grave.'

Pancho took a few hesitant steps towards the corpse. 'Is that Lubis?' he asked, incredulous. 'Who else could it be?' sobbed Sebastián. 'Oh, God!' cried Ubanbe. 'It's late. Let's get this over with,' said the captain of the civil guards from the path. He clapped twice to make it clear that this was an order.

Virginia was lying face down on her bed, crying so quietly that sometimes I had to look to see if her back was still shaking or if she'd fallen asleep; but, no, she was still crying, stopping and then starting again, entirely undramatically, her sobs creating a kind of furrow in the darkness of the room. Everything was still. The only other sound to be heard was the hiss of the river, which, at times, was louder than her weeping.

I listened to Virginia, I watched the course of her tears, and gradually, the barrier that had been stopping my voice gave way and I began at last to talk, to tell her what had happened to Lubis: 'He was trying to catch a trout, he slipped and hit his head really hard, and as bad luck would have it, he fell over in Urtza, where the water is deepest. Lubis couldn't swim.'

These were poor words, which only repeated what the young civil guard had said, but they did me good, they helped me to recover my voice. Virginia took my hand and rested her wet cheek on it. 'Esteban couldn't swim either. I told him he should learn, that it wasn't wise to work on a boat without knowing how to swim, but he was old-fashioned about certain things, and he just couldn't see himself doing a swimming course at the local pool. And then a boat collided with his when they were fishing off the Brittany coast. Two out of seven of them were saved, one of them was the captain. And in a letter the captain wrote to me, he said: ". . . when he saw the boat was going down, out at sea and in thick fog, Esteban made his way over to me as best he could and asked: 'What do we do now?' The boat gave a lurch and he slipped and fell into the water. I never saw him again."'

Virginia continued talking about what her life had been like during the days and months that followed Esteban's death, waiting to receive news that his body had at last been found. 'A corpse was washed ashore in a place called Brest, but it wasn't him.' 'He and Lubis will be together now,' I said. Whatever it was trammelling my feelings dissolved completely then, and I burst into tears.

I woke up at around seven in the morning, and I could see daylight through the cracks in the shutters. Beside me, Virginia was breathing quietly. Outside, in the river, the water flowing towards Urtza was busy erasing the marks of the previous night, so that the pool would be, as it had been until then, a place where people enjoyed themselves in summer, not the scene of a death.

Oki barked in his kennel. 'Who can that be?' asked Virginia, opening her eyes. 'David! David!' someone called very softly, trying not to make too much noise. A few pebbles struck the shutter. 'Well, whoever he is, he's in a hurry,' Virginia said. I looked out and saw Joseba. 'Come down. Please.' He looked distraught. 'Take him into the kitchen,' Virginia said from the bed, alarmed by my friend's behaviour.

'You do know, don't you, that they killed Lubis,' Joseba told me when I went downstairs and before I could even say a word. 'Last night, two civil guards came for him when he was at Adela's house, and then they tortured him to death. That's why he turned up later on in Urtza. They threw him in there to cover things up.' Joseba was terribly pale. 'You've got to go to Iruain, David. Otherwise, they'll kill our friends. The whole valley is crawling with civil guards. I got through because I showed them my ID and they could see that I live at the sawmill.' He was still breathing hard. 'There's no escape,' he said. 'The only thing that can save them is the hiding-place.'

Lubis had told them about the hiding-place, but, out of respect for my Uncle Juan, hadn't wanted to show them where it was in the house. 'He told us that if we got into trouble, he himself would hide us. We never thought for a moment that he'd die first!' 'Are they there, at the house?' I asked. 'Yes, all four of them, but the civil guard have already

304

started searching the valley. If they don't hide soon, I dread to think what will happen. Papi has given them total freedom to do as they see fit, but he says they won't take him alive, that he knows too much. And Triku told me he feels the same, that it's better to die in a shoot-out than to die the way Lubis did.'

'Papi, Triku . . . who the hell are you talking about?' I asked tetchily. I realised who they must be, but the nicknames irritated me. Everything that was happening irritated me. All the more so when I remembered that, a moment before, I'd been asleep beside Virginia. 'Yes,' said my inner voice, 'you were asleep beside Virginia, but shortly before that, where were you? Standing by Lubis' corpse. Isn't that right? Well, remember that too.'

'I'm sorry,' Joseba said. 'Papi is Jagoba's political alias within the organisation. Triku is Agustín's.' 'Agustín, Komarov, Triku . . . our friend certainly doesn't lack for names,' I said in a friendlier tone of voice, and I felt better. 'Papi is in charge. He was the one who was behind the fire at the hotel, right from the start.' 'The entomologist!' I said, surprised. 'Yes, although, believe it or not, he really is an entomologist.' We both seemed calmer. 'Will you go?' he asked me. 'Yes, I'll go,' I said.

We walked to the other side of the bridge. My motorbike was parked by the playground. 'Go quickly. Iruain is your family house, and the guards will let you through. You'll save our friends' lives.' I looked at Virginia's bedroom window. There was no one there. I thought she must be lying in bed. 'It'll work out fine, and nothing will happen to you. Show them the hiding-place, and I'll take care of the rest.'

The way he spoke betrayed the fact that he, too, was involved, 'organizado' to use the word of the time. 'And what's *your* name?' I asked him. 'Etxeberria,' he replied gravely. 'But it's not official yet. I'm still only new.' I couldn't bring myself to start the bike. 'All this frightens me,' I said. 'Besides, although I realise you won't understand this, I want to be with Virginia.' Joseba swore. 'Look, I may not have your success with women, David, but please, I'm not a fool.' Virginia's bedroom window remained a blank.

Joseba walked round to the other side of the bike. 'Do you know why the civil guards went after Lubis?' he said. 'Bikandi reckons it was a tip-off, but I think it was our fault. Lubis first fell under suspicion the night they let that donkey loose at the hotel dance. There was a rumour in the village that distributing the Miss Obaba leaflets was a form of training exercise. That's what happens when you build sports-grounds in villages like this. Now everything is training. People think that in order to be a political activist, you have to train.' 'Lubis had been a marked man for some time. Ask Ángel,' I said. But I felt guilty. What Joseba was saying made sense.

In most of the houses, the kitchen light was now on. In Villa Lecuona too. My mother always had plenty to do. As she herself put it, at fiesta time because it was fiesta time, and afterwards because it wasn't and there were still dresses to be made. On the road, there was a constant toing and froing of cars – people on their way to work.

'The tip-off could have come from Ángel,' I said. 'He's had it in for Lubis ever since Uncle Juan's horse was killed.' Joseba looked doubtful. 'If you want my opinion, the person behind all this is Berlino. He was like a madman when he saw the hotel go up in flames; he started shooting at anything that moved. And I'll tell you something, David, if it's proved that he was responsible for Lubis' death, he'll pay for it.' I felt even more guilty than I had a moment before: for having played the accordion at the hotel dances; for being the son of Ángel, Berlino's friend; for having contributed to the whole stupid business with the donkey and having thus increased the suspicions that may already have existed regarding Lubis.

The church clock struck once. It was half past seven. 'But if you'd rather I went, just tell me where the hiding-place is, and I'll sort things out.' 'You'd have problems at the road-blocks. You have no reason to be going to Iruain at this hour of the morning.' 'I could try. I don't want them to kill Triku, Komarov, I mean. It's enough that they've killed Lubis.'

I got on my bike. 'I don't know if I'll be able to hold my nerve,' I said. He tried to smile: 'While I was on my way here, I imagined I was

306

the lead singer of Creedence Clearwater Revival and that I was performing "Suzie Q". That's how I overcame my fear.' 'Right, then, I'll hum "Padam Padam". That was Lubis' favourite tune.' But I knew I wouldn't be able to. I set off without looking back at Virginia's house.

The deck of cards

Papi's apartment in Paris was very close to Parc Montsouris. It was quite small, but very pleasant, despite the lack of light. From the bedroom window, you could see the trees in the park and a group of elegant houses that seemed to form a kind of village. 'I think Ben Bella lives around here. Sometimes I pass him in the street,' Papi said, looking out of the window. At the time, the former Algerian president lived in exile in France.

The record-player was on, but so low we could barely hear the music. Papi turned up the volume. 'There might be microphones,' he said, sitting down on the sofa. 'Do you know this?' He was referring to the music. 'It's Guridi, isn't it?' I said. 'That's right. The eighth melody, the prettiest of them all, I think.' He then passed seamlessly on to speak of politics. He told me that the Spanish dictatorship's days were numbered, and asked if I had any views on the role to be played by a revolutionary group should Spain set up a democracy. He used that verb 'set up' as if he were talking about a market stall.

Two hours later, we were once again in Parc Montsouris, at one of the entrances, waiting for a bus. He took a deck of cards out of his pocket and showed it to me. The pack bore the photograph of an orange butterfly. I read: *Euskalerriko Tximeletak*, 'Butterflies and Moths of the Basque Country'. 'You never believed that I was an entomologist,' he said, 'but while we were in Iruain, I really was studying insects as well. Here's the proof. It was published last month.'

I tried to take the cards out, but they were so tightly packed I couldn't. 'The cards are for you,' he said, placing his hand over mine. 'If you don't want them, then leave them in the hiding-place in Iruain, next to the American's hat. As an ex voto.' His expression never changed, even when he was joking.

*   *   *

The deck of cards Papi gave me is now in my study at Stoneham, not in the hiding-place, or *zulo*, in Iruain. They've always been here, ever since my first day at the ranch. Uncle Juan liked them too, and often, sitting in his rocking chair on the porch, he would enjoy himself going through the deck, as if it were a collection of picture cards. Liz and Sara used to do the same. When we played with them, I'd sometimes pretend to be a wizard and read their fortunes: if I turned up a dark moth, that was a bad omen; if a yellow or a red butterfly came up, we had reason to celebrate.

I stopped typing for a moment and went to fetch the cards. I've just shuffled them. I want to spread them out again on the desk, not as I did when I used to play with my daughters – Liz and Sara have grown up, and they no longer believe their father is a wizard – but in order to awaken my memories.

The first card is on the desk. It's a brown and yellow butterfly, with six black spots. Its name is *Pararge maera*. I associate it with Adrián. In our Obaba days, he could have worn it on the lapel of his jacket, as an emblem.

I've put down another card, and the butterfly this time is large and beautiful, a kind of pearly white, with a number of black spots on its forewings and four bright red spots on the hindwings. Its name is *Parnassius apollo*, and is clearly a perfect match for Ubanbe. I think of him all the time. At the trial held after Lubis' death – fifteen years later, in 1985 – he was the only one who dared to name the murderers, and he was denigrated for doing so; there was a lot of talk at the time of 'the boxer Gorostiza's physical and mental deterioration'. We didn't believe that, Ubanbe. For us, for all of those who were Lubis' friends, you will always be *Parnassius apollo*, and, by your side, we'll always see Sebastián, the first to weep for Lubis. Sebastián's card, his butterfly: a small saffron yellow one. *Colias croceus* by name.

The fourth: *Eudia pavonia*. It's a moth, and a mixture of gold, blue and grey, with two black lines on the hindwings. It has four spots, like real eyes. I thought of you, Teresa.

What kind of butterfly are you, Virginia? I intended to put one card down on the table and instead put down two: *Leptidea sinapsis*, which is pure white, and *Euproctis chrysorrhoea*. It's not a very pretty name, but the moth itself is. It has small, whitish wings, quite ordinary, I suppose, but – and this is the characteristic from which it derives its name – it has a golden abdomen. Virginia, if you need an emblem, wear it as a brooch on your dress.

Lymantria dispar is white and pink. Its forewings look as if they'd been painted by someone, its hindwings are like two small skirts. I think of my mother.

The eighth card has fallen face down, and I've left it like that. I said to myself: 'That's Joseba. I don't yet know which card suits him.' He may well think the same about me.

The ninth: *Plebejus icarus*. Small and blue. Lubis.

The tenth: *Gonepteryx rhamni*. Very intense yellow with orangish spots. Without a muse, there is no song, Mary Ann.

August days

1

At noon today I went with Mary Ann to the airport at Visalia to meet Joseba. On the way out, in the queue to pay for the car park, a woman who had apparently just flown in from Chicago started complaining about how tired she felt after long flights. She was muttering about this to herself, and then she noticed Joseba and me: 'You two don't look too good either. I bet you've been travelling a long time.' She couldn't have put it more plainly. We both had the same travel-worn appearance, but while Joseba had been travelling for more than thirty hours and had crossed the Atlantic and the whole of the United States, I had left Stoneham at mid-morning, having enjoyed a quiet breakfast on the porch of my house. This, however, was no surprise. The mirror reminds me of the truth every day.

The unfortunate nature of the woman's remark wasn't lost on Mary Ann and Joseba, and the memory of it cast a shadow over our conversation. In the end, I decided to broach the subject myself and talk about my illness. We were nearly at the ranch, and Joseba was full of praise for the beauties of Lemmon Valley. 'It's the land of the golden apples,' I told him. 'There's no better place to recover from long journeys. You'll see, the jet-lag we're both suffering from will disappear as if by magic.' Mary Ann didn't beat about the bush; she quickly brought Joseba up to date on my state of health: 'David hasn't been feeling very well lately. The doctor says he'll have to have another operation on his heart.' 'Unless I learn to cope with flying better,' I added lightly. But Mary Ann, a worried look on her face, continued her explanations. 'We'll certainly have to do something,' she concluded. 'At the moment, he can't even carry a box of books upstairs.'

I thought: 'Joseba won't let an opportunity like this slip.' And so it was. Frowning furiously, he said to Mary Ann, almost shouting: 'What exactly are you suggesting, Mary Ann? Are you expecting me to lift boxes, cut grass, chop wood? No way! I've come here for a holiday, and I warn you, I don't intend to lift a finger.' Joseba was very good at playing the grouch, and Mary Ann burst out laughing. 'No, I wasn't expecting you to do piddling little jobs like that, Joseba. I was going to give you the stables to clean out. You don't imagine you're going to spend the whole of August just gabbing, do you?' 'Look, Mary Ann,' Joseba said, feigning irritation. 'I just hope you adopt a more positive attitude. If you don't, I warn you, David and I will go and watch baseball every Sunday.' Mary Ann laughed again. She likes writers, and one of Joseba's books is among her favourites.

'All right, I won't ask you to do any work, but I do have a favour to ask,' she said very seriously. 'As you know, in the United States, every town has its Book Club, well, Donald, who's in charge of the Three Rivers Book Club, asked me if you'd be willing to do a reading. I'd help you with the English.' 'Yes, fine,' Joseba replied, 'but let's talk about it later, shall we?'

Back in Stoneham, Rosario and Efraín made sure he had a warm reception. They welcomed Joseba and took him over to Uncle Juan's old house to show him his room. Liz and Sara, on the other hand, behaved appallingly. Sara wouldn't say a word, in 'a fit of shyness' as she calls it, while Liz retired to her bed and would have nothing to do with us. When Joseba went over to her, she hid her head under the pillow, and I got annoyed and called her *tuntuna*, which, in Basque, means 'silly'. Then she yelled: 'Shut up! Don't speak Basque to me!' In the end, I had no option but to leave her alone.

I don't know what's wrong with Liz, but lately she seems to be angry with me. She turned thirteen last weekend, and at the party we held here at Stoneham, her friends bought her some of those huge monarch butterflies. It's the latest fashion. You buy them at butterfly farms and release them as soon as the candles on the cake have been blown out. Anyway, during the party, I started telling them about how the Basque language has hundreds of names for butterflies and that one of them, *pinpilinpauxa*, was really strange, because instead of reproducing a sound,

312

which is what onomatopoeic words do, it imitated the actual flight of the butterfly. Thirty seconds into this story, Liz unleashed one of her 'shut ups' and I had to stop. In front of all her girlfriends too; she made me feel just like an old man who's always repeating the same story. I didn't expect such behaviour from her.

Mary Ann assures me it's her age, that our eldest daughter behaves like that because she's entering adolescence. This may be true, but there are other possible explanations. I fear she may have inherited a certain hardness of heart, the same as runs in Ángel's veins and in mine. I fear, too – and this is a worse hypothesis – that Liz sees the future far more clearly than anyone else and that, horrified by what she sees, she's distancing herself from me, preparing herself for the moment of final separation. *The moment of final separation*, or death, if we dispense with euphemisms. Anyway, this business with Liz only deepens my pessimism about love. We want to place it on a pedestal above everything else, but it's just not possible. We're not angels. I'd like Liz to be closer to me, but it doesn't seem exactly logical to demand such affection after the problems I had with my own parents.

In the afternoon, we sat out on the porch talking and drinking lemonade to combat jet-lag. Mary Ann and Joseba are still out there. I should have stayed with them. My thoughts have slithered off into dark corners, and I've ended up writing black letters on this white computer that Mary Ann gave me for my birthday.

2

After a light lunch, we went swimming in a pool in the upper part of the Kaweah river, and it was like sloughing off all my tiredness. It was such a pleasure to get into the cold water and an equal pleasure to be able to speak in the language which, since Juan died, I can only use to speak to myself. Besides, both Joseba and I opted to remember the happy things from the past, although the shape of the pool did remind Joseba of the place in our village where we used to bathe and the death

313

of Lubis. 'I've never regretted the way we responded to the people who killed him,' he said suddenly, in a tone of voice Mary Ann wouldn't recognise. I thought he was going to continue along that route, but he changed the subject. Just as well. He only arrived in Stoneham yesterday, and it's too soon to deal with all that.

The breeze from the mountains meant that it didn't feel quite so hot. We left the shores of the Kaweah and, like two idle vacationers, in swimming trunks and with towels slung round our necks, we walked over to Rosario and Efraín's house, intending to collect the guacamole they'd promised Joseba. It was too early for supper and so we lingered for a while in the ranch's small cemetery.

It was really pretty. The wind stirred the grass and the flowers very gently, as though afraid of bruising them. 'Let's stop for a moment, while I smoke a cigarette,' Joseba said, and we sat down, he on one rock and I on another. Joseba smokes black tobacco now and not the aromatic herbs he used to smoke.

He fell silent, and so did I. The wind had suddenly dropped, and the grass and the flowers had stopped moving. Then, as if it had been waiting for that precise moment, a butterfly emerged from one corner of the cemetery and flew straight towards us. It seemed about to perch on my forehead or on Joseba's, but, instead, it flew over our heads and disappeared among the leaves of a tree.

I felt happy and wanted to explain to Joseba that the butterfly, doubt-less one of the monarch butterflies released on Liz's birthday, had, oddly enough, emerged from the same corner of the cemetery where I'd buried the word *mitxirrika* – 'butterfly' in the language of the country people of Obaba – as if it had come back to life, or more precisely, become flesh, in order to fly up from its tiny grave. But I said nothing. It wasn't easy to explain to an old friend this custom of burying words in matchboxes, however simple the explanation. Mary Ann understands: I did it for purely pedagogical reasons. I wanted my daughters to take an interest in my mother tongue, a desire which, unless things change radically, isn't going to be fulfilled. Liz's attitude certainly doesn't leave much room for hope.

After the butterfly had flown over our heads, I noticed that Joseba

314

seemed even more sunk in thought. I asked him what he was thinking about and he replied as if he were quoting from someone: 'My vagabond thoughts come and go.' But with Joseba you never can tell. His 'quotations' are often inventions to get him out of an awkward spot. It's an old habit. 'Hm, "vagabond",' I said, 'I like that word.' And our conversation took on the tone of the talks we used to have thirty years ago in Bilbao.

He went over to Juan's tomb and read the epitaph out loud: 'I could have done with two lives, but I only had one.' He asked if I'd written it. 'With Mary Ann's help.' 'Well, you're on good form. I like it.' Then he continued on until he reached the hamsters' little graves. 'And what about here? Whose are these?' 'Tommy, Jimmy and Ronnie. My daughters' hamsters.' He jumped over the small area in which the matchboxes are buried, and left the cemetery. Why did he jump like that? Perhaps he felt the presence of the *mitxirrika* and the other words from Obaba.

'Do you know who I thought of while we were in the cemetery?' he said later, when we set off again. I had to ask him to walk more slowly because I couldn't keep pace with him going up the hill: 'You're obviously getting over your jet-lag,' I said, 'but I'm still having difficulties. Go on, then, tell me. Who did you think of?' He slowed down to match my speed and walked alongside me. 'Redin, our French teacher, I mean, Monsieur Nestor.'

It occurred to me to mention the memoirs I've written, but it isn't the moment. I'll give him a copy on the eve of his departure from Stoneham so that he can read it if he wants to and then deposit it in the library in Obaba. 'I often remember him,' I said. 'Really?' 'Yes, really.' 'You're a very loyal pupil, David. I'd forgotten all about him. But in March, I was in Cuba, and there was our Redin.' 'You're joking,' I said. Joseba burst out laughing and flicked me with his towel: 'Don't look like that, David, I mean that I saw him in a photo!'

He told me that he's studying the relationship between the Basque colony in Cuba and Cuban writers, which is why he went to Havana. The poet Eliseo Diego took him to visit Hemingway's house. 'It's really beautiful,' he said. 'It's on the top of a hill and entirely surrounded by trees. As soon as I went into his living-room, I found a big poster advertising a bullfight

315

in San Sebastián. It was hanging over the fireplace, and to the left and right were other photos taken in the Basque Country. One of them showed Hemingway himself in party mood, smoking an enormous cigar and grasping his companion round the neck in a kind of wrestling hold. Well, guess who that companion was.' 'Redin?' 'The very man! And smoking an equally huge cigar,' Joseba said. 'So everything he told us was true.'

I started laughing out of sheer pleasure. My French teacher suddenly seemed an altogether worthier man, not as he had been when we were students, a poor, pathetic creature who invented stories to make himself seem more important. 'I remembered my trip to Havana when I saw the graves of Tommy and the other hamsters,' explained Joseba. 'Hemingway used to do the same with his cats. There were four small white graves about twenty yards from the house.'

I didn't go into Efraín and Rosario's house, but I saw Liz and Sara's backpacks on the porch. Mary told me later that our two daughters have decided to move in there: Liz, because, she says, that is where she wants to live, and Sara, because she wants to be with her big sister. They're entirely innocent, but how they wound me. We were probably innocent in Redin's day, but I'm sure we wounded him too. In a way, we despised him. I believed in him more than Joseba and the others did, but even I issued some very harsh judgements on his behaviour. He seemed to be a man of little character, almost servile sometimes, especially in his relations with the people at the Hotel Alaska. Or with Ángel. That's why I was so glad when I found out that his supposed friendship with Hemingway was true. Confronted by our incredulity, Redin would think: 'Laugh all you want, young ones. But your lives will never be as brilliant as mine was.' He would have been right. If partying with Hemingway isn't brilliant, what is? Right now, I think about that photo and immediately feel like lighting up a cigar.

3

Last night, in my dreams, I saw an old man sitting outside the front door at Iruain. He was wearing a cream-coloured suit and a maroon tie. He must have been about eighty. 'It's you! What are *you* doing here, Redin?' I asked when I recognised him. 'What do you think I'm doing, David? Can't you see? I'm waiting for the last train.' I smiled broadly and told him that he looked really well and that he shouldn't think about taking the last train until he was a hundred. He took off his glasses and looked straight at me: 'One has to resign oneself, David. What else can one do? Strain at the rope like an animal that feels the knife at its throat?' 'You're right. It's best just to wait quietly,' I said. 'Of course! Look, there's my train now!' I turned and saw a group of people silently waiting for the train to arrive. Suddenly, the station master grabbed my arm: 'On you get!' Frightened, I pulled away. 'It's not my train. I just came to keep this gentleman company!'

'It's all right, David. It's me,' Mary Ann said. It took me a while to calm down. 'I was dreaming I was wrestling with a bear, trying to defend my flock,' I said at last. 'You Basque shepherds are all the same. This time, though, the bear is going to win.' She rolled over on top of me, and we kissed.

The night and its sombre dream were followed by an extremely happy day. Mary Ann was very busy. She phoned our friends at the Three Rivers Book Club to organise the reading. Joseba, for his part, is still in excellent spirits. The Mexican horsebreeders had a high old time watching his attempts to get on a horse. 'I hate these gigantic creatures!' he kept saying. 'Leandro, bring him a pony,' Efraín asked one of his companions. Joseba started shouting: 'No, not a pony, Leandro, a dog! Or better still, a cat. They're even smaller!' We all laughed. Later, I saw Joseba emerge from the paddock wearing a broad-brimmed hat.

In a sequence of memories, I suddenly recalled a fact about our lives that I'd completely forgotten. Triku, Joseba and I went to a fortune-teller once and the card that came up for Joseba was the ace of pentacles. 'You have the sun with you,' said the fortune-teller, Señora Guller. 'Whatever you do, you will always succeed.' 'So he won't go to prison, then,' said Triku gravely. He'd had total faith in Señora Guller ever since, when he was a child, she had correctly guessed the medical history of each of his classmates. He often went to her for advice and followed it to the letter. Señora Guller again spread the cards and immediately looked worried. 'They say that all three of you will go to prison.' She passed me the deck. 'Shuffle them, please.' Then she asked Triku to do the same. Finally, she turned to Joseba: 'Pick a card, any card, and place it on the table.' Joseba did as she asked. 'Excellent!' cried Señora Guller. The ace of pentacles had reappeared. 'You have a very powerful sun. You will save yourself and you will save your friends as well, even from prison.'

Joseba wagged his finger at us: 'From now on, a little respect, please, for the one who gives you light and heat.' He was as sceptical as I was. But Señora Guller wasn't just any fortune-teller. Our consultation took place at the beginning of 1976, seven or eight months before we were arrested and put in prison. Not long afterwards, in May 1977, we regained our freedom. Thanks in large part to Joseba.

The memory vanished at once and left me feeling slightly sad, but calm too. If Señora Guller was here, I'd ask her to get Joseba to choose another card. I could really do with an ace of pentacles now!

4

Today we visited Sequoia National Park. Joseba is still on excellent form, and Mary Ann and I laughed out loud when he went over to the information desk to enquire, in all seriousness, where he could find the big trees. The employees looked at him incredulously and pointed to the sequoias all around. But Joseba didn't give up: 'No, no, not the ordinary ones, the others, the really big ones.' He seemed so earnest that the employees couldn't be sure, as they suspected, that he wasn't merely pulling their leg. 'Do those sequoias look ordinary to you?' one of them asked. 'In my country most of the trees are that size,' he said, poker-faced. 'Well, if you want, go over to the window, and they'll refund your entrance fee,' the employee said at last. He moved off with the look of someone who feels a migraine coming on.

We went to see the 'oldest living organism in the world', the sequoia which is said to be nearly three thousand years old, and Mary Ann explained to us that it hasn't always been called General Sherman as it is now; a century ago, it was called Karl Marx. The change of name gave rise to a series of jokes, but being close to the tree itself moved us to silence. It's frightening to think that it was born some 3000 years ago and that, at the time, a goat could have swallowed it whole, along with its tender little leaves. But it was stronger than goats, storms, frosts and people. And there it is, still growing. Blessed be the tenacity of trees.

Before we left, we sat for a while at the food stand in the park and ate some sandwiches. 'Do you remember, David? We came here the day we found out I was pregnant with Liz,' Mary Ann said. 'It was one of the happiest moments of my life,' I replied.

How could I possibly forget that day. We were coming back from Stoneham after visiting the doctor in Three Rivers, and we both felt like going for a drive. We wanted to savour the news, without sharing it with anyone, not even with Juan. That night, when we did finally tell him, my uncle was so overcome with emotion that he wept for joy, and then we felt guilty for not having told him earlier.

Mary Ann lit a cigarette; now she only smokes when she's happy. 'Speaking of Liz, I know now why she's angry with us,' she said. 'Angry with me, you mean, not with us,' I said, correcting her. 'No, with us, David. She's been snapping at me for days now.' 'What's wrong, then?' 'She wants to go to Santa Barbara on vacation, like her schoolfriends.'

Compared with the reasons I'd been imagining, this seemed unimportant, frivolous. I asked Mary Ann if there was some way of solving the Santa Barbara problem, if we could find a family who'd be able to take our daughters for a week. Mary Ann stubbed out her cigarette and stood up: 'Let's go into town. Perhaps we can sort everything out in one fell swoop – Santa Barbara *and* the reading at the library.' So we set off to Three Rivers and, two hours later, it was all arranged. Liz and Sara will stay in Santa Barbara with the head teacher's sisters, and Joseba will read to the members of the Book Club next Wednesday, in about a week's time. Mary Ann will translate the texts into English.

319

Joseba and I have spent the day alone, because Mary Ann has taken the girls to Santa Barbara and will stay there until tomorrow. We got some beers out of the icebox and sat on the porch, looking across at the mountains. 'You know, last Christmas, I went to Morocco for a few days,' Joseba said as he took his first sip, and for a while, he spoke about the customs of the country like any other tourist; then, when he described the journey back and the foul weather – 'I had to drive with my head-lights on even during the day' – his voice changed. 'What is it you want to talk to me about, Joseba?' I said. I imagined it must be something to do with our shared past. And so it was. He wanted to tell me about meeting Ubanbe.

'Like I said, on the way back, the weather was appalling. In Morocco, it rained non-stop, and the roads were flooded. And in Spain, it was even worse. It started to snow and everything turned white, even the olive groves. Then, as I approached Madrid, the weather deteriorated still further, and I had no alternative but to spend the night in a motel. A real dive. The cafeteria was a vast place packed with people. On the back wall, a giant screen was showing endless images of boxing. I was just going to my room, when I saw Ubanbe on the screen in that fight with the German. Do you remember? God, he was handsome, our Ubanbe! I felt so happy, and it set me thinking about our times in Obaba.

'Suddenly, the screen went dark, and the lights in the room all focused on a stage made to look like a boxing-ring. "Tonight, dear friends, is a very special night," announced a man dressed up to look like a trainer. And on came Ubanbe, looking as fat as a pig. His face was all puffy and he was almost bursting out of his suit, as if he'd put on forty pounds since he bought it. I couldn't bear it and went up to my room.'

Joseba sat for a moment in silence, gazing out at the mountains. It was as if he could see those images in the distance, amongst the trees and the rocks, and that he was half-closing his eyes to be able to see them more clearly. I asked him to go on. 'It's best not to drag this kind of story out too much,' I said. 'Wait until the end,' he replied, 'and then draw your conclusions.' He drank the rest of his beer and continued talking.

'I woke up at about three in the morning, and I could stand it no longer. I got dressed, went down to the cafeteria, and there was Ubanbe at the corner of the bar, alone, drinking some sort of yellowish liquid. He looked like a well-thumbed book, as if everyone at that evening's event had slapped him on the back. I stood about three feet away from him, and addressed him as if we were in Obaba, in pure dialect: '*Ze it-te'ek emen, Ubanbe, etxetik ain urruti?*' – 'What are *you* doing here, Ubanbe, so far from home?' He spun round with unexpected vigour. It took him about a second to recognise me. 'Don't you know what day it is today, Manson?' he said. 'Yes, Ubanbe, it's 28 December.' '28 December! Are you mad? It's the Day of the Innocents, Manson, our All Fools' Day! And I've celebrated it by making fools out of a load of imbeciles.'

'Blessed be the rough tongue of the woodcutters!' I cried. Ubanbe's reaction seemed entirely worthy of him. A proof that they hadn't managed to defeat him. 'Then he became even more impossible,' Joseba went on. 'He flung out his arms and asked if I thought he looked handsome. I said he did, and in exchange received a punch that very nearly dislocated my shoulder. 'You liar!' he said. 'I'm fat and disgusting, but then you're not exactly handsome yourself. You look like an old donkey with those big teeth of yours and all that grey hair. You were better off with your hair long.'

Joseba laughed and said Ubanbe was quite right, and that whenever he looked in the mirror now, he always saw a donkey. Lots of things sprang into my mind, among them the image of Sebastián and his twin brothers in the days when Uncle Juan used to have fun joking with them. 'Adela's three sons are important people now,' Joseba told me when I asked after them. 'They set up a repair shop for trucks on the industrial estate in Obaba and it's worked out incredibly well for them.

321

Now they're the owners of a huge depot. I think they repair about a hundred trucks a month.'

The phone rang, interrupting our conversation. It was Mary Ann, phoning to say that they'd arrived safely. Then Liz came on the line: 'Hi, Daddy, how are you?' she asked, as if we hadn't seen each other for ages. I told her I was fine. 'I love you lots, Daddy,' she added. And Sara, in the background, said: 'Me too.' I was so touched I felt like crying. A slightly over-the-top reaction certainly. I must be a bit punch-drunk – the boxing term comes from having Ubanbe on my mind. 'I had nothing to do with it. It was their idea to call,' Mary Ann assured me, when I asked the reasons behind that declaration of love. 'What are you up to?' she asked. 'Joseba was just explaining to me why he looks so much like a donkey.' Joseba let out a braying noise. 'Sounds pretty authentic,' said Mary Ann from the other end.

A truck was coming from Bakersfield to pick up a horse, and I had to hand over some documents to the driver. On the way to the stables, we met Efraín. 'I want to ask you something very serious,' Joseba said. Efraín laughed: 'Oh, yeah.' 'Take a good look at me, Efraín. Do I look very much like a donkey? I don't mean do I look a bit like a donkey, because I realise I do. What I want to know is do I look a *lot* like a donkey.' 'You clown!' cried Efraín. We ended up at his house, eating the tortillas Rosario had made for us.

6

In the morning we went for a swim at the pool in the Kaweah river, and Joseba got a real fright when he went to grab hold of what he thought was a root in the water, and it slithered out of his hands. Snakes terrify him. I remember that once, when we were at nursery school, we visited a stable to see a snake which, so they said, used to suckle milk from a cow every night, and Joseba suddenly started screaming blue murder because he had felt something slimy brush past his ankle. And later on, when we were working with Triku for the organisation,

322

his phobia intensified. On hot days, he hated having to walk through scrub, and Papi had to keep telling him to worry less about toad-eating reptiles and more about the civil guard. The Kaweah river suddenly seemed to him a most unpleasant place. He got out of the water and sat in the shade, smoking a cigarette.

'Well, obviously he'd say that,' Joseba retorted when I reminded him of Papi's advice. 'He liked butterflies. And what is the greatest enemy of the butterfly? The toad. And what is the number one exterminator of toads? The snake. He was very much a *frentista* – in favour of forming tactical alliances – not so much in political terms, but certainly as an entomologist.' *Frentista*. It seemed to me a very old-fashioned word, with no sheen to it. Like other words from the same era: 'privatisation', 'imperialism'. In order to estimate the damage done by time, it isn't enough to look at the rose or the lame dog, one has also to study the glossiness or otherwise of words.

'Have you seen him recently?' I asked. I suspect he has. He put his cigarette to his lips. 'Papi? Yes, I have, but we'll talk about him later.' 'When?' 'Are you coming to the reading on Wednesday?' 'Yes, along with the other forty members of the Three Rivers Book Club.' 'Right then, after the reading.' He laughed. 'You know the kind of questions people usually ask at these meetings,' he said. Then he parodied some of the prospective members of that imaginary audience: '"Is the novel autobiographical?" "Are your characters based on real people?" Well, you and I could do the same.' 'Now don't start playing the naughty boy,' I said. 'I didn't mean to, David. It's just that I don't know how to speak frankly. I always have to put on an act.'

I don't know how to speak frankly. Joseba has been saying this for twenty or twenty-five years now. Moreover, he makes a big thing of it, and considers that this same impossibility affects everyone, whether they admit it or not, whether they conceal it or not. When we were in prison, the ordinary prisoner who was in charge of the infirmary asked him once why he wrote stories. 'It's a way of telling the truth,' Joseba answered. The prisoner wasn't convinced. 'I think the best way is to be straight with people,' he said. Joseba laughed and patted him on the back: 'Verily I say unto thee, it is easier for a prisoner to pass through the eye of a keyhole and escape than it is for a mere mortal to tell the truth or, as you put it, be straight with people.'

'What are you thinking about, David?' 'About your obsession with keeping secrets.' He laughed out loud. 'All your efforts are in vain, David. I will only speak in the presence of my public. Make sure you're there.' He hesitated over how best to dispose of his cigarette end and finally stuck it in a crack in the rock. 'Don't get so serious, David,' he said. 'You're a devious creature, Joseba, and you always have been.' 'A typically Yankee sentiment, comrade. I forbid you to drink any more Coca-Cola.' He imitated Papi's voice when he said this. Then he changed the subject and started talking about the current scene in the Basque Country.

I couldn't follow him. I didn't recognise any of the names, not even the names of politicians. 'From now on, you'll be better informed,' he said. 'They're going to start broadcasting our TV programmes by satellite. So that the diaspora doesn't disappear entirely, if you get my meaning.' I told him that I'd try to keep myself up to date. 'Wait till you read the credits at the end of the most popular programme of the evening: "Costumes by Paula Iztueta".' 'So our Paulina has become Paula.' I remembered how my mother used to say that she'd be a fine dressmaker one day. 'The odd thing is that Paulina always puts women in long dresses,' said Joseba, this time parodying the way Adrián used to speak. 'She's betraying her own youth. At the dances, she was always the one wearing the shortest skirt.'

Joseba cut a branch from a bush and started trimming off the sidebranches to make a stick. 'I was with Adrián not so long ago,' he said. I told him I'd kept in touch with Adrián on and off and that I knew about his marriage to the Romanian woman and how he'd adopted her little girl. 'A few years ago he sent me two dolls for Liz and Sara.'

Joseba struck the water with the stick 'to frighten off the snakes' and then jumped into the river. 'His wife is called Rulika and the little girl Iliana,' he told me from the water. 'Adrián's besotted with the child. He's very happy.' He swam energetically from one side of the pool to the other. He enjoys excellent health. 'Do you know what Pancho says?' he shouted. 'He says that Adrián has turned into a poof, because he used to make magnificent penises and now he only makes dolls.'

'You've obviously seen a lot of people,' I said. 'You're very well informed.' He explained then that he wanted to write a book about our lives, about the fate of all those who appear in the photos taken at the school in Obaba. 'Is that why you've come to Stoneham?' I asked. 'And is that why you tracked down Ubanbe? To take notes?' He protested that he'd met Ubanbe purely by chance, and that he didn't need to take any notes about me. 'I've written all the pages that are to do with you. In fact, you'll be able to hear them at the reading next Wednesday.' I told him, not entirely jokingly, that he'd better be careful because Mary Ann would be amongst those listening. 'You come out of it quite well, David. So don't worry, your wife won't leave you, and your daughters won't hate you.'

I thought of mentioning my book of memoirs, but again it didn't seem the right moment. I've always hated people who, as soon as they hear about a project, respond with: 'I've been thinking of doing something similar myself.' Besides, I was tired, and didn't feel like saying any more. I got into the water and swam for a while.

Dr Rabinowitz hasn't called. I wish he would. Knowing the exact date when I'll have to go to the hospital in Visalia would be a relief. The uncertainty won't let me rest. When I'm with Joseba and Mary Ann, I can hear a little noise inside my head, something like a cricket singing. And now, at night, that song has a metallic edge to it.

7

Today, I woke up very early, at about six, and I was immediately struck by the silence. I got out of bed and discovered the reason: it was raining. When I opened the window, the sound of the rain came into the room. Or, rather, the sounds, in plural. When they were small, Liz and Sara used to say that the rain had different sounds, the sound of all the drops together and the sound of each individual drop. Rather an acute observation, I think.

I remained standing at the window. Underneath the grey sky, the trees looked tense, as if they were waiting for something. It occurred to me that old General Sherman would be a great deal calmer than them; after 3000 years, nothing could startle him. Certainly not the rain. If he could speak, he would say to the other sequoias: 'When I was young, there was always talk of terrible rains, of a flood that would sweep everything away. I don't believe in such stories any more. Don't worry, no flood will uproot you.' But it's hard to place yourself on his level. It's hard to overcome fear. Perhaps you have to live for 3000 years in order to achieve calm.

I noticed a butterfly on the ground, next to a trail of water formed by the rain. It was a monarch butterfly. Probably one of those given to Liz on her birthday, like the one we saw the other day in the little cemetery. Or perhaps the same one. It looked dead, as if the rain had torn its wings, grounding it for ever. Into my head came a Mancini tune I used to play on the accordion, a very sad song: 'Soldiers in the rain'. Butterflies in the rain. At first, those two images don't seem to go together, but they've become linked in my head, no, more than linked, fused together. It took me hours to get rid of the tune.

The day has followed the pattern set by those early hours. It's been a particularly silent day. Joseba noticed too. He was at Juan's house preparing for the reading, and when I went to see him during a break from work, he said: 'Here I am, brother, copying out the incunabula of our monastery.' It's the silence that led him to identify Stoneham with a monastery. 'Is it burdensome work?' I asked. 'Worthy of a heavy-laden donkey, brother.' I leaned towards the computer to see what he was working on, but he covered the screen with his hands to stop me. 'This mania for creating suspense is most unacceptable, brother, most rude,' I said. 'Once I was more subtle, brother.' 'And now you're more of a donkey.' He tossed his head like a donkey.

I returned home and saw that Mary Ann was also preparing for the reading. I asked her about the texts she was translating and if they contained any treacherous material. From behind her glasses, her eyes revealed surprise. They're still as blue as ever: *North Cape*. She pointed to some sheets of paper: 'This one is about snow.' 'That's a subject Joseba's been drawn to ever since we were at nursery school,' I said. She took off her glasses to rub her eyes: *North Cape One, North Cape Two*. 'The other text I've translated is kind of tragi-comic,' she said, 'about a Japanese man.' 'Toshiro?' 'No, he's called Yukio.' 'Does it take place in Bilbao? In a small boarding-house?' 'Yes.' 'In real life, he was called Toshiro, not Yukio,' I explained. Mary Ann took my hand: 'Why don't you tell me your version while we go for a walk around the ranch? It's stopped raining now.' She got up from the desk and planted a smacking kiss on my cheek. 'Ah, the sound of Thule!' I cried. 'I've always liked the name you gave my lips,' she said and kissed me again. Mary Ann to the rescue again. Once she helped free me from my past, and now she's taking away my fear of the future. She breaks the silence. She drives me forward.

We walked along the path that leads to Three Rivers. After the rain, the air was clean and it was a pleasure to breathe it in. I found the walk very easy. I told her the story of Toshiro, and I wondered where he was now. Would he still be working in the shipyards of Osaka? Would he finally have married his fiancée? I'll never know. We simply passed in the air. We were following very different routes.

'Joseba's version is quite similar,' Mary Ann said. A mischievous smile played about her Thule lips. 'Mind you, he does give quite a long-drawn-out description of the final party. Apparently, the two of you danced all night.' 'We were so happy.' 'And I believe that a young woman, a fellow economics student, was particularly friendly towards you.' 'Joseba's fevered imaginings.' We'd reached the Kaweah river now and were walking back up the hill to the house. 'I think Joseba wants to write a memoir too,' I said. She asked me then if I'd said anything to him about my book. I told her I hadn't. Mary Ann wishes I had. She has more faith than I do in my writing.

When we returned home, she suggested phoning Helen. 'Why don't we invite her to come. It would be nice to spend a few days together.'

'It was thanks to her that we met,' I said, 'and I'm eternally grateful for that.' Mary Ann kissed me again. 'It's true. If it hadn't been for her, I wouldn't have gone to San Francisco and I wouldn't have asked you to take our photo.'

It's an odd thought, but death and love get on quite well together. Love takes on different forms when we know that death is hiding behind the bedroom door: sweet, almost ideal forms, oblivious to the frictions and conflicts of everyday life.

I left Mary Ann talking on the phone to Helen and went over to the trickle of water made by the rain. There were small leaves, small stones, trails of small white petals, but not a trace of the butterfly. Not even nearby. This means that it wasn't dead when I saw it from the window this morning. The rain had brought the butterfly down, but the butterfly had managed to beat its wings again. Not even General Sherman could have done more.

Addenda. I opened the computer file containing my memoir, and I searched for the name 'Toshiro'. I couldn't find it, though, and it looked as if I'd lost him. Then I remembered that I'd spelled his name 'Tosiro', and I refreshed my memory of events by re-reading what I'd written about him. Contrary to my expectations, I enjoyed going back to the days when Joseba, Agustín and I were involved in the underground struggle and called ourselves Etxeberria, Triku and Ramuntxo. It must be as the ancients said: time passes, and what once gave pain gives pleasure. Or as Joseba says: in fiction, truth takes on a gentler, more acceptable nature.

My feeling that what I'd written about Toshiro had become slightly lost has not gone away. Amongst all the other pages, they seemed irrelevant. I've decided that the story of our friend from the past deserves a more fitting place, and I'm going to place him here amongst these notes. He'll be better there.

Toshiro

In the communiqués issued by the movement for the liberation of Euskadi, it was stated that the two fundamental problems to be resolved were, on the one hand, the national question, and on the other, the social question, and to shore up the legitimacy of their twin objectives, they quoted from a few of Lenin's writings; the various Communist parties – the Third International, the Fourth International, the Maoists – did not, however, share this view and reproached us with acting in a way likely 'to favour the bourgeoisie'. 'The workers,' they said, 'aren't concerned about the nation, still less about the Basque nation!' When, in some pamphlet, we propounded the Leninist doctrine on oppressed nationalities, they would riposte with a flyer bearing only the famous slogan: 'Workers of the world unite!' It felt as if they were throwing a bucket of cold water over us.

Their criticisms were seriously damaging our movement. Many young people didn't want to risk ending up dead or in prison merely 'in order to benefit the bourgeoisie' and so refused to work with us. This problem was aired in all our internal publications. If we didn't build a stronger workers' front, the organisation itself could be in danger of collapsing. This concern reached a peak during a strike at the biggest shipyard in Bilbao: we weren't involved in that struggle, and this, in the eyes of society, meant that we were very much relegated to the background. In future, we would come to be considered just another marginal, militant group.

The thousands of workers at the shipyard were on strike for a long time, but, in the end, they returned to their jobs without having their claims met. They occasionally stopped work or held demonstrations, but it was clear that the battle was lost. The Communist parties weren't powerful enough to overcome the problems created by the strike. After many years of dictatorship, the strike funds were empty. Moreover, the police continued to respond with their usual degree of violence.

329

Papi came to see us. 'We mustn't miss this opportunity. The *españolistas* – the anti-separatists – have compromised a lot of people and all for nothing,' he said. He then started explaining to us about the workers' front and the possible consequences that might arise from any weakness there. Joseba interrupted him: 'We've read your article, Papi. Let's get down to more concrete things.' 'We're preparing a special action,' Papi said, changing subject without a flicker of annoyance. 'If it's successful, neither the shipowners nor the other bosses are going to want to waste any more time arguing. However, it's vital that this action should be attributed to *our* workers' front.' We said nothing, waiting for him to go on. But Papi remained silent too. 'Do you want us to carry out this special action?' Triku asked at last. Papi shook his head. 'You don't have enough experience, well, *you* might, but Etxeberria and Ramuntxo don't.' Ramuntxo was my alias at the time, just as Etxeberria was Joseba's and Triku was Agustín's. 'You have to distribute propaganda in the shipyard itself,' Papi went on, 'and believe me, it won't be easy. Since all the trouble, there are really strict controls.'

He opened a file adorned with a drawing of Mickey Mouse, and showed us a plan of the shipyard, indicating where we would have to leave the 10,000 pamphlets so that our contact, a colleague who worked there, could safely pick them up. He also gave us the address of the place where we would hide during our stay in Bilbao. I remember it exactly: Calle del Pájaro, 2, Apartment 6. 'Do you know a discotheque called Kaiola?' asked Papi. Joseba and I knew it from our university days. It was famous among the Bilbao student population. 'Well, the boarding-house is very close. We chose it because the owner works in the shipyard. You might get some useful information out of him.' He told us that we had a room reserved, and that the pamphlets were already there, in cardboard boxes, disguised as student hand-outs. We were to pass ourselves off as undergraduates studying to retake our exams. We would have about ten days to carry out the action.

The boarding-house didn't really merit the name. It was just an ordinary three-bedroom apartment. Antonio and Maribel, the couple who

330

owned the place, slept in the first room; a Japanese man called Toshiro slept in the second, a tiny room that gave on to the central courtyard; and we slept in the third. Maribel, who did all the work in the house, introduced us to Toshiro: 'He's from Osaka. He works at the shipyard too. He's come here to fit the ship's propellers.' Toshiro gave us a curt nod and immediately withdrew to his room. 'He's sad. He doesn't want to talk,' Maribel told us. 'He feels lonely, you see, and misses his girl-friend.' Maribel was a very nice woman.

Fortunately, our room had two large windows with a view over the river, and we spent a lot of time staring out and smoking 'just the one cigarette', as Triku used to say, although it always ended up being four or five. It did us good contemplating that landscape. It relieved the sensation of claustrophobia provoked in us by the fact of hiding, as well as easing the sheer weight of the risk we were running, because, as time goes on, a risk increases in weight and volume. Anyone can face a danger that lasts only ten seconds, but almost no one can withstand one that goes on for days.

The ships went up and down the estuary, either out to sea or into the city. Sometimes, one of them would sound its siren, and we, by some strange association of ideas, would find ourselves staring at the cardboard boxes containing the 10,000 pamphlets. The days passed, and we still couldn't find a way of carrying out our plan.

It wasn't going to be easy. Maribel's husband, Antonio, was extremely reactionary, and at supper time, when we all gathered round the table, he would constantly mutter against the 'factions' who stirred up trouble and the 'stooges' who were taken in by the slogans of the provocateurs. There was no way we would ever get any information out of him. The slightest suspicion would have him phoning the police. It occurred to us, for lack of any better idea, to turn to Toshiro, and Joseba made a vain attempt to get to know him. 'The man from Osaka' – as we called him – would slip away as soon as he'd eaten dessert.

'I know what's wrong with Toshiro,' Joseba said after supper on the fifth or sixth night. 'He spends all day working in the belly of a ship and he's simply not used to the light.' Maribel smiled: 'It's true he gets sadder and sadder, but that's not the reason.' 'He's depressed,' put in her husband Antonio. 'It's only logical. He's a long way from home.' A look passed accross Maribel's face, indicating that this was not the reason either, far from it. Later on, while we were helping her with the dishes, Joseba returned to the subject. 'So what *is* wrong with him, Maribel? What's the truth about Toshiro?' he asked in a jokey tone. 'I'd tell you if I could, but I can't. He asked me not to tell anyone.' We went to bed with that small mystery.

Our investigations at the shipyard brought almost no progress. There were groups of police everywhere, as well, it seemed to us, as a lot of secret police and plain-clothes policemen. It would be impossible to get 10,000 pamphlets past them. In these circumstances, we thought, there were only two possible options: to cross the river by boat and reach the shipyard via the wharf, or to hijack one of the trucks that were constantly driving in and out. Whichever option we chose, we had to be quick. The days were passing.

We started to get nervous when our contact in the shipyard phoned us to say: 'Are you studying hard? The exam is fast approaching.' He spoke with a strong Vizcayan accent. 'Yes, we're studying hard, but we still can't see how we're going to pass,' I said. 'Well,' our contact told us, 'the teacher's getting very impatient. As you know, we've got another even more difficult exam soon afterwards.' Triku grabbed the phone from me: 'Why can't we do the exam outside?' Our contact obviously didn't understand, and Triku could contain himself no longer: 'Why can't we distribute the pamplets outside? We'll get in amongst the workers going into the shipyard and it will all be over in a minute, before anyone has even realised what's happened.' Triku listened to the man's reply for about twenty seconds. 'He doesn't want to do that,' he said when he hung up. 'He says the pamphlets have to be distributed in the shipyard itself, otherwise the workers will consider it outside interference.'

We opened the windows in our room and sat smoking and talking until most of the lights in the houses opposite had gone out. In the end, we decided we would use a truck, and we chose one that usually went to a fairly isolated industrial estate to be loaded up. We would devote the following day to preparations, and then, very early on the day after that, we'd carry out our plan: Joseba and I would take care of the driver, and Triku would drive the truck into the shipyard.

That night, at about four o'clock in the morning, a ship sounded its foghorn. 'It must be for some sailor who hasn't returned,' I said. The foghorn wheedled its way into the last fold of the brain. It was impossible to sleep. Joseba turned on the light and started leafing through the newspaper. 'Of course, high tide is at half past four. That's why it keeps sounding the foghorn.' In order to navigate downstream to the sea, the water had to be at its highest level.

The ship sounded two very long notes, and then allowed a few minutes to pass before the next call. At first, that interval of silence was a respite, but, soon, after the ninth or tenth blast, it became more distressing than the sound of the horn itself. 'If that sailor doesn't come back soon, I'll go and find him myself!' exclaimed Joseba. It was half past four in the morning and we were all up, with the windows open. A lot of lights were on in the houses nearby. 'What happens to sailors when they lose their ship? Do they become stateless?' asked Triku. 'This sailor will have no choice. He's going to get lynched. Look, he's got half the city out of bed.' More and more lights came on in windows. A lot of people had given up trying to sleep.

I went to the bathroom down the corridor, but, as I passed the room that faced on to the central courtyard, I glimpsed something through a crack in the door that made me stop short. Toshiro was kneeling on the tiled floor, wearing nothing but a pair of shorts, and with his arms stretched out to the sides. Suddenly, his arms and his head dropped down. He tried to lift them again with an agonised moan, then collapsed. 'What's wrong, Toshiro?' I asked, going into the room. Nothing was wrong. He was fast asleep and his breathing came in rasps. Not even the foghorns of a hundred ships would have woken him.

I met Maribel in the corridor. 'Oh, dear God, the poor man!' she cried. Joseba and Triku joined us. 'Look at the state of his knees,' said Maribel. The skin had been worn away, leaving traces of blood and scabs.

333

'What's wrong with him? Tell us the truth, Maribel,' Joseba said. The woman put her finger to her lips indicating that we should speak more softly, and then gestured to us to follow her into the kitchen. The coffee was already made.

'I'll tell you what's wrong with him.' Maribel poured the coffee into the cups. She was pleased to have kept the secret, but pleased, as well, to have a good reason to reveal it. 'He's madly in love with his fiancée,' she said. 'She's a very pretty girl. You just have to look at the photos. Her name's Masako. At first, he devoted every free moment to her. He wrote her letters or went to the telephone exchange to call her. But one day, on his way back from the shipyard, he had the bad idea of dropping in at that discotheque, the Kaiola. And, of course, the inevitable happened. He fell into the hands of a bad woman, and she took all his money. When I saw him arrive home, I couldn't believe it. He was drunk and dirty . . . he didn't look like the Toshiro I know.' Maribel fell silent. Outside the window not a sound could be heard. The ship's foghorn had stopped. 'Go on, Maribel,' Joseba urged her.

She didn't speak at once. She glanced at the door of her bedroom. 'Sorry, I thought I heard a noise,' she said. 'I don't want my husband to know anything. He can be very unbending, and, who knows, he might put Toshiro out in the street.' We exchanged looks. We thought it most unlikely that Antonio would give up Toshiro's rent over something like that. Maribel was too kind.

'Anyway, Toshiro was filled with terrible remorse for what he'd done,' she went on. 'He confessed to me, almost in tears, that he'd betrayed Masako. He said he was unclean and must cleanse himself before returning to Osaka.' 'Through suffering,' I said. 'Exactly. For the first few days, he whipped himself with a belt. But I told him not to. I used Antonio as an excuse, and said that he'd realise what was happening when he heard the sound of the lashes, and that this could get Toshiro into trouble. The real reason I did it was because I felt so sorry for him. And ever since then, well, you've seen what he does. He kneels in his room until he keels over from sheer exhaustion. That's no way to live, spending all day down amongst the propellers of a ship and all night on his knees with his arms outstretched.' 'How long is he going to go on like this?' asked Triku. 'Until he goes back to Osaka. He thinks he isn't punishing himself enough. He's always telling me that he should do more and wants me to give him permission to go to bed without any supper. But I'm not going to do that. Never. In my house, no one goes to bed without supper!' Joseba gently patted her on the shoulder: 'What I wouldn't give, Maribel, to have a mother who looks after me the way you look after Toshiro!'

We poured ourselves more coffee and stayed there chatting until dawn. Triku explained to Maribel about harakiri, and Maribel showed us some photos of Masako. She was, indeed, very pretty, and the green and yellow kimono really suited her. She was holding a chrysanthemum in her hand and smiling at the camera.

We were watching the trucks going in and out of the shipyard. The one we'd chosen was driven by a young man about our age ('It's a pretty dirty trick you're pulling on me, but I understand why you're doing it,' was the response of nearly all the young drivers we 'called in'; the older drivers got more agitated). I wasn't convinced the plan would work. 'You don't like it, do you?' Joseba said to me. He knew at once what I was thinking.

I set out to them the idea that had been going around in my head since that morning. Toshiro could take the propaganda into the shipyard instead of us. After all, as Maribel had told us, he felt he wasn't being punished enough, so why not ask him to make a larger sacrifice. 'We just tell him that we're fighting for the rights of workers and that if he helps us, his debt will be paid.' Joseba gave a wry smile: 'Especially if the police get hold of him. They'll give him such a beating that, as well as paying for this sin, he'll be in credit for the next.' 'I'd prefer to use the truck,' said Triku. 'Toshiro won't want to take a risk like that, and we'll have blown our cover.' Joseba, however, liked my idea, and liked it more with each minute that passed. 'He's from a country where people commit harakiri, Triku. You yourself explained that to Maribel. He won't be frightened.' 'Let's try,' I said. 'And if it doesn't work out, we can always go back to the truck idea.' 'Who's going to talk to the man from Osaka, then?' asked Joseba. 'You are!' cried Triku and I simultaneously. Joseba had a way with words. Papi always used to say that with such a persuasive person at our disposal, it was a shame the organisation didn't have a diplomatic front.

According to Joseba, Toshiro read the pamphlet and asked him for ten minutes to consider, during which time he sat on the floor in the lotus position. Then he stood up, gave a brief bow and said: 'I believe I will do this with greatest of pleasure, comrade.' 'He called you "comrade"!' Triku and I were equally surprised. Joseba nodded vehemently. 'That's what he said, word for word: "I believe I will do this with greatest of pleasure, comrade. I also feel hatred for third international revisionists. I proud Trotskyist."'

We needed to smoke a lot of cigarettes at our bedroom window in order to absorb the surprise. I remarked that what had happened proved our organisation's analysis to be correct: that you couldn't separate a supporter of Lenin or Trotsky from his or her own culture. It was impossible to imagine a Trotskyist from Ondarroa or Hernani, for example, spending the night on his knees. 'Although, you never know, they might for Masako's sake!' said Joseba drily. 'It's a beautiful night,' said Triku. Despite the city lights, we could still see the starry sky.

We spent the morning strolling round the city and then had a cheap meal in a café. I called our contact at around three o'clock. He was euphoric. '*Artistak sarie!*' – 'You're real artists!' – he exclaimed admiringly. 'We didn't go to the exam ourselves,' I said, 'we sent someone else.' 'Well, *he's* an artist.' 'So he put everything in the right place at the right time, then?' 'Not only that, he himself took charge of the distribution. It rained.' I asked him to explain in more detail. He told me then, in an oblique, roundabout way, that our 'artist' had used the propellers of a ship to send the pamphlets flying up into the air so that they landed on the heads of the workers: '*Eurixa les, barriro esanda*' – 'Like I said, just as if it was raining!' 'So it went well?' 'Brilliantly!' said our contact. 'They only made one arrest, a Japanese fitter.' I started to sweat. 'Well, that's our job done, then,' I said. 'Let's see how the next exam goes, the really difficult one.' I put the phone down.

Triku had a friend in a student apartment, and we asked if he could give us a place to sleep. Once we were safely installed, we phoned the boarding-house. 'It's been a very strange day,' Maribel told me when I explained that we were out of town and wouldn't be back for a few days. 'Why's that?' 'The police came and searched the apartment, but they didn't find anything.' 'Really?' I cried. She lowered her voice to a whisper: 'They've arrested Toshiro.' 'Really?' I said again. I've never had Joseba's facility with words. He would have expressed his amazement in five different ways. Maribel went on in a low voice: 'And it wasn't for getting drunk or because of some incident with a woman. According to the police, it was political.' 'It was lucky we weren't there. If we had been, they'd have arrested us all. That's what tends to happen in these cases,' I said. 'They asked me about you, but I told them you were always studying and hardly left the house, not even to go to the Kaiola with the other students.'

After the phone call, we had a meeting. We agreed that we would stay in the city until Toshiro was sent to prison, then we could find out, through the prisoners' committee, what information the police had got from him. We didn't hold out much hope: the police had our photographs. Toshiro would have no alternative but to identify us, for he longed to go back to Osaka to be with Masako again.

I phoned the second day, in the evening. As soon as she heard my voice, Maribel let out a shriek: 'He's here!' 'Toshiro?' 'Of course! They released him without charge, although he is limping a bit.' It took Toshiro ten seconds to reach the phone. 'Where are you? At the Kaiola?' he asked. At first, his question seemed absurd, but then I realised that it hadn't even occurred to him that we might be in hiding, fearful of what he might tell the police. 'We're on our way there now. We want to buy you a glass of champagne,' I told him. 'All right, but we must not stay late. Tomorrow, I must work,' he said. I looked at Triku and at Joseba. They understood at once what had happened. 'Toshiro kamikaze!' shouted Triku down the phone.

Toshiro was, as Maribel had said, limping slightly, and his face, beneath the bright lights of the discotheque, was that of someone who has endured several rounds in the ring. We embraced. 'How are you, kamikaze? Did they give you a hard time?' Triku asked him. 'I am very happy,' Toshiro replied. 'Joseba was right. Now I have paid all I had to pay and can return with tranquil heart to Osaka.' In the noisy discotheque it was impossible to know in what tone of voice he said this, but he clearly meant what he said. 'I told you that you would pay not only for what happened before, but be in credit for the next time. And that's exactly what happened,' Joseba said. We ordered a bottle of champagne, and Toshiro explained to us that he'd played the innocent with the police. He told them over and over that he thought the leaflets were publicity for a fiesta, not political propaganda. He said he'd been duped by a woman who approached him on the way into the shipyard. 'I tell them Japanese men like women very much and women play tricks on them. I said this not first time I been tricked. Tricked before too.'

We ordered a second bottle of champagne and returned to the boarding-house feeling distinctly tipsy. 'Phone Masako and tell her you're staying with us, kamikaze!' cried a euphoric Triku. 'The bird from Osaka always return to Osaka,' replied Toshiro. He was repeating, in his own way, a Basque saying that Joseba had taught him: *Orhiko txoriak Orhira nahi* – 'The bird from Orhi dreams of Orhi'.

The following morning, while we were having breakfast, we saw an old photo of Papi in the newspaper next to a picture of a collapsed building. The headline stated that over 650 pounds of dynamite had reduced the Yacht Club of Bilbao to rubble, and that the attack bore all the hallmarks of one of the organisation's most dangerous militants.

8

On a day just like today, twenty-three years ago, I found out that my mother had died.

Joseba, Triku, another colleague whom we called Carlos, and I were at 'the reserve' in the French village of Mamousine, near Pau. We were

338

working on a dairy farm along with other *émigrants espagnols*, killing time until, as Carlos put it, 'the moment to continue the struggle arrived'. Papi had written us a letter telling us that, in the autumn, we would have to cross the frontier for another special operation.

Joseba found the life we led at Mamousine disagreeable in the extreme, and he was always complaining. I remember that one morning, while we were mucking out the cowshed, he lost his temper completely and started cursing so furiously that our Andalusian colleagues stopped work and stood staring at him. I tried to behave as if nothing was wrong, and said reproachfully that there was no basis for his complaints; I told him that manure can smell as sweetly as roses. He threatened me with a pitchfork, saying that if I ever said that again, the 'manurist' front of our liberation movement would have its first martyr. He was joking, of course, but it was what he really felt. He was very angry. Not so much because of the work, which he loathed. Nor because of Papi, who had sent our group to that dairy rather than, for example, to Paris. The cause of his malaise was Carlos; there lay the source of all his discontent. As they used to say at the time, there were 'bad vibes' between them.

Carlos was very serious and very taciturn and terribly meticulous. The day he introduced us, Papi said: 'With him in charge, you'll be perfectly safe. He doesn't like surprises. He's capable of spending five hours planning something that will take only five minutes to carry out.' He wasn't exaggerating. Carlos was obsessed with 'preparation', and when he finished his work in the dairy, he'd shut himself up in his room to examine plans (those of a ministerial building in Madrid, for example) or to study theory (I remember the title of one of the books he was reading: *The Consequences of Colonialism in the Third World*). At the other extreme, Joseba spent not a single moment on politics or 'the struggle'. He'd just discovered American detective fiction and devoted all his free time to reading the works of Ross McDonald, Raymond Chandler and Dashiell Hammett. He was also about to publish his first book, under the pseudonym Ramón Garmendia. At meetings, he would start glancing at the clock after about twenty minutes, and, from then on, find a

339

thousand ways to make his boredom painfully clear. Carlos found such behaviour intolerable.

Things came to a head towards the end of July, when we'd been in Mamousine for nearly a month. After supper, Carlos used to go for a run, because, according to him, preparing oneself for the struggle meant, first and foremost, 'being in peak physical condition'. That day, he returned to the attack and demanded that we follow his example. It seemed to him that we were getting lazy and flabby. We should do some exercise and go running with him. Joseba started laughing: 'That's all we need after a day spent shovelling shit!' He got up and left the meeting, dismissing the whole subject with a wave of his hand. 'I'd go running with you, but I have work to do,' Triku said, by way of an excuse. He was working in the kitchen at Mamousine. 'I'm sorry, Carlos, but I think Joseba's right. We do quite enough exercise as it is,' I said, thus reinforcing Joseba's position. 'Well, all I can say is that you're a very undisciplined lot,' said Carlos brusquely. From then on, he became still more taciturn and would have almost nothing to do with us. He preferred to spend his free time chatting to the Andalusian emigrants, because, as he so often told us, it was important to know about 'other social realities'.

Everything seemed to indicate that the four of us would have to continue living together in that strained atmosphere until the day came to leave Mamousine. However, during the first week of August, something odd happened to me, something which, in the end, would alter everything. I can find no better way of putting it than to say that I experienced a change of personality. I first noticed this one day while I was doing the washing-up with Joseba. I made some completely banal comment and was amazed, because the words emerged from my mouth exactly as my mother would have said them, as if I'd picked up her accent instead of the Bearnais accent of the people of Mamousine or the Andalusian accent of our colleagues on the dairy farm.

At first, I didn't give it much importance. After all, I often thought about my mother. I felt for her. I knew how depressed she'd been since the day the police came looking for me at Villa Lecuona, both because

340

of what that visit meant and because of the brutal way in which they'd carried out the search. Apparently, they turned the sewing workshop upside down, and, when they'd finished, left the floor strewn with dresses, remnants, buttons, thimbles and even bullets, because one of the civil guards had accidentally emptied the entire contents of his magazine when he dropped his machine-gun. Sometimes, I'd go to a phone box and call her, but we never managed to speak for more than a couple of minutes, because she always ended up crying. I found the experience too distressing, and my calls became less frequent.

The days passed, and the spirit of my mother continued to take possession of me. One morning, when I woke up, I made some perfectly ordinary remark: 'Let's see what the weather's like today, then.' But what came out of my mouth was: 'Let's see what weather the Good Lord has sent us today.' Just as my mother would have said. By then, I'd noticed other similarities. My gestures when I smoked, for example: I exhaled the smoke exactly as she did.

'I've never experienced anything so strange,' I said to Joseba one night. He was the only person I could talk to about it. Triku, given his penchant for the esoteric, would have taken it too seriously. 'What form does it take?' Joseba asked, ready to listen.

'I don't know exactly what astral travel is,' he said, when I'd finished speaking, 'but I've heard Triku on the subject, and it does sound like that's what happened to you.' I didn't know whether he was being serious or joking. Probably half and half: joking about astral travel, but serious because he could see how concerned I was.

That night, I had a dream. I was in an aquarium, in the area where the deep-sea fish were kept. Someone said: 'You see that shadow? It's a fish called a *Chiasmodon*. It lives in the darkness on the sea bed.' I sighed: 'Fancy having to live like that, never leaving those slimy pebbles, not even knowing that light exists!' I heard Lubis' voice: 'Do you mean because of the darkness? But you used to like it. I remember how much you enjoyed bathing in the pool in the cave in Obaba.' I looked and saw my mother standing beside Lubis: 'Ah, if that were all it was!' she cried. 'But this son of mine has changed a lot. He used to love his mother so much, but now he hasn't even come to say goodbye.' 'Don't talk like that, Mama.' 'Oh, I'm not reproaching you, David. It's just that I would like to have said goodbye.' 'Goodbye?' 'Didn't they tell you, David? I'm dead. But I'm quite content. I won't always be in the area for the deep-sea fish. The Lord will soon raise me up to the warmer waters where the clown fish and the other goldfish live. That's why Lubis is here with me. He'll guide me there.'

'Wake up, David!' whispered Joseba, shaking my arm. He got out of his bunk and sat down beside me. 'You were whimpering,' he said. 'I really envy your ability to dream. If we end up in prison, you'll at least be able to spend your nights outside.' 'It was awful,' I said. 'I dreamed that my mother was dead.'

He became thoughtful. 'I can see only one way of reassuring you,' he said at last. 'Phone home and speak to your mother.' 'I can't phone her from here. It would be dangerous.' He looked at the clock. 'It's a quarter past six. If we leave now, you could be in a phone box in Pau by half past seven.' 'Without telling Carlos?' 'Of course.' 'Let's go,' I said, and we quickly pulled on some clothes and went to fetch the old Renault we used in Mamousine.

As we left the room, we thought we could hear someone in the bathroom and we waited until the door opened. But it wasn't Carlos, it was an Andalusian worker called Antonio. Joseba knew him quite well. He told Antonio that if he saw *monsieur le patron*, he should tell him that we'd had to go out, but that we'd be back at the dairy by nine o'clock. Antonio nodded and offered us a couple of cigarettes. 'For breakfast,' he said, in the gruff voice of someone who has just woken up. We set off for Pau, smoking the cigarettes.

Paulina picked up the phone, and I knew what had happened as soon as I heard her voice. It wasn't usual for her to be in my house at that hour. The girls who attended my mother's workshop arrived at Villa Lecuona at around nine, never before. 'She died yesterday afternoon, David,' she said. 'We've spent the whole night crying.' From her voice I could tell that her grief had been long and exhausting. She spoke to me easily, using my name quite spontaneously, despite my three-year absence from Obaba.

342

'The funeral will be at five o'clock in the church up the hill.' Then she suddenly realised the situation and added: 'Oh, but you won't be able to come!' 'How did it happen? Had she been ill?' I asked. I couldn't remember when I'd last spoken to my mother. 'She went out on to the terrace in the evening, as she always did. Your father found her there at supper time. At first, he thought she'd fallen asleep, because she was sitting slightly slumped in the wicker chair. Alas, though, she was dead. Her heart must have given out.' 'Thank you, Paulina, I'm very grateful.'

Those words could have been my mother's too. It was her way of speaking: 'I'm very grateful', 'if you don't mind my asking', 'if it isn't too much trouble' . . . She valued courtesy greatly. I was sure that the funeral, doubtless organised by Don Hipólito, would be beautiful and worthy of her. It would take place – Paulina had told me – at five o'clock. In ten hours' time.

On the way back to Mamousine, Joseba didn't stop talking once. He finally knew what we should do when we returned to civilian life. We would open a consulting room like Señora Guller's – for money, of course – and he and Triku would drum up custom while I played the medium and told people's fortunes. He kept up this chatter until we reached Mamousine. 'Are you going to the funeral?' he asked me then. 'Yes, I am.' I'd decided when I was on the phone, but I surprised myself when I put that decision into words. It was a serious move and contravened all the rules. 'I'm on your side, and I'll tell Carlos that I am,' said Joseba. 'Let's go straight to Monsieur Gabastou.' I thanked him. I would need his support later on.

Monsieur Gabastou was the owner of the dairy farm and lived in Mamousine itself. '*Bien sûr!*' he said when I asked his permission to absent myself in order to attend my mother's funeral. The Andalusians, who had known him for a long time, said that he'd been in the French resistance during the Nazi occupation. He was a very decent man. He always treated us well; our fluent French betrayed the fact that we were not genuine emigrant farm labourers, but he never asked any questions. Possibly out of sympathy, or simply so as to avoid complications. '*Allez! Partez tout de suite!*' – 'Go on, off you go!' – he said.

Joseba dared to ask him another favour. He asked if they happened to have a dark suit I could wear, since, in Obaba, one couldn't attend a funeral wearing just anything. 'My son André's suit might do,' said Monsieur Gabastou, and he sent us off to find his wife.

'Yes,' Madame Gabastou told us, 'I should think it would fit you. My son's like you, thin and big-boned. He's living in Paris now.' The woman was right. I was quite slim at the time, about thirty or so pounds lighter than when I was at university. 'Your son's in Paris, we're in Mamousine . . . it seems that all of us young people are far away from home,' said Joseba. With a sigh, the woman left the room to fetch the suit.

'André is obviously your double,' Joseba remarked when I put the suit on. And it really did look as if it had been made for me. Madame Gabastou was of the same opinion. She disappeared again and returned with a black tie.

When we left the house, Monsieur Gabastou once again showed his generosity and consideration. He offered me his blue Peugeot 505, a respectable car. Joseba and I both thanked him. The vehicle could prove a great help when crossing the frontier. 'What kind people!' I said. 'Not like some we know,' replied Joseba, doubtless thinking of Carlos.

When we walked past the dairy, Joseba went in search of further 'accessories' and placed on my nose a pair of imitation spectacles with very thick lenses. 'Put this on too, and see how it suits you,' he said, putting a black beret on my head. 'Perfect. No one will recognise you in Obaba.'

Joseba looked at his watch. 'It's eleven o'clock. Shall we arrange a time to phone?' 'I should be across the border by one o'clock.' I agreed to phone him at half past one to let him know that I was safe. 'Don't get to Obaba too early,' he advised. I started the car, and we shook hands. His fingers squeezed mine. We were more than comrades in the struggle, we were friends.

My mother looked very tranquil, as if she'd closed her eyes in order to listen more carefully to the music of the organ. Or to concentrate on the perfume from the flowers. 'I'm here,' I said to her. Someone placed a hand on my shoulder. 'Forgive me, but we've got to set off for the cemetery now.' It was Don Hipólito. He was about to close the coffin. 'Just a moment,' I said, lifting the lid again. I bent over to kiss my mother. Don Hipólito was watching me, trying to identify who I was. I don't know if he recognised me or not. Perhaps he did. But he said nothing. He addressed the congregation: 'Her soul, I am sure, is now in heaven, let us give thanks to the Lord.' Everyone waited for the procession to move off. There they were in the front row: Geneviève, Berlino, Uncle Juan and Ángel; behind them, in the second row, were Paulina and the other girls from the sewing workshop.

When I left the church, I went to the car, intending to get back to Mamousine as soon as possible, but a sound reached my ears, the singing of the choir, who, like everyone else, were walking up to the cemetery – *Agur, Jesusen ama, Birjina Maria* . . . Farewell, mother of Jesus, Virgin Mary . . . – and I opened the door of Monsieur Gabastou's Peugeot in order to hear them more clearly. *Agur, Jesusen ama, Birjina Maria* . . . It was my mother's favourite hymn. A gentle breeze was blowing, carrying with it the melody, which grew ever fainter as the procession moved off.

I ran in the direction of the cemetery until I could hear the song again, more loudly this time: *Agur, Jesusen ama, Birjina Maria* . . . Then I walked along, keeping pace with the cortège. The landscape around Obaba seemed lovelier than ever: fresh green hills, white houses. The cemetery, too, resembled a white house, broader and larger than the others.

A dozen or so men were standing at the entrance to the cemetery, smoking cigarettes, and I hung around behind them until the burial was over, and the people attending the funeral began slowly to return to their homes, each with his or her own thoughts, partly sad to have witnessed another victory for death, partly glad to feel the warmth of their own body ('we're still here in the world'). Amongst the people I knew, I saw, first, Opin and other workers from the sawmill, followed by the manager, Joseba's father, who looked very downcast ('Don't worry,' I would have liked to say, 'your son is safe in France'). Then, with tear-filled eyes, came Adela, the shepherd's wife, our neighbour in Iruain ('Give me a hug, dear Adela,' I would have liked to say). She was followed by a large group of mourners, as if Adela really were a shepherdess and they the sheep who had been saved. I saw Adrián and his Romanian wife, and Isidro, Adrián's father, and Gregorio from the hotel; then, almost bringing up the rear, came Virginia, walking arm-in-arm with a tall man (my mother had told me on the phone: 'Virginia's going to marry the new doctor in Obaba'). She was wearing a very sombre, purple dress, doubtless made at Villa Lecuona, and she looked rather pale. A little behind them came Victoria and Susana accompanied by two men I didn't know, and then the members of the church choir, who were still singing, but very softly now: '*Agur, Jesusen ama, Birjina Maria . . .*'

The group of smokers at the entrance to the cemetery dispersed, and I was left exposed to the view of those coming out. I was about to leave when Paulina appeared. She was flanked by two colleagues from the workshop, and each had linked arms with her as if to hold her up. She wasn't crying, but she seemed on the verge of fainting. I realised suddenly that since the day of my disappearance, she had been like a daughter to my mother. Thanks to her, my mother's last years had not been entirely solitary and sad.

I was still watching Paulina, when Berlino and Geneviève emerged from the cemetery, accompanied by Colonel Degrela's daughter. When they saw me there alone, all three of them looked at me, and I was afraid of what Berlino might be thinking behind his green glasses. I took off the beret that Joseba had given me and went into the cemetery. I looked back; they were walking away quite normally; Berlino was stooped now, like an old man.

It wasn't hard to spot my mother's grave. It was heaped with flowers and, beside the other graves, looked almost luminous. Ángel and Uncle Juan were there, heads bowed, as still as two stone figures. I didn't have the courage to go over to them, and I went instead to the place where my good friend Lubis was buried.

His tomb was decorated too; someone had placed a bunch of wild

346

flowers on the stone. 'How are you, Lubis?' I whispered. 'How do you think he is!' shouted a man seated on the ground, and the surprise made me take a step back. 'He was my brother, and those pigs killed him.' Pancho had grown fat and was almost bald, but his voice was the same. I wondered if my voice was the same too. I didn't dare say anything to him. 'Do you think it's all right for me to put them there?' said Pancho, pointing at the wild flowers. 'My mother wants it all to look neat and tidy. Anyway, if you don't like it, you can lump it.' I left without a word.

Ángel was alone now by the tomb. I told myself that it would be best not to cross the frontier at night, that the controls were more rigorous outside of normal hours, but I kept walking. Ángel was crying. I suddenly remembered the letter I'd found once in Villa Lecuona: 'Dear Angelito, I don't know how I could bear the work in this restaurant if it weren't for the lovely things you tell me . . .'

It was strange being there, surrounded by the cemetery walls and by all those who had once been alive. They were at peace. And I wanted to be at peace too. 'I came,' I said. It took him a while to identify the person speaking to him. He looked me up and down, his eyes wide. 'David! What are you doing here?' He gesticulated, but no other words came out. I embraced him. And he returned my embrace.

I reached Mamousine by supper time, and, after asking me about the funeral, Madame Gabastou gave me a tray of raspberry tartlets. 'You can eat them with those friends of yours who've just arrived,' she said. I didn't understand what she meant. 'That nice young man who came with you this morning told us that some friends have come to give you their condolences.' I quickly changed my clothes and set off to the dairy. 'Don't forget the tartlets,' Madame Gabastou called from the door of her house. I had, indeed, forgotten them. I returned to thank her once more, then set off again.

A couple were standing at the entrance to the dairy, and, as soon as they saw me, they indicated that I should go straight to the house where we were staying. There, in the large hall, where the tools were kept, Carlos was waiting for me. He took three steps towards me and struck

347

the tray. The tartlets scattered over the floor. 'You've put us all in danger!' he shouted. I grabbed the pitchfork hanging from a hook. 'How would you like me to stick this in you?' I said. Again, my voice sounded to me like that of someone else. Not my mother's voice this time, but Ángel's. Ángel, I thought, was also inside me, and always had been. That thought distracted me, and Carlos took advantage of my distraction to grab another pitchfork.

A man with white hair appeared and stood between us; he looked like an artist. 'I feel like taking a photo of the two of you, to be distributed among our younger militants,' he said, laughing. 'Then they can see the current state of the armed struggle.' He took the pitchforks from us. 'Honestly, Carlos, fancy throwing away the only thing we have for supper.' He took the tray and started picking up the tartlets. Carlos helped him. 'I'm sorry, Sabino, but these people just drive me mad,' he said humbly. 'If you like, we can make something to eat for supper. Triku's a very good cook.' 'No, don't worry, Carlos. We're in a bit of a hurry,' Sabino replied. 'Let's try to sort this matter out and then we can leave.' He beckoned to me, and I followed him upstairs. 'Wait in the corridor,' he said and went into the bedroom where we had our bunks.

From the end of the corridor came the murmur of conversation, and when I went to find out who it was, I found Joseba and Antonio. They were both smoking, and the room was full of smoke. Antonio shook my hand: 'I'm so sorry to hear about your mother. This morning, I didn't realise what had happened.' I thanked him. 'Have a cigarette,' he said, offering me the pack. 'We were talking about death,' Joseba told me. 'Antonio says he's not afraid of death.' 'Afraid of death? No!' exclaimed Antonio.

He was a thin man, with bright, intelligent eyes. He began regaling us with anecdotes about his life. He'd been a shepherd since he was eight years old. He and his brother had often had to fight off marauding wolves. Despite everything, though, they used to compare how they lived and how their father lived, and would feel happy. Because their father worked in the Riotinto mines. 'Do you know what mercury is? It's the worst mineral there is. The men have to work naked because of the heat, and if one drop of the stuff falls on them, it burns their skin.' We confessed that we knew nothing about this, and he explained to us the history of those mines. They were owned by Englishmen. 'And English capitalists are terrible, heartless. I mean it,' he sighed. 'That colleague of yours, Carlos, has told us a lot about the things that have happened to you Basques, but we Andalusians haven't exactly had an easy time of it either.' We agreed, and Joseba asked after his family. Antonio smiled for the first time during the whole conversation. He told us that he was lucky, because he had a good wife. I didn't hear what he said next. His words took me back to the cemetery in Obaba. The day was about to end, and I would never again see my mother.

'You can come in now,' Sabino said from the door. We put out our cigarettes. 'Perhaps we can continue our conversation another day,' said Antonio, and Joseba patted him on the back. 'Any news of Papi?' he whispered to me. 'Not a word.' He looked worried. 'Come in,' said Sabino. We went into our room. There was a girl my age looking out of the window. We didn't know her, and that worried me. It worried Joseba even more. 'Where's Papi?' he asked. Sabino said brusquely: 'Papi couldn't come. He says he'd get all weepy because you're his favourite pupils, and he prefers to leave us to mete out the necessary punishment.' The girl at the window still didn't move or look at us. 'That's enough, Sabino,' said Papi. He was hidden behind the bunks in the room, leaning over a bedside table, writing. He wore his hair brushed forward and was wearing contact lenses rather than glasses, but his eyes were the same, like two small cracks. 'Go and speak to Carlos,' he said to Sabino and the girl. We felt enormously relieved.

Papi shook us by the hand. 'Pack your bags,' he said. 'Tomorrow you're off to Biarritz, and you'll stay there until you get the order to cross the frontier. You're being put in charge of a special action.' 'You're getting soft, Papi,' said Joseba. 'You may not have bothered to say hello, but you did at least get up from the table before speaking to us.' He was recovering from his fright, and his face was a better colour now. 'Make sure it doesn't happen again,' Papi said in his soft voice. He was wearing a pale-green Lacoste polo shirt with short sleeves; his trousers

349

were beige and neatly pressed; his shoes were a pair of leather sandals. It would not have been easy to attribute any particular job or status to him, but he nevertheless looked like a local, someone you could trust. 'If you ever pull a stunt like this again, you'll get no help from me,' he warned us. We thanked him. 'This action we're in charge of, is it difficult?' asked Joseba. Papi handed us the piece of paper he was holding. 'Here are your instructions.' Amongst various other notes was the name of a village on the Mediterranean coast. 'Ah, the summer campaign,' said Joseba. 'All three of you will go,' Papi told us. 'The ideal thing would be for Triku to get work in a hotel kitchen.'

Papi started going down the stairs, and we followed him. 'Can I try one?' he said to us in the hallway. The raspberry tartlets were on the shelf, rather the worse for wear, but still, apparently, all there. Papi left the house with one of them in his hand.

I went to look for Triku. 'We're leaving,' I told him. He embraced me: 'I'm so sorry about your mother. OK, you broke all the rules, but I'd like to know what Carlos would have done in your place. How would he react if he learned that his mother had died?' Without even thinking, I replied: 'He'd probably go jogging.' Triku burst out laughing. 'Let's go and get our things. Joseba will be waiting for us,' I said.

When we went back to the house, we found Joseba and Antonio sitting in the room at the end of the corridor. They'd placed the tray with the tartlets and other provisions – cheese, bread, a tin of foie gras – on the lid of an old suitcase. 'We can't leave without a farewell supper,' said Joseba. 'Why don't you bring something from the kitchen, Triku? And don't forget the wine.' He was rubbing his hands, already enjoying the banquet. Triku dug me in the ribs with his elbow: 'Look how happy he is now that he knows he's never going to see Carlos again.' Joseba threw a raspberry at him. 'Be quiet and go to the kitchen.'

The supper brought that long, decisive day to a close. A week later, the police arrested us on the express train to Barcelona and put us in prison. Not for very long, though. Thanks to an amnesty, we regained our freedom fourteen months later.

*   *   *

I wrote these lines today without feeling the slightest fatigue. I was driven on by the memory of my mother; I was driven on by what Joseba told me: that the texts he's going to read the day after tomorrow in the library are based on memories of our time as militants. I've spent all of today in front of my white computer.

Mary Ann and Joseba have worked hard too. They were preparing the texts for the reading at the Book Club until gone three o'clock in the afternoon. Then they went to Visalia airport to fetch Helen.

9

The day began with a phone call from Liz and Sara. 'I love you lots, Daddy,' Liz said. 'I love you too,' I replied. 'You know, Daddy, Mom has given us permission, and we wanted to know if you do too.' 'Permission to do what?' I asked, although it was easy enough to guess. 'Our friends here in Santa Barbara have invited us to stay for another week, and we think it's a pretty cool idea.' 'Aha! Now I understand that declaration of love,' I said, putting on the voice of someone very smart. 'I'll still love you, Daddy, even if you don't give us permission.' Of course she knew the answer would be in the affirmative. 'Is little Sara there?' 'What about the permission?' 'If your Mom thinks it's all right, then it's all right with me too.' There were whoops of joy on the other end of the phone. '*Egun on, aita*' – 'Good morning, Daddy' – Sara said, coming on the phone. She likes her father's language. 'Do you love me lots too?' I asked. 'Yesterday, we took the kites on the beach,' she said, ignoring my question. I could see her on the seashore, in her green swimsuit, holding the strings of the kite. She continued her explanation for about two minutes, then abruptly brought the call to a close, with a hasty 'Bye'.

Talking to Liz and Sara gave me strength, and I joined Joseba, Helen and Mary Ann on the porch for an 'old-style' breakfast. We were just finishing when the phone rang for a second time. Something told me that it would be the hospital, and I was right. 'How have you been feeling lately?' Dr Rabinowitz asked me. I said that I'd been feeling well, better than for the past few months. 'Yesterday and the day before, for example, I spent nearly all day working at the computer, and I hardly felt tired at all.' 'Great,' said the doctor. I waited. 'How would the 23rd suit you for the operation?' he asked. 'What day is that?' Obviously, it didn't matter in the least which day it was, but the cricket living inside my head started whirring as soon as it heard the word 'operation', and I couldn't think of anything else to ask. 'It's a Monday,' he replied. I told him that was fine, and not to worry, that I'd be sure to be there. 'Of course. The 23rd it is, then. As you know, you'll have to come in the day before.' 'Should I not eat beforehand?' 'No, you can eat, Mr Imaz.'

I waited for a while before going back out on to the porch, but I couldn't deceive Mary Ann. She guessed what had happened at once. 'Don't worry,' said Helen. 'They do these operations every day, all over the world.' 'Oh, I'm not worried,' said Mary Ann, but there was barely any light in North Cape.

I went back to my office to get the ranch accounts up to date, and to be alone. I did hardly any work and had a feeling I could scarcely remember having before: my gaze would fix on a stone, a branch, a cloud, and I had to force it to move – the way one does with a lazy dog – and go off in search of other things. For a moment, in a state of mind more appropriate to Triku, I started looking for signs, and I thought it would be a good omen to see the same butterfly from the other day come fluttering by. But that didn't happen. I thought then that I'm different from Triku, and that signs, good or bad, are a matter of indifference to me.

At midday, Joseba came to the office. He informed me that Mary Ann and Helen have decided to hold a barbecue 'next to that snake-infested river', and that he had been delegated to bring me the good news. I told him that Juan's rifle was in a box in the cellar, and that he could use it to finish off any snakes. He folded his arms, the way Toshiro used to do: 'I believe I will do this with greatest of pleasure, comrade. I also feel hatred for third international revisionists. I proud Trotskyist.'

He told me that he and Mary Ann have almost finished their preparations for the reading the day after tomorrow. Mary Ann will read the texts, because Joseba thinks it would be hard for people to understand him reading in English. He will simply introduce them. 'I know you chose the story about Toshiro,' I said. 'No comment. Sorry, comrade.' He bowed Japanese style and asked me to follow him.

10

Sometimes we're like Russian dolls. The first and most visible doll is followed by a second, and the second by a third, and so on until we reach the last, the most secret. I first became aware of this with Geneviève, after Teresa's illness. She didn't seem to be the person I'd known up until then, but somehow smaller and more shrunken. And it happened again with César, our science teacher, when he told me that his father had been shot.

I wonder how many Josebas there are, and if he, too, is not some kind of Russian doll. I know that he has at least two personalities. Depending on who he's with, he puts on one voice or another and reveals a different mood entirely. He doesn't speak to me in the same way that he speaks to Mary Ann or Helen. And the change can't just be put down to language.

This afternoon, I was in my office, finishing the stories I began yesterday, and his words drifted in to me through the window. He was explaining to Mary Ann, Helen, Donald, Carol and another three or four members of the Book Club about the 'Basque question' and 'the end of terrorism'.

I closed my eyes the better to analyse his tone of voice, trying to determine its current composition as if it were a liquid. I thought I could distinguish four components: conviction – about thirty to thirty-five per cent; despair – twenty per cent; candour – ten per cent; and sincerity. What he said was very convincing. This was, without a doubt, a third Joseba. Not the one from Obaba, nor the one who had been part of the organisation, but another Joseba who has only surfaced in the last few years: 'The joker', the one who never speaks frankly and resorts to stories and metaphors.

'Have you ever seen one of those great steel balls that hang from a crane and which they use to knock down buildings?' he said in his hesitant English. 'The crane lifts up the ball and lets it fall on the building. That's exactly what's happened in the Basque Country. Except that there the ball is out of control.'

There was a murmured response, but no one wanted to interrupt his explanation. Joseba's voice changed slightly, and the percentage of candour doubled to at least twenty per cent. He mentioned Franco and Hitler, saying that they were hand in glove, and that the bombing of Guernica – 'the first civilian bombing in history' – had been their work. 'Amongst the dead that day were, just to give you an example, the grandparents and two aunts of a friend of mine called Agustín; now what can you expect from Agustín given such a precedent, and in a political environment in which it was forbidden to use the Basque language even on gravestones.'

Joseba went on explaining that the peons of the military dictatorship, borne along by their hatred for the people of the Basque Country, had hung the steel ball very high, and that is how everything had started. Over time – 'It's impossible to direct the steel ball exactly where you want to' – those who had been the victims became the executioners; for example, another friend, who had also been his teacher – 'his name is César' – had received death threats for no other reason than that he belonged to the socialist party, and despite the fact that he was a decent person, a progressive and a democrat.

My body reacted more quickly than my head. Before I knew it, I was out of my office and standing on the corner of the porch. 'Hasn't David ever talked to you about the Basque Country?' Joseba asked when he saw me. Donald smiled mischievously: 'There's a book going around of which only three copies have been made, but it's in Basque and so I can't understand it.' Like Mary Ann, Donald wanted me to become a writer. When he first saw my memoir, he got slightly annoyed with me

354

for using 'a language no one understands'. Mary Ann nudged him, he took the hint and said nothing more.

Joseba's tone of voice changed when he spoke to me. It became firmer, and more desperate too. 'I didn't tell you about César because I didn't want to depress you,' he said. 'César has received death threats? How is that possible?' I exclaimed. 'That's the way things are, David.' Without intending to, I sat down next to them. I did so automatically.

Carol thought we were still talking about my book. 'David, when are you going to read something for our club? We haven't read anything by you yet,' she said. 'That's not quite true,' replied Mary Ann, trying to avoid the subject of the memoir. 'You all read the story he published in the Visalia anthology.' 'The story about Obaba's first American?' said Carol. 'Yes, but I mean new work!' 'I really liked that story,' said Donald. Both he and Carol are very tenacious. The situation was quite absurd.

When we were alone, Joseba put his arm around my shoulder. 'Let's not be naïve, David! It was inevitable that things would end like this!' 'I can understand Berlino receiving death threats, but César! That's a very bad sign.' 'Now don't copy Triku and start talking about signs.' I noticed something more than resignation in his voice. 'I'm just the messenger, David. It's not my fault. Besides, we paid our dues.'

His tone changed again, and for a moment, he was once more the rather theatrical Joseba who makes Mary Ann or Efraín laugh: 'Although, the truth is we didn't pay very much. A year in prison and then the amnesty. We were lucky, weren't we, David?' 'What are you talking about exactly?' I asked. 'I'm thinking about the main theme of my reading: betrayal,' he said. 'But let's not talk about that now, please, comrade.' Then he said again that he found it impossible to speak frankly, and that nothing made him more nervous than the confiding tone of voice. 'I can only confess to a large audience,' he went on, without giving me the opportunity to disagree. 'That's why I've never been to a psychiatrist. I'd need a minimum of twenty psychiatrists before I could even start talking, and I don't earn enough royalties to pay for that.' He went on in this vein until we rejoined Mary Ann and Helen.

355

11

Today was the day of the reading. There were about forty of us, more or less the expected number, and I noticed that Joseba looked very serious when he came into the room. He was wearing a reddish-brown jacket and a white shirt. Mary Ann was in her pearl-grey dress. Donald gave a brief introduction, and, after a 'thank you for coming', Joseba got straight to the point. He talked about the Basque Country and referred to Picasso's *Guernica*, since it was something everyone there would know. 'David and I are from there, from Gernika. We were born very close to that town.' From 6000 miles away, the statement could be construed as accurate.

Despite his accent, he made his case very clearly and the audience applauded him. Mary Ann went up to the lectern to read the first texts. 'These are three short stories, or, rather, confessions.' Joseba must have become suddenly aware of the 6000 miles that separated him from the audience, because he returned to the microphone to give a little additional information: 'Perhaps, here in the United States, it is worth mentioning that the war in the Basque Country did not end with the bombing of Guernica; in one way or another, the conflict went on. So much so, that, at the end of the sixties, many of the young people who decided to take up arms considered themselves to be at war with the Spanish state. The stories you are going to hear have as their protagonists three such young people. The stories are about something that happened at the end of the dictatorship, something quite special.' Joseba gave me a smile, and added in his somewhat eccentric English: 'I'm sorry for this tricky way to create suspense.' The members of the Book Club all smiled.

I awaited the reading of the stories with some nervousness. I could imagine what Joseba meant when he referred to 'something quite special'. Gladys, who, at eighty, is the oldest member of the club, noticed my constant foot-tapping. 'Your shoe will fly off if you tap your foot much harder, David,' she said slightly mockingly. When I apologised, she added: 'Oh, don't worry about me. I lost my fear of flying shoes a long time ago.' She is a little like General Sherman. Her life has been a long one, and now she is perfectly calm.

The audience warmly applauded Joseba's stories – the three confessions and the stories about snow and about Toshiro. Afterwards, during the question-and-answer session, Joseba had recovered his usual good humour. 'Do you think you need a special gift in order to be a writer?' asked a club member. 'No, not in my case. I'm a little like the donkey in the fable: I make the flute play purely by chance. In reality, I'm a donkey, a donkey who writes.' Everyone laughed.

At around seven o'clock, we had a light supper on the porch outside the library. By nine, we were back at the ranch.

Before going to bed, I turned on my white computer and found an e-mail from Joseba. He was sending me the stories we'd heard at the library. 'So that you can analyse my truth more closely,' he said. 'I wasn't that surprised by it, you know,' I replied. 'But I'll read the stories and give you my opinion.'

'Did you cope all right, David?' Mary Ann asked me when we went to bed. She's worried. She's afraid that events like today's, which she and her friends have put on solely to entertain me, may prove harmful to my health. 'Well, in a way it was quite hard,' I told her. 'It seems like it's impossible to free oneself from the past. We remove the fly from the soup, and then, when we're not looking, there it is again. But I really enjoyed it as well. And you know why too.' 'No, I don't,' she said, kissing me. 'Because I could compare my life then with the life I've had since I met you.' And I kissed her back.

Three confessions

TRIKU'S CONFESSION

Everything was going well, but then, unexpectedly, something went wrong, and just as happens when a spaceship develops a tiny fault, we hardly noticed at first, and then suddenly, one day, before we knew it, we were spinning out of orbit. It's sad watching the astronauts in those lovely white spaceships disintegrate, sadder still to see the ship slowly land and know that the crew are all dead, asphyxiated in their cabins before they've even touched down. That second alternative, the sadder one, was ours. In the end, Ramuntxo, Etxeberria and I, members of the same revolutionary group, were asphyxiated by the lies and rumours invented by the police instead of being blown up by a bomb or felled by a bullet. We were hiding in a small French village called Mamousine, but we felt really uncomfortable there because of the new leader Papi had chosen for our group, Carlos. We didn't like him. Carlos was, of course, an exemplary militant, a real soldier, a comrade who would have been welcome in any organisation. It was said that, before he went underground, he had single-handedly placed five bombs in one night. But he was very strict and far too serious; he never joked or laughed. He never allowed himself a moment's rest.

Etxeberria found this attitude particularly hard to bear, because it was diametrically opposed to his own anarchic temperament. In meetings, he started winding Carlos up and calling him 'Super', as in 'super-militant': 'As Super has told us', 'although Super doesn't share my opinion' and so on. As was to be expected, Carlos didn't like the nickname at all, and this led to the first argument. That first argument was followed by many others, and it became ever clearer that the two men simply couldn't stand each other.

One day, Carlos informed us that it was our duty to do exercises and jogging, and that Ramuntxo and Etxeberria had to stop smoking, because any militant who wasn't in peak physical form would only cause problems. Etxeberria flatly refused and stormed out of the meeting. This annoyed Carlos, and, with Etxeberria gone, he started laying into me instead: he said I should abandon all my superstitions and get rid of the piece of cloth I sewed inside my shirt. I stood my ground: 'For your information, that piece of cloth is a sacred relic from the bombing of Gernika.' 'A "sacred relic"!' said Carlos angrily. 'And he calls himself a revolutionary! A "sacred relic"!' he went on, hoping to get Ramuntxo on his side. Of course, Ramuntxo took my part. We weren't just members of the same organisation, we were friends too. He said to Carlos very gravely: 'You should show more respect for a comrade who lost half his family in Gernika!' 'God, you're impossible, you lot!' cried Carlos.

Unfortunately, the stars were not in our favour. Barely a week after that bitter spat, Ramuntxo's mother died. Ramuntxo had driven into Pau with Etxeberria and thought he would phone home, which is when they gave him the news. It might have been chance, or possibly telepathy. Musicians, especially accordionists, make very good telepaths. At midday, Carlos came into the kitchen and, without a word, went over to the drawer where I kept the pistols. When I saw him put them in a bag, I asked him what was going on. 'Something very serious,' he replied, without looking me in the eye, or, rather, looking at me, but not seeing me. His thoughts were elsewhere. He went over to the kitchen door, taking the pistols with him, but I blocked the way and wouldn't let him leave. 'I need my pistol,' I said. He might be the leader of the group, but he had no right to take my weapon from me. He hesitated for a moment, then took it out of the bag and placed it on the table. 'This one?' he snapped. 'I want to know what's happened,' I said. Then he told me that Ramuntxo had crossed the frontier, that he'd gone to his mother's funeral without asking permission first, and that he would pay dearly for this betrayal. The word 'betrayal' frightened me: it was

359

something the organisation didn't forgive. 'It's not a betrayal,' I said. 'At most, it's irresponsible. What does Etxeberria think?' He gave me a piercing look: 'Whose side are you on?' 'At the moment, no one's,' I said. He left the kitchen, slamming the door behind him. Our spaceship was already out of its orbit.

It was Papi who saved Ramuntxo and Etxeberria. I was so relieved when I saw him arrive in Mamousine. He's always said that we were his favourite colleagues and that he owed a great debt to Ramuntxo for having hidden us at Iruain when we were surrounded by civil guards. Carlos could scream and shout until he was blue in the face, but he wouldn't get the punishment he wanted for my two friends: what the boss says goes.

After talking to Carlos, Papi came into the kitchen and started looking at the recipe books on one of the shelves. Four very long minutes passed, then he said: 'What should we do, Triku?' 'Why don't you tell me what you think, that would be quickest,' I replied. He spoke then of us going back into active service. That was the only way out. Otherwise, Ramuntxo and Etxeberria would have to take their punishment. 'I'll go with them,' I said, making my mind up there and then. 'We've been together a long time now, and I'd like it to continue like that.' 'That's what I wanted to know,' said Papi, putting the book he was holding back on the shelf.

I noticed that our spaceship was starting to change direction. From now on, we would have to pass through some very dangerous places, but the crew would remain the same. There would be no strange pilots amongst us. That night, when Etxeberria asked me to choose the best wine from the kitchen and prepare one last supper at Mamousine, I felt intensely happy. Then, before going to bed, I sewed the relic from Gernika inside my favourite shirt. I couldn't care less what Carlos thought. Contact with that piece of cloth was important to me. It reminded me of the reasons for the struggle. And, besides, it brought me luck.

But there was no luck, no change of direction. Things continued to go wrong. Ramuntxo was deeply affected by his mother's death, and

360

when we asked him to bring his accordion, he refused so vehemently that we found it very hard to insist. Nevertheless, we asked him again. Etxeberria said: 'The accordion would be more useful than ever. Bear in mind that it's over 350 miles to Barcelona, and we're going to have to go by train. If we're singing, they'll just take us for three young guys out on a spree.' Ramuntxo grunted an answer. He would take the accordion if we considered it necessary, but would we, please, just leave him in peace. He wasn't in the mood for talk.

In the train, he got angry again. We were joined in our compartment by two drunks, attracted by the music. They kept asking him to play the latest pop songs, and Ramuntxo was worried because he didn't know what songs were popular in Spain at the time. 'What about that song Antonio used to sing? *Eva Maria se fue buscando el sol en la playa*,' said Etxeberria, humming the tune. '*Con su maleta de piel y su bikini de rayas*,' sang one of the drunks, joining in. 'Yes, play that one, go on!' said the other drunk, getting up and starting to dance. 'Right, that's it! I've had enough!' said Ramuntxo and put the accordion back in its case.

We sat in silence for the next hour, and even the drunks seemed to have calmed down. At a certain point, the train slowed, and one of the drunks leaned out of the window. 'We're coming into Zaragoza,' he said. And the other one commented: 'Yes, there are a lot of reds there too.' I was surprised to hear these words. Or perhaps I was only surprised shortly afterwards, when I saw the two supposed drunks pointing their guns at us. I had mine in my bag. I started to get agitated. I didn't know what to do. Suddenly, Ramuntxo struck the hand of the policeman in front of him – because they were, of course, policemen – and the gun fell to the floor. Instinctively, I crouched down and tried to pick it up, but I couldn't. By then, there were three other men in the compartment. They were young and athletic, probably special officers of some sort. One of them gave me a karate chop to the neck that left my arm dead. It was 19 August, a Saturday. After almost five years on active service, our group had just been caught.

I've no idea where they took us, because they put sacks over our heads so that we couldn't see. I'm sure, though, that we didn't stay in

Zaragoza, because we were driven in a car for three or four hours. They may have taken us to Madrid or to San Sebastián. During the journey they kicked me repeatedly. For example, I would ask for a drink of water and before I could even finish the sentence, I'd receive a kick in the ribs or the head. One of these blows left me feeling dazed. 'Be quiet, Triku,' Ramuntxo said and he, too, got a kick.

When they took the sack off my head, I found myself in an empty room. There were no windows, just a fluorescent light on the ceiling. Three policemen were there too, none of them particularly young. I made as if to scratch myself on my left side and was thrilled when I felt the scrap of cloth from Gernika still sewn inside my shirt. I thought of the nearly 2000 people killed in the bombing, especially my two aunts, who were only children then, and I braced myself for the inevitable beating. What frightened me most were the steel-capped shoes; I mean, what I feared most was that one of the policeman might be wearing steel-capped shoes, like those worn by the notorious torturer Melitón Manzanas, but I soon learned that none of them was. The kicks they dealt me left no actual wounds.

After that initial session of kicking and beating, they made me stand to attention against the wall, with my knees stiff, and then they put a telephone directory on top of my head and started hitting it. Each hard, sharp blow sent a kind of electric shock all the way down my spine to the soles of my feet. I felt as if my brain was going to explode at any moment. In between, while they held me up so that I didn't fall to the ground unconscious, they asked me questions, they wanted names: who was in charge of the prison 'committees', who coordinated the hunger strikes, who was responsible for the commando groups. I couldn't simply collapse, because every time I did so, two of the policemen would hold me up, while the third yelled those same questions at me: 'Who's currently in charge of the prison "committees"? Who coordinates the hunger strikes? Who's responsible for the full-time terrorist cells?' On the third or fourth time of asking, I said without blinking: 'Why don't you look in the Yellow Pages?' This provoked such a rain of blows that I lost consciousness.

362

They took me to a small room, and I slept for a while. In my dreams, as if it were the most normal thing in the world, I had the impression that I was in a spaceship, floating in a brilliant blue sky. Suddenly, I saw beside me Vladimir Mikhailovich Komarov, the astronaut I loved best: 'We've left our orbit. The situation is very dangerous,' he said with great serenity. At that moment, I understood precisely what my situation was, and I said to myself that perhaps Vladimir Mikhailovich Komarov's words were not part of a dream, but a sign that I was falling into a coma.

Then, close by me, I heard another voice, not the cosmonaut's, the voice, apparently, of an older person: 'Your resistance is most praiseworthy, Triku, but I hate to see you suffer in vain. Your colleagues have told us everything. More than that, your colleagues have betrayed you.' When I opened my eyes, a man with very white hair was sitting on one corner of my bed. His hair was neatly parted and he was impeccably dressed. He looked like a priest from Opus Dei, but, of course, he was a policeman, the one they call 'the soft cop', because that's the role he plays in the interrogation. 'What did my friends say?' I asked him at last. Now, as I write this confession, I see everything clearly, but at the time I found it hard to follow the thread of my thoughts. 'As I said, Triku, your friends have betrayed you.' He gave an unconvincing smile. 'My colleagues are really giving you a hard time. To be honest, I'm against such drastic methods, and besides, in most cases, they're quite unnecessary. Your case is just such an example. All you have to do is give me a few names and everything will be fine. And believe me we only need the names as corroboration. As I said, they've told us everything. And they did so before they even got here. You understand me, I'm sure.' What he was implying was very grave indeed. 'I don't believe you,' I said.

He gave a sigh and stood up: 'Didn't you think there was something rather odd about your capture? Didn't you find the arrest just a tad too easy? And another thing: have you heard your colleagues in the next cells cry out? No, you haven't, have you? You, on the other hand, have been squealing like a stuck pig.' 'Well, we're all different, aren't we?' I

363

said. He slowly closed the door, then opened it again. 'I believe this time they're going to give you the plastic bag treatment. Be careful, now, and don't suffocate,' he said. This time he closed the door more quickly. He didn't want to hear my response. 'You're finished, and anyone can smell it a mile off!' I shouted.

Back in the room with the three policemen, I noticed a plastic bag on the table, and my palms began to sweat. I would prefer a thousand beatings to being unable to breathe. 'Right, let's have a look at the album,' said the policeman in charge of the interrogation. He placed a series of photos on the table. The other two policemen stood behind me, slipped the bag over my head and then immediately took it off again. 'He's got kind of a big head, but it'll do,' said one of them. The man in charge pointed to a group of young people on a *bateau-mouche* in Paris, and asked: 'Who are they?' I said I didn't know, and, besides, the photo was taken from too far away. 'Let's see if we have more luck now.' He showed me a detail of the same photo. I saw Carlos together with a female colleague who was known as Lucía. 'Who are they?' he asked again. 'If those two put down that bag, I'll tell you.' 'The names!' he said, gesturing to the others to move away. 'He's Busca Isusi,' I said. He looked at me, surprised. It seemed too easy. Nevertheless, he made me repeat the name and he wrote it down in his notebook. 'And the girl?' 'She's Nikolasa.' He showed me more photos. 'Perucho!' I said, or 'Luján' or 'Castillo' or Montalbán', the names that appeared on the spines of my cookery books. But once when I said 'Cándido', he asked 'Which Cándido?' Without even thinking, and because I was still in a daze, I said: 'You know Cándido's recipe for roast suckling pig, don't you?' Then one of the policeman behind me, clearly shaken, shouted out: 'Don't you get it, Jesús? All this time, he's been giving us the names of chefs!' Jesús began to curse – 'Bastard . . .' – and punched me several times. The other man said: 'Wait, Jesús, use this instead,' and they put the bag over my head, and I felt as if my heart would burst.

Vladimir Mikhailovich Komarov was sitting beside me. He pointed to the red light on the control panel of the spaceship. 'A valve seems to have failed. The cabin is losing oxygen.' 'That's bad, isn't it?' I said.

364

'I reckon we have enough oxygen for about twenty minutes, and we still have to go round the planet seven times before we land in Siberia.' I looked out of the spaceship window: from there, the Earth seemed a very peaceful place. I saw the outline of North America, and shortly afterwards of Greenland; a little more, and I could make out the pony-tail formed by Norway, Sweden and Finland. 'We're going very fast, aren't we?' Just at that moment the red light went off, and I shot Vladimir a hopeful glance. 'No, my friend, nothing has been fixed,' he said, seeing the expression on my face. 'I was the one who turned the light off. We don't need it. We know the situation we're in.' 'Meaning that there's less and less oxygen.' 'Exactly.' 'What do you think, Vladimir? Do you think we're going to die?' 'Yes, I do.'

In the front part of the cabin, there was a rectangular panel, apparently made of glass, and through it, if you looked slightly upwards, you could see the stars, thousands and thousands of them, forming patches of golden dust. It was a marvellous sight, but, despite that, I was more drawn to what I could see through the window, the succession of different places on Earth: first, the coast of China with a kind of hook that must have been Korea, then Japan, which, from that height, resembled a scarf. 'I don't know if you know, Vladimir, but the saint who evangelised Japan was a Basque. His name was Francisco Javier.' He smiled faintly. 'Don't ask me about saints. I don't like religion. It's the opium of the people.'

We were flying over the Pacific Ocean, a vast black expanse beneath us. 'There's something that saddens me, Vladimir. I would love to see the Basque Country again before I die, but that won't be possible.' 'Why not? What parallel does it lie on?' 'No, that's not the problem,' I said. 'It should be visible from this orbit, more or less. The problem is the size. The Basque Country's so small that you can't see it from space.' Vladimir gazed at me sadly: 'That's one problem we can't solve, my friend. But if you look with your inner eyes, you'll see everything. There are no limits for our inner eyes.' 'A friend of mine, Ramuntxo, used to say that we have other eyes behind our first eyes,' I remarked. Vladimir smiled: 'I can see the Red Square in Moscow right now. I can see my wife walking among the crowds. She's probably going to buy some currants. Then she'll make roast lamb with currants, Armenian style. It's delicious.' In other circumstances, I would have asked for the recipe, but this was not the moment, and I preferred to do as he had done, to open my inner eyes: I saw a green hill, and my grandparents' white house at the foot of the hill, and a little further off the *ría* of Gernika and the Bay of Biscay. My eyes filled with tears, both my inner eyes and my outer eyes. 'From the spiritual point of view, you're stronger than I am, Vladimir,' I said. 'You saw your wife in Red Square and you didn't cry, whereas here I am weeping for a house.' 'Don't worry, my friend,' he said. I realised then that he, too, was moved. We sat on in silence, each immersed in his own thoughts.

Below us, I could see California, where Ramuntxo's uncle lived. 'Forgive my asking, but why are you called Vladimir? After Lenin?' 'Yes, I believe so,' he replied. 'My father is a party member. But it was also the name of one of my grandfathers.' I wondered if I should ask him about the national question, to see what he thought about the right to self-determination of Georgia and the Ukraine, but I decided not to. The lack of oxygen was becoming very marked now, we had to breathe in twice to fill our lungs. And the more we talked, the less oxygen we would have left. Besides, it was good not to talk: silence is the music of the heavens. I saw Newfoundland and the southern part of Canada whose lakes looked like tiny black specks. It was as if all these places were asleep. I would have liked to fall asleep too, but the lack of oxygen prevented me.

When we passed over Europe again, breathing was becoming really painful. 'The truth is, Vladimir, I don't mind dying at all,' I said. Vladimir turned his deep eyes on me. 'For any reason in particular?' 'Because of something they told me when I was arrested. I don't know what inter-rogations are like in Russia, but the Spanish police take different roles: some are "hard cops" and they beat you, and the others are "soft cops" and they feed insidious ideas into your mind. The "soft cop" fed the idea of betrayal into my mind. He said that Ramuntxo and Etxeberria had betrayed me, which is why it was so easy for us to be caught. At first,

I didn't want to think about it, but some words are like worms in cheese, and once inside your head they just get fatter and fatter. And I've reached the conclusion that it might be true, because the fact is Etxeberria did behave pretty strangely after we left Mamousine. Ramuntxo didn't, but Etxeberria did. I really think he might have betrayed us, Vladimir. And if that's so, I'd rather die. Just thinking about it makes me ill.'

We were flying over the ocean. On the control panel a few green lights came on, and the spaceship began a sharp descent. 'We're on our way home,' said Vladimir. He found it hard to speak. Our faces were drenched in sweat. 'What are you thinking about, Vladimir?' I asked. 'I'm thinking that unless something is done to prevent it, I'm going to be the first astronaut to be killed while on a mission.'

I stopped to think. There was no way of knowing what number I was. Not exactly. The first were my grandparents and my aunts. And the 2000 other people who died in Gernika. And all those who had died in the war, especially the entirely innocent people who were shot, like the schoolteachers in Obaba Ramuntxo was always talking about. And Lubis, the first martyr of our group of friends, who had also been suffocated by a plastic bag. And many others. But it was impossible to calculate, and so I concentrated instead on the window.

We passed over California again, and I waved goodbye to Ramuntxo's uncle. 'He worked for many years for the liberation of Euskadi,' I said to Vladimir, 'but now he's angry with us. He says he doesn't approve of our methods. Like all the members of his party, he's a bit too willing to contemplate a peace agreement with the enemy, but he still deserves my respect.'

'It's beautiful to die beneath the stars,' said Vladimir suddenly with a sigh. The slight tremor of his nostrils stopped; his deep eyes remained fixed for ever on one of those stars. The spaceship plunged downwards, this time in free fall, as if the death of its pilot had taken away its will to carry on flying.

We hit the ground, and the spaceship shattered into a thousand pieces. Two nurses immediately appeared and took me to hospital. I opened

367

my eyes. Before me stood a grave-faced man dressed as a doctor. 'The worst is over,' he said. 'Am I in Siberia?' I asked. 'No, you're in San Sebastián hospital,' he said. 'The worst is over.'

I closed my eyes and Vladimir Mikhailovich Komarov appeared before me again. He was in Red Square in Moscow, in an open coffin, and hundreds of people were waiting in line to honour him. Where was his wife? What would she think when she returned from the lavish ceremony and found the currants she'd bought on the kitchen table? Many men and women raised a clenched fist in the air as they passed the coffin. I did the same. I energetically raised my fist in honour of Vladimir Mikhailovich Komarov.

'Excellent, you've recovered the use of your arm,' said the doctor. 'How are my friends?' I asked, coming to. 'Not too good, but better than you. We discharged the one called Joseba the day before yesterday,' he said. I felt a rush of happiness. Joseba is Etxeberria's real name. If they really had roughed him up, that meant he hadn't betrayed us.

My eyes again filled with tears, but this time, they were tears of joy. 'It's all right, the worst is over,' repeated the doctor. 'Where's my shirt?' I asked, trying to sit up. I had tubes everywhere. 'Why do you want it? Clothes from outside are not allowed in intensive care,' said the nurse. 'I just want to see something. Please!' I begged. In the end, they brought it to me, and I told the nurse to show me the inside. The scrap of material from Gernika was still there, in its place. I asked them to look after it for me, and then I went to sleep. The doctor was right, the worst was over.

II

RAMUNTXO'S CONFESSION

We had to travel by train to the Mediterranean coast in order to carry out a series of actions. According to the leaders of our organisation, tourism was, at the time, the mainstay of Spain's economy, and attacking the tourist industry meant attacking the dictatorship, striking at one of its principal pillars of support. The aim seemed perfectly achievable:

just place ten bombs on ten beaches, and the hotels would empty. The only difficulty lay in the fact that we would have to make ten separate sorties in a very short space of time. But, as Joseba declared, the accordion could prove to be our best ally. The music would help us in our travels. More to the point, we could transport the explosives in the accordion case.

The eve of our departure coincided with a *xaribari* in Altzürükü, about forty miles from Biarritz, and Etxeberria suggested that we go to the fiesta to see that 'unique performance, that theatrical remnant of the Middle Ages'. I was against the idea. I wasn't in the mood. Besides, a lot of people from San Sebastián and from Bilbao used to go to the Basque fiestas on the French side of the border, in the 'Pays Basque', and it seemed imprudent to be seen there. We were bound to meet someone we knew, and that person was sure to tell his circle of friends: 'The other day I saw Etxeberria with two other guys. They were in Altzürükü.' And that wasn't good. Sabino, the organisation's instructor, was always saying: 'Sooner or later, everything reaches the ears of the police. If it's the Spanish police, that's bad, but if it's the French police, that's even worse.' But Etxeberria can be very persuasive, and, in the end, he got me and Triku to agree. Triku agreed because he loves Basque fiestas, and I agreed because I didn't feel like arguing.

The *xaribari* began with a procession. The dancers and musicians, the actors disguised as judges, civil guards or lawyers, and all those with a part in the farce, paraded down the streets leading to the square. The weather was beautiful, the sky was blue; the atmosphere was enlivened by the sound of piccolos – *xirulak* – and the people's laughter. However, after a quarter of an hour standing on a street corner, watching the procession, I had to leave. I couldn't stand the sight of Joseba chatting to an old friend from Bilbao, or Triku flirting with some girls from San Sebastián; but even more unbearable, for some reason, were the piccolos. The notes filled my head like so many squeaking mice. I told my friends I'd come back when the *xaribari* was over, and I set off along a path that led up to a hill overlooking the village.

The path ended at a farmhouse. It was a humble dwelling with white walls and window-frames and doors painted blue. In front of it, on the edge of a flat piece of land, were two hayricks and a small red tractor that looked like a toy; further off, was a maizefield that extended as far as the foot of the next hill. The maize was tall and already in flower.

Next to the small red tractor was an old lady, sitting on a wicker chair with her back to the village. I went over to her and greeted her cheerily: 'What's this? Aren't you going down to the village to see the *xaribari*?' She was a very sweet old lady, of a type we in Basque would call *amañí*. Small and slender, she couldn't have weighed more than ninety pounds. She wore her hair caught back in a bun. 'I couldn't care less about fiestas,' she said. I noticed that she was holding a rosary in her hands. 'So you prefer to pray, then?' I said. 'If you'd like to pray with me . . .' 'Pray?' Her invitation made me feel like laughing. The days were long gone when, as the harmonium-player, I was a regular at the church in Obaba or the chapel at La Salle. Nevertheless, it was pleasant being there with that pretty *amañí*. 'You carry on saying your rosary, and I'll be happy to listen.' I sat down on the ground and leaned against the little tractor.

The prayers were like small wheels. First I heard the words *Agur Maria*, 'Hail Mary', then a murmur, then, shortly afterwards, *amen*: one turn. Followed, again, by *Agur Maria*, a murmur, and *amen*: another turn. And so on, over and over, with no aim, simply turning for the sake of turning. My thoughts flew to Iruain, and I saw Lubis in the stables, and the happy peasants who used to come up to me, saying '*caballo, caballo*', and Ubanbe, Opin, Pancho, Sebastián and Adela. All those friends I'd left behind.

I remembered the *zulo* in Iruain – the hiding-place – and a voice that joined in the murmur of prayers reproached me for the ill use we'd made of it: 'For more than a century, it had no other function than to give shelter to the persecuted, but you and your friends despoiled it by using it for something quite different, for hiding people who'd been kidnapped.' I recognised the voice. The person speaking was my Uncle Juan. 'That's because Papi didn't keep his word, Uncle,' I thought. 'He promised they'd only use it to hide colleagues in trouble, but soon afterwards they imprisoned an industrialist who'd failed to pay the revolutionary tax. But I had nothing to do with all that. I've always respected Iruain's history. Sometimes I still wear the Hotson hat.' 'Your intentions were good, David, but you've been far too weak. You've never been able to master your feelings, and sentiment on its own never makes for good company. In that respect, you're like your father.'

These memories were making me feel anxious, and I tried not to let myself be swept along by them. But the little wheels kept turning – *Agur Maria*, a murmur, *amen* – and I found myself once more in the past. I saw Adela leaving the cemetery in Obaba, followed by all those who had come to say a last farewell to my mother: Adrián and his Romanian wife, Paulina accompanied by the girls from the workshop, Virginia in her purple dress, the members of the choir at Obaba . . . I realised that I was the one who had distanced myself from and abandoned them, not the other way round, as I'd at first thought. And I realised, too, that when I joined the organisation and went underground, Virginia did the only thing she could, and when I phoned her from Paris, her response was unanswerable: 'I don't want to see you again. I had enough unhappiness with my husband.' For a moment, Virginia's voice silenced the old lady's prayers. Then it vanished.

The wheels began to turn again. I saw Triku in the bar in Obaba on the day when Neil Armstrong and another astronaut walked on the Moon. 'I'd have to be born again to believe that story,' said a peasant who was watching the moon-landing on television. Triku and I tried to convince him that the news was true. But the peasant clung to his views. 'You should listen to them,' said the owner of the bar. 'These young people know a lot.' To which the man replied: 'They know a lot and they know nothing. That's the law of the young.'

The peasant's words were trite perhaps, but there, in Altzürükü, with my eyes fixed on the maizefield and accompanied by the murmur of the old lady's prayers, they seemed to me full of meaning. I thought to myself that many of the mistakes I'd made in my early youth had been made out of pure ignorance, because I didn't know the simplest of truths, namely, that life is the most important thing there is and one

371

should take it very seriously, 'just as a squirrel does', as Nazim Hikmet wrote. But there was still time. I could put my life right. I could redeem myself by visiting the kingdom of Death. I would have to visit Gethsemane and know the cross, but the happy day of resurrection would arrive and then I would be free of all my past debts.

Metaphors apart, my plan implied that I would hand myself over to the police. Once across the border, I would take the first opportunity to lose my friends and go to a police station. 'I've come to give myself up,' I would say. 'Why?' 'Because I don't want to go on.' The old lady finished her prayers. The wheels stopped. The decision was made.

I didn't get a chance to put my plan into practice. Three days later, in a train compartment, a policeman pointed a gun at Triku and me, and, out of pure reflex action, I struck him on the wrist and disarmed him; fortunately, though, I didn't succeed in foiling the arrest. I had plenty of doubts in the days that followed, especially when I heard Triku's screams from the torture cells, because those screams made the decision I'd taken on the hillside above Altzürükü seem ridiculous and repugnant. But I went ahead anyway. I declared myself responsible for all the actions mentioned during the interrogation and, more than that, in order to leave nothing out, I informed the police about the existence of the hiding-place in Iruain. My colleagues wouldn't be able to make use of it in the future. Those doubts pursued me even when I was sent to prison, and all the other political prisoners – accusing me of being a traitor and blaming me for the arrest of our group – excluded me from the community and ostracised me.

One day, Triku and Etxeberria decided to break the rules laid down by the prisoners' collective and turned up in the infirmary of the prison where I was working out my sentence. They wanted my permission to send a message to Papi in my defence, to tell him that this business about betrayal was a calumny. I refused. I told them that the punishment was necessary if I wanted my soul to heal. 'Don't do anything,' I told them. 'Let's just allow the butterfly to return home.' 'Can I borrow that line for a poem?' Etxeberria asked me. I said it wasn't mine, that

I'd taken it from a book. Ostracism at least had that advantage: I could read constantly, and poems, stories and novels were to me like pure water.

III

ETXEBERRIA'S CONFESSION

What happened inside me was a reversal, just as when love turns to hate, to use the language of the agony columns. Overnight, I started to loathe everything – my political affiliation, the sentimental songs and, above all, certain words in our day-to-day lexicon: 'the people', 'national', 'social', 'proletariat', 'revolution' and others in the same vein. From that moment on, all the organisation's communiqués seemed to me absurd, the attacks that were carried out even more absurd, and my colleagues remote and unpleasant.

This reversal was confirmed during the time we spent in the French village of Mamousine, when the organisation passed sentence on us after we were denounced by a colleague we knew as Carlos. I was filled with hatred, and I promised myself that I would finish with it all as soon as I could. I had to leave the organisation. Otherwise, I would go mad. Because the life I was leading was, literally, enough to drive a person mad. Exposing yourself to great danger because of an ideology you carry in your head and in your heart may be admirable – although sceptics, or realists, see no merit in this at all, believing that grand words are always followed by grand disasters – but putting yourself at risk against all the dictates of your head and heart, that's pure folly: the pathetic fate of some carnival character.

Around that time – it was 1976 – there was no way of cutting your links with the organisation. There were rumours of splits, and there were constant bitter arguments between those who believed in the 'purely political' route and the militarists. The militarists said that all those who defended moderate points of view were traitors,

373

counter-revolutionaries, and that they weren't prepared to take such a route. Since that was how things were, I set about thinking things out for myself, without the empty rhetoric, puerile ideas, etc. and I ended up making a decision: I would hand myself over to the police. Or, to put it more crudely – without the empty rhetoric, puerile ideas, etc. – I would betray the organisation. Papi's decision to send our group to the Mediterranean worked in favour of my plan. It was just over 370 miles from the Basque Country to Barcelona, and we would be travelling by train. It was a long journey, and I would simply have to wait for the right moment.

Once I'd decided, the doubts began. There was something that got in the way of my plan. I didn't know what to do about Triku and Ramuntxo. On the one hand, I didn't want to put them in danger and deliver them to the police, but, on the other hand, I felt sorry for them. They would remain inside the organisation, trapped by their past, getting deeper and deeper in. I didn't like that idea either. I wanted to be a good shipwreck victim and share my lifeboat with them.

In the end, the good shipwreck victim won out. Ramuntxo and Triku had probably not suffered such a reversal of feelings as I had, but I could see that they were tired and self-absorbed. Triku spent half the day trying out recipes, and the other half listening to esoteric programmes on the radio or reading magazines about astronauts. He'd become very obsessive too. He had a piece of cloth, which, according to him, came from the dress an aunt of his was wearing on the day they bombed Gernika, and whenever we went out on a mission, he'd sew it inside the shirt he was wearing; if he didn't have it, he'd get really upset, like a savage who's lost his amulet. As for Ramuntxo, he was concentrating on learning English. Whenever he could, he would take his books and tapes and go to his room to study. On one occasion, Papi told him that he should get more involved in the organisation, but Ramuntxo refused point-blank. He just didn't want to know. He merely carried out the orders he was given and that was that. Perhaps he was depressed. Ramuntxo has always been prone to depression. And he'd been very low since the death of his mother.

When we left Mamousine, I said to myself: 'I've got to get them out of this hole. The Spanish dictatorship can't last much longer. The change in the political situation will doubtless bring an amnesty and the prisoners will be set free. The situation of any militants still active, however, will be very complicated indeed.' I was convinced that militarists like Carlos would take over the organisation, and that the armed struggle would go on and on. And militants would once again end up being sent to prison, to the very prisons that had just been emptied. And when was another amnesty likely to be granted? It was impossible to know, but not for many years – perhaps ten, perhaps twenty. It was important, therefore, to go to prison as soon as possible.

I won't describe our arrest in detail. As soon as we left San Sebastián, I told my friends that I was going to the toilet, and I asked the conductor to summon the railway police. When he came, I told him I wanted to speak to some high-ranking officer, that it was a matter of life and death, and that if all went well he would earn a month's leave and possibly even a medal. I made the phone call from the station of Alsasua and agreed the conditions with the governor of Navarra: there would be no violence during the arrest and no torture at the police station. There would be no need. I would supply them with all the information that was at my colleagues' disposal. The governor gave me his word, and I gave him the only fact he needed at that moment: one of my companions would be playing the accordion. Locating our carriage would be easy. 'We'll arrest you at Zaragoza, shall we? I just need to make sure everything is ready. I don't want to rush things,' said the governor. I told him that this seemed fine and asked him, please, to send some intelligent policemen. 'It's always easier to work with intelligent people.' 'You're a cool customer,' he said, with a nervous laugh. He didn't get phone calls like mine every day.

Fourteen months, two weeks and five days later, Triku, Ramuntxo and I were freed thanks to an amnesty; free, at last, of the organisation, and ready to start a new life. At the time, it seemed to me that the price we paid was a low one. Many of our colleagues had only been freed

375

after ten or more years in prison, and so, by comparison, we got off lightly. But time has passed, and life has taught me one lesson after another, and I can no longer deceive myself. The price was high for all of us, especially for me.

I can hear the voices of Triku and Ramuntxo. They disagree and are outraged by my last statement. 'What do you mean, *you* paid a higher price than anyone, Etxe?' asks Triku. 'How can you say that? Have you forgotten that they tortured me so mercilessly I very nearly died?' And Ramuntxo, equally angry, declares: 'You've always been such an egotist, Etxeberria. You always place yourself at the centre of the universe. During the fourteen months, two weeks and five days that followed our stay in the police station, I was in constant danger of my life, accused of being a traitor and an informer. More than that, the prison committee dragged up my whole unfortunate past. I became once again the son of a fascist, the last representative of an odious line. If someone so much as spoke my name in the exercise yard, everyone would spit. And it was no better when I came out of prison. I would go into a bar, and people would look the other way. I saw my name painted on walls: I was a traitor and, as such, deserved to die. I wouldn't wish those weeks and months on my worst enemy, Etxeberria. But what happened had its good side, I do agree with you there. Without all that suffering, I would never have come to Stoneham and would never have touched paradise with the tips of my fingers. That, however, is no thanks to you, but to the people I found in this part of the world. If it hadn't been for my uncle, and if it hadn't been, above all, for Mary Ann, I would have ended up like that astronaut Triku was always talking about, going round and round and gradually suffocating to death.'

Triku and Ramuntxo might be right, and if they ever actually said the words I've placed in their mouths, I would immediately lapse into a shamed silence. But then I would urge them to look at the scar on the left side of my forehead.

I was in the cells, and I heard screams, especially Triku's, but Ramuntxo's too, and I was awaiting my punishment, a few blows, the odd punch. I was not so ingenuous as to believe the governor's promise.

Instead, though, the police spent all their time telling jokes and laughing; they offered me cigarettes and brought me sandwiches and beer for lunch and supper. One policeman said to me: 'You'll leave the police station fitter and fatter than when you arrived,' and this looked set to be true.

My first reaction was gratitude, but the night they took Triku to hospital – the one night when there was silence in the basement where the police tortured detainees – I understood the reasoning behind their behaviour. The police were sending out a message: 'Etxeberria is the traitor.' Obviously the organisation would be suspicious of the ease with which we'd been captured and would start to ask questions. When the prison committee wrote their report – 'Etxeberria emerged from interrogation in great shape' – the suspicions would gain credence. I would be submitted to another interrogation, this time in prison, and my colleagues would not be easily satisfied. I started to sweat. I saw myself in a prison cell, lying on the floor.

At that moment – 'Just as well,' I thought – a policeman opened the door of my cell and told me it was breakfast time and suggested we have a cup of coffee together. I started to drink my coffee, and I noticed a heavy iron door, rather like a safe door, which led down to the basement. I jumped up and hurled myself headlong against it.

I woke up twenty hours later in hospital. 'There have been a lot of street protests about how you and your friends have been treated,' the male nurse told me. I realised I was safe, and I felt glad. I didn't know at the time what damage I'd inflicted on myself: a deep cut to the forehead, which would leave a permanent, purple scar.

I've suffered in many ways since I left hospital. First, because of Triku, who remained in a coma for several days, with a risk that he might never wake up at all. Second, because of Ramuntxo, who for a whole long year had to carry the burden that was, by rights, mine. Third, because during that long year, I had to put up with my colleagues in the organisation. And fourth, because, almost up until the present day, my scar, my stigma, has condemned me to a life of loneliness.

Condemned to a life of loneliness. Again the language of the problems page. But it doesn't matter, we're all far more banal than we think. I certainly am. And speaking of those condemned to loneliness, on TV recently, I saw a girl who weighed about nineteen stone to whom a very pretty presenter – eight and a half stone, green eyes – was saying in amazement: 'What do you mean, no one loves you? Why wouldn't they?' She would have had a similar reaction if confronted by me. She would have affected the same astonishment. As if she hadn't seen my purple scar. And I would have felt like that nineteen-stone girl. I wouldn't have burst into tears, of course; I would have reacted far more strongly than that. I am, after all – need I say it? – a violent person.

On her first visit to see me in prison, my girlfriend of the time – her name was Niko, a newspaper photographer – couldn't take her eyes off the scar on my forehead. 'It will change colour, won't it?' she asked at last. 'Sure it will,' I said. But it didn't. It remained the same for five or six years. After that time, it became less vivid and turned a dull lilac colour. Meanwhile, it had scared off Niko. And it scared off all the other women too. It makes me laugh: I read in one of the Sunday supplements that men are very concerned about how a woman looks, but that women give far less importance to a man's physical appearance. What a joke! Stick a good scar on your face, and then we'll talk.

But solitude has only been a small part of the price to pay, no more than twenty or twenty-five per cent of the total price. Indeed, as well as the scar on my forehead, I have another one, though I'm not sure where, perhaps on my soul, on my spirit, or perhaps on my mind: that of the traitor.

We traitors are foul beasts. He who forgave everything did not forgive the treachery of his disciple. And the disciple hanged himself. I, on the other hand, far from doing that, wished to redeem myself and wanted to gain forgiveness by means of some exemplary act. In prison, I would say to myself: 'I'll confess the truth and bear the cross that Ramuntxo is carrying now,' but I feared they would kill me. Then I decided that I'd sort everything out when I left prison. I'd write a confessional letter to Papi and leave the country. But my friends left before me: Triku to

Montevideo and Ramuntxo to the United States. My confession would bring them no advantage. I decided to say nothing.

The years passed, and the story of the betrayal on the train was lost amongst a thousand other stories. Triku and I will remember it; Ramuntxo, Papi and a few others too. But no one else. Triku was reborn in Montevideo, and has gone on to become a wealthy citizen, the owner of one of the best restaurants in the city. And Ramuntxo is doing equally well, or even better. In his case, it was love that rescued him from hell. I, on the other hand, am only so-so. At least my second scar is changing colour and starting to fade like the one on my forehead, and I have not yet lost hope.

12

In the morning light, the computer looked really white, and I had the feeling that the papers, photos and other objects that have accumulated around it were somehow getting in its way. I immediately started tidying my desk, and everything ended up in a large cardboard box. For a moment, I thought of taking all these things down to the dump at Three Rivers, just as I had with the gorilla notebook. The thought saddened me a little, though, and so I left it all where it was. Well, almost all, because I separated out two of the photographs and put them in a much nicer box: the picture Joseba's father took of us on the day of our first class with César and Redin, and the photo taken at the inauguration of Adrián's workshop at Samson's Bath. I did this, more than anything, because of César and Lubis. I often think of them both. Lubis would have hated the people now threatening César.

Now there's only the white computer on the desk. I wondered if it would allow anything else to share the desk with it, and so I took Mary Ann's butterfly – the one called *Gonepteryx rhamni*, yellow with orange spots – from the deck of cards given to me by Papi. I placed it on the table and waited. The air didn't move; nothing broke the silence or disturbed the peace. The only effect it had was a favourable one: the study seemed more cheerful. A short while later, as if something had summoned her there, she appeared at the door, and we went for a walk.

We spent the afternoon on the shores of Lake Kaweah. Yachts and small boats skipped across the water. We sat out on the terrace of a café and ordered lemon cakes all round. Then Helen mentioned yesterday's reading. 'Everyone was staring at your forehead. They were surprised not to see a scar there,' she said to Joseba. 'I do have a tendency to the autobiographical, but I don't go that far,' replied Joseba.

But his tendency to the autobiographical does go that far. The scar exists, not on his forehead, but on the back of his neck. When he threw himself against the iron door, he didn't do so head first, as in his story, but backwards. The doctors said that if he'd hit himself only slightly harder, he wouldn't have lived to tell the tale.

'I think people enjoyed the reading,' Helen went on. 'The story about Toshiro even made them laugh, which is remarkable really. I mean, Trotskyists don't exactly get a good press in California.' Helen is convinced that this is the most reactionary of all the states. More even than Texas or Alabama. 'The people who laughed most were Carol and Helen,' I said. 'But they were just in the mood to have a good time. They were biased.'

As they say in Latin, Mary Ann then tried to work *pro domo sua*, using the situation to her own advantage: 'Carol and Helen do indeed want to have a good time, which is why they'd like to attend a reading by you. It would be here at the ranch and there'd only be a few of us.' 'They're trying to cheer up the invalid in the group,' I explained to Joseba. 'No, David,' protested Mary Ann, 'Donald truly appreciates your writing. He's given lots of people copies of that story you published in Visalia.' 'Ah, yes, "Obaba's First American",' said Joseba, demonstrating how good his memory was. 'I'd like to hear it too, or at least read it.' 'We'll see,' I said, eager to drop the subject.

The water in the lake was a bluish colour, and the sails on the boats looked like white handkerchiefs ready to wave hello or goodbye. But they went on their way, indifferently, gently scooping up the breeze. 'I no longer see the green boats and happy sails on Kaweah,' quoted Joseba.

380

'All I see is the giant net of the fisherman.' He added: 'A genuine quote this time.' 'Well, I can't see any giant nets, only the little hut where they hire out boats,' said Mary Ann. Five minutes later, she and Helen were rowing on the lake.

When we were left alone, Joseba and I talked some more about the reading. I told him that, in my opinion, his stories kept pretty close to the truth, and he needn't worry about me. My stay in prison had given me the opportunity to pay for my mistakes, and also, independently of that, to start a new life in America. Agustín's case, however, was more awkward. He would always be younger than us. In a way, he would always be twenty. And, being stuck at that age, he would find it hard to understand what had happened. 'I find it hard to understand too,' he said. 'And I don't just mean what happened after we left Mamousine, but the day I went to fetch you with the Guzzi. I still can't comprehend why I dragged you from Virginia's bed in order to get you involved in that whole mess, and that's the reason, really, why I have to write the book.' It would have been a good moment to mention my memoir, but I couldn't bring myself to do it. 'The only alternative is to make an exhaustive analysis of the circumstances,' I said. He nodded, but only out of politeness. At this point, he doesn't need such advice.

I remembered the rose Teresa gave me and which I put in a glass vase, and I remembered the decision I took then: I would wait for a reply from Virginia until the rose had lost all its petals, and if I didn't hear from her by then, I'd forget all about her. I couldn't help but laugh at the joke life had played on me. The rose was intact when that letter arrived, but it was equally intact on the day Joseba came to fetch me and I left Virginia's house for ever.

A motor-boat came past. In it, as well as a man and a woman of about sixty, was a chihuahua wearing a life jacket. 'This is America!' exclaimed Joseba.

'Can I say something else about the reading?' I said. He indicated with a gesture that I should continue. 'There's one bit of Etxeberria's story that strikes me as weak. The business about the railway policeman and the phone call to the governor . . . The people in Three Rivers might believe that, but I don't. You'd been preparing the operation for some time.' 'If you want to know the truth, I started thinking about it the day your mother died, on the drive back from Pau to Mamousine.' 'And you put the finishing touches to the plan with that "friend from Bilbao" whom you "happened to bump into" in Altzürükü.' *'Bistan da!'* – 'Of course!' – cried Joseba, imitating the Altzürükü accent. 'But, you see, a writer always has to transform things,' he added. 'The scar on the back of the neck moves to the forehead, for example. It's more obvious on the forehead, easier to remember.' I gave a few other examples. We wouldn't have noticed the boat unless the chihuahua in the life jacket had been there. Joseba has always had a taste for literary theory.

Luckily, at that point, Mary Ann and Helen returned. I wanted to go home and sit down in front of that white computer. Its docility amazes me. I pass my hands over the keys, and on the screen appear letters, words. 'Rose' appears, and 'glass vase'.

13

Panic. When I got up this morning my feet felt as if they were made of stone, so heavy that I couldn't even drag myself over to the phone. Mary Ann rang Dr Rabinowitz, and, on his instructions, I took a double dose of Dablen. 'You'll get better,' Mary Ann said to me. With her help, I managed to calm down. Then Joseba and Helen arrived, and they helped too. Besides, my feet no longer felt as if they were made of stone, more like plaster of Paris. At midday, I was able to get up and go out on to the porch.

At about two o'clock, Dr Rabinowitz phoned to see how I was, and he asked if I'd like to bring forward the date of my operation. 'It could be on the 18th. That's a Wednesday.' 'That would be best, wouldn't it?' 'If you lived here in Visalia, I wouldn't suggest a change of date, but I'm worried about the time it takes for you to get here from Three Rivers. It's best to be prudent.' I agreed. 'As you know,' he said before hanging up, 'you have to be here the day before, on the 17th.'

In the afternoon, in my study, I got more photos out of the cardboard box – well, three to be precise. The one of me and Virginia on the day of the ribbon race; a photo that Teresa sent me from Pau; and the picture taken on the occasion of the unveiling of the monument in Obaba – Uzcudun, Degrela, Berlino, Ángel, Martín . . . I didn't play the accordion at the ceremony and, for the first time in my life, showed a little dignity. That's why I like the photo.

When I went out on to the porch, Helen, Joseba and Mary Ann were also looking at photos. 'You're very elegant in this one, David!' Joseba said. He was referring to the picture of Mary Ann and me in Sausalito. 'It's the first picture of the two of you together,' remarked Helen. I thought Mary Ann looked lovely. 'Mary Ann,' I said, 'what did we do with that postcard of the Guernica Restaurant? You remember, don't you? We tore it in half.' 'Of course, I remember. More than that, I still have my half.' 'What about you, David?' asked Helen. 'Oh, I still have mine,' I replied. 'Just as well!' all three of them chorused.

We were very comfortable out there on the porch. And I'm comfortable now too. My feet are back to normal; I can feel my toes inside my slippers. But the cricket inside me is watching. At the first sign of alarm, it will start rubbing its wings uncontrollably, like an insect gone mad.

14

This afternoon I noticed there were ten seashells on my desk and that the card with the yellow and orange butterfly had been moved. I soon understood the reason: I heard Liz and Sara laughing in the garden. 'You're looking very pretty,' I said when I went out to give them a hug. They're the colour of Santa Barbara. 'The beach was neat,' Sara said, 'but I got homesick.' We went to see the horses, and from there to Efraín and Rosario's house. I felt a little weak.

A while ago – it's seven o'clock now, and I'll be joining the others soon to watch the movie they're showing on TV – I did something odd. I wrote the epitaph I'd like to have engraved on my headstone and then

I wrote the funeral oration. The words floated effortlessly into my mind, as if they were writing themselves, as if they were intended for someone else. I must tell Mary Ann that she can find it here, under the entry for 14 August. If I die, I want it to be read in three languages: Mary Ann will read it in English, Efraín in Spanish and Joseba in our Obaba language.

Epitaph: 'He was never closer to paradise than when he lived on this ranch.'

Funeral oration: 'He was never closer to paradise than when he lived on this ranch, so much so that he found it difficult to believe that life could possibly be any better in heaven. It was hard for him to leave his wife, Mary Ann, and his two daughters, Liz and Sara, but, when he left, he had just the tiny necessary sliver of hope to ask God to take him up into heaven and place him alongside his Uncle Juan and his mother Carmen, and alongside the friends he once had in Obaba.'

15

Sunday. I spent all morning doing puzzles with Liz and Sara. In the afternoon, they went off down to Efraín and Rosario's house, and I got together in the living-room with Mary Ann, Joseba, Helen, Carol, Donald and other friends from the Book Club. It was too stiflingly hot to sit out on the porch. When I arrived, they were talking about last Wednesday's reading, but Donald immediately started praising 'Obaba's First American' and suggested I read it. I told him I couldn't, but that he could – if he wanted to, of course.

Donald was expecting my answer, and was prepared. He had with him the anthology published in Visalia, with a post-it marking the first page of my story. In fact, they were all prepared. They had obviously agreed everything beforehand. Donald started reading: 'When he returned from Alaska and set about getting the hotel built, Don Pedro was a very fat man who, it was said, used to weigh himself each day on a modern set of scales he'd brought with him from France . . .'

I indicated to him that he should continue reading, and I went into my study to find the letter that Don Pedro Galarreta wrote to my Uncle Juan describing what happened before Juan concealed him in the hiding-place at Iruain. I read it a couple of times and went back into the living-room. Donald's reading finished a quarter of an hour later.

'If you applaud too warmly, I'll think it's out of sympathy for the afflicted,' I said, and they fell silent. Then I explained that the story Donald had just read was based on the letter I had in my hand. 'This was written by Don Pedro Galarreta himself, Obaba's first American. I'll translate it as I go along so that you can compare his testimony with my invented version.' 'How interesting,' said Donald.

I sat down in an armchair and started translating Don Pedro's story, which is very simple, and devoid of intrigue and metaphors.

DON PEDRO'S TESTIMONY REGARDING HIS PERSECUTION

(. . .) The car was driving along very fast and suddenly we reached the outskirts of Obaba. We stopped there, and another car immediately joined us. Everyone, except the man in charge, got out, and other men got in. The new driver asked the driver who was getting out: 'Where are we taking this lot?' And the man said a name, which wasn't the name of any village I know, and which I'd never heard before.

Our car set off after theirs. We immediately left the road and started driving along a track into the countryside. All my doubts ended there. They were obviously going to kill us. I didn't know the mountains in that area, but I was sure there would be precipices where I could throw myself out of the car and kill myself. It horrified me to think how they might kill us, how they might make us suffer, because it seemed unlikely they would miss an opportunity to torture us, and so I felt pleased with my decision. But the car ahead was travelling very slowly and I could see no suitable precipice to throw myself off.

We reached the pass and drove on for about 800 yards. Suddenly the car in front swung round and parked across the road. Ours stopped a few yards behind. 'Right, this is it! Everybody out! You first!' they said.

(I had to stop writing for a few hours. The memory of what happened is so distressing it made me feel quite dizzy, then I recovered and lay down on the bed for some minutes, after which I started writing again.)

They said again: 'You first! Out!' I didn't want to get out and, since I was next to the door, the others couldn't move and there was a struggle inside the car. The men in the other car had already got out, including the teachers. A man came over, leaned in through the other window, and, before I could defend myself, struck me with the butt of a heavy rifle, hard enough to kill a weaker man. He raised the rifle and was about to shoot me. One of his companions said: 'Don't shoot him until he's got out, otherwise you'll splatter the whole car with blood. Remember what happened yesterday.'

Two more men from the other car tried to drag me out. I shook them off and threw them to the ground. In the end, though, I had no alternative but to get out. The two teachers were standing a few yards away. They lined us up, first Don Mauricio, then Don Miguel, then Don Bernardino, and, lastly, me. The boss stood next to me, holding a big gun, with the ten or twelve other men about two yards behind him, their rifles at the ready. The man in charge said to me: 'Right, Galarreta, you're going to be the first to die.' I asked him to listen to me first. 'Talk fast, I'm in a hurry,' he said. I told him that I'd done nothing wrong and would do nothing wrong in the future, that I had a small fortune which I would give him to dispose of as he wished. He gave the order: 'Fire!' I grabbed hold of him, picked him up and held him in the air. 'Run for it!' I shouted to the others. Then I dropped him and started running downhill into the woods, and they all opened fire on me. Don Mauricio shouted: 'You go, I can't, let them kill me here!' I was running like mad. I tripped over my own feet and fell to the ground. They fired another five shots.

They assumed I was dead. The boss said: 'Right, let's deal with these other smart-arses.' I got up quickly in order to continue running, and then I saw Don Bernardino drop to the ground, letting out a loud scream as he fell. Then two more screams, from Don Miguel and Don Mauricio. I didn't see them fall. They shot them through the heart.

386

They delivered the coup de grâce to each of them almost simultaneously, and when the man who came to finish me off couldn't find me, he yelled: 'He's not here!' The boss screamed back at him: 'I should shoot *you* in the head for letting him escape, and I might just do that.' I started running again, but my espadrilles fell off and the laces remained tied about my ankles, preventing me from running.

I ripped off the laces and started running barefoot. I was afraid they'd hear me and follow, because they were all young, some less than twenty . . .

I interrupted my reading at this point. 'The letter continues, but I think you've probably got the idea. It's easy enough to compare the two texts,' I said. 'In real life, things ended far more tragically. In the fiction, we see Don Pedro putting up a fight, firing a gun to defend himself, regretting having killed his fellow man and, finally, we see him safe. And one of the teachers, Don Miguel, was also saved because he left for Bilbao in time. None of that actually happened. Don Pedro was at the mercy of the murderers. We hear his account and he seems to us like a lamb staring in horror at the slaughterman.' 'What are you trying to say, David?' asked Donald, looking worried. 'That real life is sad,' I said, 'and that all books, even the harshest, embellish life?'

A silence fell, provoked perhaps by the vehemence with which I'd spoken and perhaps because they were all thinking about my imminent departure for hospital. Joseba deployed his histrionic gifts. Putting on a scowling face, he boomed: 'Would you have us believe that real life is always sad? And what about the day you met Raquel Welch and her horse wearing nothing on top? Was *that* sad?' I started to deny this, to explain to Donald and the others that this hadn't happened to me. But the lie was already flapping round the living-room, and any attempt at an explanation was pointless. 'Raquel Welch naked? Where?' asked Carol, surprised. 'It was the horse that was wearing nothing on top,' replied Joseba, 'Raquel Welch was wearing a bikini.' Donald was equally surprised: 'Did you really meet Raquel Welch?' he asked. In the end, Mary Ann had to tell them the true version of events. But this still didn't sort out the muddle. Carol found it hard to return to reality. 'You mean Raquel Welch was at Lake Tahoe?' she said to me, a whole half hour after Joseba's comical remark.

I've been wondering what it was that made me read the dramatic excerpt from Don Pedro's account, which, when I was writing my own story, I'd decided to discard. And why I went on to make that pessimistic comment. I have the answer: I am now Pedro Galarreta. It's night, I'm in a car, and I don't know where they're taking me. I only know that some of those who were travelling with me are already dead. I used to see them in Dr Rabinowitz's consulting rooms, telling him about their symptoms, and the doctor would say: 'Great. I'm glad to hear that.' It's impossible to escape, that's the hardest thing. Even if we do escape, they always catch us up, and we always come back to the car. And one day, suddenly, we hear the inexorable words: 'Right, this is it! Everybody out! You first!' I don't want to think any more. I can hear the cricket singing inside me. It's not a merry song: it's frightened. If it could escape, it would run away and hide among the white keys of the computer.

16

Mary Ann helped me prepare my things ready for the hospital, and then we went to the park in Three Rivers, so that Liz and Sara could say hello to their friends. Joseba and Helen came with us. In the park, a kite-flyer or *cometista* – if such a word exists in Spanish – was explaining to a group of children how to fly a kite. Liz and Sara joined the group, as did Mary Ann and Helen. I think Mary Ann did this on purpose. She assumes Joseba and I want to go on talking about 'our past lives', and tries to leave us alone.

I told Joseba that, before going into hospital, I wanted to finish our review of the past, and for him to tell me what he knew about Papi, Triku and the others. 'Do you know where the nickname Papi came from?' he asked. 'I always thought he was called Papi because he was slightly paternalistic,' I said. 'That's what I thought too. But apparently it comes from the film *Papillon*. I didn't tell you the other day, but I was with him in Havana.' I had thought as much.

We talked about Papi for quite a while. Then it was Triku's turn. Joseba had seen him in Montevideo. 'His restaurant's a huge success,' he told me. 'Do you know what it's called? "The Spiceship". As you can imagine, he intended calling it "The Spaceship", but the man who made the sign misread his writing, and it's stayed like that ever since.'

I'm sure Joseba will write a good, well-documented book, and I told him so. He looked doubtful. 'I'm not so sure. I wanted to talk to Papi and Triku about the betrayal, as I have with you. But the problem is they don't read stories. With Papi I ended up talking about Steve McQueen, and with Triku I simply chatted and strolled about the city.' 'How are they? I mean mentally and otherwise.' 'Well, Triku's completely lost. As I told you the other day, he's basically stuck in his twenties. Do you know what he does every day? He walks past the Casa Vasca just to hear the sounds from the pelota court. He says that he closes his eyes and feels like he's back in the Basque Country. As for Papi, what can I say? He assures me that his one aim in life now is to write a book about the butterflies and moths of Cuba. But who knows?'

The 'class' in the park had finished, and a crowd of kites, about twenty of them, were moving about in the air. Two of them, green ones, belonged to Liz and Sara. Mary Ann beckoned us over. 'We'll finish our review of the past when you come out of hospital,' Joseba said.

We had supper early. I intended going to bed immediately afterwards, but instead I sat down in front of the computer, as I've been doing every day throughout the month of August, and I managed to write a little. Now I'm going to watch a video with Mary Ann and the girls. And tomorrow, to Visalia.

With thanks to
Asun Garikano
Txema Aranaz
the family of Don Pedro Salinas, and especially his daughters,
Carmen, Beatriz, Laura and Sara

Translator's acknowledgements
I would like to thank Bernardo Atxaga, Annella McDermott, Palmira
Sullivan, Antonio Martín and Ben Sherriff for all their help and
advice.